North

CW00376235

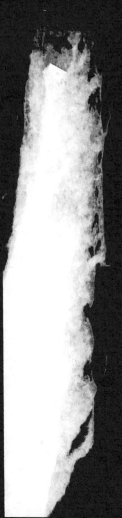

Farperoo

Book One of the Dark Inventions

Fairperoo

Book One of the Dark Inventions

by

Mark Lamb

with

Illustrations by Matthew Armstrong

Cover Graphics by Claudio Grilli

Farperoo

Book One of the Dark Inventions

Volume Three

Published in Great Britain by
The Madriax Press

This illustrated, limited edition first published
October 2007

ISBN 0-9548356-3-8

Printed and bound in Great Britain
by Biddles Limited, King's Lynn, Norfolk

Set in 13pt Garamond

10 9 8 7 6 5 4 3 2 1

To Niddy

Forever…

Arcanum the Sixth

Arcanum the Seventh

Mumtaz Gubbins

Lucy was quite certain that Zenda had drowned.

She was equally sure that Quim and Madimi must have plunged over the eastern falls, along with Doctor Dee. And with the river level still rising and the remains of their raft turning to porridge, it wouldn't be long before they all joined them.

There was just one option remaining.

'*Surrender*?' said Toby, with a look of horror. 'Are you mad?'

'We don't have much option,' said Tenby.

'But who are we surrendering to?' said Toby, his feet sinking into the waterlogged planks.

'Does it matter?' said Pixy.

Henbeg, who was towing them ashore, gave a grunt as he reached the bank and the raft nudged against the pier legs.

'Come on now,' yelled a voice from above. 'They's all waiting for you.'

'Is they?' said Lucy. 'I mean *are* they?' She was surprised by the sound of escaping steam, which seemed to be coming from the back of a canvas-covered wagon on the pier.

'I've seen that cart before,' said Lucy, as they climbed up.

'So who's the suspicious looking bloke in the driving seat?' said Toby. He smiled as he watched the remains of the raft slip beneath the surface.

'This is Weazenock,' said Lucy, 'and the other one is Bony Crumpet, and any minute now they're going to tell us what they're doing here – aren't you Mister Weazenock?'

'Following you,' grinned Weazenock. 'We thought you might need help. And judging from the state of your raft thingy we was just in time.'

'So the commotion back there in the trees was you?' said Lucy, eyeing the cart.

'It's our secret weapon,' grinned Bony.

'Only it's not a secret any more,' sighed Weazenock. 'Not now you've gone and frigging-well *blabbed* about it.'

'But they don't know the details, do they?' said Bony, turning to Lucy. 'See?' he said. 'I told you we had some interesting exhibits.'

'What kind of exhibits?' asked Toby.

'They're showmen,' explained Lucy. 'They wanted Pixy and me as part of their freak exhibition.'

'That was all just an accident,' said Weazenock.

'Yeah,' agreed Bony, 'we got confused.'

'I see,' said Lucy, 'and are you still confused?'

'*Deff-nit-lee* not,' said Weazenock. 'We're on an important mission.'

'Just suppose I believe you,' said Lucy. 'Why are you following us? And how did you know where to find us?'

'We heard you needed a special kind of help,' said Weazenock.

'Like being locked up in a cage?' said Pixy.

'Umm, sorry,' said Weazenock, shuffling uncomfortably.

'It was Boaz that finally convinced us to help you,' said Bony. 'He was asking all sorts of nosey questions. He wanted to rescue you from the palace and everything.'

'There's nothing wrong with that,' said Lucy. 'We were trying to escape from there ourselves.'

'True,' said Weazenock, 'but you wouldn't have been properly free if *he'd* got you out. That's a case of out of the Loppit pan and into the fire.'

'Yummy,' said Pixy. 'I knew there was something I'd forgotten.'

'As for knowing your whereabouts,' said Weazenock, 'we've got eyes and ears everywhere, haven't we Bony?'

There was a growl at their feet. Henbeg sniffed at Bony's boots – a smell that brought back a few unpleasant memories.

'Yeah,' said Bony, eyeing Henbeg nervously.

'So what have you got on the cart?' said Lucy.

A cloud of water vapour rose from the simmering tarpaulin, as if there was something hot concealed below its folds.

'That'll be for *me* to know,' said Weazenock, making sure the flaps were secure. 'But I promise you it's something interesting.'

'*Interesting*?' said Lucy, keeping one eye on Henbeg. He gave another deep growl, this time sniffing at Weazenock's trousers.

'Hey, gerroudovit,' he said. 'Gerrofmerottenkekks.'

'You were saying,' said Lucy, 'about the thing under the canvas?'

'Well it *must* be interesting, mustn't it?' he said. 'Otherwise you wouldn't be wanting to poke your nose in.'

Lucy fiddled with a rope-knot. She failed to untie it, so tried to force a corner of the tarpaulin up.

'Don't even think about it,' said Bony.

He laid a massive hand on hers, and she felt an intense heat coming from him, even through the opera gloves.

'Why won't you let us look under your stupid canvas?' said Pixy.

'Well firstly,' said Weazenock, '*we* haven't asked to look inside that stinky coat of Miss Lucy's.'

'Good point,' said Lucy. 'And *secondly*?'

'And secondly,' grinned Weazenock, 'there isn't time.'

'Why?' said Pixy.

'Because there's a steaming pile of Loppit stew waiting for us at the Bright Byrde – with side orders of noggin-lungs and crispy mumble-guts.'

'Will you be providing sick bags?' said Toby.

'Yummy,' said Pixy, licking her lips. 'Well I don't know about *you* lot, but that's about all the proof *I* need.'

When they were all safely installed below the driver's seat, Weazenock went back to check on the cargo. The deck of the wagon was divided in two and covered by a single tarpaulin, with Lucy and her friends hidden up front, and their fellow passenger stowed in the rear compartment. The creature breathed slow and deep, snorting each time Weazenock whispered to it.

'*Heh-Shi, Heh-Shi, Bezooga, Bezooga,*' he called softly.

'What do you think that means?' whispered Toby.

'I'm hoping it means stop snorting on the girl,' said Lucy.

'Eh?' said Toby.

'It's breathing through the boards,' said Lucy. She placed a hand over the gap in the planks that separated them from the rear section.

'It's like being stuck under a blanket with a big kettle,' said Pixy.

'Or a giant, overflowing toilet,' said Tenby. 'I don't know what that thing had for dinner, but I'm willing to bet it didn't die recently.'

'If we slid one of these planks out of the way,' whispered Pixy, 'we could see what was causing the stink.'

'I don't think so,' said Lucy. 'It might be dangerous.'

'Are you scared?' said Pixy, trying to lever a plank loose.

'Hey,' said Weazenock, poking his head through. 'You're not messing with those planks are you?'

'Of course not,' lied Pixy.

'Good,' said Weazenock. 'Because our special passenger hasn't been fed yet, and you know what *that's* like.'

'I certainly do,' said Pixy as she gave a deep, malodorous belch.

Eventually they got underway, with Weazenock and Bony sitting up top in the driver's seat and all the others crammed below with the stinking, foul-breathed mystery. They sat in darkness, lulled into silence like parrots under a cover and gently nudged towards sleep by the swaying motion of the cart.

But after a while, they were roused from the doldrums by the sound of Weazenock's voice. He was whispering to Bony, who sounded worried.

'What are they talking about?' asked Pixy.

'Dunno,' replied Toby, 'all I could make out was *con-joinment* and *woo*.'

'I heard that too,' said Lucy. 'And I think they know we're listening.'

'They don't trust us then?' said Toby.

'The feeling's mutual,' whispered Lucy.

The cart creaked as they rolled over a bump.

'Can you see where we are?' said Pixy impatiently.

'It's all narrow passages and pointed roofs,' said Toby, lifting the canvas. 'But there's a covered market coming up – and it's quite busy.'

'The Sisters haven't frightened everyone off then?' said Lucy.

'Not yet,' said Toby, 'but they don't look too happy.'

'Hey, you lot down there,' hissed Bony, 'keep *quiet* will you?'

Toby peeped out again. He wanted to get some kind of a bearing – but there was just so much of the city he had never seen.

Outside, there was a narrow passageway lined with hundreds of doors, each barely a yard wide. Most of the vendors sat well back on embroidered cushions and looked ready to close the shutters at the first hint of trouble.

'I know where we are,' said Pixy, squeezing her head into the gap. 'These carpet shops are near the Bright Byrde.'

Weazenock leaned down, poking his head through a gap in the canvas.

'Keep your heads inside, and be quiet,' he whispered. 'We're approaching the church of the Blessed Margaret, and if we're going to have problems then this is where they'll be. This is one of the few old churches left – the Sisters destroyed the rest.'

'Why's that then?' said Pixy. 'Why didn't they burn them all?'

'I wish I could see inside,' said Lucy, peering through the flap. She had a strange feeling that the church building contained all the answers she needed, and all she had to do was ask.

'You can't,' said Toby. 'Even if you could get over there without being seen, it's all chained up.'

'He's right,' said Pixy, 'and all the windows are covered.'

Toby allowed the canvas to flap into place, and as darkness fell inside the cart they heard some children singing a rhyme. Curiosity got the better of him and he lifted it again to reveal the youngsters playing near the rear wall of the church. Five young girls sang and skipped over a rope, as if the city's problems didn't exist. Only the scarab hovering nearby and the words of their rhyme gave anything away.

Dark angel, dark angel, don't take my life,
Dark angel, dark angel, don't take my wife,
Dark angel, dark angel, spare my brother too,
And leave us all in peace, when you flee to Farperoo.

Lucy pushed her way to the gap in the canvas, looking on in horror as the scarab slowly descended on the children.

'It's going to take one of them,' she screamed.

'Will you lot shut up down there?' hissed Weazenock. 'Or perhaps you want to get us all killed?'

'But the girl,' squealed Lucy, 'the scarab, it's... she…'

'Oh *great*,' sighed Weazenock. 'Now we really *are* in trouble.'

Toby swallowed hard as the scarab turned its attention away from the skipping girls.

The Khepri Mistress in charge of the beast made her way to the cart.

'You'd better think of something fast,' he hissed to Lucy.

'What have you got under the cover?' demanded the Mistress.

'Just spice,' said Weazenock innocently, 'see for yourself.'

'Unfasten the ropes,' she said with a confident sneer.

As Weazenock loosened the ties, the Khepri Mistress walked around the cart, scrutinising every tiny detail for a clue that might betray them.

'I *know* you, don't I?' she said, pointing an accusing finger at Weazenock.

'I doubt it,' he said. 'I'm just a simple tradesman.'

'With a sideline in freaks,' said the Mistress. 'I saw you trundling your crappy cart around the palace market a few days ago. What exactly are you hiding?'

As the Khepri Mistress loosened more ropes, the passengers flattened themselves against the wooden floor of the cart, not daring to look up in case the morning light caught their faces.

'What's happening?' whispered Pixy.

The sound of wing-beats filled the air.

'Shush,' whispered Lucy, pointing at the light streaming in from outside.

The insect nudged its head under the tarpaulin, dripping mucous and slime on their heads as it probed the friends' hiding place.

'I think we'll have the cover off completely,' said the Mistress.

'Sorry,' said Weazenock, 'but we can't do that.'

'And why not?' demanded the Mistress.

'Why was it we can't do that again Bony?' said Weazenock.

'Umm, regulations,' said Bony helpfully.

'*Regulations*?' said the Mistress. 'And just where are these regulatory laws written down?'

'It was one of Dragonard's new rules,' said Weazenock in a sudden fit of creativity. 'And we don't want to disobey *him*, now do we?'

'Do we not?' said the Mistress. 'The last *I* heard, his tiny pathetic majesty was being pitched bodily over the city walls. And the Sisters don't recognise his authority in any case, the runty, fart-arsed, puke-faced little windbag.'

'Ah, well now you come to mention it,' smiled Weazenock, 'we never really liked him *that* much, did we Bony?'

'Eh?' said Bony, slightly preoccupied. He was trying to pass a handful of powder to Lucy without being seen.

'I said we didn't like Dragonard, *did* we? We've always had a soft spot for the Sisters.'

'Yeah, right between the eyes,' whispered Toby.

'How touching,' said the Khepri Mistress. 'In that case you won't mind if one of their representatives has a look inside your cart, *will* you? Now pull back that cover. Unless you want my scarab to eat your head.'

As the cover rolled back, Lucy blew the spice into the scarab's snout. The insect's mouth dropped open like a coal chute and sprayed gallons of sticky green snot into the cart. Then it sn-sn-sn-sneezed like a firecracker and shot backwards, colliding with a heavily barred gate. A curious head appeared at a tiny window, wanting to know who was knocking.

'I told you, didn't I?' said Weazenock. 'It's the spices we're carrying. I can't help it if he doesn't like them, now can I?'

The Mistress glanced over at the gate where her charge was trying to pick itself up. Two of its hairy legs had broken off and were twitching where they fell. The insect was too dazed to fly, so it limped towards them like a battle-weary soldier.

'You're going to be *very* sorry you did that,' yelled the Mistress.

'But he just sneezed from the spice,' whinged Weazenock.

'We'll see about that when we get the rest of this cart uncovered,' said the Khepri Mistress. 'In the meantime, I'm going to call for reinforcements.'

'No, don't,' said Lucy. She threw back the cover and stood up in full view.

'*You?*' said the Mistress. 'But you're the one we're looking for.'

'Not quite,' smiled Lucy. 'I'm one of the official decoys.'

'Decoys?' replied the Mistress. 'I didn't hear anything about that.'

'Ah, well there wouldn't be much point if everyone knew about them, now would there?' said Weazenock, winking at Lucy.

'I suppose not,' said the Mistress. 'But how do I know you're not the *real* Lucy Blake?'

Mumtaz Gubbins

'That's where they were really clever,' said Lucy. 'Because all of us decoys have one thing in common.'

'And what's *that?*' said the Mistress, calming her injured beast.

Lucy took off an opera glove and held out her hand for inspection.

'The real Lucy Blake has got five fingers,' she said.

'Yeah,' said Weazenock, joining in enthusiastically. 'And the look-alikes have only got four – see?'

'Oh,' said the Mistress, feeling Lucy's stump. 'So you really are a decoy?'

'I know it's a bit extreme, chopping our fingers off,' said Lucy. 'But it's the only way to make sure we can be told apart. There are a lot of people who want to get their hands on that rotten-stinking Lucy Blake, and we all have a duty to work together and stop them, *don't* we Mister Weazenock?'

'That's right,' said Weazenock. 'And since we've got official business to be getting on with we'll let you continue your search. Oh, and by the way, I think your scarab might be coming down with a cold. I should get him wrapped up nice and warm if I was you.'

'Alright then,' said the Mistress, 'thanks for the advice.'

'Brilliant,' grinned Toby as they drove away. 'Do you think she fell for it?'

Lucy peeked back. The Khepri Mistress scratched her head, then pulled the insect's long tongue out, as if she was examining it for spots.

'I think she *might* have,' said Lucy. 'But we'd best get out of here, just in case she changes her mind.'

It was mid-morning when they arrived at the Bright Byrde, which wasn't the best time to sneak into a tavern unnoticed. But they tried anyway, sliding in amidst a crowd of street-entertainers.

'Hey, I got all that food you wanted,' shouted the innkeeper.

Weazenock winced, as everyone turned to look. Pixy snuffled the air like a tracker dog, twitching at the odour of mumble-guts. Toby, Tenby and Lucy all covered their noses, trying to keep out the disgusting stink.

'Thanks for blowing our cover,' grumbled Weazenock.

'Umm, sorry,' said the innkeeper. He winked at Lucy.

'Hey,' yelled someone from the grog-room. 'Look who's trying to sneak in without us noticing – it's *her* again.'

'Yeah,' said another. 'I didn't expect to see her with Weazenock though.'

'Shut your face, Handy Forceps,' said Bony. 'You give Mister Weazenock some respect – and don't go telling people we're here.'

'It's a bit late for that,' said Lucy, recognising some of the faces. The one called Mongy Twelve-Trees was announcing their arrival to anyone who would listen.

'Look, she's brought that *thing* with her,' he shouted, 'the *snappy* monster.'

Henbeg swished his tail, as if he approved of the name. But his pleasure turned to a nasty snarl when Mongy got too close.

'I wouldn't do that if I were you,' said Lucy. 'Look what he did to my face, and I'm his friend.'

'I see what you mean,' said Mongy, examining Lucy's scars. 'Well you'd better keep him under control, that's all *I* can say.'

Henbeg's eyes narrowed, a low growl building inside him – like a Lectric water pump connected to his lungs by ten feet of rubber tubing.

'On second thoughts,' said Mongy, 'maybe you should just let him do whatever he wants.'

'Actually he's with me,' said Weazenock. 'Lucy here was just looking after him for me, *weren't* you?'

Lucy tried narrowing her eyes like Henbeg, but only succeeded in giving herself a slight headache. Instead she contented herself with a special look that she hoped would turn Weazenock into a quivering pile of toad guts.

'Just my little joke,' said Weazenock. 'We can still be friends though, *can't* we Henbeg?'

The crocodile set up a growl to match the first, like an outboard motor in his stomach. It went perfectly with the rows of sharp teeth he was displaying, giving an overall '*vicious creature*' effect that Weazenock found it difficult to ignore.

'Acquaintances perhaps?' said Weazenock.

'Never mind that,' said another drinker, 'why don't you tell us about this river thing? I heard it just turned up out of nowhere.'

'It's none of your business, Detritus Scumbucket,' said Weazenock. 'It's sorcery stuff that is, and it's not intended for the likes of you.'

'Yeah?' said Scumbucket scowling at Lucy. 'Well being eaten by scarabs wasn't for the likes of us either, at least not until *she* turned up. That's when it all started to go apple-shaped right enough.'

'*Pear* shaped you mean?' said Weazenock.

'Obviously you ain't seen none of my apples,' said Scumbucket.

'Yeah,' grinned Mongy. 'So what're you doin' here Weazy? Have you got one of your clever schemes on the go?'

'And what makes you think that?' said Weazenock.

'You're hauling that freak wagon around,' said Scumbucket. 'I reckon you must've worked up some kind of wheeze for getting rid of them scarabs, and maybe the Sisters too.'

'Either way we won't be telling *you*,' said Bony, looking uncomfortable.

'See?' said Scumbucket, turning to his drunken friends. 'They're too good for the likes of us. I've a good mind to go and find the nearest Vooghul and tell it what's going on.'

'Oh, yeah?' said Bony. 'Well just as a matter of interest, purely scientific like, are you any good at walking on broken legs?'

'Dunno,' said Scumbucket, 'I never tried it.'

'There's a first time for everything,' said Bony, flexing his muscles. 'Now does anyone else want to go and warn the Sisters, or are we going to settle down and have a nice drink together?'

'I'm feeling a *bit* thirsty,' admitted Mongy. 'Maybe we should listen?'

'Alright,' sighed Scumbucket, pulling up a stool. 'I'll have a tankard of Blue Squeezed Wibbley, and some Nogg-Lip stew if there's any going.'

The innkeeper dragged four tables together to form a banqueting bench that soon groaned with dishes and platters. There were sauces that looked blue from one angle but turned green if you moved your head. There were wobbly piles of stuff that looked like horse dung in gravy, and side dishes piled with delicacies that hadn't realised they were dead, even though they were wrapped in various rancid dressings.

'And I've got something for you too,' the innkeeper whispered, trying to attract Lucy's attention without alerting anyone else.

'For *us*?' said Lucy. 'But you didn't know we were coming, did you?'

'I hope it's chips,' said Toby.

'It's not food,' said the innkeeper.

He led them to a dark recess that seemed faintly familiar.

'It's *this*,' he said, indicating a filthy cloth that was draped over something big and bulky.

As they tried to work out what was concealed beneath the dustsheet, Lucy recalled the details of their previous visit, when they met the woman with the cards.

'You remember that day you disappeared?' said the innkeeper. 'Well she knew all along what was going to happen.'

'Who did?' said Lucy.

'Miss Pubrane,' he replied. 'She was a fortune teller, so it stands to reason she knew it all in advance.'

'That's a very good point,' grinned Toby.

'And what *was* going to happen?' said Lucy.

'This,' said the innkeeper, whipping off the sheet.

Beneath the covers was a familiar-looking cabinet. It had ornate wood panelling below and glass windows above.

'It's Princess Mumtaz,' said Toby.

'No it isn't,' sobbed Lucy, 'it's Miss Pubrane.'

'Actually, it's only her head,' grinned the innkeeper.

'I can see that you idiot,' snapped Lucy, her eyes filling with tears.

Exotica's face was just as she remembered. It was covered with powdery makeup, only now it was laid on even thicker. It looked like the fortune teller was sleeping, even though she lacked a body to be sleeping *with*. All that remained was a gathering of cloth that suggested a torso, and a wooden arm and dull silver hand that was connected to a spring.

'Why do you think they did this to her?' said Toby.

'Perhaps the sign is something to do with it?' suggested Lucy. She picked up the rough piece of cardboard and pressed it against her nose, as if it might still have Exotica's scent on it.

'*The head is the sinner, the body is merely the servant,*' she read aloud.

At the sound of her voice, a dim glow appeared around Exotica's head, as if she was powered by some strange form of Lectric. Lucy expected the mechanical hand to activate, or the eyes to spring open as they did on her Uncle Byron's machine. Nothing of the kind happened, but the head seemed to recall a task it had been set, and began to describe the world according to the Sisters.

'*Assiah is indivisible.*'

'*Assiah is immutable.*'

'*Assiah is perfection.*'
'*And the stealers of food and mongers of filth shall be destroyed.*'
'*Assiah is purity.*'
'*Assiah is…*'
The ranting stopped, and the eyes twitched slightly.
'*Assiah is…*'
'*Assiah is…*'
'*Assiah…*'
'*Ass…*'

Some inextinguishable light at the core of Miss Pubrane's existence had recognised Lucy's presence. And Exotica was fighting for control of her own mouth.

'*A creature is sitting on an island,*' she whispered, almost inaudibly.

'What is it doing?' said Lucy, moving closer.

'*Waiting for me,*' whispered the Pubrane head.

'Did you hear that?' said Lucy. 'She must still be alive – she's thinking about Lundrumguffa.'

'I don't think so,' said Toby, squatting to examine Miss Pubrane's neck in detail. 'It looks like a clean cut. And I think it might have been done with the blade that Thomax showed us.'

'So this really *is* Miss Pubrane's head?' said a dejected Lucy.

'I'd recognise her anywhere,' said the innkeeper. 'She had that little mole on her chin. You can just see it, there, under all the makeup.'

'You knew her well then?' said Toby.

'Of course,' said the innkeeper. 'She owed me a lot of money.'

'*Not owe money,*' hissed the head.

'Eh?' said the innkeeper, trying to look innocent. 'What did she say?'

'*No money owed,*' said the head. '*Now go, or trouble will haunt you.*'

'Alright,' he said nervously. 'I'll see about adjusting your account.'

'*Remember,*' hissed Exotica as he scuttled away, '*no money owed.*'

'You're in there, *aren't* you?' said Lucy, pressing her nose on the glass.

'*I am in there,*' said the head.

'See Toby? I *told* you – now if only we can get her out…'

'*No time,*' said the head, '*but what of Henbeg?*'

There was a disturbance behind them, as if the creature had been waiting patiently for a mention of his name.

'He's here,' said Lucy.

Henbeg reared up on his hind legs and leaned against the cabinet, his sad eyes focused on Miss Pubrane. He tried desperately to lick her face, but the glass prevented him from kissing his mistress. An entire yard of disappointed tongue wound up like a mad spring, disappearing into his mouth with a liquid snap.

'*Yours now,*' said Miss Pubrane. '*Look after – always protect.*'

Exotica looked Lucy in the eye as the wooden arm began to move. The metal hand flipped over a small pack of cards that Lucy hadn't noticed until now. Then it spread them out and passed a finger over each one, as if trying to make an important decision.

'*Henbeg,*' whispered the head. '*Will of his own.*'

'We noticed,' said Lucy, watching closely. 'Weazenock wants him too.'

'*No,*' snapped Exotica, '*your creature – not belong Weazenock. And not belong Dee. Watch him, watch…*'

Miss Pubrane's eyes fluttered, and when she examined the face closely, Lucy saw the real reason for the movement. There were weevils under the eyelids that squirmed and made her eyeballs move. Then she noticed a ring of dried blood around the neck, and the thin glassy sticks, almost invisible, poking up from below. They were attached to the corners of Exotica's mouth and moved to make it look like she was talking.

'But I *heard* her,' sighed Lucy, 'and it all made some kind of sense.'

'Hey,' someone shouted, 'what are you doing talking to *that*?'

Lucy turned to find a packed room, with everyone craning their necks to see what the young sorceress was doing. Most were simply curious, but one groundling in particular pushed his way to the front. He had just three hairs that he combed across and stuck down with spit, in what he considered to be a pleasing effect.

'You can't talk to her about stuff like that,' he said. 'Them cabinet heads is for preaching the truth, not chatting about water monsters and the like.'

'And what truth is *that* then Barnet?' said Bony.

'Well *you* wouldn't know it,' said Barnet, 'not even if it was explained to you with a large lump of wood.'

'Eh?' said Bony. 'Are you threatening me?'

'Not exactly,' said Barnet, suddenly sounding a lot less brave.

'Yeah, well *I* saw inside one of those head things once,' said a particularly ugly looking groundling.

'No you didn't Grog, you no good liar.'

'I *did*,' said Grog, 'I was stuck inside it for days.'

'Prove it,' shouted another.

'I don't need to,' he yelled. 'I can show you.'

With Barnet's help, he rocked the cabinet back and forth until it crashed to the floor in a cacophony of breaking glass and splintering wood.

'I reckon that's about done it,' said Grog.

'I rather think it *might* have,' said an astonished Lucy.

At first she thought she'd imagined it, but when she looked at Toby it was obvious that her friend was equally shocked. The cabinet had fallen in the exact way that the Mumtaz Machine in Byron's workshop had toppled. And poor Exotica's head had rolled out just like Princess Mumtaz's, coming to rest in a corner of the room.

'Hey, lets have a look in the bottom,' yelled Barnet.

Everyone seemed to agree that looking inside the machine was a great idea, but nobody wanted to be the first to move; they were too busy watching Pubrane's head in case she blinked. Eventually, Grog stepped up and kicked the panelling, breaking the thin veneer away to reveal what lay below.

'Wow, just *look* at all them gubbins,' said Barnet.

'It's downright, absolutely, flipping-well *disgusting*,' said Grog.

'You sound surprised,' said Toby. 'I thought you'd been inside one of these things?'

'I have,' insisted Grog.

'I don't see how you could fit,' said Barnet. 'Not with all *that* lot.'

The onlookers stood quietly, staring at the purplish-red squishy thing that looked like it had fallen from a butcher's window. It was connected to the severed head by a tube-like umbilical cord – and it was pulsing and moving the push rods that had been connected to Miss Pubrane's mouth.

'I don't think it was her talking, do you Luce?' said Toby.

Lucy nodded weakly, her eyes searching the wreckage for evidence that it really *had* been the fortune teller's voice.

'I know it's hard to admit,' said Toby tenderly. 'But it really does look as though she's dead. Which is a pity, because I could swear she was going to tell us something important.'

Lucy picked up the fallen cards as a memento, stowing them away in her pocket. She wanted to cry, but instead her sadness was channelled into anger, her fists tightening around the cards like they might tighten around Raziel's neck. She was certain he was responsible for all this, even though she didn't know exactly how.

'What are you so upset about?' said Pixy. 'I thought you said you hardly knew her.'

'Yeah, *I* knew her better than you did,' said Grog. 'And anyway, she was already dead – unless you count *that* as living.'

He pointed at the bloody mess that had kept Exotica's head alive, and then pushed it around with his foot. It was still throbbing, but looked a lot weaker now, oozing sticky phlegm and bile every time he prodded it.

'This is absolutely *brilliant*,' said Tenby, pushing in from the back. 'I just *have* to get a shot of this.'

Phoomph…

There was an eye-watering flash, followed by an ear splitting whine that sounded like a mosquito being charged up with Lectric.

Zoo-weeeeeee…

Everyone in the tavern froze in the brilliant light from the flashgun.

'He's a wizard,' shouted one of the drinkers.

Phoomph…

'What, *another* one?' said someone else.

Zoo-weeeeeee…

'Will you please stop doing that?' said Lucy. 'And anyway, where did you get that camera?'

Phoomph…

'I'm a professional,' said Tenby. 'I always carry a spare.'

Zoo-weeeeeee…

'So much for your word of honour,' sighed Lucy. 'I suppose you *do* remember promising?'

'There's no such thing as a promise in the newspaper business,' said Tenby. 'Don't get me wrong, we have words like honour and integrity, but they mean what *we* want them to mean. Now, I just need to get another shot of you both alongside the ugly one. Just move a little bit to the left will you Grog?'

'Is he saying I'm ugly?' said Grog, moving just as he'd been told. 'I'll have him know I was the handsomest in our family.'

Phoomph…

'Lovely,' said Tenby. 'I think that about covers it for now.'

Zoo-weeeeeee…

'*Hey*, wait a minute,' said Grog. 'You haven't sucked my brains into that thing, have you?'

'We'd never know if he had, *would* we?' grinned Barnet.

'Watch it,' said Grog. 'Unless you want one of those three remaining hairs pulling out.'

'Never mind my hair,' said Barnet. 'I thought you wanted to know if your brains had been sucked up?'

'Yeah, that's right,' said Grog, turning on Tenby. 'Give me a look at that magic flashy bangy thing.'

'Can't,' said Tenby, 'this camera is the property of Her Majesty's Press.'

'Just hand it over,' said Grog, 'and we promise Her Majesty will never find out.'

'Hey, give it here,' yelled Barnet, 'I want a look too.'

Before anyone could move he snatched the camera from Tenby and held it upside down, as if he expected Grog's brains to pour out.

'Give me that,' shouted Tenby.

'No, give it to me,' screamed Grog. 'I saw it first.'

'Smine,' shouted Barnet, holding onto the prize, if only for a moment. As he pulled out of Grog's way he lost his hold and the camera bounced onto the floor where Henbeg promptly swallowed it.

'Great,' sighed Tenby. 'My editor is going to kill me — that's *two* cameras I've lost on this job. Not to mention losing Zenda.'

'This isn't a *job*,' snapped Lucy. 'Haven't you realised that yet?'

Tenby grabbed Lucy and demanded the camera, but she simply shrugged and looked at Henbeg to show that the situation was out of her control.

'Hey, stop fighting for a minute,' shouted someone at the back. 'I think I heard something.'

'Get lost Pokey Warburton, you're just upset at being left out again.'

'I'm not imaging it,' insisted Pokey. 'Come out here and listen.'

Everyone listened for Pokey's noise, which grew and grew until it sounded like four hundred elephants doing synchronised walnut crushing.

'It's Pentabonce,' said Pokey, peering out of the window.

'Hide,' shouted one of the ale drinkers. 'It's the Emperor's men.'

'Ah,' said another, who was obviously better informed. 'But there isn't any Emperor any more, *is* there?'

'I vote we hide anyway,' said Pokey. 'I don't care *who* they work for, and I don't like those sharp-spiky-pointy things they're carrying either.'

The door crashed open with such force that one of the hinges came away and plopped into a nearby glass of ale. The owner fished it out, sucked the ale off and threw it back towards the door. It landed at Pentabonce's feet.

'Don't worry,' said the Shieldmaster, staring at the quivering hinge-chucker. 'There are much more important things requiring my attention. For instance, there's *you* sir – why don't you start by taking your hands off the young lady?'

'Or what?' said Tenby, stepping away from Lucy.

'Or I'll find some interesting and amusing things to do with the sharp end of this pole,' said Pentabonce. 'We've been using them on the scarabs we found on the palace road, but I'm sure we can find a tender enough piece of skin to test it on you.'

'It's alright,' said Lucy. 'He just wants his camera back.'

'Kam-er-ah?' said Pentabonce.

'*This* thing,' said Lucy, as Henbeg vomited it up. 'Here,' she said, handing it to Tenby. 'And I don't want to see you using it again – next time, Henbeg can keep it.'

'But it's covered in puke,' said Tenby.

'Perhaps you'd like to lodge a complaint?' suggested Pentabonce.

'Maybe not,' said Tenby, eyeing the Shieldmaster's pole. 'Puke is all the rage these days – it's very sought after.'

'Very wise,' smiled Pentabonce.

'It's good to see you,' said Lucy, smiling at him, 'but, umm…'

'We were following you,' said Pentabonce.

'*We?*' said Lucy.

'Me and a few men,' said the Shieldmaster. 'Not the cowards who fled from the tortoise when they were supposed to be protecting you – these are brave and true men, from the forests.'

'I see,' said Lucy. 'And were any of them responsible for what happened to Blueface and his friends? That certainly didn't take much courage, did it?'

'The brand of shame will rest forever on my brow,' said Pentabonce.

'So it *was* you?' said Lucy.

'No,' said Pentabonce, clearly horrified. 'We abandoned the palace as soon as we heard about the executions. That's why the scarabs were able to breach the defences.'

'But you said you were ashamed,' said Lucy.

'For not reaching the performers in time,' said Pentabonce. 'We tried, but many stood against us and casualties were high. They were outnumbered, and confused too, being asked to fight against their friends.'

'Hmm, well I *still* don't know,' said Lucy.

'It's alright,' said a familiar voice, 'you can trust him.'

'*Gusset* – it's *so* good to see you,' grinned Lucy. 'Where have you been?'

'Good to see you as well,' he said, pressing through the ranks of guards. 'I reckon a few things have happened since we all left the Braneskule.'

'They have,' chimed Toby and Lucy together. 'We've…'

'Later,' said Gusset. 'There's a time for stories and a time for action.'

'But sometimes they have a habit of coming together,' smiled Lucy. 'Can you at least tell us where you've been?'

'Gusset has been helping to gather forces,' said Pentabonce. 'We aim to rid the world of the Sisters once and for all.'

'You haven't been back to the Braneskule then?' said Toby.

'No,' said Gusset, his smile looking like a split passion fruit. 'There is bad news. The Sisters have received information about your movements.'

'They know where we are?' said Toby.

'Not exactly,' replied Gusset. 'But someone appears to be helping the Sisters with magick.'

'I'll bet it's Boaz,' grinned Toby. 'His eyes are too close together.'

'You're right,' said Lucy, recalling Boaz's missing ear. 'It probably *is* him.'

'So,' said Pentabonce. 'Now that you know *our* purpose, are you going to tell us why *you* came here?'

'We think our friend Fenny is being held in the tower,' said Lucy. Then she lowered her voice and added, 'by someone called Raziel.'

'Never heard of him,' said Pentaboncc. 'But if your friend is in the tower then why come to the tavern?'

'We're hungry,' said Pixy.

'That's *not* why we came,' frowned Lucy. 'Mister Weazenock offered to help, and this is where he brought us.'

'I wouldn't say it was the safest of places,' said Gusset, 'and even if it *was* safe I wouldn't recommend accepting help from *him*.'

'Don't worry about us Gussy,' said Weazenock. 'We've turned over a new leaf. We rescued them from the river.'

'And what river might that be?' said Gusset.

'The Isis,' said Pixy. 'But we were already ashore.'

'So they *half* rescued you from an imaginary river?' frowned Gusset.

'They had a cart,' said Lucy. 'And they got us here safely.'

'And they promised us Loppit stew,' said Pixy.

'Ah, yes,' said Gusset. 'I *thought* I could smell cooking.'

'There's Crimped Eel,' said Pixy enthusiastically.

'Glad to hear it,' said Gusset. 'But there's more to life than food.'

'Is there?' said Pixy. 'I hadn't noticed.'

'Try to think of it another way,' suggested Pentabonce. 'You need to be alive in order to eat don't you?'

'The last time I looked,' said Pixy.

'Well *we* tracked you down with very little effort,' said Pentabonce. 'How long do you think it will take the Sisters?'

'We need to move,' said Lucy.

'And fast,' agreed Toby.

'But what about Dee?' said Lucy. 'He won't know where to find us.'

'The river currents were powerful,' said Pentabonce with a knowing look. 'Your friends were probably carried away to the eastern wall by the flow.'

'*No*,' said Lucy, 'they just *can't* have been swept away.'

'Tragedies happen all the time,' said Pentabonce. 'Just because something is beautiful or valuable, doesn't mean to say it can't die or become lost.'

'But not like that,' said Lucy. 'It's so…'

'Stupid?' said Toby.

Lucy nodded and looked at Pixy. The groundling was always saying how she didn't want to die just now, and she could imagine Dee and Madimi and Quim thinking the same thing. The sorcerer and his daughter would want to die in blazing glory, battling serpents with ancient magick. Quim meanwhile would probably dream of being crushed by a toppling wardrobe filled with the finest clothes. They certainly wouldn't want to go falling off the edge of the world on some crumbling old raft.

'So are we going to get a move on then?' said Weazenock.

'Well *we* are,' said Pentabonce, 'but we can do without your kind.'

'If you let us help,' whinged Weazenock, 'I'll show you our secret.'

'I think not,' said the Shieldmaster. He watched Lucy from the corner of his eye. It was obvious that she'd developed a soft spot for old Weazenock, even though the rogue still coveted her handbag.

'There's going to be trouble,' said Bony, 'and I reckon if you *don't* let us help then there's going to be more trouble than you can handle.'

'Oh?' said Pentabonce. 'And how do you work that out?'

'You can't beat the Sisters by sticking spears in them,' said Bony, 'you've got to be cleverer than that.'

'Yeah, well you're the one for that job,' said a voice in the crowd. 'He's really clever that Bony is.'

'All the same we'll take our chances,' said Pentabonce.

'Where will we go?' said Lucy. She thought about the postcards and what they said about the Sisters – and wondered which, if any, of them, were true.

'Somewhere safe,' said the Shieldmaster, 'at least for the time being.'

'What about all this food?' said the innkeeper. 'Will you take it with you?'

A look of panic spread over Toby's face as he tried to think of an excuse – but Pentabonce beat him to it.

'The smell would leave a trail a mile wide,' he said. 'We might as well lay on our backs in the market square and wait for the scarabs to feast on our intestines.'

'We'll bring it on the cart,' said Weazenock hopefully.

'I told you, you're not coming,' said Pentabonce. 'You can't be trusted.'

Weazenock slumped like a melting candle, but Bony Crumpet grabbed one of Pentabonce's men by the neck, threatening to twist his head off if they weren't allowed to come.

'I think you should release him,' said Lucy, watching the Shieldmaster's iron stare. His men were readying spears, and swords were sliding noiselessly from their scabbards.

'Alright,' said Bony, glaring at Pentabonce. 'But only because it's you, Miss Lucy. And if you change your minds, you know where we both is.'

'We're quite capable of looking after them,' said Pentabonce. 'Now sling your hook, before I'm tempted to see just how unruly my men can be.'

'Yeah,' grunted one of the ugliest ones. 'Unruly *and* violent.'

'We know when we're not wanted,' said Weazenock, heading for his cart. 'But you ain't heard the last from us – not by a *long* streak of chalk.'

Zarofi

They paused outside the Bright Byrde to make sure there were no scarabs in the vicinity. But for once the skies were clear.

'It's too quiet,' said Pentabonce. 'And this lot know something.'

The shield men were surrounded by a small but curious crowd, some of them wondering why Dragonard's men were here, and others, knowing that the Emperor was dead, wondering what the ones who *used* to be his men were doing here.

'Listen to me,' said Pentabonce, shouting at the crowd. 'My friends and I are about to leave. And I want you all to face the wall and close your eyes.'

'Yeah?' said a bright spark. 'What if we just wait until you're gone, and then follow you?'

'You could try,' said Pentabonce dryly, 'but you might find it difficult to navigate these narrow passageways with a spear through your neck.'

'But you won't be here to do the sticking, will you?' said the smart Alec.

'Not personally,' said Pentabonce. 'But some of these men will remain, under the command of Shield Bearer Frembley.'

'Ah,' said the smart Alec. 'Well in that case we'll be watching the insides of our eyelids, very quietly.'

'I knew you'd see sense,' said Pentabonce. 'Now, are we ready?'

The men in the escort party tied sacking over their boots, in order to deaden their footsteps. Pentabonce did the same, and offered bits of torn cloth to Lucy and her friends. And when they were all suitably equipped they were scarcely able to hear their own footfalls.

Their route took them through a complex maze of covered, fly-blown alleyways, many of which seemed to double back, as if trying to lay a path of confusion for anyone brave enough to follow. The party did get some rest though, pausing to take water whenever they encountered a well that hadn't been poisoned by the Sisters.

'We need to make better progress,' said Pentabonce, eyeing a shadow in a nearby alley. 'At this rate it'll be dusk by the time we reach the house.'

'House?' said Lucy.

'I've said too much,' said Pentabonce. 'We need a safe place where we can talk without being interrupted or overheard.'

'But we're heading to the tower,' said Lucy, as Pentabonce disappeared for a moment. 'I keep catching sight of it between the rooftops.'

'Our destination is near the Migdal,' admitted Pentabonce, as he returned wiping blood from his sword. 'Now walk quickly, and remain silent. There are troops still loyal to the Emperor, and they may be following us.'

As they resumed their journey, a flash of light reflected from a wall up ahead. Something was waiting around the corner, and from the disgusting noise it made, Lucy had a good idea what it might be.

'Mister Pentabonce?' she whispered. 'Are we expecting any of those slurg things?'

The Shield Master flattened himself against the wall.

'Don't make a sound,' he hissed.

'But we've got them outnumbered,' said Tenby with a smile.

As the slurgs moved into view they saw that the photographer was right. There were two creatures tethered side by side, and they were attached to a single large cart, manned by a driver and a pair of stunted assistants.

'Don't move until I say so,' whispered Pentabonce.

The cage on the cart contained a single groundling. He was dressed in rags and sitting on the floor in chains. And he wept loud enough for a hundred of his kinfolk.

'If you don't shut the fekk up,' yelled the driver, 'I'm going to climb down from here and frigging-well gut you with this.' He brandished a huge knife that glinted in the sunlight, but the sobbing continued unabated.

'That's it,' yelled the driver, unbuckling himself from the saddle. 'You've really gone and done it now, and no mistake. I *told* you to shut up, didden I?'

He slid down from his perch and leapt onto the cart, opening the cage with one of the dozens of keys that jangled on his leather belt.

'Please, *do* something,' hissed Lucy as the driver lifted his arm.

Pentabonce raised his spear. And as the knife was about to strike the groundling, the Shieldmaster's weapon impaled the driver's hand.

He fell to the floor of the cage screaming.

'Sling those two into the cage,' said the Shieldmaster, pointing at the assistants. 'In fact let's all get in — we can pretend to be prisoners.'

'Not me,' sobbed the groundling, 'but I can show her how to drive.' He pointed at Lucy, who was eyeing up one of the saddles. Then he raised a hand and one of the slurgs brought his head down and nuzzled him.

Pentabonce looked over at Lucy and saw her nodding.

'Alright,' he grumbled, 'but one false move and I'll be the one doing the gutting.'

Lucy climbed up the slurg's neck, which was cold but not as slimy as she expected. From the comfort of the tiny saddle she could see into the upper storeys of the surrounding houses. There were people inside, lying on the floor, and every so often one of them would take a peep when they thought they weren't being watched.

'Come on,' said Lucy, jiggling the reins, '*move*, will you?'

The slurg stayed put, even when she kicked it behind he ears.

'You don't want to do that,' said the groundling, as the creature's screams died away. 'That's the way the trappers treat them. It's not their fault they have to pull the death carts.'

'I suppose not,' said Lucy. 'But how do we get them to move?'

The groundling took a spare saddle from the cart and shinned up the other neck.

'I always wanted to have a go on one of these,' he said, grinning as he strapped himself in.

'I thought you knew how to control them?' said Lucy.

'Well you wouldn't have let me up here otherwise,' he said. 'I'm Gripple by the way.'

'Pleased to meet you,' said Lucy. As she spoke, the head she was sitting on craned up over the rooftops, as if it had smelt something. In the distance was a group of spear bearers, and they looked decidedly unfriendly.

'We have to get these things moving,' she yelled. 'Pentabonce was right about us being followed.'

'Don't look at me,' said Gripple.

'Oh, great,' sighed Lucy.

Curtains twitched furiously, and a few brave people ventured from their houses. Then, to Lucy's relief, an upstairs window creaked open.

A young girl stuck her head out and shouted to the slurgs.

'*Agribbo,*' she yelled, '*agribbo, negribbo, palumbo.*'

Lucy smiled and waved at her as all four slurg heads bobbed into action and they moved off. As they picked up speed, the slurgs occasionally leaned towards each other, exchanging sparks between their antennae.

'That's more like it,' said Lucy.

'Umm, yeah,' said Gripple, 'just so long as it's what you really want.'

'What do you mean?' said Lucy.

'It depends where you want to go,' said Gripple.

Lucy glanced up at the dark towering shape ahead.

'Not there,' said Gripple. 'The slurgs only know one destination.'

'Oh?' said Lucy. 'And what's that?'

'Piranesi's Perpetual Purgatorium,' replied Gripple.

Lucy leaned back in the saddle and the slurg reared, taking her above the rooftops. Gripple was right. The dark threat of the Migdal was visible in the distance, but their immediate destination was a lot closer. It was a massive stone walled palace laid out according to a geometrical design that might be easy to divine from the air, but which looked hellishly complex from the ground. Its walls were hewn from dark, damp granite that absorbed light.

But strangely, they didn't seem high enough to make a prison.

Lucy leaned forward and the slurg's head dipped to street level, where the thoroughfare had broadened into an irregular square with a well at its centre. To her right was the low, outermost wall of the prison, and ahead of her, the drawbridge entrance, where other slurg carts were converging.

'Let us out of here,' said a voice from the floor.

'Down there,' yelled Toby, 'look, at the bottom of the wall.'

Lucy leaned over so far that her slurg's head almost grazed the cobbles, where she found dozens of iron-barred gratings set into the wall. Each one was packed with desperate faces that clamoured for the light and begged for bread and water. And one of those faces belonged to the woman who had lost the drawing of her dead daughter. Her face was haggard and lined, made ugly by her grief and hopelessness.

'It might be easier to sympathise if you were all a bit prettier,' yelled one of Pentabonce's men.

'Faggenboom,' hissed the Shieldmaster, 'hold your filthy mouth.'

'*You* again?' the woman yelled to Lucy. 'You promised to free us once before and you never did.'

'Yeah,' yelled someone from the next grille. 'You made a promise and then you broke it, and umm, well, er, that means you have to help us escape. And if you don't…'

'Then we'll just have to stay here,' added another.

The twisted logic was almost as inescapable as the prison.

'Can't we do anything?' said Lucy, turning to the Shieldmaster.

'It's too well guarded,' replied Pentabonce.

'But the Emperor has gone,' said Lucy, 'surely…'

'It doesn't make a single bit of difference,' said Pentabonce. 'The people hate groundlings and that's all there is to it.'

'Yeah,' yelled Faggenboom, 'the lazy good-for-nothing food stealers. It's not worth risking your life to help them – or mine.'

'He's right,' said Pentabonce. 'At least about the risk – you'd never get them out of that place.'

'But it must be worth a try,' said Lucy.

'No,' said Pentabonce firmly, as the slurg turned towards the gate. 'And now we have to get off this thing, before it takes us inside.'

He gave Lucy a long, hard stare as she slid down from the saddle and opened the cage.

'Don't even think about it,' he said, noticing the glint in her eye.

The Purgatorium eventually receded from view, although the memory of the captive groundlings stayed with Lucy for a good while longer. As the rags wore down and began to drop from their feet, they approached a darker area where the alleyways narrowed and the eaves of the houses kissed overhead.

'This is the footings,' said Pentabonce. 'It's where…'

'I think I can see why,' said Lucy, her blood chilling.

A massive structure was visible in the gap between two houses. It was a small part of one of the Migdal's feet. And it plunged into the bare earth like a knife into dead flesh.

Pentabonce remained silent, signalling his men who filtered away into the surrounding buildings, like mist flowing amongst river rocks.

'Strange house,' said Lucy as they squeezed through a narrow door. The windows on the ground floor were barred, reminding her once again of the groundlings in their grisly cells.

'This was formerly the dwelling of Exotica Pubrane,' said Pentabonce. 'We should be safe here, at least for a day or so.'

'But it's so close to the tower,' said Lucy. 'Won't they think of looking on their doorstep?'

'The agents of the Sisters are accustomed to dealing with cowards,' said Pentabonce. 'It will take them a while to realise that we are bold enough to hide in the shadow of the Migdal.'

'And what will we do whilst we're here?' said Lucy. She glanced at the graffiti on the walls and the initials carved into the furniture. The soldiers had obviously been here before and got bored.

'Nothing,' said Pentabonce. 'You must be kept safe until we can gather enough forces to mount an attack. In the meantime you might like to sleep.'

But Lucy was too curious to rest.

Being brought to Miss Pubrane's house was like a second chance to get to know Exotica, and she was eager to explore the contents of her parlour. One item in particular caught her eye. It was a pot phrenology head, like the one Lily had installed in the hallway at home.

'Ah,' she sighed. 'Home. Now that would be nice, wouldn't it?'

'If you say so,' said Toby. 'But try to remember what Percy and Lily are really like before you start getting all misty eyed.'

'And Tarquin too,' said Lucy, running her hand across the pot skull.

'What's this you've found?' said Gusset.

'Just a piece of nonsense,' said Lucy. 'People collect all sorts of rubbish, don't they?'

'Not Miss Pubrane,' said Gusset. 'If she has something then there's likely to be a good reason. This is one of those things that tells you what people are like by feeling the bumps on their head.'

'They'd have a job,' smiled Lucy. 'The lettering is rubbed off, and Miss Pubrane has written Henbeg's name in lipstick in all the various positions – now that *is* strange.'

They carried on around the room, poking amongst tigers' heads, finger-vices and make-up cabinets. And then, having pulled out a bizarre machine that looked as though it belonged in a museum of Lectric, they came across a picture album with a single pencil drawing inside. A middle-aged woman sat on the grass next to a dried-up riverbed. And lying next to her, looking quite content, was an oversized and hauntingly familiar handbag.

Underneath, the scrawly handwriting said: -

'EAP and a young HO, GreenWitch Starr-Gaze-Atorium - Year 1.'

'It's a holiday drawing,' said Gusset. 'You could have them done in the old days. This one is from the very first year of the world.'

'So I see,' smiled Lucy. 'And Miss Pubrane looks to be about fifty years old, even then.'

'Yes,' said Gusset. 'It's all to do with the uni...'

'...versal mysteries?' said Lucy, completing his sentence.

Gusset grumbled as they passed from parlour to kitchen, where they discovered food on the table. There was even a handy knife nearby.

'It's bread,' grinned Lucy, 'almost an entire loaf.'

'It looks a bit green,' said Toby.

'And blue,' said Tenby. 'It definitely looks a bit blue.'

'I don't really care,' said Lucy, rubbing her aching stomach.

'I'll see if I can find something to put on it,' said Gusset.

He opened the larder but swiftly closed it again, turning to lean against the door. It shook violently, as if something was trying to escape.

'Nothing of interest in there,' he said nervously.

But Pixy had spotted something in the darkness.

'That's what happens when Star-Gazey sauce goes rancid,' she said. 'The fish-eyes come alive again. Then all the other stuff in the larder starts to get ideas.'

'I think I'll stick to the mouldy bread,' said Lucy.

'Maybe not,' said Toby. He cut the end crust off the loaf to reveal a slimy pile of maggots inside, each one a different shade of yellow.

'Oh *yummy*,' said Pixy, 'I love mixed ambers.'

'I'm going to vomit,' said Lucy. She ran from the room, her face the same colour as the squirming delicacies.

'I'm next with the bucket,' said Toby, yelling after her.

On her return, Lucy found Pentabonce slumped in an armchair.

'So how do you propose to get inside the Migdal?' he said. 'There are no doors you know.'

'What do you mean?' said Toby.

'Just that,' said Pentabonce. 'If you were to count the doors leading from the outside of the tower to the inside then you'd come up with a number slightly less than one.'

'Like *none* you mean?' said Pixy proudly.

'Correct,' smiled Pentabonce. 'So unless you can fly, I suggest we look at some alternative plan.'

'But that's where Fenny is,' said Lucy. 'What's the point of an alternative plan if it doesn't achieve what we want?'

'And you're sure that's where she is?' said Pentabonce.

'Not absolutely,' said Lucy, 'but Doctor Dee thought he recognised the room – something to do with removing heads.'

'Well that's something we know about,' said Pentabonce. 'Especially poor Snagrot.'

'And Exotica,' said Lucy solemnly.

'So where does that leave us?' said Toby.

'Tired,' said Lucy, yawning. 'Very, very tired.'

'Then perhaps we will dream a solution,' said Pentabonce. 'Toby can take the fainting couch in the parlour, and Gusset and Tenby will share the bedroom down the hall.'

'But it's freezing in there,' said Tenby, 'and it smells of wee.'

'Don't shout too loud,' grinned Pentabonce, 'or everyone will want it.'

'What about me?' said Pixy.

'You can sleep in the big basket in the kitchen,' said the Shieldmaster.

'And where will you be when all this is going on?' moaned Tenby.

'Outside the door of Miss Lucy Blake's room,' he replied seriously. 'And I shall be armed with a drawn sword, to see off all cowans and intruders.'

Tiredness had ambushed Lucy, who clumped up the stairs as if she as wearing lead slippers. Henbeg followed behind, growling at the thought of all the strangers in his house. They had looked in his mistress's cupboards, and eaten his mistress's food and now they were even going to sleep in her bed.

'Will you show me where to go?' smiled Lucy.

Henbeg reluctantly nuzzled the bedroom door open and waited by the window for Lucy. The room was surprisingly plain – just three bare walls washed in a kind of maggoty yellow, and a fourth punctured by a tiny window with bulls-eye glass that distorted the scene outside. Lucy squinted through one of the thick panes and was shocked to see the tower twisted into an even more grotesque form by the contours of the glass. She hadn't though it possible, but the Migdal seemed even more threatening, perhaps because of the dark storm clouds that were accelerating the onset of night.

She turned to the bed – a fabulous four-posted specimen of the type that one might like to die in, but only after a long and fruitful life. The quilt was covered in wild-yellow and gold embroidery, and decorated with tassels and sequins, and Lucy had no trouble in imagining Exotica lying there, perhaps with Henbeg stretched alongside her. And even though she was tired, Lucy leaped onto the bed and jumped up and down, squeaking the ancient springs that were buried deep in its foundations.

Henbeg gave an excited yelp.

'What was that boy?' said Lucy.

He gazed at the coat-hook on the back of the door. Then, when he had Lucy's attention, he stared at the space below the bed.

'You want something from under there?' said Lucy.

Henbeg returned a stare that might have meant '*yes*', but might also have been '*I fancy a game of cards*', or '*I'm going to bite your ankle*'.

Lucy reached underneath and pulled out a heavy wood and gilt structure that looked like a basket for a pampered dog. Henbeg gave another of his inscrutable grins and then looked at the coat hook, then back at the basket, then at the hook again until Lucy caught on.

'I see,' she smiled. 'So the basket is for when you're a crocodile, and the hook on the door is for when you're a handbag?'

Henbeg gave an unmistakeable snort, looking backwards and forwards between the two spots.

'You want to know which one to use?' said Lucy. 'Is that what Miss Pubrane did? Well on this occasion I'll let you choose. Wherever you think you'll dream about your mistress the most.'

Without hesitating Henbeg leapt into the basket, flipping onto his back and wriggling all eight legs in the air.

'I'm glad that's sorted out,' said Lucy. 'Now, can we get some sleep?'

Henbeg laid still, his legs in the air, gazing longingly at Lucy.

'What is it now?' she said. 'A tummy tickle?'

She reached down and rubbed Henbeg's belly, and was surprised to find that he was quite soft underneath. He gave a low, contented growl, like a refrigerator with a noisy motor, then flipped over onto his side and curled up into a tight ball.

It was time for them both to slip into the arms of darkness.

When Lucy woke, she expected it to be light outside, but the candle had burned barely halfway and night was still looking in at the window. Above the sound of Henbeg's snoring she heard a noise like the rustling of leaves, only louder.

'Henbeg?' she whispered, as she crossed to the window. 'Are you awake?'

In an instant the creature was beside her, standing on his four hind legs with his nose pressed firmly to the window. His breath left a pattern on the glass where Lucy was surprised to see four rings, even though he only had two nostrils.

'What is it boy?' she said. 'Is it dangerous?'

Henbeg sniffed at the glass but was unable to get a scent, so Lucy opened the window just a crack. Three shadowy shapes flew in and circled the room before landing on the bed canopy. They looked like bats without faces – a triangular flap of leather, folded in the middle. Henbeg sniffed the air and went back to his basket. Whatever they were, he judged them to be friendly.

'I hope you're sure about that,' said Lucy. She watched the dark shapes settling on the canopy, like a set of animated roof tiles.

Henbeg grunted and began to snore, so she snuffed the candle and went to the window where dozens more of the creatures flapped against the glass. It was as if they had been told she was giving out free seed, or whatever it was they ate with their non-existent mouths. Lucy soon tired of their antics though, and opened the window to shoo them away. And it was then that she noticed a more sinister shadow lurking in the road below. If she'd had any money she would have bet it all on Weazenock being out there.

The next time Lucy woke it was still night, but there was a different kind of disturbance outside. A band of musicians had gathered below, but instead of tossing pebbles at the window to attract her attention they were playing their instruments very, very quietly. But not quietly enough – candles were flickering into life in the surrounding houses.

'Do you think this'll do it?' said one of the shadowy figures.

'I rather think it might,' said Lucy as she threw the window open.

'See? I told you it would work,' said the shadow. 'That's her, innit?'

'I know I'm going to regret asking,' said Lucy, 'but what do you want?'

'I'm Khibri,' shouted the horn player, rather too loud for comfort.

'And I'm Snooker,' yelled the ugly one with a mouth organ. 'We followed the slurg trails.'

'Did you see any soldiers on the way?' whispered Lucy.

'A long way back,' yelled Khibri. 'Otherwise we wouldn't be able to do this would we?' He picked up his horn and blew a tune that reminded Lucy of where she had seen them last – at Dragonard's command performance.

'Do you mind?' whispered Lucy. 'We're supposed to be hiding.'

'Yeah, pack it in Khibri,' yelled a man in a green tunic. His instrument looked like an old kettle on the end of a hose. 'Otherwise I'm going to come across there and shove that Nollidge right up your…'

'Phlange, *please*,' said Khibri. 'We're all in this together remember? We're supposed to be helping her.'

'We heard about you in the Assembly of the Dead,' said Snooker. 'You tried to get them groundlings out of their cages. So we came to help.'

'By playing loud music and giving our position away?' said Lucy.

'Yeah,' admitted Khibri, 'umm, sorry about that.'

As Lucy got dressed she glanced at the bed canopy, expecting to see the dark shapes – but they were gone. As she ran downstairs and into the street she made a note to ask about them, but promptly forgot when she laid eyes on the mayhem caused by the musicians. They had arrived on three carts draped with tarpaulins, covering what looked like packing crates.

As Lucy approached, the drivers dismounted from their carts and the one called Snooker explained to Toby why they had left the palace.

'Yeah, well when we heard what they done to Snagrot we said we wasn't going to hang around playing music for the likes of them,' he said.

'So you decided to inflict it on us?' said Toby with a wink at Lucy. 'If you really wanted to teach them a lesson then you should have stayed behind.'

'After what they did to Terranus?' said a boy carrying a huge drum. 'He was our favourite – present company excepted of course.'

'Arnold's right,' said the hurdy-gurdy man. 'Nobody could match Miss Lucy Blake and her famous Venter Lokey.'

'I'm glad you liked it,' smiled Lucy. But her smile disappeared, as she recalled leaping over a shape outside her bedroom door. It was Pentabonce, and he must have been asleep, which didn't seem right.

'Yeah, we liked your act alright,' said Snooker. 'But we liked Neebophilus Blueface too. It was a pity what they did to him.'

'Don't tell me,' said Lucy.

'They cut him into hundreds of slices,' said Arnold.

'I *said* I didn't want to hear,' hissed Lucy, her expression turning to a frown as she realised that nobody else in the house had woken.

'You need to hear,' said Phlange, 'so you can hate proper – you can't just hate for no reason, can you? We all wanted to do the same thing to old skin and bones Dragonard, but that angel thing got to him first – carried him off kicking and screaming it did. He sounded a bit like Quim the day they ripped all the seats out of the theatre. You know Quim, don't you?'

'We did,' said Toby, 'but the last we saw of him, he was floating off down the river.'

'And what's one of them?' said Khibri.

'An old thing,' said Pixy appearing in the doorway. 'Full of water.'

'Like a bucket you mean?' suggested the kettle man.

'It'd have to be an old bucket,' said Snooker.

'*Ye-es*,' said Lucy, deciding not to follow the deteriorating course of their conversation. 'Umm, did the Emperor say anything before they dropped him over the side?'

'Nothing I can repeat in front of you,' grinned Snooker.

'He didn't say sorry then?' said Lucy.

'Unlikely,' said Snooker. 'Did you hear anything Nurk? You was at the baskets when the skinny Majesty got dropped over the side.'

'There wasn't no kind of apology,' said Nurk. 'Just a sort of whizzing sound as he went by.'

'I see,' smiled Lucy. 'So tell me, what exactly is it you're doing here?'

'We're on a mission,' said Snooker.

'Anything to do with what you've got under the tarpaulins?' said Lucy.

'We're not allowed to tell,' he replied.

'Who says?' said Toby.

'The chap with the strange hat,' said Snooker. 'He's the one what gave us the destructions. Well he didn't actually give *us* the destructions; he gave them to Frumble, the carpenter. But we're the ones with the carts, so we got to bring them along. Whatever they are.'

'The destructions?' said Lucy.

'I thought you was supposed to be clever?' said Snooker. 'I heard you was a sorceress on account of...'

'Yes, I know,' interrupted Lucy. 'Tell me about the man in the hat – was it Doctor Dee by any chance?'

'Dunno,' said Frumble, 'he just turned up at the manufactory and gave us this.' He unrolled a large blueprint and spread it out on the ground. 'It's the destructions for building some kind of trap.'

'These are instructions for making an Angelic Cabinet,' said Lucy. 'And it looks as though they were torn from a big book.'

'Do you reckon it was one of Dee's?' said Toby.

'Perhaps,' said Lucy, turning her attention back to the carts. 'And that's what you've got under here is it? Angelic Cabinets?'

'I don't know nuffink about names,' said Frumble. 'I just made them perzackerly as I was told.'

'But that's not why we're here,' said Snooker.

'Oh?' said Lucy, raising an eyebrow.

'That's why we had to drug the others,' said Khibri. 'We sneaked some green stuff into their supper.'

'Uh-oh,' said Toby. 'I don't like the sound of this.'

'Don't worry,' grinned Khibri. 'They'll wake up eventually.'

'Yeah,' said Snooker, 'but we'll be on our way.'

'To the prison,' said Khibri. 'We're going to get them all out.'

'I wanted to try,' said Lucy, 'but Pentabonce said it was too dangerous.'

'We know,' said Snooker.

'But won't it be quite difficult getting in?' said Toby.

'That'll be easy,' grinned Khibri. 'It's getting out that's the hard bit.'

'Shouldn't this place be guarded?' said Lucy, gazing up at the dark stone walls of the Purgatorium.

'What's the point?' said Snooker. 'Nobody ever gets out of here alive. It ain't possible to, wotsisname.'

'Escape?' suggested Toby.

'Yeah, that's it,' said Snooker. 'Excape.'

'I find that hard to believe,' said Lucy.

She heard the words emerge, but didn't really believe them. Piranesi's Perpetual Purgatorium had the look of an impenetrable fortress, even if they *had* run out of building materials half way through. The low circular wall was punctuated by a single arch, and didn't seem high enough to keep anyone in, at least until Lucy and the others passed through the gate. Then everything became clear – a madman had designed the prison. The ground inside the walls sloped away from them like the crater of some long extinct volcano, and criss crossing this depression were hundreds of ladders and walkways. Most of them were concentrated at the centre, where ropes dangling from huge windlasses descended into a massive sheer sided crater.

'That's the furca,' said Khibri.

'The *what*?' grinned Toby.

'A big hole,' explained Arnold. 'It's guarded by four stone lions.'

'Oh,' said Lucy, as they approached. 'So it is.'

Rising through the centre of the cylindrical shaft was a massive structure that resembled a lighthouse, but with no visible means of support – it simply reached up from the void to a point just below the rim.

'So that's why the outer wall isn't very high,' said Lucy.

'It's huge,' whispered Toby, peering into the dark. 'Can you imagine how much effort it took to excavate a hole that size?'

'Nobody knows,' said Khibri. 'Not even the jailers. They say the hole was here before the world began.'

'*Was* it?' said Lucy. 'Now that *is* interesting.'

The furca was around three or four hundred yards in diameter. It was capped by a series of radial cables tethered to the rim wall on the outside and to the walls of the lighthouse at the centre. It resembled a giant bicycle wheel tipped on its side – the tower forming the hub, the cables looking like spokes and the outer wall of the shaft taking place of the rim. Lucy squinted at the tiny lighthouse portholes. There was movement inside, which meant only one thing – they had been spotted, even in this dim half-light.

'Where are the prisoners?' she asked.

'Asleep,' said Khibri.

'Yes, but *where* are they asleep?' said Lucy.

'Down there,' replied Snooker with a sombre look. He leaned out and pointed to the wall that gently curved away from them on either side.

Lucy steadied herself and leaned out as far as she dared. The shaft was lined with rough stonework and punctuated by cells whose doors faced out into the void. The only access to these one-man prisons was by ropes that dangled through the radial spokes like a mass of tangled knitting.

A terrible moan emerged from the void. It sounded like the cell in Dragonard's palace, but Lucy knew that this time it wasn't the wind. As her eyes got accustomed to the gloom she was able to follow some of the shorter ropes to their end.

'There are people,' she said, with a slight sob. 'There are prisoners dangling on the ends of those ropes.'

'Maybe we can get down to them?' said Toby, indicating a nearby door.

They all piled onto a stone staircase that spiralled down inside the skin wall of the cylinder. Each time they curved back to the excavated edge there was a narrow window where they could see the cables, and, in the distance, the walls of the lighthouse at the centre.

'A few more storeys yet,' said Toby.

Lucy paused at the window, staring silently at the prisoners, the topmost of which they were almost level with. Each of the groundlings was bound into a wickerwork cage and suspended from a thin hemp rope, whose hairy cables swayed gently. Every so often the baskets would touch, allowing the prisoners to join hands for a moment. They were the lucky ones. Many of the wicker coffins were frayed at the bottom, the groundlings inside them clinging on for their lives. Others less fortunate had already succumbed and fallen out, their constant tears and weak-as-water pee having rotted away the lower parts of their cages.

Lucy peered further into the gloom, and was shocked to find that some of the fallen victims were still visible. They were clinging to various narrow ledges by their worn-out fingernails.

'That's not natcherel that isn't,' said Snooker. 'People like us groundlings isn't designed for the air.'

'So why don't they mutate into birds and escape?' said Lucy.

'Yeah, *right*, change into something else,' grinned Snooker. 'That's just one of them myth thingies that everyone believes – but it's not true.'

'S'right,' agreed Khibri, 'but if we *did* happen to find someone like that – someone who could change shape – then there'd be a lot of trouble.'

'We'd probably have to kill 'em,' said Snooker.

'That's right,' said a voice from the pit. The groundling dangled just a few yards away in a relatively new basket. He had a narrow face and slit eyes that made him look like a moneylender.

'Kill them?' said Lucy. 'But why?'

'Because they's different,' said the moneylender. 'That's why.'

'But that's why you're in prison.' said Lucy. 'You're being persecuted because you're different, and yet you want to do the same thing to your own kind.'

'Snot the same,' said Snooker.

'Yes it is,' said Lucy.

'No it isn't,' yelled the moneylender.

'Alright,' said Lucy, losing her patience. 'Well frankly I don't *care* what you think. We're going to get you out of there, so keep your stupid opinions to yourself or I might just change my mind.'

'Rescue?' said the moneylender. 'Oh, well I'm all in favour of that.'

'I thought you might be,' said Lucy. 'Only it's not going to be easy.'

'Snot gunner be easy at all,' said Snooker.

'Has anybody got any ideas?' said Lucy.

'We were kind of hoping that'd be your department,' said Khibri, 'what with your reputation for talking your way out of trouble.'

'So who do we need to talk to?' said Lucy.

'Clinker,' said Snooker. 'The chief warden.'

'Alright,' said Lucy. 'You lot stay here and I'll have a word with him.'

'No fear,' said Khibri, staring up at the disc of open sky. 'We're coming with you – can't you hear them?'

'*Scarabs*?' suggested Toby, peering through the web of ropes.

'Could be,' said Lucy. She tilted her head. There was a vague buzzing in the distance, like a swarm of flies inside a cardboard tube. 'You'd best stay here in any case,' she added.

'Not bloody likely,' said Khibri. 'We've come this far together, so we're going to help you with the rest of it.'

'Oh, goody,' said Toby.

'Gentlemen,' said Khibri, 'take up your instruments and follow me.'

They carried on down the spiral staircase for a dozen or so storeys before coming to a flat landing with a wooden door in the inner wall. Lucy expected to find it locked, but it swung aside noiselessly, revealing a gently bowed bridge that reached out towards the lighthouse. It was a delicate affair, built from light wood and thin ropes like the one they crossed near the Forest of Skeels, but this one was smaller and much older, and a great deal of care had been taken in its construction. The handrails were carved with snake forms, and the newel posts were capped with a huge glass marble, inside which was a pair of twisted serpents. Lucy paused to consider the other bridges. She could see two more running at right-angles to this, but was certain there'd be a fourth on the other side – and it didn't take her long to guess what symbols might be carved onto those others.

Lucy steadied herself against the serpent marble and leaned over, hoping to see the bottom of the void. But there was nothing – it simply went on forever, the sheer sides fading from view along with the lighthouse.

'That's a long drop,' said Khibri. He blew his horn gently, but the sound reverberated around them, amplifying as it bounced off the cylinder walls.

'It certainly is,' grinned Toby. 'Why don't we throw your instrument over the side and see how long it takes to get to the bottom?'

Khibri ran across the bridge and squashed himself against the red painted door, cradling the instrument in his arms in case anyone tried to snatch it.

'Don't worry,' said Lucy. 'There are more important things to be doing than ridding the world of questionable music.'

'Well if there are,' grinned Toby. 'I'd like to hear about them.'

Zarobi

There was a sound of flushing from above. Seconds later, the contents of a toilet shot from a pipe and covered Khibri and his Nollidge in twelve different-smelling types of effluent.

'I think you should stay here,' sniffed Lucy. She tried the nearest door but it was locked, so the orchestra followed her around the gantry until they found another entrance, this one decorated with a golden eagle.

'Just as I expected,' said Lucy.

'Yeah, me too,' said Snooker, as the latch clicked.

The warden sat behind a desk in his sparse office, puffing on a huge pipe. He reminded Lucy of Malcolm, and for a moment she felt homesick – a feeling that was reinforced by the sweet smell of tobacco.

'Hello,' she said meekly, 'Mister Clinker, is it?'

'Warden Clinker to you,' he snarled. 'And anyway, who wants to know?'

His blown up cheeks glowed like apples, and were surrounded by a fuzz of crumb-flecked whiskers. 'Umm, is that thing with you?' he said, pointing at Henbeg.

'He might be,' said Lucy. 'But you're in luck, he had a big supper.'

The crocodile licked his lips, indicating that he could probably find room for another course if it was absolutely necessary.

'Yeah?' said Clinker. 'Well make sure it stays where I can see it. Now what do you want? I'm a very busy man.'

'We'd like to come to some arrangement,' said Lucy.

'What kind of an arrangement?' said Clinker. 'And don't think you can influence me by playing soft music and all that stuff. I hate music, so you've wasted your time bringing that lot with you.' He pointed at the orchestra who were shuffling about in the doorway behind her.

'It's quite simple really,' said Lucy, motioning the musicians away. 'I want you to release all the prisoners.'

'Oh, well if you say so,' said Clinker. He gave a great bellowing laugh that reminded her of Beaksheaf.

'What, really?' said Lucy.

'No, *not* bloody well really,' he yelled. 'What do you take me for, some kind of idiot?'

'Ah, well,' said Lucy, 'I'm not quite...'

Zarobi

There was a sound of flushing from above. Seconds later, the contents of a toilet shot from a pipe and covered Khibri and his Nollidge in twelve different-smelling types of effluent.

'I think you should stay here,' sniffed Lucy. She tried the nearest door but it was locked, so the orchestra followed her around the gantry until they found another entrance, this one decorated with a golden eagle.

'Just as I expected,' said Lucy.

'Yeah, me too,' said Snooker, as the latch clicked.

The warden sat behind a desk in his sparse office, puffing on a huge pipe. He reminded Lucy of Malcolm, and for a moment she felt homesick – a feeling that was reinforced by the sweet smell of tobacco.

'Hello,' she said meekly, 'Mister Clinker, is it?'

'Warden Clinker to you,' he snarled. 'And anyway, who wants to know?'

His blown up cheeks glowed like apples, and were surrounded by a fuzz of crumb-flecked whiskers. 'Umm, is that thing with you?' he said, pointing at Henbeg.

'He might be,' said Lucy. 'But you're in luck, he had a big supper.'

The crocodile licked his lips, indicating that he could probably find room for another course if it was absolutely necessary.

'Yeah?' said Clinker. 'Well make sure it stays where I can see it. Now what do you want? I'm a very busy man.'

'We'd like to come to some arrangement,' said Lucy.

'What kind of an arrangement?' said Clinker. 'And don't think you can influence me by playing soft music and all that stuff. I hate music, so you've wasted your time bringing that lot with you.' He pointed at the orchestra who were shuffling about in the doorway behind her.

'It's quite simple really,' said Lucy, motioning the musicians away. 'I want you to release all the prisoners.'

'Oh, well if you say so,' said Clinker. He gave a great bellowing laugh that reminded her of Beaksheaf.

'What, really?' said Lucy.

'No, *not* bloody well really,' he yelled. 'What do you take me for, some kind of idiot?'

'Ah, well,' said Lucy, 'I'm not quite...'

924

'Don't bother insulting me again,' he growled. 'I have no intention of freeing any of them.'

'But why?' said Lucy. 'Now that the Emperor has gone there's no reason to keep them here.'

'Oh you *think* so, do you?' said Clinker. 'Well I know otherwise see? It's not just the Emperor that wanted this worthless bunch of scrag-ends banged up in choky for the rest of their naturals.'

'Isn't it?' said Lucy. 'I mean, wasn't it?'

'Course not,' grinned Clinker. 'Everyone hates them.'

'But only because they were taught to dislike them,' said Lucy.

'People are *designed* to hate,' sneered Clinker. 'It's just buried a bit deeper in some of us. Even you.'

Lucy shuffled uncomfortably. She'd intended to claim the moral high ground, beating him about the head with her unassailable logic, but Clinker had managed to make her feel guilty for hating Raziel. He was right – the capacity for loathing was in everyone.

'Hey, wait a minute though,' said Clinker. 'What's that you've got poking out of your pocket?'

'You wouldn't be interested,' said Lucy, sensing an opportunity. She pushed the end of the vellum roll back inside her coat.

'I'll be the judge of that,' said Clinker. He leaned over and grabbed the map, spreading it over his desk before Lucy had chance to protest. It tried to burst into life, but Clinker rolled it up immediately, his eyes blazing with greed.

'I've changed my mind,' he said, tearing off a small piece of vellum. 'I'll take this, and in exchange you can have the prisoners.'

'Is that all?' smiled Lucy, reaching for the desk.

'Of course not,' grunted Clinker, '*this* is your bit.' He pressed the smaller fragment into Lucy's hand and shoved the rest into a cabinet, padlocking it with such speed that she had barely managed to get her mouth open.

'Ber, ber, but...'

'No ber, ber, ber, buts,' snarled Clinker. 'I was thinking of getting out of this business anyway – there's too much anxiety.'

'Yours or the prisoners?' said Lucy.

'Mine,' grunted Clinker. 'I told you, nobody cares about the scum-bag prisoners.' He opened a cupboard to reveal a signalling device, which he blew into. When a tinny voice responded he bellowed into the mouthpiece.

'Open the gates.'

'What, all of them?' squeaked the voice at the other end of the tube.

'Just do it,' bellowed Clinker.

'There,' he said, turning to Lucy, 'will that do you?'

'Very nicely thank you,' she said with a frown.

It had all been too easy. There was something else going on, but she couldn't think what it might be.

'Come on Luce,' said Toby. 'We've got what we came for.'

'And lost a map,' said Snooker, as they backed out of the office.

The warden was as good as his word. Baskets were being winched up the shaft and cell doors were creaking open. Hundreds of ropes were lowered into the shaft, and groundlings were spilling from their cages and climbing toward the sky.

There was a lot of whooping and cheering, but Lucy remained silent.

'I don't like this,' she said.

'Me neither,' said Toby. 'Something stinks.'

'But we've got what we came for,' said Khibri, looking puzzled.

'We'll see,' said Lucy, wrinkling her nose at the horn-player's smell.

They made their way back across the bridge and climbed the stairs that would bring them back to ground level. Each time they reached a window Lucy paused to check on the escape.

'I'm still not convinced,' said Toby, as they set off on the final leg.

'Me neither,' said Lucy, returning to the window.

The cheers had ceased, and as she peered towards the top of the shaft the reason became apparent. The ropes were stationary, and guards with spears were positioned all around the rim. A few feet in front of her were three dangling baskets, one of which was occupied.

'Hey, get us out of here,' said the groundling, 'or you'll be sorry.'

He reminded her of Percy but without the pipe. Or at least how he might have looked if he had been left out in the rain for two years and his skin had turned to prune-leather.

'If you speak to me like that again, I might just leave you,' said Lucy. 'Don't you have any manners at all?'

'Yeah,' said the groundling, 'but they got worn away, what with us being under the threat of death and everything.'

'Sorry,' said Lucy, 'I suppose that might be a good excuse now you come to mention it.'

'I reckon,' whinged the groundling. 'So how about letting us out?'

'We're working on it,' said Lucy. She clamped her hands over her ears as a deep clanging noise split the air all around them. It sounded like the gates of hell were open and all the devil's church bells were ringing at once.

'What's going on?' yelled Toby.

'I don't know,' said Lucy, 'but I don't think we should wait to find out. They don't ring bells like that without a good reason.'

'Hey, what about me?' yelled the groundling in the basket.

'I'm sorry,' yelled Lucy. 'I'm really very sorry. I'm sure it'll be alright in the end.'

'Yeah, right,' screamed the groundling. 'Well run away then, you stinking, shitty fart-arse. And I hope you drown in a vat of diarrhoea and your whole family dies of snot-gobbler's face rot.'

Lucy was in tears as they ran up the stairs and emerged into the prison yard. The skies buzzed with scarabs and armed guards surrounded the compound. And the warders were bringing out manacles and fetters and other grisly contrivances that certainly hadn't been designed for the comfort and convenience of the prisoners.

'It's a trap,' said Toby.

'You're in trouble now,' grinned a nearby guard.

'It's alright,' said Lucy in desperation. 'We have an arrangement with the chief warder.'

'Not any more you don't,' shouted Clinker, as they winched him up from the pit on the end of a rope. 'Hey,' he yelled, waving the map in the air, 'that girl you wanted me to find – she's over here.'

'You bloody filthy lying pig,' hissed Lucy.

'Now, now, don't be like that,' grinned the warden.

'Umm, hey, wait a minute,' said Lucy, scanning the area. 'Who were you shouting at just now?'

'I think that might have been me,' said a dark-clothed man.

He pushed his way through the orchestra and stood before them.

'And you are?' said Lucy.

'Do you not recognise me?' he said.

Lucy studied his gentle, soft-skinned face and saw that it wasn't a man after all. There was no beard to speak of, and the line of the jaw was delicate and gently defined, like a woman's.

'Have we met before?' said Lucy, trembling slightly.

'I am Zarobi,' said the angel. 'Our paths crossed briefly at the palace – and then once again, when I spied you on the ground.

'Is this one of the Sisters?' said Toby. He ducked to pick up a fallen spear, but before he had a chance to level it the wooden shaft turned to flames, blistering his hands and singing his eyebrows.

'Looks like it,' said Snooker.

'I thought you might be tempted to free the prisoners,' said Zarobi, 'so I prepared these simple people for my plan and then I waited.'

'Hey, less of the simple,' said Clinker.

The angel ignored him, and continued to address Lucy.

'You will come to find,' she said, 'that servants such as these can often be useful, despite appearances to the contrary.'

'Hey,' grunted Clinker, 'I told you about that, didn't I? You can't talk about me like that – I'm important.'

'Be *silent*,' hissed Zarobi. '*Forever.*'

The angel closed her eyes and tilted her head back, parting her lips as if to whisper. But as she blew the softest of breezes, her breath burned blue in the air.

'Look out,' shouted Toby.

It was too late for warnings. The air crackled and hissed as its component molecules bent to the angel's will. Clinker held the map in front of him like a shield, but a cloud of blue fire swallowed it instantly. The vellum writhed in the flames like a dying bird, and for a moment it seemed that a model of the entire world was suspended in the fizzing air. But the vision of Assiah soon vanished and the flames turned their attentions to Clinker. They wrapped his body, taking his hair first and his clothes and finally his skin. And then, as everyone looked on in horror, the flames intensified, swirling and swooping around his exposed skeleton and swallowing him up.

'You have led the representatives of heaven on a merry dance,' said Zarobi, without any hint of emotion. 'But your time of flight is at an end. You will submit, Lucy Blake, and come with me.'

'And if we don't?' said Lucy, trying not to look in Clinker's direction. Not that he was there anymore. All that was left was a glowing pile of ash.

'We are under instruction from the irresistible might that is God,' said the angel. 'Would you dare to defy the creator?'

'Was it God's idea to kill Clinker?' said Lucy. 'Or was that just for your own pleasure?'

Zarobi snorted.

'And another thing,' said Lucy, noticing that the ground had begun to shake. 'This God chappie you say you're working for.'

'Yes?' said Zarobi uncertainly.

'Well he's not really the creator, is he?' said Lucy.

'You presume too much,' said Zarobi. 'Have you ever heard the human expression, *'a little knowledge is a dangerous thing'*?'

'It's not as dangerous as no knowledge at all,' said Lucy, 'and in any case we're learning all the time, aren't we Toby?'

'What? Oh, umm, *yeah*,' said Toby, following the line of Lucy's gaze.

The cobblestones under Zarobi's feet were jostling around, as if being drilled out from underground.

'More of your trickery?' said the angel.

She spread her arms and unfolded her dark feathered cape to reveal a great pair of wings. The stench of droppings emerged from her clothing like a cloud of despair. Lucy turned her nose up, leaning back to avoid the sweep of feathers as the wings unfolded to their full height. There was a sense of relief when they were out of her face, but the emotion was replaced by an unwelcome feeling of admiration for Zarobi's gracious, flowing movements. The angel's body brightened and glowed as powerful wing-beats lifted her clear of the ground – just enough to avoid the mysterious excavations.

'I think we've had it,' said Toby, glancing at Clinker's ashes.

'Unless we can think of something quickly,' said Lucy.

'Well don't look at me,' replied Toby.

'Excellent,' said Zarobi, 'then you will submit?'

'Yes,' whispered Lucy, still staring at the vibrating cobbles.

'I'm sorry,' smiled Zarobi, 'I didn't hear – was that a *yes*?'

'Just a minute,' said Lucy.

She moved to where the angel had just been standing. Toby and Henbeg moved to join her and the ground shook even more violently, raising a cloud of dust around their feet.

'What will happen to the others?' said Lucy, playing for time.

'You and the boy will accompany me,' said Zarobi, slightly puzzled. 'And the rest may go free.'

'Then we'll come quietly,' said Lucy.

Zarobi snorted again.

'No, this is all too easy,' she said. 'Raziel is my sworn enemy, but despite that, he warned me that you would slither and turn like an eel coated in olio of slipperum. So just what is it that I have failed to see?'

But there was no reply from the three friends – just the sound of the wind and a nebula of dust that had risen around their feet. And when that cloud finally settled, they were nowhere to be seen.

Indistinct
Rumblings

The light of Zarobi was extinguished, and as they plummeted down a smelly, root-lined shaft, Lucy had visions of ending up in an underground cell. Or perhaps the passage they were tumbling into went to the edge of the world or even beyond?

'Try to keep calm,' yelled a voice from below.

It sounded familiar, but she couldn't quite place it.

'I'm *very* calm,' said Toby, dropping like a stone. 'This is such a pleasant way to go – it was nice knowing you all.'

'Don't panic,' shouted the voice, 'the shaft will flare out soon.'

As the voice promised, the vertical drop turned into more of a diagonal plummet, then flattened out slowly until eventually they were skidding along on their backs. As they came to a halt amidst clouds of dust, Lucy caught sight of their rescuer. It was Groffin, and he was yelling at the crocodile that had fallen alongside them.

'Leave Groffin alone,' he begged. 'Groffin has done nothing to you.'

There was a great deal of growling, followed by some tail thrashing, but at Lucy's signal the handbag released his grip and revealed a set of bright red indentations in Groffin's ankle.

'You'll be alright,' smiled Lucy, dusting herself down. 'That was just a play bite, wasn't it boy?'

'Then Groffin would not like to see him when he's being vicious,' said their rescuer.

'Well that's the introductions over with,' said Toby. 'Where are we?'

'Underground,' said Groffin helpfully.

'Hey, wait a minute,' said Toby, with a suspicious stare. 'I've seen those eyes before – you were spying on us from a manhole cover at Smiff's Fields.'

'We was keeping a friendly eye on you,' admitted Groffin.

'You were *spying*,' said Toby. 'I don't call that friendly – and dragging us underground isn't very friendly either.'

'Nobody asked you to stand there,' said Groffin. 'And anyway, you perscaped from the angel thingy, and I'm not promising anything, but we *might* just be able to get you inside the Migdal – umm, you *do* want to get inside, don't you?'

'Is there *anyone* in this place who doesn't know our plans?' said Lucy.

'I expect they're written on our foreheads in crayon,' smiled Toby. 'And we're the only ones who can't see them.'

'Crayon?' said Groffin.

'Never mind,' said Toby, 'what was that thing we fell down?'

'I don't know what they are where you come from,' said Groffin, 'but in these parts we call them holes.'

'Yes, *very* funny,' said Lucy. 'And will the angel Zarobi be able to follow us through this wonderful hole technology?'

'Only if she's good at digging,' grinned Groffin. 'Just before that beast of yours savaged me I knocked the ceiling props out.'

'Great,' said Toby, 'I've always wanted to be buried alive.'

'It's better than being buried dead,' said Lucy.

'Only just,' said Toby, staring at the roots growing out of the ceiling.

'Come on,' said Groffin. 'The GM wants to speak to you.'

'I expect that'll be someone else who wants us to surrender,' said Lucy. 'Or lock us in a box, or make tacky souvenirs out of our intestines.'

'Yeah, who *is* this GM?' said Toby.

'You'll see,' said Groffin.

'I don't suppose we have a choice,' said Lucy. She waited for Henbeg to turn into a handbag, then picked him up and strode off down the tunnel.

'It looks like she knows the way,' said Groffin, as Lucy disappeared.

'But there's only one way,' said Toby, staring at the collapsed tunnel.

'You been here before then?' said Groffin.

'Yes,' lied Toby. 'But that time I was heading in the other direction.'

'Ah, an *explorer*,' said Groffin. 'What some might call an adventurer.'

'Don't do that,' whispered Lucy as Toby caught up.

'What?' grinned Toby.

'Don't make fun of him,' said Lucy. 'He may not be the sharpest knife in the box, but at least he rescued us.'

'I owed you a favour,' said Groffin.

Lucy nodded and smiled weakly, recalling their last meeting, which hadn't exactly been a success.

'Umm, about this GM,' she said nervously.

'You'll see,' said Groffin.

Emerging from the narrow confines of the tunnel, it was as if they had entered another world, where rock walls marked the edges of the universe and everything in between was hewn from stone or fashioned from mud.

'This is the under-domain,' explained Groffin.

'And you live here?' said Lucy. 'In *this*?'

'Mostly,' he said. 'But we go upstairs sometimes.'

'But it's, umm, well, it's *underground*,' said Lucy.

'Well spotted,' grinned Toby.

'But how do you grow food and heat your huts?' said Lucy. 'And where does all the light come from?'

'Glowstone,' replied Groffin. 'It comes out of the walls, like everything else. Right, here we are – the residence of the most-honourable grandparent.'

Number One, Gruntfondle Mansions was a grandiose mud hut with a wicker gate and a circular wooden door that was painted green, unlike the others, which were all the same burned-earth colour as the walls. Lucy and Toby ducked through the tiny opening, and waited for their eyes to get accustomed to the murk. And it was only then that they spotted the figure in the rocking chair. He was surrounded by a cloud of blue smoke, and had a pickled onion head that was even bigger than Groffin's – like the really huge one that always lurks at the bottom of the jar.

'So this is your grandfather?' whispered Toby.

'Don't be so rude,' hissed Groffin. 'This is my grand*mother*.'

'But she has a beard,' grinned Lucy. The old lady's face hadn't seen the sun for years, and it was bleached a perfect white.

'Good, isn't it?' whispered Groffin. 'Granny Moon's beard was voted the best in the village, two years running.'

'You must be *so* proud,' grinned Toby. 'Will she be entering next year?'

'*Groffin?*' said a gravelly, ancient voice. 'Is that *you* whispering over there?'

'Yes, Granny.'

'Ah,' she growled. 'Yes, I recognise you now the pipe smoke has cleared. But that's not *all* I can see – who the grocking hell is that with you?'

'Why is it nobody is ever pleased to see us?' whispered Toby.

'They're visitors,' explained Groffin meekly. 'From *above*.'

'I can see that, from the ugly pink heads on them,' spat Granny, staring intently at Lucy's handbag, 'but what the grocking hell are they doing down here in the grocking-well under-domain?'

'They saved my life,' said Groffin.

'What, *both* of them?' spat Granny.

'Just the one with the things stuck on her face,' said Groffin.

'They're glasses,' said Lucy.

'Some kind of jewellery is it?' said Granny.

'They're for seeing better,' said Lucy. 'But I don't really need them.'

'Oh?' said Granny.

'No,' admitted Lucy, 'they're a disguise.'

'Well they're not working,' said Granny. 'I can see you, plain as anything.'

'I'll see about having them fixed,' said Lucy. She was staring at the walls, which were decorated with blue-green scarab elytra.

'Do you like my collection of wing cases?' said Granny.

'They're lovely,' said Lucy, as ironically as she could manage. 'And what is it that you do with them?'

'*Do?*' spat Granny. 'You don't *do* anything with trophies – you just sit and look at them and think of the old times.'

'But don't you normally keep the head as a trophy?' said Toby.

'Well *that* wouldn't be very decorative, would it?' said Granny.

She stared at Toby as if he was mad, then pulled a face that would shame a gurning champion. And it was then, whilst her features were screwed up like the map of a very wrinkly country, that Lucy spotted the beetle around the old woman's neck.

The insect was attached to her by a length of gold chain.

'That's little Pimbo,' said Granny. 'It's good luck to wear at least one of these somewhere about your person.'

'Really?' said Lucy.

'Of course,' said Granny. 'Like when you're out walking and you meet a beetle on its back. If you want luck then you have to turn it up the right way again, and if you don't then your house will get struck by lightning.'

'But we live underground,' said Groffin.

'That's the trouble with youngsters,' sighed Granny, 'always trying to put logic in the path of progress. Well don't fret yourself young Groffin. If that lightning has a mind to then it'll find a way down here, don't *you* worry.'

'And what about the Sisters?' said Lucy. 'Will *they* eventually find a way?'

'That's where you come in,' said Granny. You're the girl who's going to save the world.'

'So people keep telling me,' said Lucy.

Granny led Lucy and Toby into a smoky room at the back of the hut, where they found a smouldering fire in the middle of the room. Above the stone grate was a hole that served as a primitive chimney.

'You'll be needing this,' she said, handing Lucy a mirror the size of a dinner plate. 'I suppose you've heard of a Perry Scope?'

'Of course,' said Lucy.

'I *thought* you might have,' said Granny, sniffing at Lucy's clothes, 'what with being educated and everything – but I'll bet you haven't seen one like this before.'

'Like what exactly?' said Lucy.

'Hold the mirror above the fire,' said Granny, 'and tilt it towards you.'

'*Oh*,' said Lucy, feeling the warmth of the embers against the back of her hands. 'There's a pair of hands up your chimney.'

'And are they holding another mirror?' said Granny.

'Yes,' said Lucy, 'it's a bit smoky up there, but...'

'*Ahooberee*,' screamed Granny, nearly bursting a blood vessel.

'Ahooberah,' came the much more relaxed reply from the chimney.

'What's happening?' said Lucy.

'The periscope monkeys are moving the mirrors,' said Granny.

As she spoke, the person up the chimney rotated his mirror with some kind of crank and toothed-wheel affair. And when the mechanical creaking and squeaking was finished, Lucy could see slightly further up.

'*Ahooberee*,' yelled Granny, almost bursting the stays in her comprehensive undergarments. 'Can you see anything yet?'

'A bit further,' said Lucy.

'*Ahooberee*,' shouted Granny.

'Ahooberah,' came the reply.

'That's it,' said Lucy.

'A*hoo*beree, *boo*beree, *boo*beree, *bee*,' coughed Granny.

'More adjustment?' said Lucy.

'No,' said Granny, 'just a bit of loose phlegm – can you see anything?'

'Yes,' said Lucy, her voice trembling slightly. 'I th-think so.'

The view wasn't clear, due to imperfections in the glass and the thick smoke hanging in the chimney, but what little she could see was enough to make her heart quicken and finally bring tears to her eyes.

'It's the Purgatorium,' sobbed Lucy. 'Everything has gone back to how it was before we freed the prisoners.'

'What's happening Luce?' said Toby.

'It's some kind of torture,' replied Lucy.

'Let me look,' said Granny, grabbing the mirror.

'But what are they doing?' said Lucy.

'They're measuring that poor oaf to see how beautiful he is,' said Granny.

'Really?' said Toby.

'Or not, as the case may be,' said Granny seriously. 'As soon as they get the beauty measuring machine out, it'll be thank you and good night for him. They'll have him in one of those wicker baskets quicker than you can say pig-snot-ugly.'

'A machine for measuring beauty?' said Toby.

'It's more like a piece of cardboard really,' said Granny. 'If they can find a face wrinkle that's big enough to trap the card then the person is ugly.'

'Oh,' said Lucy taking the mirror, 'well he has got rather large wrinkles.'

'Then it's a wicker cage for him,' said Granny. 'And I think you know what happens after that.'

'Someone should say something,' said Lucy.

'It'll give the periscope position away,' said Granny. 'But I suppose we can afford to lose one of them in a good cause.'

She screamed up the chimney again.

'Ahoobereee, booberee, squidgery pooberry.'

'More phlegm?' said Lucy.

'Do you mind?' said Granny. 'Those were precise instructions. Now, just say what you want them to hear and the periscope monkeys will repeat it.'

'Hey,' said Lucy.

'Hey,' said a faint voice in the chimney.

'Hey,' said an even fainter one.

'Hey,' said a voice that was so faint she almost didn't hear it.

For a while nothing happened, but then the person wielding the piece of cardboard turned around, obviously shocked. He stared fixedly as he made his way over to where the periscope was hidden. And when he finally worked it out, he stuck his nose against the glass.

It was Pongsqueal.

'What the flip is going on here,' he yelled. At least that was what Lucy thought she could read on his lips.

'This is Lucy Blake,' she yelled. 'Stop what you're doing this minute.'

Her words were repeated, fainter and fainter, until Pongsqueal heard them and framed his reply. Lucy didn't repeat it for Granny because it had far too many 'F's in it.

'Is that old Pongsqueal?' said Granny. 'I thought I recognised the back of his head. You won't get any joy out of him.'

'Stop doing that,' yelled Lucy undeterred.

'Stop doing that,' repeated the chimney monkeys.

Pongsqueal wasn't impressed. He picked up a plank and clobbered the upper end of the periscope. The glass shattered into hundreds of pieces, but just before the image disappeared Lucy thought she saw a familiar face.

'Damn and blast,' she hissed. 'I wanted to see more.'

'There's plenty where that came from,' said Granny. 'We've got hundreds of mirror-routes, and one you particularly need to see.'

'*Afooberee, nooberry, slobbery booberee…*'

The mirrors changed orientation according to Granny's commands and another frightening vision flickered into view. The angel Zarobi was floating above the prison courtyard, her wings raging like a forest fire.

'She's spreading flames everywhere,' sobbed Lucy. 'And the scarabs, they, they're eating the poor pris… no, I can't even say it – it's too awful.'

'She knows you're watching,' sighed Granny. 'And she's burning those innocent creatures because she knows how it makes you feel.'

'Like everything inside me has turned to fat, cold stones,' said Lucy. Her hands trembled on the mirror, sending the horrific images shimmering off into nowhere. 'And I hate her for doing it. I *hate* her.'

'Be careful what you hate,' said Granny. 'It might make things difficult if you choose to love it later.'

'And the other way,' said Groffin. 'You shouldn't love a thing too much either – just in case – *you* know.'

'Yes,' smiled Granny, 'but try to think of the first idea more often than the second, now *there's* a good girl.'

'I can't watch,' said Lucy, throwing the mirror aside. 'There's *so* much pain out there – I have to stop it. I have to give myself up.'

'But that's exactly what they want,' protested Toby. 'You *can't* give up after all we've been through.'

'People are in torment,' cried Lucy. 'Because of me they're being burned and tortured and hung up by their heels and eaten by insects and I just can't stand it any longer – it's all my fault.'

'It is *not* your fault,' hissed Granny. 'They are suffering because of others.'

'But if I go,' sobbed Lucy, 'then all of this will stop.'

'Are you *sure*?' said Granny.

'There's always chance they'll keep their word,' said Lucy.

'And a bigger chance they'll continue with the persecution,' said Granny.

'She's right,' said Toby. 'We have to stick to our original plan and get into the tower.'

'And then?' said Lucy. 'We don't even know what we'll find.'

'But if we don't try, we'll never find out,' said Toby.

'You're right,' said Lucy, drying her tears. 'They're doing everything they can to stop us getting in.'

'That's the spirit,' said Granny. 'We've finally got a chance to get rid of them once and for all. It would be *lovely* to live on he surface again.'

'Again?' said Toby. 'You mean you haven't always lived down here?'

'Would *you* prefer to live in a hole in the ground?' said Granny, raising an eyebrow.

'They set traps,' said Groffin. 'To keep the numbers down.'

'Are you telling us that they *kill* you?' said Toby.

'Can you think of a better way to get rid of your enemies?' said Granny. 'If you exterminate the people you don't like often enough then the problem eventually goes away.'

'It's true,' admitted Lucy. 'We rescued Groffin from a trap.'

'But it's not right,' said Toby. 'They can't kill you because of the shape of your head.'

'It's not *just* our heads,' said Granny. 'Some of us have certain talents – and the people on the surface don't like it.'

'I know,' said Lucy with a smile.

'You do?' said Granny, looking distracted. An ugly, hump-backed man sidled up to her and whispered a silent message. 'Yes, I *see*,' she said. 'Well, I'm glad we've got that sorted out, because another matter has come up.'

'Oh?' said Lucy.

Granny retrieved the mirror and locked it in a velvet-lined box. Then she took them back to the other room, where there was a surprise in store.

'*Gusset*! *Pixy*!' squealed Lucy. 'You *made* it. Umm, what about the others?'

'They escaped,' replied Gusset, 'but so did the angel.'

'And we've got the tea on,' said Pixy, pointing at the kitchen range.

Lucy sat next to Gusset and smiled at Pixy. She couldn't have been in Granny's house for more than a minute, and already the kettle was wheezing like a fat boy on a cross-country run.

'Wait a minute,' said Groffin. He stared at Pixy as she tended the kettle. 'This is *her*, isn't it? The one who wanted to leave me to the trappers.'

'Hmm,' said Granny. '*Did* she now?'

'Ye-es,' admitted Pixy. 'But that was before I knew I was one of you.'

'One of us?' said Groffin. 'Is this a joke?'

'Her head doesn't look like a pickled gherkin,' said Granny, 'but I *can* see a family resemblance. Do you by any chance know of the Astronomers?'

'Don't talk to her like she's a friend,' whimpered Groffin. 'She was going to let me die. She was a different shape then, but I'd recognise those eyes anywhere.'

'Was it you?' said Granny, gazing into Pixy's purple eyes.

'Maybe,' admitted Pixy.

'And you were going to leave him in the trap?' said Granny.

'I was thinking like them upstairs,' said Pixy.

'I see,' said Granny. 'Well that's alright then.'

'You *what*?' snarled Groffin. 'But she…'

'Is it really alright?' interrupted Pixy. 'Am I forgiven?'

'What's done can't be undone,' said Granny. 'The world is full of those who want to get rid of people because they don't like the look of them, or they fear what's inside their heads. And *that's* not right either, but we can't change it, can we? Now, would anybody like some tea?'

'Me,' said Pixy. 'And something to eat too.'

'You *can't* be thinking about food already,' said Lucy.

'I'm not,' said Pixy, 'but my stomach is.'

'Nothing for me,' said Lucy.

'So you don't want any of my special bread then?' drawled Granny.

'Bread?' smiled Lucy. 'Oh, well that sounds alright.'

'It's got raisins,' replied Granny.

'We don't care what's in it,' said Toby. 'We'll have a loaf each.'

'A loaf each eh?' said Granny. 'I *like* a boy with a sense of humour.'

'He's serious,' said Lucy. 'We really are very, very hungry. And there can't be much wrong with bread, can there?'

'*Grundle*?' shouted Granny. 'Fetch me a couple of those raisin and bat squeezing loaves. And bring some of the dung tea whilst you're at it.'

'I'll pass on the tea,' said Lucy.

'Me too,' said Toby.'

'There's no actual dung in it,' explained Granny. 'It's mostly rat water and Loppit droppings – but I don't think they count as dung, do they?'

'Course not,' grinned Groffin, 'them's *garnish*, that's what them is.'

Lucy nibbled the bread and was just about to sip her tea, hoping it would take away the taste of the rat water. But as the drink was about to pass her lips there was a knock at the door.

'Sounds like a knock at the door,' said Groffin helpfully.

'Who is it?' screamed Granny. 'We're conducting essential business.'

'Well this is sort of essential too,' said the voice outside. 'It's one of those emergency thingies you told us about.'

'Then you'd better come in, hadn't you?' shouted Granny.

The door creaked open slowly, as if the underling had changed his mind.

'Right, who's in charge?' said Zenda, stooping to get through.

'*Quim, Dee, Madimi!* You're *alive!*' beamed Lucy. She took the opportunity to slide her teacup over to Henbeg, who slurped it down like a drain cleaner.

'Who's running the show here?' said Zenda. 'I want a full inventory, and nobody is to move anything – this is all newspaper property.'

'What the *grock* is the big eared one talking about?' growled Granny.

'Don't worry,' said Lucy. 'She had a bump on the head, but she'll be alright soon, *won't* you Zenda?'

'You managed to find her then?' said Toby with a broad grin.

'She was floating face down,' said Quim. 'Doctor Dee considered leaving her for dead, but I managed to talk him round.'

'That was lucky,' grinned Toby.

'Yes, *wasn't* it?' said Zenda.

'Has she been insulting you again Master Dee?' said Lucy.

'Once or twice,' said Dee. 'She questioned my competence as a sorcerer – and a navigator – and an oarsman.'

'And she cast some doubt on your parentage,' added Madimi.

'Only because he was so obsessed with his books,' said Zenda. 'He was more concerned with saving that stinking pile of garbage than rescuing me.'

'Yes,' chortled Granny, quickly assessing the situation. 'I'm beginning to see how that might be.'

'So did you save the books?' said Lucy.

'Of course,' smiled Dee.

'Oh yes,' moaned Zenda. 'We spent ages scrabbling around in the mud and wearing blindfolds so we couldn't see what was going on. *I* thought he was supposed to be a sorcerer, but he's more like a bloody lunatic dog if you ask me, digging things up and then burying them again.'

'And where was all this burying going on?' said Granny.

'They washed up near the Palace of Water-Pumping,' said Groopley.

'I wanted to visit the haberdashery shop on the Island of Growling,' said Quim, 'but we were dragged away and spirited down a stinking hole.'

'You can go if you want,' said Granny, 'but you won't last five minutes out there – unless you're a lot braver than you look.'

'More scare stories,' scoffed Zenda. 'I fought off an angel and didn't even get a scratch.'

'Is that so?' said Granny.

'No,' said everyone together.

'She was going to get pulled through a window,' said Toby.

'So we used my pinking shears,' said Quim.

'And then she very bravely fainted,' said Lucy.

'Shut your face Blake,' said Zenda. 'Why don't you make yourself useful and tell me what's going on? Tenby and me have got deadlines to meet.'

Tenby offered a thin smile, and scratched his nose.

'Granny is going to help us get inside the tower,' said Lucy.

'*Is* she?' said an astonished Dee. 'Then you have won the trust of the groundlings already?'

'I wouldn't exactly call it trust,' said Granny. 'But she hasn't persecuted me for the last fifty years, so I don't mistrust her – yet.'

'Then might there be another reason?' said Dee.

'There might,' snapped Granny. 'But I don't think this is the right time to be discussing it.'

'I do,' said Groffin.

'Me too,' said Gusset.

'Yes,' said Granny. 'I rather thought you might.'

'I know,' yelled Groopley. 'She's the one in the holy book, *isn't* she?'

'Book?' said Dee, his interest aroused. 'Did you say *holy* book?'

'Yes,' sighed Granny. She cuffed Groopley around the ear. 'Actually we do *have* books, thank you very much. Not everything down here is made from rock and soil.'

'I'm sorry,' said Dee, 'I didn't mean to offend you – but I do have a very special interest in books.'

'We know,' said Groffin, 'we've seen inside your library.'

'You have?' said Dee, raising an eyebrow. 'How exactly?'

'Through the invention of Perry Scopes,' said Groffin.

'And tunnels,' said Gusset.

Granny beamed at him. She was proud to see him back underground after all this time – he was so *handsome*.

'You spied upon Master Dee in his library?' said a shocked Madimi.

'Only slightly,' said Groffin.

'*Slightly?*' said Dee. 'How can you spy on someone slightly? Did you only look with one eye? Or did you deliberately forget half of what you saw?'

'I never felt as though I was alone in that place,' said Madimi. 'And now I know why.'

'So, you have tunnels all over the city?' said Dee.

'We *might* have,' said Granny, desperately trying to keep the secret, even though it had already exploded in their faces.

'Aren't we straying from the point?' said Toby. 'We were talking about the holy book.'

'Oh well,' sighed Granny, 'I suppose there's no harm telling you about it, now the secret's out.'

'Wonderful,' enthused Dee. 'A hitherto unknown holy manuscript – what a *triumph.*'

'It's only a grocking book,' said Groopley. 'You'll see.'

'Nobody is allowed to see the sacred jotter,' said Granny. 'Not even me. It has been passed down through countless generations since the beginning of the world – and it has never been read out loud.'

'Oh?' smirked Zenda. 'And how does *that* work then?'

'Simple,' said Granny, looking down her nose at the reporter. 'So simple in fact that even you might be able to understand it.'

'Then *tell* us,' snorted Zenda.

'The new guardian of the jotter learns the story from the previous one,' said Granny. 'I told you it was simple.'

'So where's the book now?' said Groopley.

'It's kept in the Satchel of Prophecy,' said Granny, her face completely straight.

'This *is* a joke, isn't it?' grinned Toby.

'We do *know* about jokes,' said Granny, 'but as far as I remember they are only used on ceremonial occasions.'

'Remind me never to come to one of your parties,' said Zenda.

'Don't mind her,' said Toby. 'I'm dying to hear the story about Lucy.'

'We don't know it's about me,' said Lucy. 'They're just guessing, aren't they Granny?'

'That's right,' replied Granny. 'They *are* guessing – although the subject of the story *is* a young female from another world.'

'Oh, how *very* convenient,' said Zenda.

Lucy looked at Dee, who stroked his chin thoughtfully. He had known all along that she wasn't from Assiah, and this merely confirmed his suspicion. But he still looked shocked, unlike Madimi who seemed to have accepted the fact without question.

'What else?' said Pixy.

'I think she was sent to take back a prize,' said Granny uncertainly.

'That could be Fenny,' suggested Toby

'But her way home is blocked,' said Granny.

'And that could be the gate,' said Toby. 'We can't go home because...'

'Ye-es, alright,' said Lucy, fearing he might reveal too much. 'I accept that the story might be about me – but it could just as well be about Zenda – *she* fits all three conditions, doesn't she?'

'Apart from the fact she's not a girl,' whispered Toby.

'I *heard* that,' said Zenda, taking out her notepad and licking her pencil. 'So come on, tell us the rest of the story then.'

'It's quite simple,' said Granny. 'You won't need to write it down.'

'Then stop stalling and just tell us,' said Zenda.

'The girl in the story makes her way to the Migdal,' said Granny. 'And when she is there she finds her way.'

'Is that *it*?' snapped Zenda.

'I left some of it out to save time,' said Granny.

'I see,' said Zenda. 'And exactly how big *is* this holy jotter?'

'Massive,' said Groopley.

'How would *you* know?' said Granny.

'Just guessing,' admitted Groopley.

'Actually you're right,' said Granny. 'It *is* massive, but the story only takes up the first few pages. Oh, and there was some other thing about the sunset on the day of ascent.'

'Well *that's* a fat lot of use,' said Tenby. 'Fancy having a guardian of secrets who can't remember what the secrets are.'

'It'll come to me eventually,' said Granny. 'There was something about how and why the world was created. Oh yes, and there was something about underground rumblings too. Now, just let me think a minute.'

'And whilst you're thinking, people are dying,' said a well-built newcomer with a face like a squashed frog. He was flanked by henchmen who stood with their arms crossed. One of them was only *slightly* uglier than frog-face, but the other poor soul had a mug like an explosion in a pickle factory.

'*Gripe*,' mumbled Granny, 'what in grock's sake do *you* want?'

'I'd have thought *that* was obvious,' sneered Gripe. 'We're going to hand the girl over to the Sisters.'

'Yeah,' said one of his heavies, 'and then they'll leave us alone.'

'That's right,' grunted the other, 'and no more trouble with subsidence either – all those shafts and tunnels caving in – snot natural.'

'Yeah,' grumbled Grout. 'The place has been falling to pieces ever since we heard about the girl and her performances. So, here's the deal – we hand her over and the earthquakes will stop – and maybe the Sisters and everyone else will go away and leave us alone.'

'And what about you Gripe?' said Granny. 'Do you want to give an innocent girl to these fiends?'

'She's not so innocent,' snapped Gripe. 'What about all the trouble she's caused?'

'And she *stinks* too,' said Grout. 'Like a fetid length of loose-bowel.'

'Thanks a lot,' said Lucy.

'But she has to go to the tower,' protested Groffin. 'It's written in the holy jotter.'

'Oh well *that's* alright then,' said Gripe. 'Only nobody has ever *seen* this famous jotter, have they? We've only got the old woman's word that the thing even exists.'

'And isn't my word good enough?' said Granny.

'Well,' said Grout, 'umm...'

'No, it *isn't*,' shouted Gripe, 'the girl's going upstairs and that's final.'

'Well *I* think you're just a bully,' said Groffin. 'You should try *thinking* before you start flexing your muscles.'

'That's rich,' laughed Gripe, 'especially coming from mister no-brains – although you *have* got a point.'

'So, you'll think it over then?' said Granny.

'No,' said Gripe, turning to Lucy. 'I meant he was right about me being a bully – it's the only way to get things done – *so* Miss Lucy Blake, are you going to come quietly?'

'Leave the girl alone,' said Gusset, stepping from the shadows.

'I'm quivering,' sneered Gripe. 'Look at me shaking.'

He pushed Gusset into the arms of his henchmen, then punched him in the stomach.

'Is this what we've come to?' wheezed Gusset as they threw him to the ground. 'One groundling persecuting another?'

'I don't *hacksherly* mind,' grinned Gripe. 'As long as the groundling what's getting percy-cuted is you.'

'Be quiet Gripe,' hissed Granny, 'or if you must speak, then *try* not to sound so stupid. Violence doesn't settle anything.'

'That's not what *we've* found,' said Gripe, grabbing Lucy by the arm.

'So the strongest person is always right?' said Lucy.

'My, you *are* clever,' said Gripe. 'You've hit the nail on the head with that one.'

'Alright, Mister big-mouth' said Lucy, 'why don't we see how tough you are without your friends?'

'But I'm at least a cubit taller than you are,' laughed Gripe.

'Then you won't be scared of being beaten,' said Lucy.

'Take a look at these muscles,' said Gripe, rolling up his sleeve. 'I could fold a little pipsqueak like you in half with one hand.'

'So what are you like at arm wrestling?' asked Lucy.

'Brilliant,' said Gripe. 'And if I win you'll give yourself up?'

'Yes,' said Lucy, taking her coat off.

'Right then,' said Gripe. 'This is going to be over *very* quickly.'

'First hand on the table loses,' said Lucy, with a dark frown.

Her joy at discovering that Dee and the others were safe had numbed her mind, but the anaesthetic was wearing off now, and she was reminded of the terrible visions she had seen in Granny's mirror. And just for a moment, all the boiling anger she felt for Zarobi was directed at Gripe.

'*Luce?*' whispered Toby. 'I hope you know what you're doing.'

She smiled and sat opposite Gripe, positioning her elbow in a handy dent in the table and gripping his rough-skinned hand in her own.

'Are you both ready?' grinned Grout.

They both nodded.

'Then take up the strain,' said Grout.

Lucy grimaced as Gripe began to push against her, but she had a surprise for him. She was pumped full of anger, and wasn't as weak as he'd imagined.

'Ready?' said Grout. 'And *go*.'

Gripe's face twisted into a disgusting purple blob as he threw all of his strength into the first attack. In contrast, Lucy was more relaxed, locking out her shoulder and expending just enough energy to stop him winning. Byron had taught her not to go for the kill straight away – it was all about tiring your opponent.

Gripe looked worried when his arm began to tremble uncontrollably, but when he realised what was going on he slackened his efforts to match Lucy's.

'Kill her,' screamed Grout.

'Smash the big oaf's knuckles to bits,' yelled Pixy.

'Kick her head in,' yelled one the henchmen.

'Is that in the rules?' whispered Granny.

'You want to give up now?' said Gripe. He squeezed Lucy's fingers until they felt like mashed putty.

'What do *you* think Genjamin?' she said, her brow glistening. 'Should we give up?'

Gripe looked puzzled, and as his concentration lapsed, Lucy pushed with all her anger-driven might.

'Has anyone got a choc-lit giscuit?' said a muffled Genjamin.

'What the grocking hell was *that*?' said Gripe.

'The sound of you losing,' said Lucy. She gritted her teeth and gathered all her remaining strength – and with Zarobi's horror film still playing in her mind she forced his hand onto a sharp sliver of wood, pushing with all her might until it punched through the flesh and jabbed into her own palm.

'She *cheated*,' screamed Gripe, blood pouring from his wound. 'Grout? Grundle? You saw what happened, didn't you?'

'I reckon we all did,' said Granny. 'The girl won it fair and square.'

'Yeah? Well you haven't heard the last of this,' yelled Gripe. He stormed out of the hut, leaving a trail of crimson blobs on the dirt floor.

'Maybe not,' yelled Lucy, as the door slammed. 'But we're not planning to be here when you get back.'

'I won't argue with that,' said Toby with a relieved sigh.

'Me neither,' said a voice from deep inside Lucy's coat.

Mother
of Vinegar

The explorers huddled together, whispering amongst themselves whilst Granny consulted the back of her eyelids. A steady drip, drip, drip of water came from the slime green bricks above, and a cold, doom-filled sigh echoed all around them.

'Umm, yes, I *think* I know where I went wrong,' said Granny, her eyes springing open suddenly. 'Try to keep close, and don't go wandering up any side tunnels – and keep *that* thing where I can see it.'

Henbeg gave a grunt and wandered over to Quim, whom he had taken a liking to.

'We've had it, haven't we?' whispered Pixy.

'I read a book once,' whispered Tenby. 'The victims wandered around in tunnels like these, and got picked off one by one in really gruesome ways.'

Zenda gave a nervous laugh and kicked him in the shin. Dee smiled at Madimi, as if to assure her that his magick would protect them all. But as the sorcerer turned away from his daughter his expression changed.

'How about this way?' said Granny. She pointed up a slimy brick tunnel that looked just like all the others.

'We've been that way three times already,' yawned Zenda. 'Haven't you got *any* sense of direction?'

'Ah, you noticed then?' said Granny, shuffling uncomfortably.

'Yes,' chimed everyone at once.

'We should have left the groundlings behind,' said Zenda. 'But especially her – she's so old her brain has turned to mush.'

'And how would we have found the secret way in?' said Lucy. 'Granny was the only one who knew how to open the earth-pile door.'

'And that's where we should have left her,' said Zenda. 'Him too,' she added, pointing at Gusset. 'There was nothing in the holy jotter story about them going up the tower.'

'But there was nothing that forbade it,' said Granny, 'and I always wanted to take a look inside this place.'

'And now you have your reward,' sneered Zenda. 'Because we're going to be wandering around this place for the rest of our lives.'

'Umm, Lucy?' said Granny. 'Have you any ideas?'

Lucy shook her head.

'Don't ask her,' sighed Zenda. 'She'll have us diving out of windows.'

They were standing in a brighter area, where the ceilings were higher and the gravelly floor smelt of cat-pee.

'We should head towards the light,' said Pixy. She indicated one of the five arched exits where a path headed upwards and the walls glowed.

'I like the upwards bit,' said Lucy. 'But the light makes me nervous. Like it might be coming from burning bodies, or something worse.'

'What could be worse than that?' said Zenda.

'I don't know,' said Lucy. 'I'm sure the Sisters will think of something.'

'Yes, I forgot the famous sisters,' said Zenda. 'And when is it exactly that we're going to meet them?'

'I wouldn't be in too much of a hurry if I were you,' said Pixy.

'She's right,' said Gusset. 'They'll eat your brains with a big spoon if they get half the chance.'

'Just a teaspoon would do for Zenda,' smiled Toby.

'I *told* you about that, didn't I?' hissed Zenda. She took out her notebook and underlined Toby's name again, forcing the nib through the paper.

'I think we should follow Granny's recommendations,' said Dee.

'I agree with father,' said Madimi. 'The groundlings are experts on what exists below the ground, so it makes sense.'

'It makes sense,' mocked Zenda.

'But we're not underground anymore,' said Granny. A look of triumph spread across her wrinkled face.

'How do you know?' said Zenda. 'You were lost twenty seconds ago.'

'Nevertheless, I think she is correct,' said Dee, consulting his brass phial.

'But how can you tell?' said Toby.

'It stinks of above-grounders,' said Granny. 'No offence.'

'None taken,' said Toby, 'but you don't smell so fresh yourselves.'

'We need directions,' said Tenby helpfully. 'I had a special pair of shoes when I was a boy. They had a compass in the heel.'

'But a compass is no use without a map,' said Toby.

'Good idea,' smiled Lucy. She searched her pockets and produced a small canister that looked like it once contained a movie reel.

'What's that?' said Zenda

'It's a piece of a map,' grinned Lucy. 'I stole it from the Emperor.'

'And what is it a map of?' asked Madimi.

'Well that's just it,' smiled Lucy. 'I *think* it can be a map of anything you like – or it used to be, when it was still in one piece.'

She removed the lid and eased the vellum out. But when she unfolded it to less than the size of a handkerchief, there was a collective sigh of disappointment.

'The last time I saw it work properly,' explained Lucy, 'it was about the size of a tablecloth.'

'Are we going to have a picnic then?' said Pixy.

'Let's concentrate on the map, shall we?' said Zenda.

The reporter took out her notebook and wrote '*One map – ex-property of ex-emperor*'. Then, when Toby stopped peering over her shoulder, she added '*Blake's pocket – get it off her.*' Then she underlined the word 'off' three times.

Lucy settled on the floor, looking somewhat uncertain.

'It's blank,' said Pixy, sitting beside her.

'You have to tell it what you want to look at,' said Lucy.

'Ah, the old model, is it?' sneered Zenda.

'Shall I try?' said Dee, adjusting his robes and clearing his throat. 'If you would be so kind as to show us the palace,' he said politely.

Everyone sighed when nothing happened, but Zenda was loudest.

'What if it needs batteries?' suggested Tenby.

Zenda frowned, then realised there might be truth amongst the stupidity.

'Umm, well *does* it?' she asked quietly.

'Of course not,' said Lucy, smoothing the vellum. '*Palace of the Emperor*,' she said firmly. The air surrounding them spat and crackled with the smell of

Lectric, and the smoking remains of the palace appeared. Alongside it, the proud structure that had been Dee's library was reduced to ash and rubble.

'My b-books,' sighed Dee, wiping away a tear.

'But parts of the palace are missing,' indicated Madimi. 'This is where the great gate should be, and here is where the Tetravox once stood. We should at least be able to see the ruins of the great horns.'

'We're lucky it works at all,' said Lucy, recalling how Clinker evaporated in the furnace of Zarobi's breath. 'This is just a tiny part of the original.'

'Then you had better find the rest,' said Zenda making another note. 'I'm holding you responsible.'

'Try looking at something else,' suggested Pixy.

'I know,' said Toby. *'The Sign of the Bright Byrde.'*

The smoking palace ruins were replaced by the more welcome sight of the tavern. Just the front entrance was visible, but in microscopic detail, as if the map was trying to make up for a lack of quantity. A tiny face appeared at an open window and vomited into the street.

'Now that's more like it,' grinned Toby.

'But it doesn't help,' said Zenda. 'We need to see the tower.'

Dee wrinkled his brow and gazed lovingly at the fragment of vellum, as if he was thinking of having another try. Or perhaps taking it for himself.

'Migdal,' said Lucy, placing a hand on the map to steady it.

Her fingers tingled as a towering edifice shot from the vellum, twisting this way and that as it formed staircases and halls and ramps and buttresses in a wild frenzy of construction. But when they went to examine it there was a sound like a liquid fart and the image folded into a sludgy brown mess.

As the sewage faded it left a stain on the map and a foul smell in the air.

'Looks like it doesn't do cursed towers,' said Tenby.

'Maybe it was too big?' suggested Toby. 'You asked for the whole tower and it just conked out.'

'What if we just ask for a small part of it?' said Gusset.

'Like the place where we are now,' said Zenda.

'If we knew that then we wouldn't need the map,' said Tenby.

'Oh, umm, yeah,' grunted Zenda.

'Does anyone mind if I make a suggestion?' said Quim.

Everyone turned, as if a stranger had suddenly come amongst them.

Mother of Vinegar

'Oh, don't worry about poor little me,' he said, interpreting their various looks. I'll just keep quiet and let you play your ruffians games.'

'Don't be silly,' said Lucy generously. 'Tell us your idea.'

'We're probably inside one of the four legs of the tower,' said Quim, 'because we're above ground level – but we can't be *that* far above can we?'

'So?' said Zenda.

'So we probably haven't reached the place where the legs fuse together to form the main body,' said Quim.

'Tower leg number one,' said Pixy.

Nothing happened – the map refused to co-operate.

'Tower leg number two,' said Pixy, slightly louder.

Nothing happened again.

'Tower leg erm, number, erm...'

'Three,' grinned Toby.

This time the map twitched, but remained unhelpfully flat.

'Perhaps it needs a name,' said Madimi.

'*Perhaps it needs a name*,' said Zenda, in her best mocking tone. 'So we're back to square one.'

'There was a rhyme we sang at school,' said Granny. 'Back before the world began, when I was a young girl.'

Pixy cracked a grin, but stopped when she saw old Moon's frown.

'Which one?' said Quim. 'Did it feature red-cheeked schoolgirls and a basket of corn-cobs?'

'No, it *didn't*,' frowned Granny.

'Oooh, I know,' said Quim, 'was it the 'Virgin from the Forest'?'

'No,' she said, wrinkling her brow even further.

'Oh, erm, I know,' said Quim. 'It's the one about farting underwater.'

'Not that one either,' snapped Granny. 'It's where you spin a blindfolded person around and they have to guess which direction they're pointing.'

'I remember it,' said Gusset, bursting into song.

'Lukey, Sobble, Boggage, Grass, fly through the air, then land on your arse.'

'That's it,' said Granny. 'But can you remember the second verse? I think it was about puking up, or maybe it was...'

'About the tower,' said Gusset. 'And how you should never say its name.'

'*Migdal* you mean?' grinned Pixy.

Vⱶⱴⱴ67   955

'Are you related to the outer-wall Scalybeaks?' hissed Gusset. 'Because they were a bunch of contrary sods too,' he snarled.

'The angels had a word for tower,' said Dee, hoping to calm the situation. 'Now, if only I could remember what it was.'

'It was Umadea,' whispered Madimi.

'Then let's try it,' said Lucy. '*Raas Umadea.*'

'Enochian for east tower,' said Toby. He was about to explain how he knew, but the ground shook and chunks of masonry fell from the ceiling.

'Stop,' yelled Lucy.

The earthquake stilled immediately, much to everybody's relief.

'Recite the name once again,' said Dee, 'but in reverse. There is so much power in certain incantations that you must pronounce them backwards in order to avoid destruction.'

'*Umadea Raas,*' nodded Lucy.

The map erupted once again, showing a cross section of the tower. One part of the image showed the outer surface and the remainder represented a complicated system of corridors. They were full of dark, steaming soil, and looked most uninviting.

'You could grow some nice root veggies in that,' said Granny.

'*Umadea Lucal,*' said Zenda, just to prove she'd been listening.

The soil filled corridors disappeared and were replaced by a vision of the northern leg of the tower. It consisted mainly of twisted and distorted metal, and was surrounded by a great deal of fresh air.

'Nice view of the countryside,' sniggered Zenda.

'See those holes in the walls?' said Granny. 'They were made when the place was captured from old Dragonard.'

'It looks like cannon damage,' said Toby.

'Worse,' said Granny.

'Much worse,' nodded Gusset.

'*Umadea Sobol,*' said Lucy.

The map groaned, as if the effort was too much to handle, but eventually it managed to form an interesting new image.

'There,' yelled Toby, pointing at a feature near the ground. 'Here's where we came in, and there's the rats' nest of corridors where Zenda got us lost.'

'Granny got us a lot more lost than I did,' said Zenda.

'A map of where we have already been is no use,' said Dee plainly.

Lucy nodded.

'*Umadea Sobol — outer layer*,' she said.

The map flickered, then showed them hundreds of birds clinging to the irregular outer walls of the tower. A scarab swooped through the scene like the shadow of death, sweeping chicks and eggs from the nests and gathering their squirming bodies in its jaws.

'Ugh,' said Lucy. '*Umadea Sobol — inner layer and rise up.*'

'Brilliant,' yelled Toby, 'look, we've just come through that bit.'

'And this is the chamber we occupy presently,' said Dee, indicating an empty room. The room bore an uncanny similarity to their surroundings, but it showed no signs of life.

'Then where are we?' said Zenda.

'Umm, I do not know,' admitted Dee.

'A-*ha*,' said the reporter. 'So if this is where we are now, then why aren't we on the map?'

'I *hate* it when she's right,' said Pixy.

'She isn't,' said Toby. 'If you could zoom into the place where the map was then you'd be able to see an even smaller map.'

'And we'd all get sucked in,' giggled Pixy, 'when the map disappears up its own bottom.'

'The child has a point,' said Dee, 'even if she does have an unfortunate way of explaining herself.'

'So we're saved,' said Zenda. 'We know where we are.'

'Not exactly,' said Lucy, 'but at least we know where to go next.'

They followed a set of twisting passages, each of them having memorised as many changes of route as they could manage — all except for Pixy, who claimed she couldn't remember anything, and Zenda who didn't want to play silly games. And finally, after a few false turns and dead ends, they came to the iron door that had been so clearly displayed on the map.

'This is it,' said Lucy. 'And behind this door is the rising chamber, where we saw the spiral ramp.'

'Then it's time for me to rescue us all,' said Zenda.

'What, again?' said Toby. He smiled, and so did the others, but as the door creaked open a stench of sulphur assaulted them, forcing tears from their eyes. They were standing at the foot of a vast spiral ramp that was big enough to drive a truck up. Arched alcoves punctured the heavy metal walls at the outside edge of the incline, each containing a grimy statue.

'This must be the fire hall,' said Granny. 'I seem to remember it gets a mention in the story.'

'Then we're in the east,' said Toby. 'Fire is in the east.'

'We know,' yawned Zenda.

'Sorry,' said Toby, 'I forgot you had all the answers.'

'So what's all this stuff on the floor then Zenda?' said Tenby.

'Yeuk,' said Pixy, 'it's like walking on earwax.'

They halted whilst their eyes adjusted to the dim yellow illumination that seeped from the walls. Their feet made sucking noises in the waxy substance as they shuffled about.

And then the iron door swung closed with a loud clang.

'Umm, yeah, what *about* that stuff Luce?' said Toby.

Lucy gave a little cough, and stuttered. She had her suspicions about the wax but didn't like to say anything.

'Shh,' she said. 'I think I can hear breathing.'

'What is it?' whispered Pixy.

'I don't know,' said Madimi nervously. 'But perhaps if we stay quiet then they will remain asleep.'

'They?' said Tenby, a little too loud for comfort.

'Umm, do you mean the statues?' said Pixy.

They were used to the dim light now and could see further up the ramp. The statues were more and more battered the further away the alcoves got – and the last of them that was clearly visible contained just rock and rubble.

'We have to push on,' said Lucy, glancing back at the sealed door.

'But the breathing,' said Dee.

'Then we'll all have to keep quiet, *won't* we?' hissed Zenda.

'I can't wait to see that,' whispered Toby.

As they made their way up the ramp it was clear that someone didn't appreciate the statuary. The alcoves containing them were gradually being cleared in preparation for new occupants. And as the breathing up ahead got louder, Lucy realised who those new residents might be. She had heard this sound before, in the Forest of Skeels. It was like three gallons of snot being forced through a narrow pipe, but here in the mucous-yellow shadows of the tower it didn't seem all that funny.

She put a finger to her lips and moved noiselessly towards the slumbering shape in the closest niche. The figure that occupied it was draped in stinking rags that fluttered slightly, even though there was no trace of a breeze. She was standing less than three feet from a Vooghul.

Toby ran ahead and scanned more of the alcoves.

'They're everywhere,' he hissed. 'Hundreds of them.'

'Thousands,' whispered Pixy, her eyes widening.

'But they're dead,' said Quim. 'Why do they need to sleep?'

'Perhaps they aren't sleeping?' said Granny.

'My God, they're *watching* us aren't they?' said Zenda, stifling a scream. 'I just knew it didn't feel right.'

'No,' said Quim. 'I'm quite accustomed to people staring at me and it's not them – someone else is watching us.'

'Then we have to be doubly quiet,' whispered Pixy.

'And doubly careful,' nodded Lucy. She turned to resume her journey, but her path was blocked as a dark shape stepped from a hidden passage.

'Going somewhere?' said the ugly newcomer. He wore huge, lead-soled boots and carried an awesome spear that glinted in the dim light. His leather armour was spattered with sewage and pieces of half digested food.

'I know you don't I?' said Lucy. 'You were at the Braneskule.'

'I was guarding the Ornithopter,' he grumbled. 'And then I got demoted.'

'I thought so,' said Lucy. 'I never forget a handsome face.'

'You were right,' said the guard, speaking into the shadows. 'You said she was going to try and soft soap me.'

'Who are you talking to?' said Lucy. 'And how did you get in here?'

'He's with me,' said Gripe. The groundling arm wrestler stepped out with a dozen supporters behind him. They all brandished four-pointed spears and stout leather shields.

'Oh,' said Lucy.

'It gets worse,' said a smirking Boaz as he stepped out from behind the spear-carriers. 'I doubt you expected that your journey would end so soon.'

'I don't know what you're doing here,' whispered Zenda, 'but can you just keep your voices down? Only there are things in the walls, and we'd rather not wake them up.'

'They will not harm us,' said Boaz. He strolled over to the nearest niche and rammed his cane into the sleeping Vooghul's stomach. A pile of stinking rags fell from the body and hit the floor with a wet slap. But all eyes were on the creature, whose naked form was folding at the waist, as if bowing to his destroyer. In the middle of its back was a gaping hole where Boaz's cane had punched through.

'Are those stars?' said Dee, with an astonished gasp. 'Are these poor creatures *really* full of stars?'

'Something for you to think about later,' said Boaz. 'If there *is* a later.'

'What do you want?' hissed Lucy.

'Isn't it obvious?' said Gripe. 'You made a fool of me, and now you're going to pay.'

'But Lucy is trying to save us,' said Dee, staring at Boaz. 'It is possible that our whole world is at risk.'

'She beat me by cheating,' insisted Gripe. 'And she's going to pay.'

'What you need is a damned good spanking,' yelled Granny.

'I'll be the one doing the spanking,' yelled Gripe, 'and *that* minx is going to be on the receiving end.'

'And when the spanking is finished,' said Boaz, 'there will be the small matter of a map.'

'No chance,' said Pixy. 'Lucy has beaten him once and she'll do it again, won't you Lucy?'

Lucy smiled weakly, taking stock of the situation.

Dee reached inside his cloak, but Boaz seemed ready to counter attack. Gusset prepared to protect Granny, even though he'd be no match for the guards. Tenby fidgeted in his pockets, and would be about as much use as Zenda. And Quim trembled like a spider-web, pretending to offer protection to Madimi. The sorcerer's daughter was the only one who seemed unafraid, at least until Gripe took a cudgel from beneath his cloak. It was tipped with steel spikes that looked capable of splintering solid oak.

'Perhaps the child was a little hasty,' said Dee. He removed his hands from his cloak and Boaz relaxed slightly.

'That's right,' said Pixy staring at the spikes. 'What if Lucy apologises?'

'She can do that with her spilt blood,' said Gripe.

The guards spread out to form a horseshoe-shaped fight ring, separating Gripe and Lucy from the others. Her only escape was over the edge of the ramp, where there was a hundred foot drop to the waxy floor below.

'I'm sorry I cheated,' said Lucy. She wasn't sorry at all, and felt like a pathetic fraud, but it seemed the only way out. It was too late to consider an invention. Stories she told now might take hours or even days to come to fruition – and the look on Gripe's face told her she had seconds at most.

The groundling gave a savage grin, circling round so he could watch the grins of approval on his minions' faces. Lucy advanced, thinking she might be able to push Gripe over the edge. She was rewarded with a swipe from a sword that grazed her scalp as she ducked.

'This isn't fair,' she said. 'I should have a weapon too.'

'That's right,' said a voice from inside her coat. 'We want a weapon.'

'I'm not falling for the talking coat trick again,' said Gripe. He took another swipe and caught Lucy a glancing blow on her arm. A sliver of pink skin appeared, quickly turning to red as her blood flowed.

'First strike to me,' yelled Gripe.

Lucy fell on one knee, clasping the wound. The blood ran between her gloved fingers as she tried to staunch the flow, but after a brief application of pressure she released the hand and cupped it against her ear.

'What was that?' she whispered.

It was the sound of boiling, but it wasn't water – the noise was rich and thick, like bubbling oil. Gripe backed up to the edge and glanced over his shoulder, then turned back to Lucy before she had chance to charge at him.

'The floor's boiling,' he grunted. 'Time to finish your sad little life and get out of here.'

'Once we have the book,' said Boaz. 'And perhaps the map as well.'

'Yeah, right,' grunted Gripe. 'Blood first, books later.'

He advanced until he was close enough to make a kill. A wrinkled sneer parted his lips and a dribble of saliva ran out and dangled from his chin.

'No *please, don't,*' begged Lucy. 'Look behind you.'

'You didn't fool me with the talking coat,' sneered Gripe, 'so what makes you think I'll fall for the oldest trick in the book. Am I thick, or what?'

A brief glance at his men shook Gripe's assurance. They were staring at the space behind his head. And they were pointing and yelling.

'What the hell is *that*?' screamed Zenda.

'I think it might be Lulo,' yelled Lucy.

'And who the frig is Lulo?' yelled Zenda.

'The Mother of Vinegar,' said Lucy. 'There was a crowd in my way back on Grimston pier, and an empty cabinet, and, umm, well, then it all gets a bit complicated.'

Lulo's giant face was a mess of boiling wax, flowing in fiery rivulets that occasionally dripped from her skin. Her neck was long and spindly, like a wax effigy of a snake, and it was attached to a thin, wasted body that had only just begun to emerge from her birthing pool. Her torso was covered with flaming streamers that searched out anchorage points with the sole intention of turning them to ash.

Gripe dropped his sword as the creature floated up behind him, the head pausing for a moment to inspect its victim. Then a massive tongue extended, wrapping his struggling body and drawing him into a smiling mouth.

There was a scream from the groundling and then he was gone.

'Oh, my *God*,' yelled Zenda. 'That is just too much.'

Toby grabbed her and flattened himself against the back wall. Then he located an alcove to his left and dragged her inside.

'Save yourselves,' he yelled to the guards.

Lulo had a taste for flesh now, and the diet obviously suited her. The rest of her mottled torso and spindly legs emerged from the wax lake, thickening as they extended and bearing her up. But her growth was suddenly halted when her shoulder caught beneath a section of the spiral ramp.

'Run,' screamed Zenda.

For once, nobody argued. They sprinted back down the slope as masonry crashed in from above, smashing into the ramp where they had just been standing.

'That's done it,' said Pixy. 'The door is locked, and the ramp is broken.'

Everyone heard, but they were too horrified to reply. Lulo's arm burst into flame, scooping terrified guards over the edge of the ramp and sending them plummeting towards the boiling wax. They screamed like firecrackers as the molten mess swallowed them up.

'We have to get that thing on our side,' screamed Zenda. 'Umm, what about a sacrifice?'

Everyone stared coldly at the journalist.

'Sometimes the forces of nature are on nobody's side,' said Dee. 'The world of creation is rich and untameable and we can only prostrate ourselves before its impartial power.'

'Oh that's *very* good,' sneered Zenda. 'I really must write that down so I can use it in an article. *If* we ever get out of this alive.'

'I think we might be alright,' yelled Pixy. 'Look.'

The uppermost parts of Lulo were cooling, leaving fire streamers stuck to the walls and her solidified head resting on the ramp. All that remained was for the rest of her molten body to drip back into the pool, leaving the air full of silence.

'You must be exhausted,' said Dee, sighing with relief and looking at Lucy. 'Your creations only have life when you have the energy.'

'I'm fine,' she said, looking somewhat haggard.

She felt wretched, but dug deep inside herself and located a reserve of strength that might be enough to take them forward. And with that, the wax lake boiled again and Lulo's hand reappeared.

But that was the utmost limit of Lucy's control, and she stood aghast as her most recent creation followed its own instincts. Lulo's hand brushed Granny and Gusset away and scooped up the rest of them, lifting them clear of the bubbling lake on an ever-growing arm.

'*Lucy,*' screamed Granny. 'I just remembered…'

'What?' yelled Lucy. She peered nervously over the side of the waxy palm that was lifting them skywards. They were too high to jump, and Granny's screaming was barely audible above the sound of slurping wax.

'Sheep sent a middle, and leafy tent peg, before the scum on your knees is a seal,' she screamed.

'I have a feeling that might have been important,' groaned Lucy.

'I heard,' yelled Pixy. 'It was something like *she who ascends the Migdal, blah, blah, must leave the temple before the sun breaks in from the east, or be sealed in the blah, blah.* Or something.'

'A deadline,' sighed Lucy, as they continued their ascent. 'That's all we need.'

A Grotesque Beauty

Lucy leaned over the edge of the waxy palm that bore them up, desperate to catch sight of Gusset or Granny. But they were too high, having passed forty or more rotations of the ramp that coiled around them like a snake. The rate of ascent was rapid, and the wind-rush whistled in her ears – but there was another, even more worrying sound. The Vooghuls were waking up and inching out of their niches, spluttering and coughing up phlegm like tramps that have spent the night under a bridge.

'We're too fast for them,' grinned Pixy.

'And what if the hand stops?' said Zenda, peering over the side. 'Or the arm stretches so much it can't support our weight?'

'She's right,' said Toby, 'it's getting thinner as we get higher.'

'Of course I'm right,' snapped Zenda.

Lulo's hand slowed down as it approached the roof, which raised a cheer from Tenby. But he groaned when he noticed that a group of Vooghuls had left the spiral ramp and were floating in the air at the centre of the coil.

'I've just thought of something,' said Quim.

'See?' said Toby. 'I knew someone would come up with a plan.'

'It's not really a plan a such,' said Quim apologetically. 'I was more sort of wondering – did anyone see what happened to our friend Boaz?'

Lulo's spindly fingers curved above them as the hand juddered to a halt and dumped them unceremoniously onto a narrow stone ledge. Just a few feet away, a green haze filtered out of a tube-like tunnel, like a bad smell creeping from a toilet. There was another similar opening at the far end of the ledge, but floating between it and them was a Vooghul. And unlike the ones that were dozing in the niches just below, this one was wide-awake.

'Get in the hole,' screamed Quim, pulling Pixy along with him.

Zenda and Tenby dived in behind, closely followed by Dee and Madimi with Toby and Lucy bringing up the rear.

'Is it following?' yelled Toby.

'Just run,' gasped Lucy, her eyes streaming from the fumes. She glanced over her shoulder as the Vooghul reached the mouth of the tunnel. It called out to her, but the words were lost in the torrent of noise from up ahead.

'We're all going to die,' screamed Quim, his voice getting closer again.

'Turn around,' screamed Zenda. She and the others were running back towards the danger they had just escaped.

Lucy pressed up against the side wall as Tenby raced past.

'Move,' yelled Zenda, running close behind him. 'Bloody-well move you stupid girl – it's coming down like lava.'

'It is *Apachama*,' said the Vooghul at the tunnel entrance. 'This is the *grease made from dust* which all life eventually returns to.'

The creature permitted them to leave the tunnel and return to the relative safety of the ledge. But it surprised them by not attacking, even when the waxy lava that burst from the tunnel and flowed out over the edge of the ramp distracted them.

'*Pixatrix*,' hissed the Vooghul, waving a skeletal hand.

'H-how do you know my name?' said Pixy, her voice trembling.

'Pixatrix,' it said again. 'Live once more in my heart.'

'It knows my name,' screamed Pixy. 'How can that be?'

'Don't listen to it,' shouted Lucy. She beckoned Pixy towards her, but the girl ignored her desperate motioning and approached the filth-clad creature.

The Vooghul bent towards her and began to whisper.

'*Come and live with me*,' it said.

'*No*,' screamed Lucy, sensing the creature's thoughts. 'You just bloody-well stay there and be *quiet* – and keep your filthy thoughts to yourself.'

The Vooghul remained where it was, but had no intention of keeping its thoughts private; instead they coiled around Lucy's mind like rusty springs, dripping dull red poison into her heart. She expected pain, but instead there came a feeling of intense emotion and the memory of unbridled passion in a sun-filled meadow. Then there were memories of Pixy, first as a baby and then as a young child. And all the time this was going on she could sense a feeling of wonderment about the world and its place in the universe.

And then it all came to an end. The scenes of anguish and torment that followed descended on Lucy like a landslide filled with razor sharp rocks.

'Murder and destruction,' said the voice in her head. 'Pain and endless suffering – and all these dark seeds were sown in the name of your cause.'

'No,' screamed Lucy, not sure if the yell was inside her head.

She boiled with anger at the scenes she had just witnessed, but there was a sadness creeping up on her as well. The Vooghul had a clear remembrance of its own capture and death, and possessed an overwhelming wish to return to its decaying body. But the deepest and blackest of all its memories was the association with Pixy.

'I can't let you tell her,' thought Lucy.

'She will be one with me,' came the reply from the creature's thoughts.

'Then I must stop you,' said Lucy.

A wisp of wax rose through the coils of the ramp, like a thread of cotton floating on the breeze. At first it was as thin as gossamer, encircling the Vooghul without drawing attention to its own presence. But then, as the thread span faster and faster, it thickened until it was like a whirling lasso.

'Pixy,' screamed the Vooghul.

The threads tightened.

'Pixatrix,' it screamed, 'my own dear daughter.'

Pixy reached out a hand, but the thread contracted, pulling the Vooghul back towards the edge of the ramp.

She held on for less than a second, just enough time to exchange glances with her daughter – and then she was gone.

'You killed my mother,' squealed Pixy.

There was a sickening splash as the Vooghul plunged into the wax pool.

'She was already dead,' sobbed Lucy, 'and she wanted you to join her.'

'But she remembered me,' screamed Pixy. 'Her memories were alive.'

'That's true,' admitted Toby.

'See?' squealed Pixy. 'You murdered her memories.'

'There was no other way,' sobbed Lucy. 'She would have killed us all.'

'She wouldn't,' screamed Pixy, 'and I wish it was *you* who were dead.'

'We should argue later,' said Toby, peering below. 'The rest of them are coming, and there are too many to fight.'

'Then we should take the other tunnel,' said Madimi.

'Why don't we send the crocodile to see if it's safe?' said Zenda.

Lucy placed the handbag on the floor and prodded it with a toe. Henbeg performed his usual dramatic transformation and sniffed the air. Then he scampered off down the passage, returning with a look of alarm on his snout and excrement covered feet.

'He's brought more of that disgusting stink back,' said Zenda.

'It smells like the waste product of beasts,' said Madimi, polite as ever.

'I vote for being safe, but up to our necks in shit,' said Tenby.

Digesting the photographer's obvious wisdom, they followed Henbeg's talon-prints that led down a wax-free passage and ended next to a small rusted grate.

'At least we won't need a key,' said Lucy. 'They've left the door ajar.'

'Nobody in their right mind would go in,' said Quim. 'Just look at that disgusting mess flooding out – and me without overshoes too.'

'Send Lucy in first,' shouted Pixy. 'If she comes back in one piece we'll know if it's safe, and if she doesn't we can sneak past as they eat her.'

'You ungrateful child,' said Madimi, fishing beneath her skirts. 'Don't you see that Lucy is trying to help us all?'

'Is that why she killed my mother?' barked Pixy.

'I told you,' said Lucy, 'I didn't know who she was until it was too late.'

'You bloody stinking liar,' screamed Pixy.

She took a mad run towards Lucy, but as she got level with Madimi the sorcerer's daughter brushed a small, bright pin across the girl's cheek. Pixy stumbled and turned towards Madimi, then fell back into Dee's arms. She soon recovered consciousness, but when she stood up, all sign of aggression had melted and she wore a smile that made her look rather simple.

'It will wear off,' smiled Dee. 'Eventually.'

Lucy leaned on the iron hatch. It gave a pained creak, setting up an eerie echo in the palace of stinks beyond. They squeezed through the doorway with some difficulty and found themselves in a space so big it was difficult to imagine how distant the walls were. The chamber was honeycombed with semi-transparent boxes, each made from a foul, waxy substance similar to that which Lulo had risen from. Some of the boxes were arranged as pens at ground level, but the majority were suspended in the air by wires, row upon row and column after column of them extending to the horizon. The only place where an end to the foul stabling was visible was about three hundred yards to their left, where roughly hewn windows admitted daylight.

'It reminds me of your library,' said Lucy.

'It *does* hint at vastness,' said Dee, 'but there is no knowledge here, only filth – putrid, disgusting filth.'

'No argument there,' said Toby, dipping a toe in the muck. 'It looks like a mixture of dung and blood and something else.' He stooped to examine it, but was beaten back by a solid wall of stench.

'And I suppose we have to walk through it,' said Zenda. 'I hate this place. My shoes have been ruined ten times over.'

'Then stay,' said Dee, 'but remember that this is the scarabs' roost, and they are liable to return at any time.'

He took a handful of dust from his pocket and blew it at the iron door. As it slammed, the rust multiplied, and before the echo had died the metal was a solid red mass, like an anchor that had rested on the seabed for a hundred years.

They headed towards the vents, carefully threading their way through the maze of boxes so that the reddish-brown filth didn't slop over their shoes. Zenda's high heels weren't suitable for poo-snorkelling though, and when they eventually reached the distant wall she was the only one with bare, chocolate coloured feet.

'I don't want a single word from anyone,' she said.

'Would you like a hanky?' smiled Quim. 'And no, I don't want it back.'

The window vents were no more than rough-edged slots that had been hacked into the thick outer shell of the tower. They obviously weren't part of the original design, and some were only just big enough to admit a scarab, many bearing signs of collision with blood and various body parts stuck to their jagged metal edges. One was bigger than the others though, and it was towards this that Lucy edged, well aware of the wind that funnelled up from the ground and sucked at the jagged edges.

They were about a thousand feet up, with a clear view of the streets near the footings and the woods that surrounded them. Lucy had no idea what was happening beneath those canopies of trees or under those hundreds of roofs, but events in the market squares and on the open ground spoke for themselves. Every bit of space was occupied by armed groundlings, who were engaged in bitter fighting with the scarabs. Above them, the air was thick with winged creatures – a humming blanket of death that looked like a delicate black-lace blanket.

'A battle,' she said quietly. There was no element of surprise in her voice, just a sigh that signalled deep weariness. She was tired of seeing people suffer because of her actions – and she wanted it to stop.

'But where did they all come from?' said Toby.

'I think we have Mister Gusset to thank for that,' said Dee. 'I believe he mobilised the groundling forces whilst you were otherwise engaged.'

'What was *that*?' yelled Toby, ducking as a dark shape flashed past.

'It looked like a scarab,' said Pixy groggily. 'But it had feathers.'

'Then we are fighting back,' said Dee, 'and not only with foot soldiers. If you look closely you will observe that the feathers on the plummeting insect are in fact hundreds of birds.'

'And their combined weight is dragging it out of the sky,' said Toby.

They stood and watched as scarabs spiralled out of control, their wings laden with small birds that clung on for dear life. And with just six feet or so to fall, the birds released their grip and the insects smashed into the ground where they were pounced on by lance-men and groundlings with pikestaffs.

Lucy and her friends cheered each time one of them was speared, their spirits lifted for the first time since they began their ascent.

But their joy was premature. Just as it seemed the scarabs were defeated, a glow appeared on the horizon.

And soon it resolved itself into six bright points of light.

'I was afraid that this might happen,' said Dee. 'They have sensed defeat and gathered to rally their strength.'

'But that's good isn't it?' said Zenda. 'If the angels are running into each other's arms it means they're scared.'

'Not so,' said Dee. 'I believe the power of angels is manifold. When they gather, their power increases in a geometrical fashion.'

'So they'll be more difficult to defeat if they stay together?' said Lucy.

'I'm afraid so,' said Dee, 'and as yet, we have not even seen what a single one of them is capable of.'

'But we escaped them earlier, *didn't* we?' said Zenda.

'I don't think they were even trying,' said Lucy. 'They still wanted me to go peacefully if you remember.'

'Well it looks like they mean business now,' said Tenby.

The points of light had grown in proportion. They were no longer mere blobs of brightness, but distinguishable figures, their massive wings beating in great bending sweeps that were the very essence of power.

'I don't like this at all,' said Tenby. '*Watch out*,' he screamed to the men below. 'Angels are coming to get you.'

Lucy and Zenda each grabbed a shoulder and dragged him in, pinning him to the ground so Toby could clamp a hand over his mouth.

'Are you mad?' he hissed. 'They could fly up and make mincemeat of us.'

'Aptly put,' said Dee.

Tenby nodded his agreement and Toby released the gag.

'I got a bit carried away,' he said. 'I thought maybe the young girly here could just tell a story and that'd be the end of it.'

'I don't think so,' said Lucy. 'We need a little more help than that.'

'And perhaps we have it,' said Madimi. 'Look down there – something is emerging from the trees.'

Winding along an old dirt track were four carts, each one covered with a great tarpaulin. The driver of the lead cart was unmistakable, even ignoring his newly acquired peacock-feather coat. It was Weazenock, and sitting next to him was a proud looking Bony Crumpet.

'I think we might have misjudged them,' smiled Lucy.

'So they *were* willing to help,' said Toby.

'You can't always judge a book by its cover,' said Dee.

'But who are the others?' said Zenda.

The drivers of the remaining wagons were more difficult to identify, but as they got nearer, Pixy recognised them.

'It's the orchestra people,' she said, 'and the carpenter.'

'Ah, good,' smiled Dee.

'So we're going to have musical slaughtering are we?' scoffed Zenda.

'No,' grumbled Dee with a frown, 'we most certainly are not.'

Events unfolded rapidly down below. Pentabonce's men surrounded the carts in a protective circle, their great lances jutting out like the spines of a porcupine. Inside the defence, the drivers leapt down to comfort the horses and remove the ropes from their precious cargo.

But when they finally drew back the covers, Zenda could hardly contain her disappointment.

'*Telephone boxes*?' she scoffed. 'What are they going to do – call the fire brigade?'

'Those are Angelic Cabinets,' said Toby, with a certain amount of pride.

'That is correct,' said Dee, a little surprised. 'They have been constructed according to a rigorous regimen, as laid down by the priests of the church.'

'And which church is that then?' said Zenda.

'Well there you have me,' said Dee. 'It has certainly never been known in this world – but I suspect it *might* have been in yours.'

'This is giving me a headache,' said Quim, who until now had contented himself with hanging in the shadows. 'Angels? Churches? Cabinets? What's next? Prayer time?'

'An excellent idea,' said Dee. 'If we fail then we will need all the prayers we can muster.'

'Prepare yourselves,' said Lucy. 'The angels have arrived.'

The six brilliant creatures hovered a hundred feet or so above the carts, but no attack was forthcoming. They seemed curious, and gradually reduced their height until they were ten feet or so above the cowering orchestra, their powerful wings raising dust-clouds from the track.

'What are they doing?' asked Toby.

'Satisfying a lust for knowledge,' said Dee. 'It would seem that even the race of angels is inquisitive.'

'Why are the musicians kneeling?' said Toby. 'And what are they doing?'

'Repeating the mantras,' said Dee. 'I left very particular instructions.'

'And what instructions might those have been?' said Zenda, reaching for her notepad.

'They are not for your ears,' hissed Dee.

Zenda grunted and put the pad away, her interest drawn back to the dirt track and the nearby woods. Three of the angels hovered, as if something had caught their attention, whilst the others peeled away and climbed higher into the sky, their colour dimming as they rose.

'What's happening?' said Zenda. 'Why aren't they flying away?'

'I believe we will soon know,' said Dee with a satisfied smile.

It was impossible to hear the chants and rituals used by the musicians, but whatever they were, they seemed to be working.

The three angels flapped wildly in an attempt to maintain height, but a thin stream of energy burst from the top of each cabinet, dimming their body glow as it made contact. A cloud of steam flew up from the first victim as he was sucked down feet first, screaming and cursing. The second angel was stronger and managed to resist the initial onslaught, but the more he struggled the deeper he became ensnared. Finally, he too was exhausted, and his wings fell like limp rags as he was pulled down. The third angel was even stronger, and although her flames had dimmed with the initial contact they brightened again as she regained some height.

'It's Zarobi,' said Toby.

The angel flapped furiously, pummelling the air in an attempt to break free – and to everyone's surprise, it worked. As the flames roared around her struggling body, her wings expanded, tearing greedily at the air and lifting her higher and higher.

'I don't like the look of this,' said Tenby.

The influence of the cabinet dwindled as Zarobi gained height – the thick stream of energy that joined them shrinking rapidly and looking as though it might break at any moment.

And still she climbed.

'She knows we're up here,' said Lucy.

Everyone moved back, but as they did so, hundreds of birds swept down on Zarobi and attached themselves to her. And when their claws were firmly embedded, they stopped beating their own wings. Zarobi screamed, but her words were swept away on the wind as she plummeted towards the cabinet. The blazing streamer thickened as she fell, dragging her ever more swiftly towards the tiny aperture on the roof of the cabinet. And then she was gone; her flaming body reduced to a cloud of ash as she was sucked inside. She was trapped, like an elegant golden fish in a tank that didn't seem large enough to contain her.

'Amazing,' said Toby, whistling through his teeth.

'But the others are getting away,' said Lucy.

She expected to feel satisfaction seeing her enemies quashed, so the wave of grief that struck her came as a bit of a surprise.

'We had sufficient materials for only three cabinets,' said Dee.

'Then how do we beat the rest?' said Toby. 'We're sitting ducks.'

'As you say,' said Dee, 'we are most vulnerable.'

'But you're a sorcerer,' said Zenda. 'And an expert on angels.'

'My secret art was designed for conversation with the angelic host,' said Dee. 'I never expected that I would ever wish to destroy them.'

'Well someone did,' smiled Lucy. 'Let's just hope they were right.'

'A plan?' said Zenda.

'Just something I picked up on the street,' said Lucy.

She pulled some stiff pieces of card from her pocket.

'*Postcards*?' sneered Zenda. 'What good are those? Or are you planning to send for reinforcements?'

'I think they might contain valuable information,' said Lucy.

'These are instructions,' said Toby, reading the first card. '*Please scratch for more information.*'

Lucy did so. There was a small explosion, followed by a puff of yellow smoke. When it cleared they were greeted by a semi-transparent image of the vendor she had met outside Dee's house.

'Who's the geek?' said Toby.

'Someone I owe a pencil sharpener to,' said Lucy.

'Many thanks for purchasing Zachary's angel cards,' said the mirage. 'All cards at cheap price, except for rare kinds at very special price. You not paid special price, so you not got special card – but very nice, all the same.'

'Wow, it speaks,' said Toby.

'Zachary speaks but he not understands,' said the seller. 'I guess what you say, then maybe leave gaps for you to say more.'

The face stopped talking for a moment.

'This is truly wonderful magic,' said Dee.

'And I do not forget the sharsen pempleners,' said the mirage.

'No,' smiled Lucy, 'I didn't think you would.'

'Zachary's cards are special,' droned the image. 'Each one comes from a magickal place, from a time that is before the world began.'

'I remember him from somewhere,' said Pixy drowsily. 'But how did he get here? And why can I see through him? Why is he disappearing?'

'She's right,' said Zenda. 'Your freaky peddler is fading.'

The image of Zachary fizzled, prompting Lucy to take out another card and scratch it. The see-through seller reappeared. He was dressed in a bizarre carpet-like shawl and wearing a soft felt hat.

'…in the west,' he said, as if he'd been interrupted, 'they are sly critters, scarcely seen, save by the reflections of murrs – but sometimes visible in the disturbance of rain-dropps and movements of the wynde.'

'Do you think I could possibly have one of those?' said Dee.

'And break up the set?' said Lucy. She glanced briefly at the sky, where the remaining angels hovered at a safe distance.

'They wonder if we have more power at our disposal,' observed Dee.

'We don't,' said Toby, as Zachary disappeared again. 'Unless of course the pencil sharpener man has any brilliant ideas.'

Lucy scratched another card, and he returned once again. He was naked this time, except for a modest rag covering his essential bits.

'Business not so good,' he droned. 'Must sell clothes to buy food. But sales will soon pick up.'

'What about the angel information?' said Toby.

'A subtle yellow thing,' said Zachary. 'It smells of the cold Hyperborean summer. He may shimmer and disappear if you hold him at certain angles.'

'Never mind that,' said Toby. 'We don't want to know about their habits or their hobbies, we just need to know how to kill them.'

'But by now,' grinned Zachary, 'you will be saying, yes, that is all very well, but can such hevven-critters be killed, and if the answer is yes then how can we be doing it, efficient and clean with best method.'

'We're all ears,' said Lucy.

'Especially Zenda,' giggled Toby.

'Well go on then,' said Pixy. 'Tell us how to kill them.'

'He can't hear you,' said Toby.

'Zachary cannot hear you,' said the mirage, 'but in any case this is not a special card, so extra information is not for me to tell. Very sorry. Please buy more cards at official angel card market stalls.'

'Oh, brilliant,' snapped Zenda. 'Trust the wonderful Lucy Blake to buy the cheap cards. Now we really are in trouble.'

'What about the others?' said Pixy. She wore a strange expression – as if she hated Lucy but couldn't quite remember why.

Lucy rummaged in her pockets and pulled the rest out into the light. The serpent card bust into flames and fizzled away in a spectacular pile of ash.

'Serpentaria,' said a fading voice. 'Hailing from east, violent and warr-lyke, constantly in fighting and bluddy messe – and all about are snayks…'

'Great,' said Zenda. 'I suppose that's the last we'll see of him.'

'So Zarobi belonged to the fire,' said Pixy.

'What?' said Zenda.

'They hail from the east,' said Toby. 'That must be fire. And Zarobi was a fire angel – that explains her burning wings.'

'And the others?' said Dee.

'There was steam as one was swallowed by the cabinets,' suggested Lucy.

'And a blast of air when the other got sucked in,' said Madimi.

'So what does that leave?' said Quim. 'Did the tendrils that grabbed Miss Zenda belong to an earth angel?'

'Why don't we ask the cards?' said Pixy.

'We only have one left,' said Lucy.

'Then let's hope it's a good one,' said Toby. 'Because the other angels are coming back.'

They stared at the approaching lights in the sky as Lucy whipped out the last card and scratched it.

'Congratulations on a superior class of card,' said Zachary, 'coming with details on how to kill your favourite angel, especially if he is equipped with tendrils and mouths.'

'That's it,' squealed Pixy. 'That's the one we need.'

'You are a clever little girl, aren't you?' sneered Zenda.

'Go on then,' said Toby. 'Tell us how to kill the earth angels.'

'By now you are getting impatient,' said Zachary. 'Perhaps you are simply curious. But more likely you are in a situation of great stress.'

'Get on with it,' screamed Zenda. 'They're coming.'

'Patience is a virtue,' smiled Zachary, his image flickering.

'He's going to disappear before we find out,' yelled Zenda. 'Of all the stupid, thoughtless…'

'Pressure,' said Zachary, 'is the only weapon that…'

Fzzzt.

'He's disappeared,' wailed Quim, as the mirage faded in a puff of smoke.

'We're dead,' groaned Zenda. 'We're all dead.'

'Maybe not,' said Toby. 'Something is happening below.'

'I believe our luck has changed,' said Dee. 'It looks like our friends are preparing to unveil Weazenock's One and Only Grotesque Beauty.'

'*Ugh,*' said Zenda. 'It sounds like some horrible fairground act.'

'They *did* tour the city once,' said Dee. 'But the novelty soon wore off.'

'Act?' said Toby.

'This had better be good,' said Tenby. 'Those angels are awfully close.'

'And brighter too,' said Lucy. 'They're furious about the cabinets.'

'Then we must pray that Weazenock makes the transformation in good time,' said Dee.

'Transformation?' said Lucy.

'Indeed,' said Dee, glancing at Pixy. 'But this is not the talent that certain groundlings possess. There are, dotted around this city, certain unfortunate beasts who exist only because of a regrettable experiment.'

'What kind of experiment?' said Zenda.

'Ah,' said an embarrassed Dee. 'Well the intention was to create an angel from ordinary body parts – and Weazenock's Heh-Shi is one such creature.'

'Really?' said Zenda. 'Now that *does* sound interesting.'

'To you, perhaps,' said Dee, 'but a lifetime of misery for others.'

'What happened?' said Lucy.

'The experimenters were quick to see the lunacy of their meddling,' said Dee. 'But the damage was already done.'

'And that's the secret weapon?' said Toby.

'See for yourself,' said Dee.

Weazenock rolled back the canvas on his cart, revealing a wet, shivering mass of feathers, about the size of a baby elephant.

'Is that the thing that followed us in the Morty Lakes?' said Pixy.

'It is,' said Dee. 'Although I didn't realise it at the time.'

'Are you sure?' said Lucy. 'It doesn't *look* that dangerous.'

A Grotesque Beauty

Bony Crumpet climbed up to assist the creature, smoothing its damp feathers and helping it to struggle to its feet. But he appeared to stumble under its weight and the creature crashed down, kneeling over him, its head touching the floor as if praying. Its wings, if that was what they were, spread out with the impact, extending at least ten feet on either side of the cart.

'It's too late,' said Toby. 'The angels have seen it and changed course.'

'They have recognised a greater threat,' said Dee.

The others nodded, staring in horror as one of the angels dropped like a bird of prey – a lethal projectile bearing down on the defenceless beast. The force of the resulting collision was so great that the wooden cart collapsed and splintered, throwing the creature off to one side, where it crouched protectively in a wet, glossy ball. There was no sign of the unfortunate Bony, who must have perished in the wooden wreckage. The angel wheeled back into the air, preparing for another dive as the creature dragged itself under the nearby trees. But this time the process of unfolding was quicker, as if it knew that time was running out.

'It's half bird,' said Pixy, observing the process of evolution with great interest. 'And half octopus.' Then, with a total disregard for the fractions she had never been taught, she added, 'and half butterfly and half wasp.'

The proportions were all wrong, but Pixy's observations were otherwise accurate. The creature now had no legs to speak of; instead there were long arms with suckers on every surface and large leafy pads in place of hands. Any assault would therefore come from the vicious curved beak, or the huge sting attached to the tip of its wasp-like abdomen.

'Do you think he'll be able to fly on those stubby little wings?' said Toby.

'Oh I do hope so,' sighed Madimi. 'So much rests on the outcome. And he's so beautiful. If he were to…'

The Heh-Shi had rolled his wings up when he took cover, and now he needed to escape the thick brush at the edge of the wood so he had enough space to unfold them again. They were still covered with egg-damp, and if he was going to get airborne then he needed to dry them quickly. But the angels realised this and descended on the wood, and every time the Heh-Shi tried to crawl out they forced him back.

Then, one of the angels set fire to the undergrowth, and the Heh-Shi began to scream.

'We have to distract them,' said Lucy. 'To give the creature a chance.'

'From up here?' said Zenda. 'I'm not sure they'll take much notice.'

Fortunately, Pentabonce had the same idea and his men converged on the angels' position, their lances extended to draw them away from the embattled beast. Seeing they were surrounded, the angels took to the air, but the distraction provided by the Shieldmaster's men had been enough.

The Heh-Shi screeched in triumph, flapping his newly dried wings to show off their brilliant butterfly scales. He took to the air with surprising speed and agility, assuming a collision course with the lead angel and daring him to flinch. The angel kept a steady course, confident that he could out-fly the monster, but the Heh-Shi flew straight and true as well, and at the last moment he brought his sting underneath himself so by the time they collided he was flying backwards. It was impossible to see the expression on the angel's face, but he must have been surprised as the great barb pierced his chest at the front and emerged from his back a fraction of a second later.

'Kill them all,' screamed Pixy, surprising everyone with her death-lust.

The Heh-Shi reversed his course and the bloodied barb slid out of the angel who fell a short distance to earth, raising a cloud of dust when he crashed.

'So, are angels immortal or not?' said Toby. 'Only if...'

There was no time to consider the question. The Heh-Shi pursued the second angel who had broken off his earlier attack and was flying directly towards Lucy and her friends.

'Has he seen us?' said Toby.

'I don't think so,' said Dee, 'but we had best hide, just in case.'

They sat on the floor, their backs to the wall below the vent. There was no way of seeing what was happening from this position, but in the event it was probably just as well.

'Do you think he's still coming this way?' said Tenby.

Before anyone had a chance to answer the angel flew through the vent, his wings flattened to fit through the gap. Even so, feathers scattered as he clipped an edge and gouged a wing, spraying Pixy with blood in the process.

The Heh-Shi was close behind, ducking and diving as the angel threaded through the maze of Scarab nests. He was trailing tendrils now, and as he flew deeper into the scarab stable in order to turn around, the vegetation thundered through the vent like the carriages of a speeding train. When he turned, the momentum in the tendrils disappeared and they dropped to the floor, so when he flew back towards the vent they trailed scarab-filth and slowed him down.

'Two things,' said Toby. 'First, everybody move, because when he gets back we're going to get covered in crap. And secondly, give me a hand to tie some of these things up.'

He grabbed an armful of the thinner growths, wrapping them around the pillar between two vent holes to form an anchor. Quim took out a couple of hankies and did the same, once he had wiped them down.

'That'll make him think,' said Toby.

The angel was flying back towards the vents and soon spotted the group of friends. The look on his face said it all. Rules or no rules, if he had the time then they would all be dead. But there *was* no time. He was flying and couldn't stop, and the Heh-Shi was close behind.

'Bye,' said Toby, waving as the angel flashed through the vent and into the outside air.

The Heh-Shi had a smaller wing area than the angel so he took longer to turn and was less manoeuvrable. But he seemed to be just as clever. He'd seen the tied tendrils on the way in and now looked as though he wanted to smile, if only his razor sharp beak would allow it.

'Look out,' said Zenda, making a grab for Quim's scissors. 'The great ugly thing is coming for us.'

'No,' said Dee. 'He's coming in to land.'

The Heh-Shi slowed his flight to a walking pace, alighting with such care that it wouldn't be fair to call it a landing. It was more like a snowflake coming to rest on an eyelash.

'He's beautiful,' said Lucy.

'That's why they call him the one and only,' said Madimi.

'Does it speak?' said Zenda.

The Heh-Shi shook its head, cupping a leafy pad against the side of his head, as if listening for something. The angel's tendrils were still flowing out of the vent but there was little slack remaining and it was obvious what the Heh-Shi was waiting for. Seconds later there was a satisfying thunk as the owner of the tendrils reached the end of his leash and stopped flying. Instead he had begun to fall, and when the tendrils reached their limit he was dragged down and smashed against the side of the tower, dangling like a marooned climber at the end of a rope.

'I think that's sorted him out,' said Toby, peering outside.

'There is still danger,' said the Heh-Shi.

His thin, fragile voice sounding hauntingly familiar.

'I thought you couldn't speak?' said Zenda.

'Only when it is necessary,' said the Heh-Shi.

'That's a good idea,' said Toby. 'You should try it sometime Zenda.'

Zenda frowned and turned on the Heh-Shi.

'Haven't you got a job to do?' she snapped.

'I would give chase if I could,' said the Heh-Shi. 'But the remaining angel has taken refuge in the upper reaches of the tower.'

'Then get *after* it,' said Zenda.

'I cannot,' said the Heh-Shi, lowering his head to show the patches of brilliant colour around his eyes. 'The air is too thin, and I am exhausted.'

'Well then *what?*' said Zenda. 'You *must* be able to do something.'

'He's already saved your skin,' said Lucy. 'Isn't that enough?'

'I can do no more,' said the Heh-Shi, slipping to the floor. 'I have no more life. But what is the loss of a single creature, if the cause is noble?'

As he slumped down onto his leafy pads, Lucy looked closely at him and had the strangest feeling that all was not as it seemed. And then she realised where she'd heard the beast's voice before.

It was Bony Crumpet.

Weazenock's assistant was part of the beast.

Phoomph…

Zoo-weeeeeee…

'Right,' said Tenby, as his flashgun recharged, 'that's a great picture of the bird thing with all those textures and colours in its coat. Now, if I can just gather everyone into a group with the thing dying in the foreground?'

'Tenby, you heartless brute,' screamed Lucy. 'Give me that camera.'

'Leave him alone,' squealed Zenda, 'he's got a job to do.'

'Be quiet, *all* of you,' shouted Dee. 'The Heh-Shi gave his life to help save us. And from what I have just heard I wonder if it was a price worth paying.'

A Grotesque Beauty

Lucy sighed and approached the Heh-Shi, admiring the ivory sheen of his beak and the tatty, felt-covered antlers that looked as though they had seen a thousand battles. She placed a hand on his quivering abdomen. It was embroidered in red and yellow silks, to warn those who might dare to fight him. But a warning was unnecessary now – the creature was exhausted, the leather lids drawn back to reveal a look of sadness in his huge liquid eyes.

'You truly were a thing of beauty,' wept Lucy.

She let her tears drop onto his leaf sacs, hoping that her sorrow might give him strength. But as she stroked the feathery scales, Weazenock's one and only beauty folded his wings, and went to sleep for one last time.

The Obsidian Blade

It was Pixy who found the concealed door, but Dee who finally managed to get it open, burning through the congealed mucous with one of his magic powders. And it was Toby who first ventured into the dark corridor beyond, eager to discover the source of the bitter-almond smell. The tunnel was less than four feet in diameter, so they had to crawl for hundreds of yards, all the time arguing about what to do next.

By the time they saw the light ahead, the argument had turned into a verbal boxing match, with Zenda in the blue corner and Lucy in the red. It was an appropriate colour too, because underneath a relatively calm exterior she was boiling with rage at Zenda's reaction to the Heh-Shi's death. Tenby too, for that matter, taking his stupid snaps when the creature lay dying.

The tunnel flared out into a large, well lit corridor that rose in a spiral, like the ramp in Lulo's chamber. But the walls here were flanked by dozens of glass-fronted cabinets of a type all too familiar to Toby and Lucy from the Grimston amusement arcades.

'Look at this Luce,' said Toby, winding a handle. The machine clunked and a gangly spring jumped out of the fascia. Fastened to the end of the wobbling coil was a model of a baby wrapped in a moth eaten blanket.

'If we're going to escape then we haven't got time to be playing around with *these* things,' said Zenda. 'And anyway they never pay out.'

'They're for amusement only,' said Lucy, 'just like it says on the label. And in any case, aren't you just the slightest bit curious as to how they got here? Or why?'

'You might as well ask me how the scarabs came to be here, or why the locals are all so ugly or incredibly stupid,' said Zenda. 'Why does there need to be a reason behind everything?'

'If the universe has no reason then we are lost,' whispered Madimi.

'Actually my brain is beginning to throb,' said Quim. 'Couldn't it simply be that they were put here to tell a story?'

'A story?' said Toby, sounding doubtful.

'Of course,' said Quim. 'Just stand back and look – with your eyes that is, not your mouth.' He frowned at Zenda, and got a hateful stare in return.

'It's just more stupid cabinets,' moaned Tenby. 'Like the ones they used to capture the angels.'

'Not quite,' sighed Quim.

Behind each pane of glass was a simple domestic scene rendered in bits of old card, thick yellow glue and various scraps of discarded clothing. And if this wasn't bad enough, the paint job was of even worse quality. It looked as though a monkey with a grudge had applied it.

'Ignore the lack of craftsmanship,' said Quim, 'and what do you see?'

'Cupboards with windows?' suggested Pixy.

'*Scenes*,' sighed Quim, 'like the various parts of a play.'

As soon as Quim pointed it out, it was blindingly obvious.

The first tableau represented the birth of a child. The second showed a woman in a room, and when they turned the handle on the front of the cabinet she disappeared. Later scenes showed very ordinary occurrences, like children sleeping and playing and reading – quite a lot of those in fact. But further along, the normality disappeared. The subjects acquired rudimentary wings and were surrounded by scenes of confusion and conflict, all of them animated by the simple turning of a handle.

'These are rubbish,' said Zenda. 'The ones on the sea front in Grimston are *much* better. You can't even tell what sex these figures are.'

'The faces are just little blobs of pink wax,' said Quim. 'But *that*, I believe is the whole point.'

'It is a general lesson that could apply to anyone,' said Dee. 'The faces have been made deliberately vague.'

'Well it's an awful lot of trouble to go to,' said Toby, idly turning a handle. 'Why didn't they just put the story in a book, and leave it out for us to read?'

'If a secret was written in a book then the volume would have to remain hidden,' said Dee. 'But the scenes in these cabinets would be meaningless to the uninitiated and could be left in the open.'

'Like tarot cards,' said Lucy. 'Lily once told me that there were ancient stories hidden in the pictures.'

'And when did you start believing *her*?' grinned Toby.

'Never dismiss information,' said Dee. 'Even if Lily is your enemy, she will occasionally have something constructive to offer.'

'Occasionally,' smiled Lucy.

'So who's behind the story in the cabinet scenes?' said Toby.

'I'm afraid I have no idea,' admitted Dee.

'Why don't we look at the rest?' suggested Toby. 'If Quim's right then we can find out how the story ends by following the line of machines.'

'Good idea,' said Lucy.

She approached the next display and turned the creaky handle, expecting the mechanism to burst into action. Instead, a series of small holes opened and the space behind the glass filled with hundreds of scarabs, each the size of her thumbnail.

'Ugh,' she said, standing back from the glass.

'Well at least they can't get to you,' said Toby.

'I wouldn't be so sure,' said a horrified Dee.

The insects were gushing through the holes in a steady torrent, with each newcomer finding it more difficult to find a place amongst its brothers.

'I think we had best go,' said Quim, desperately trying to make himself heard above the mournful squeal that glass makes when it breaks slowly.

'Run,' shouted Pixy.

'But what about the other machines?' pleaded Lucy.

The glass panel shattered into thousands of sharp fragments that fell around their feet.

'You do that,' yelled Toby as he ran past her. 'You can discuss the hidden story with all your new insect friends.'

The scarabs swarmed from the machine as if there was an infinite supply of them on the other side of the wall – and it was clear that they were *not* happy at being cooped up. And what they *really* wanted after spending all that time in prison was to eat twice their own bodyweight in meat.

'Run,' shouted Pixy again.

'I'm running,' screamed Lucy, pulling her coat over her head.

As she ran, the storyteller glimpsed the remaining machines and realised that her chance for knowledge was slipping away. And scraping insects from her face, she recalled a fact that hadn't seemed so important at the time. Someone had once told her that the Migdal used to be called the Tower of Self Knowledge – so what if the 'self' in that name was her?

But she didn't get a chance to consider the idea. Toby had identified their next goal, and was calling desperately to her.

'It's an entrance of some kind,' wheezed Quim.

'More like a lift,' said Toby, batting away a squadron of tiny scarabs. He saw that both Dee and Madimi were wearing puzzled looks, so offered a few words of explanation. 'The Mericans call them elevators,' he added.

'That cleared things up,' said Lucy, running to join them. 'They're even more confused now.'

'Indeed,' said Dee, spitting out an insect. 'But the Miracle Lellavators are not important – we must concentrate on opening the doors before we are consumed in body, if not in mind. Now, can anyone think what these symbols might represent?'

He stood back for a clearer view. The area around the sliding doors was studded with twenty-one ornate panels, each containing a single symbol.

'It looks like a puzzle,' said Zenda.

'And only the worthy can pass,' said Madimi.

'Is it something to do with your Enochian language?' said Zenda.

Lucy raised an eyebrow. Tenby shuffled uncomfortably, to the sound of tiny, glistening insects being crunched underfoot.

'There are twenty one letters in the language of angels,' said Dee, shaking his head, 'but these symbols do not correspond to them.'

'That's a pity,' said Toby. He combed a scarab out of his hair and shook a few from his pockets, but the threat had subsided. The swarm was reluctant to venture any further along the passage.

'Any ideas?' said Lucy.

'Not a clue,' said Zenda.

'And it's far too clever for me,' admitted Quim.

'We guessed,' said Zenda.

'Well I think you're *all* too clever,' said Pixy. 'Why don't we just press a button and see what happens?'

'No,' said Dee, 'you might...'

Before anyone could stop her, Pixy touched a symbol.

The doors slid apart with a gentle hiss.

'There you are,' she said, as they entered and the doors closed behind them. 'Easy.'

There was a sound of metal wheels rolling on oily rails and the soft hiss of water under pressure. There was an aura of smugness too, and it was coming from Pixy.

'I suppose you think that was clever?' said Zenda.

'Just obvious,' grinned Pixy.

'Then perhaps you also know where we're going?' said Zenda.

'I got the door open like you asked,' said Pixy. 'I didn't offer to give you a guided tour.' She rubbed her cheek and stared at Lucy, like a doddery professor attempting to remember the name of a prehistoric fish. She was annoyed about something, but couldn't quite place her anger.

It was clear that the lift was rising from the moving patterns of light visible between the doors, but there was no indication of how far they had travelled. The only clue was the frequent interruption of the light as they passed through various levels.

'How does it know we want to keep going?' said Pixy finally.

'Well?' she repeated.

Nobody wanted to answer, because they were all too busy wondering the same thing. What marvels or horrors were they missing on the intervening floors, and why wasn't the lift stopping at them? And why was there a lift at all, for that matter? It simply didn't fit with the rest of the world.

'I've counted at least four hundred storeys,' said Zenda, sounding a little nervous and glaring at Pixy.

'Four hundred and seventeen,' said Quim. 'If we go any higher I'm going to need a little something to calm my nerves. Why doesn't it just stop for goodness sake?' He stamped his foot like a small child, but the tantrum was cut short by a sudden change in the background noise.

The watery hiss faded to a whisper and was replaced by a slight ticking, as if a mechanism was measuring some precise distance.

'I don't like it,' said Pixy, sniffing the air.

'We should get out of the box,' agreed Dee. 'I have never been happy with ropes, especially if one's life depends on them.'

The doors slid open to reveal a huge portal on the opposite wall, which was rusted almost as badly as the one that Dee sealed earlier. But the wheel that locked it had been oiled recently and revolved easily, lowering the great iron shield into the floor. Everyone was grateful for the blast of fresh air that blew the smell of Lulo wax and scarab waste away, but none of them was really prepared for the sight that greeted them.

'I reckon we're about five thousand feet up,' said Toby, moving forward carefully.

A covered catwalk extended from the main body of the tower, jutting out at ninety degrees and meeting another gantry about thirty feet out. This much larger walkway was made from a pearly green metal and extended both left and right, curving out of view as it hugged the contours of the Migdal. It was caged on all sides to prevent falls, and the only point of access was the linking gantry, which, by now, they were all standing in.

'It's a long way down,' said Pixy, staring between her feet. 'Umm, how far *is* five thousand feet? Is it more than a hundred?'

'Slightly,' grinned Toby.

Zenda watched nervously as the doors closed and the elevator car moved towards the higher floors.

'Let's go,' she said. 'We don't know where that thing is going next. And we don't know why it dropped us here either. It might be a trap.'

'She's right,' said Tenby. 'We have to get out of here.'

'Just one problem,' said Toby. He indicated the end of the gantry where it met the orbital walkway. The safety fence on the outer catwalk formed an impenetrable barrier.

'We're stuck,' said Quim, his eyes flooding. 'And it's freezing out here.'

'Then we must go back inside and think,' said Dee.

'Ah,' said Tenby, 'umm – sorry.'

'You haven't gone and bloody-well *closed* it, have you?' screamed Zenda. 'What did I tell you about not closing doors? Her Majesty's press requires access to a convenient escape route at all times.'

'I suppose we'll just have to wait out here,' said Tenby sheepishly.

'But the air is so thin,' wailed Quim. 'It'll play havoc with my breathing.'

They paused to listen to Quim's chest. His tiny lungs made a noise like a piece of tissue paper that had been swallowed by an asthmatic canary.

'Tough,' said Zenda.

'Have you ever thought of becoming a nurse?' smiled Lucy.

'I might have the answer,' said Toby. 'I've been watching the shadows, and I reckon the outer ring follows the sun around.'

'And there's a gap somewhere?' said Lucy.

'If so,' said Dee, 'then we need only to wait until it lines up with the end of our gantry.'

'And can Professor Tobermory tell us how long that will be?' said Zenda.

'Why?' said Lucy. 'Do you have an urgent appointment?'

Zenda remained silent, staring through the perforated metal floor and trying to make sense of the scene far below. The smoky grey smudge at the base of the tower was a village set into a patchwork of fields and woodland that disappeared into a distant haze.

'In situations like this,' said Dee, 'I find it is always good to pass the time with a few stories.'

'Do you?' said Zenda. 'Well in that case I'd like to know what's going on with these scarabs.'

'Going on?' said Dee.

'Well they don't fit in, do they?' said Zenda. 'I can just about believe everything else I've seen in this place, but giant insects? *Why* exactly?'

'That may be my fault,' admitted Dee. 'Years ago, when I attended the Great Skule of Camm Brigg I staged a play by a writer called Ristofferknees, and years later the Empress Draconira had me repeat the performance for the imperial court.'

'And someone enjoyed the scarabs so much that they decided to copy the idea?' said Lucy.

'Perhaps,' said Dee. 'Although the exact procedure remains a mystery to me. The original beast was powered by spring works and reflecting surfaces and counterbalances. But the horrors we have seen lately appear to have a life force all of their own.'

'Are they mechanical?' asked Toby.

'Who can say?' said Dee. 'Are we not merely mechanisms ourselves?'

He reached into his cloak, and extracted a thimbleful of powder that he threw into the air. The particles hung for a moment, as if strangers to gravity. But when they began to fall, they twinkled and swirled like a night filled with restless stars, eventually gathering to form a tiny incandescent scarab. The creature visited each person in turn, hovering by a nose here, nudging an ear there; even settling in Zenda's hair briefly. Henbeg watched every movement with a hunter's concentration, waiting for the right moment to attack. The scarab hovered, then revisited each member of the group, slowing a little with each adventure. And then, when it seemed the end was coming, it used its remaining potency on aerobatic stunts, flying inverted, then performing a loop and some barrel rolls. Then it landed, flipped on its back and died. And even though it reminded them of the horrors they were fleeing, everyone felt just a little saddened.

'We ought to have turned it the right way up,' said Lucy, as the fizzling insect disappeared into Henbeg's mouth. 'Granny Moon said so.'

'And what if we didn't?' said Zenda.

'Granny says your house will get hit by lightning,' said Toby.

'Well she'd know all about *that*, wouldn't she, the wizened old bag. Did you see the food she tried to palm us off with? I played safe with the tea.'

'An excellent choice,' smiled Lucy.

'How long is it *now*?' said Zenda. 'We've been listening to these bloody silly stories for hours, and it still doesn't seem to be getting any closer.'

Toby checked the position of the gap in the safety fence that would allow them access to the orbital walkway.

'About ten minutes,' he said.

'More stories,' said Pixy.

'Get lost,' said Zenda. 'We've had enough.'

'But I was under the impression that you told stories for a living,' said Dee. 'Or have I misunderstood what the Phibber is about?'

'Most of hers are made up,' grinned Tenby.

'Well when we get back I won't *need* to,' said Zenda. 'I'll have the greatest story ever, complete with an attractive heroine.'

'Luce?' said Toby. 'Is she talking about you?'

'Of *course* not, you stupid boy,' snapped Zenda. '*I'm* the heroine.'

'I think I preferred it when we were telling the tales,' sighed Toby.

'Well *you* might be happy listening to Pixy's tale of the biggest bone ever to be found in a kitchen,' said Zenda, 'or Quim rambling on about how many sandbags it takes to make a pantomime fairy fly, but Phibber readers will fall asleep if they're presented with twaddle like that. And as for that load of guff we had from the famous Lucy Blake...'

'Ah, yes,' smiled Dee. 'The story of the Bright Squadrons and the road to Farperoo. I enjoyed that.'

'How did it start again?' said Pixy. 'Everyone thought it was impossible to get to Farperoo, but one day...'

'No more,' said Zenda, 'once was bad enough.'

'Tell us about the baby ornithopters again,' said Pixy. 'They were my favourites.'

'Well I hope for their sake they last longer than the river did,' said Zenda. 'Have you seen it recently?'

They knelt on the metal walkway and peered through the mesh to get a better view. Far below, the snaking route of the river Isis was still visible, but the silvery thread of water had almost disappeared, and the riverbed was nothing more than a damp chocolate stain dribbling through the landscape.

'It's gone just like everything else,' sighed Lucy. 'I wanted a closer look at the Emperor's palace, but that burned down. Then I wanted to see the other cabinets, but scarabs chased us off, and now even the river has dribbled away. It seems like I'm *never* going to know anything about this place.'

'So?' said Zenda. 'We'll be going home soon.'

'But this world was put here to teach me,' said Lucy. 'And I haven't learned nearly enough from it yet.'

'Good *grief*,' said Zenda. 'Have you ever *heard* such arrogance?'

'Only from you,' said Toby.

'I can imagine why Lucy might think like that,' said Dee. 'From the very beginning of time people have believed themselves to be at the centre of everything.'

'Only I don't *want* to be at the centre,' said Lucy.

'Amazing,' snorted Zenda. 'When I claimed Assiah for the Phibber, she gave me a lecture on how it didn't belong to anyone – and now she's gone and crowned herself queen.'

'I've done no such thing,' said Lucy. 'I didn't say I owned the place – just that it was put here to tell me something.'

'You really *are* a treasure, aren't you?' said Zenda. 'Who else could make up a story like that?'

Lucy looked around for support from the others. Quim examined a piece of lint he'd found in his pocket. Madimi pretended to relax with her eyes closed, and although Dee met her gaze straight on, he was clearly unsure of what to say.

'Actually I disagree,' he said eventually. 'You say that Assiah was put here for you to learn from, which would indicate some mysterious hand at work. But if this world is just an invention of someone's mind, then all our history and culture and achievements count for nothing.'

'Yes, I know,' said Lucy, 'but just *think* about it.'

'I already have,' said Dee. 'We desperately seek the meaning of creation, but few if any would conclude that it revolves around them personally.'

'I didn't say I *wanted* to be the centre of attention,' protested Lucy. 'And I certainly don't want people to die because of me.'

'The deaths are unfortunate,' said Dee, 'particularly when those that we know are taken. But that is not your fault. The blame lies with those who use violent ends to support their belief – and the world is full of such people.'

'It never used to be,' said Pixy. 'I'm only nine and even I can remember when it was a whole lot quieter – before the Sisters and the Vooghuls.'

'That's another thing,' said Lucy. 'I think I was meant to see the world as Pixy remembers it. I should have met the old Empress and seen the Tower of Self Knowledge, but instead I get kidnapped by her mentally deranged son and find the Migdal turned into a stinking fortress. Assiah and its true meaning has been distorted by people who have no right to be here.'

'I knew a sub-editor once,' said Zenda, 'he was just like Lucy – and *he* used to think the sun shone out of his own arse too.'

'Oh, that is *most* amusing,' chuckled Dee.

'It's a popular phrase where we come from,' grinned Zenda. 'Especially in the newspaper industry.'

'Yes,' smiled Dee. 'I keep forgetting that you are also from Farperoo.'

Zenda gave Dee such a stare that he actually turned his gaze away, and at that moment he knew that it was all true. The reporter and her colleague and

Tobermory and Lucy really *were* from a different world – and it was one that he would never see, no matter how much he yearned for it.

Lucy saw the expression on the sorcerer's face and realised what he was thinking.

'Grim-ston,' said Dee, pronouncing the syllables and rolling them around on his tongue. 'It sounds like a truly wonderful place.'

'I didn't used to think so,' said Lucy. 'But I've missed it.'

'We all have,' said Toby. 'Even Zenda.'

Zenda's defences were temporarily down. She was on the verge of tears – the hard wing-casings dropping away to reveal the soft, vulnerable creature inside.

And then they were up again.

'Grimston is a grotesque, crap-filled dump,' she snapped. 'But I don't care anymore. When this story gets out I'll move to Lundern. I'll be offered a job on a big national paper, like the Daily Psyche or the Sunday Blether.'

There was a metallic clang as the gap in the outer ring lined up with the gantry.

'Me first,' said Zenda, barging through onto the rotating walkway.

'She'd try the patience of a saint,' whispered Lucy as they all followed.

'For the first few hours,' said Dee, 'and after that she would have the blessed ones going about each other with sharp weapons.'

'Are you talking about me?' said Zenda, turning back to eavesdrop.

'Of course,' smiled Dee. 'We were wondering if you had any views on which way we should go?'

'Oh, *were* you?' said Zenda. 'Well, what about this way?'

'Hmm,' said Dee. 'Now that would be contrary to the motion of the shadow on a sundial, wouldn't it?'

'Eh?' said Zenda.

'Anti-clockwise,' said Lucy, recalling the ritual at the palace. 'It's luckier to go clockwise.'

'Is it?' said Zenda. 'Well you'd know, wouldn't you, Miss clever pants?'

Zenda grumbled like a drain as they set off clockwise. Every so often they caught tiny fragments of her own story as the wind whipped the words from her lips and sent them screaming over the edge. From the little that Lucy could make out, it was something about the reporter's auntie who lived next to a pie shop and would only ever walk around the town anti-clockwise because of an accident with a lawnmower. One day, Lucy considered, she might even ask Zenda for the details, but for now she had to concentrate on staying upright. There was no chance of being blown over the side because of the wrap-around fence, but the wind blasted through with such force that they were sometimes left flattened up against the mesh, unable to move. And it was then that they were forced to look down, unable to avert their eyes from the pyres of smoke that rose from every woodland glade or gathering of buildings.

Three hours later, bruised and tired, they reached the next gantry and had their first bit of luck. The ring was seconds away from alignment, so they could get back into the tower and out of the freezing air. They clambered through the gap and made their way along the walkway, huddling against the fleshy outer wall of the Migdal as Toby tried the iron wheel on the outer door. It stood firm, but when Tenby lent his weight to it they managed to break the ancient seal that rust had placed on the mechanism.

The squeal of grating metal had everyone covering their ears.

'I never thought I'd be glad to be back in here,' said Toby.

They were in a small iron-clad porch, no bigger than a garden shed.

'Wait a minute,' said Zenda. 'Isn't this where we were before?'

'This is quite different,' said Madimi, looking worried. Her eyes narrowed and her nose twitched. 'This place reeks of evil,' she whispered. 'And I feel a wind of malice, blowing from there.' She pointed at a tiny window in the wall opposite the door. It was covered in greasy stains, like a toilet window in a transport café.

'I don't know about you,' said Toby, 'but whenever I see something like that, the first thing I want to do is go and look through it.'

'I know,' grinned Lucy. 'I've seen you staring into people's front rooms when the curtains are open.'

'So we're not going to have a look then?' smiled Toby.

'I didn't say that,' said Lucy. 'We'll need some kind of cloth.'

Everyone turned to Quim and stared. And they continued to stare until he gave in and produced yet another clean hanky. He spat on it, and then, with a look of deep disgust, began to clean the window.

'Can you see anything yet?' said Pixy.

'Yes,' said Quim, staring through the dim glass. 'But you won't like it.'

'Let me,' said Zenda, folding over a fresh page on her notebook.

Quim had cleaned a hole about the size of a dinner plate, so whilst Zenda had her head stuck to the window nobody else could see a thing.

'Is it worth a snap?' said Tenby eagerly.

Zenda turned back from the window, her face ashen.

'What is it?' said Pixy. 'What did you see?'

'Nothing,' said Zenda. But her voice was trembling.

'Let me look,' said Lucy, unable to stand the suspense. She pressed her nose against the glass and looked straight ahead, and saw very little. Then she realised that what lay beyond was a tall room and the window was near the ceiling, like a high level spy-hole. The floor was a long way below, lit by rows of candles that were insufficient for the job. Even so, she could make out a rough wooden table, fitted with straps and raised up from the floorboards. At one end, where a head might rest, there was a cushion for the neck and a long glassy pipe that led off into the shadows.

But there was something else.

It was swinging in the dark, flying possibly, but on a dead straight course, like a pendulum. It was difficult to see, being composed entirely of shadows and suggestions, but there was no doubt in Lucy's mind as to its purpose. It swung back and forth in perfect alignment with the cushion and would sever the neck it found there, dropping the detached head into the crystal tube where it would roll away to meet whatever horrors awaited it in the dark.

The Promise of Resurrection

Lucy was unable to tear her gaze from the glass tube. It was streaked inside with blood, and to her eternal shame and disgust she found herself hoping the red smear belonged to Miss Pubrane, because she couldn't bear it to be Fenny's.

'This is a bad place,' said Pixy.

'Any particular clue,' chuckled Tenby, or was it the head severing gear that gave it away?'

'Maybe it was the sign on the wall,' she replied.

'And are you going to read it out for us?' grinned Zenda. 'Or did you learn to read in the same place you learned to count?'

Pixy frowned, not sure if she was being insulted.

'It is written in the Enochian language,' said Dee. He ran a slender finger over the rusted metal plate, disturbing tiny flecks of oxide. 'I am uncertain of the exact form of words, but it says something about bad blood and water.'

'Which tells us nothing,' said Zenda. 'And since there's no way out of this poxy cubby hole I say we go back the way we came.'

'Shh,' said Pixy. 'I think I heard something.'

'Zenda's in charge of hearing things,' sniggered Toby. 'That's why she got those massive...'

'Shut it,' hissed Zenda, flicking her hair over her ears. 'She's right, there is something.'

There was a distant scraping noise, like a rusty wheel turning. They span to look at the door, which had closed without them noticing. But the wheel that locked it was stationary.

'What was it?' hissed Pixy.

Dee took a handful of powder from his cloak and blew it towards the door. Glowing balls of energy flew across the room and smashed into the frame, surprising everyone when it reflected back at them. The screaming energy fizzed as it flew over their crouching forms, bouncing off the wall behind and throwing them against the floor as it returned. Lucy pressed her ear against the cold metal. The squealing, scraping sound was still present, like a thousand field mice in a grindstone. When Dee's energy weapon finally lost momentum the scraping noise became clearer, but this too was dying away and another was rising to take its place. It was a deep rumble, like a train running in a tunnel beneath their feet, or tons of water shooting past behind the walls. Then the rumble built into thunder, and the thunder turned to an ear splitting roar that rocked the air around them, conspiring to take their breath away.

'I want to go to the toilet,' screamed Quim.

'I knew it was water,' yelled Zenda, covering her ears.

'Bad water,' yelled Madimi.

'I believe we are still safe though,' mouthed Dee. 'Despite the sound of tumbling water there is no sign of a flood.'

'And no way out,' said Toby. 'The door is fused shut and the only other possibility is through the window.'

'Ah, yes, the blade room,' said Dee.

He started out towards the window, but Lucy was already there, her face pressed against the grimy glass. There was a jagged pipe in the ceiling that she hadn't noticed before – and torrents of murky water were spurting from it, like thunder from a cannon.

'This will be your friend Raziel I suppose?' said Zenda. She pushed Lucy out of the way and stared down into the blade room. The floor was awash with murky, swirling water.

'He's not my friend,' yelled Lucy, 'and anyway, he wants me alive.'

'Umm, what if the water doesn't stop?' said Toby.

'The room will fill up,' said Pixy.

'So?' said Zenda. 'It's on the other side of the window.'

'The glass won't withstand the pressure,' said Toby. 'As soon as there's enough water it'll break, and this room will flood too.'

'I told you we were all destined to drown,' squealed Quim. 'Ever since that business with the raft, I *knew* it would all end in water.'

'You *will* drown,' said Madimi. 'I saw it in your aura when we were on the river. But it will not happen for many years yet.'

'Oh, well that's alright then,' sobbed Quim.

Toby took his place at the window and glanced into the blade room. The flood was a couple of feet deep, and swirling around the neck-cutting table.

'It's not filling as quickly as I expected,' he said.

'There were holes,' said Zenda. 'I saw daylight shining through the walls.'

'So if we can make the holes big enough,' said Pixy, 'the water will flow out as fast as it's coming in.'

'And how does that help?' said Zenda.

'She's right,' said Tenby, 'we'll still be stuck up here.'

'The answer is in purpose,' said Madimi, her voice quivering. 'I think the torrent of water is used to cleanse the room of blood.'

'And why should we care about that?' snapped Zenda.

'I see what she means,' said Toby. 'If the room can be filled then there must be a way to empty it.'

'A plug,' squealed Quim. 'Oh it's all so simple when you think about it – we're saved, we're saved, we're, *uh-oh*,' he said, suddenly looking much more worried. 'I think I see what you're suggesting.'

'It's a risk,' said Toby, 'but what other choice have we got?'

'I hope it doesn't involve damaging Phibber property,' said Zenda.

'We wait until the water rises to the window,' explained Toby. 'Then we send Henbeg in to pull out the plug and we float down as the water empties.'

'And go gurgling out of the holes with the bath water,' said Zenda.

'Or down the plughole,' said Tenby.

'And we're going to get our clothes wet,' moaned Quim.

'Maybe not,' said Toby. 'The table has broken loose and it's floating up.'

'Me first,' yelled Zenda. She took off one of her high heels and broke the window, grinning with satisfaction as the fragments fell into the whirlpool.

'So we're going with that plan are we?' said Toby.

'We don't have a choice,' said Lucy. 'Not since the owner of the entire world broke the glass.'

'I'm just a *representative* of the new owners,' hissed Zenda.

'Yes, of course you are,' said Lucy.

Zenda glared back. Blake had gazed into the depths of her greedy heart, and uncovered her secret plan. The editor of the Phibber would never hear about Assiah, because Zenda wanted the world for herself.

'Go on then,' said Lucy flatly. 'If you insist on being first.'

One by one they squeezed past the jagged remnants of window glass, lowering themselves onto the floating table as it passed beneath. When they were all safely on board, Lucy threw the handbag into the water. He thrashed back into his crocodile state and swam to Lucy to receive his orders.

'Henbeg,' she hissed. 'Go and pull the plug out boy.'

'If there is a stupid plug,' said Zenda.

'You must have faith,' said Madimi.

'I might,' snapped Zenda, 'if I wasn't about to get drowned again.'

'That is the meaning of faith,' said Madimi. 'Belief without proof.'

'Yeah, right,' chuckled Tenby.

The water rose past the window where they gained access, marooning them beneath a featureless metal ceiling with the waters swirling about them. The only sounds, apart from Quim's whimpering, were the roar from the jagged pipe and the hiss of escaping air as it forced out through cracks in the roof.

'It doesn't look good,' sobbed Quim. 'But if Madimi was right about me not drowning until later, then I'm not going to drown now, am I?'

'So it's just us that's for the chop then?' said Toby.

Lucy was about to tell him to shut up and concentrate on escaping, but noticed his grin. The currents had begun to settle, and although the pipe was still spewing water into the whirlpool, the table was no longer rising.

'Your handbag has saved us,' yelled Quim.

Lucy smiled, but the expression was forced. She scanned the turbulent waters for a sign of the crocodile, but there was nothing.

'Henbeg must be trapped,' she breathed. 'I can't see him.'

'You can always buy another handbag,' said Zenda. 'I've got a wardrobe full of the things at home.'

Lucy bent down and put her face into the water. It was like trying to see through treacle, and she came up spluttering and picking bits of weed from her teeth. And then she noticed the upper part of the blade emerging as the surrounding water fell. It had trapped one of Henbeg's middle legs, spearing him on a vicious looking barb.

'Paddle like hell,' screamed Lucy. 'We have to release him from the blade before the water sinks, or he'll be left dangling.'

As soon as they were close enough Lucy leapt onto the iron frame that supported the obsidian blades. It was cold to the touch and covered in slime, but at least it wasn't sharp.

'Luce, for God's sake, be careful,' yelled Toby.

'What on earth is the stupid girl doing?' said Zenda.

Lucy clambered into position above the impaled crocodile, then shinned down the frame as far as possible without touching the blade.

'She's undoing something,' said Toby.

'Is that not the key that holds the blade up?' said Madimi.

Her question was soon answered. Lucy prised a small metal pin out of framework, and with an ear-splitting creak the blade assembly slipped into the whirlpool like a ship being launched. But this ship was destined to sink, and take Lucy down with it.

'Oh, dear, Lucy has gone,' said Zenda, with a slight trace of a grin.

'Perhaps she was sucked down by the current?' said Quim.

'I hope she dies with slimy weed in her throat and stinking turds up her nose,' screamed Pixy. 'I've just remembered why I hate her.'

'Time for another draught,' said Dee. He motioned to Madimi, and when Pixy wasn't looking his daughter scratched the girl's cheek again.

'I hope she hasn't been harmed,' said Quim. 'For all we know the water could be poisoned.'

'Look,' said Pixy, smiling uncertainly. 'Look at the sword.'

A gloved hand held an obsidian blade out of the water, like Excalibur. Then the rest of Lucy's arm appeared, and finally her shoulder and grinning face. She swam awkwardly to the bench and dragged herself onto the deck, still holding the glistening blade.

'Where's Henbeg?' she spluttered. 'Is he safe?'

The bench wobbled as she dragged herself upright and searched for the creature. But the only sign of life was the trail of blood that spread from his former position – and it was thinning and gradually disappearing as the water swirled and gurgled around the plughole.

'It's nearly empty,' said Quim, as the table came to rest in a sea of grey-green sludge.

'And still no sign of Henbeg,' said Toby.

'Henbeg,' screamed Lucy, close to tears. 'Where *are* you?'

'Down the plughole I expect,' said Zenda, grinning like a loon.

Lucy took a run at her, but stumbled and fell off the table. The obsidian blade clanged on the floor beneath the slurry. And Henbeg, as if he had been waiting for a signal, leapt from the ooze and scampered towards her on his seven-and-a-half good legs. He leapt at Lucy, bowling her over into the sludge again and licking her face until she begged for mercy.

'Give up,' she grinned, 'and get *off* me – you can thank me later, when we've found out who tried to drown us.'

'And we've stamped on their pig-faced heads,' said Zenda. 'My clothes are absolutely ruined.'

Lucy was about to compare her own sorry state with Zenda's, but was distracted when the water stopped tumbling from the jagged pipe, which was now at least fifty feet above them.

'Whoever it was,' said Quim, 'they're still watching us.'

'Maybe the water ran out?' said Toby.

'No,' said Madimi. 'They are reminding us of their presence.'

'And they know exactly where we are,' said Lucy.

'And since we only have two ways out,' said Quim, 'they'll have a good idea where to look for us next.'

They stared at the plughole, where sludge filtered away with a disgusting snot-clearing sound. The pipe below was lined with a blue-green slime that only Henbeg could love. And to prove it he sniffed enthusiastically around the opening.

'I think I prefer the other possibility,' said Quim.

There was a domed hatch in the floor with a wheel on top that looked like it belonged on a submarine. Toby gave it a spin and the hatch flipped open to reveal a ladder.

Lucy was about to step onto the top rung when Quim called her back.

'Don't forget your trophy,' he said. He handed her the obsidian sliver and eagerly scooped up Henbeg who had turned back into a fashion accessory.

'Thank you,' said a sludge covered Lucy.

She weighed the jet-black blade in her hand. It was deceptively light, and the sides were ground to an edge that was almost invisible when turned sideways. But there was no comfortable way to hold it – the only blunt part was designed to be bolted to a frame and the rough edges hurt her hand.

'Perhaps you might like this,' said Dee. He produced a small crucifix and offered it up to the end of the blade. It glowed and fused with the obsidian and soon became an indistinguishable part of it.

'*Irae*,' said Dee. 'The Blade of Wrath.'

'A *sword*,' said Lucy, weighing the weapon in her hand. 'Umm, I'm not really certain I want it.'

'I'll have it,' said Zenda. 'It rightly belongs to the Phibber anyway.'

'Well if *you* want it, then so do I,' smiled Lucy. She tucked the blade into her belt. Her coat fell forward and covered the weapon completely.

'Hey, come on down,' yelled Pixy. Her voice had a metallic echo, like she was standing at the bottom of a long tube. 'Hurry up,' she screamed. 'I've found something.'

'Is it safe?' said Zenda, peering into the hole.

Madimi leaned over the hatch and inhaled the air that rose from it.

'It is clean,' she said.

'More than you can say for this place,' said Toby, pointing upwards.

The water pipe retched a foul yellow pus that spluttered like custard under pressure.

'I don't like the look of that,' yelled Quim, 'and the smell is disgusting.'

He scrambled for the hatch and clambered down the ladder, missing one rung at first, then two at a time and finally jumping when he was almost at the bottom. The others followed as quickly as they could, whilst Toby stayed behind to secure the hatch.

'What a *stink*,' said Zenda. 'Almost as bad as my editor's farts.'

'Through here,' yelled Pixy. 'I've found another Lellavator and I'm going to show you how to work it.'

She ran up to the doors and hit a button at random, then dived towards the gap. But the sliding panels remained shut, and her nose was flattened against the unforgiving grey metal.

'It must be this button then,' she said, pressing another.

Nothing happened.

'Any more bright ideas?' said Toby.

'I *told* you she was lucky last time,' said Zenda.

'Maybe not,' said Lucy. 'The last time wasn't a test, but I think this is.'

'I'll try the others,' said Pixy, desperately battering each symbol in turn. 'Hmm, not that one, not that one, not that one, not...'

'I think we've established it's not any of them,' said Lucy.

'It must be a combination,' said Toby. 'Isn't your friend Bentley Priory good with safes?'

'Brilliant,' said Zenda. 'I'll just run back to Grimston and fetch him.'

'Or we could work out the combaburnibation ourselves,' said Pixy.

They sat for hours, staring at the doors and feeling cold and very hungry. Madimi offered some of Granny Moon's snacks around, but only Pixy was able to keep them down, being the only one with a stomach forged from the same material they make toilet bowls with.

'You should eat,' protested Madimi. 'You will all need strength. I feel it.'

'Thanks,' smiled Lucy. 'If any real food happens to come along I'll be the first in the queue.'

'Me too,' said Pixy. 'Those snacks were *so* small. I ate twenty one of them and they only just filled a hole.'

'Twenty one?' said Lucy.

'I'm not going to apologise for having a healthy appetite,' said Pixy.

'But you said twenty-one,' said Lucy, 'which was the number of symbols on the first Lellavator, I mean lift.'

'So?' said Zenda.

'Well these doors have twenty-two,' said Lucy.

'She's right,' said Toby after a short delay.

'So we're saved then?' said Pixy.

'Think again pea-brain,' sneered Zenda. 'Twenty-two symbols means *more* combinations, not less.'

'More combaburnibations,' said Pixy, 'so more chances to escape.'

'If only we could have maths like that at home,' grinned Toby.

'But Lucy seems to think that twenty-two symbols increases our chances,' said Madimi. 'Or did I misunderstand? And I'm sorry if I spoke out of turn.'

'No,' said Lucy, fishing around in her damp pockets. 'You're right, and I think I might just have the answer we're looking for.'

'Tarot cards,' said Dee, eying Lucy's treasure. 'Where did you get them?'

'They were bequeathed to me by an old friend,' said Lucy. She held them out to Henbeg, who gave them a good sniff as he turned back into his seven and a half legged form. 'Smell your mistress,' said Lucy. 'Good boy.'

'Oh, *please*,' said Zenda, 'spare us the detail will you?'

'Henbeg?' said Lucy. 'Bite the nasty reporter.'

'Yee-ouch,' squealed Zenda, rubbing at her ankle.

'Good boy Henbeg,' said Lucy. 'Now go for her throat...'

'Alright,' pleaded Zenda, 'call him off, and I promise to just listen.'

'I have one question before we start,' said Tenby.

'Yes?' said Lucy.

'It's about that handbag,' grinned the photographer. 'Could you possibly tell me where *I* can get one?'

'Right,' said Lucy, when the sniggers had died down. 'This is a long shot, but the Major Arcanum of the Tarot has twenty-two cards, and each has a number. This one is the Magus or magician, and is number one.'

'And which other cards did your friend leave you?' said Dee.

Lucy sat down and spread the pasteboards out, announcing the name of each one as she laid it on the floor.

'Number four. *The Emperor.*'

'Number fifteen. *The Devil.*'

'Number sixteen. *The Tower.*'

'Number eighteen. *The Moon.*'

'The Moon card has a scarab,' said Pixy, 'and it's holding a golden disc.'

'That's the sun,' said Madimi.

'Forget the interpretations and just try it,' said Toby looking at Zenda.

'Yes, let's,' she said, quietly rubbing her ankle and frowning at Henbeg.

'Great,' said Toby, whispering to Lucy. 'Even if it doesn't work we've found a way to shut her up.'

They all took up a position near the doors, and at a signal from Lucy they each pressed their designated button. There was an expectant hush, followed by the squeak of a slightly rusty mechanism, but the doors remained shut.

'Excellent,' said Toby.

He slid down the wall and slumped on the floor.

'Perhaps the tower is not part of the key?' said Madimi quietly.

'Go on,' said Lucy.

'It may be a part of the lock,' explained Madimi. 'Perhaps it's there simply to tell us what the rest of the cards open?'

'It's possible,' said Lucy. 'Let's try it.'

Each of them stood by his or her designated button again, all except for the tower, and they pressed at Lucy's signal – but still, nothing happened.

'Now we really are stuck,' said Toby.

'Don't all shout at once,' said Zenda, 'but I've got an idea.'

'Go on then,' said Lucy. It was the tone of voice one might use to tempt a scorpion out of a biscuit tin.

'This is just to prove I was listening earlier,' said Zenda, 'even though I thought you were all talking the utmost twaddle.'

'Fine,' said Lucy. 'What's the idea?'

'You said this wasn't the way you were to see Assiah,' said Zenda. 'You reckon you should have met the Empress and not her scheming son.'

'Thanks for remembering,' said Lucy.

'I remembered it,' said Zenda, 'but that doesn't mean I agree with it. But what if we substitute the Empress card for the Emperor?'

'I suppose there *is* an Empress card?' said Toby, raising an eyebrow.

'Of course,' smiled Madimi. 'That would be card number three.'

Zenda had planned on looking smug when the doors opened, but as the heavy metal panels parted, all thoughts of congratulation faded. She was too busy staring into the room beyond, trying to work out what it all meant.

They entered a circular space, about a hundred feet in diameter, but with no apparent ceiling, and no floor either as far as anyone could see – just a metal gantry that ran around the cylinder formed by the walls. In the centre of the chamber was an island refuge. It was supported by four trelliswork fingers that reached up from below and held it in their fingertips. Rising from this floating island and disappearing into the blackness above them was a transparent tube. It was about eight feet in diameter and so finely poised that a careless sneeze might well destroy it – and with it, their only chance of escape.

'It looks a bit flimsy,' said Pixy.

'I *like* it,' said Quim, 'it's delicate *and* functional.'

'Me too,' said Zenda. 'But only if it's going to help us escape.'

'I reckon the glass tube might be a lift shaft,' said Toby.

'So all we need now is a lift,' said Tenby.

'And a way to get to the island,' said Lucy stepping onto the walkway.

'Not *that* way,' boomed an officious voice that seemed to come directly out of the walls. 'Can't you see I've planted new bulbs down there? And not *that* way either – the workers in that area are trimming peacock shapes out of bushes. Please just stand exactly where you are and tell me where you're trying to get to.'

Since nobody knew where they were heading, nobody had an answer – not that it mattered. The announcer had the kind of voice that asked a question just so that it could ask another as soon as you started to answer.

'Well?' it said. 'I'm *waiting*.'

'Sounds like our Ingulesh teacher,' whispered Toby.

'And my editor,' grinned Zenda.

'Who are you?' said Lucy. 'And *where* are you?'

'I'm asking the questions,' boomed the voice. 'Tell me where you are going, and I'll consider telling you whether you can get there.'

'We're trying to get home,' said Lucy, signalling to the others. She would keep the voice talking whilst they all had a good look around.

'Home, eh?' said the voice. 'Well that will be nice, *won't* it?'

'I suppose so,' said Lucy, urging the others in their search.

They circled the gantry, and on the opposite side they found a small iron gate. Beyond it, a suspended trellis-way led to the central island – except for a ten-foot gap, where the path dropped away into the void.

And guarding the gap was a head cabinet, which, judging by the scrape marks on the floor had been hurriedly dragged into position. It was occupied by an old groundling, or what little was left of him. He wasn't as ancient as Granny or as ugly as Gusset – more the kind who'd be happy eating a cream tea with soil under his fingernails. And he seemed somewhat preoccupied, perhaps because the cabinet glass had been painted over with an untidy red cross, like a door in a plague-struck village.

'I'm Gremmidge,' he said, his voice softening as they approached. 'I'm the head gardener.'

'Oh, brilliant,' snorted Toby unable to control his laughter.

'Well *you* might not think much of gardeners,' said Gremmidge, 'but we do a very important job.'

'Sorry,' said Toby. 'It was your title that made me giggle – *head* gardener.'

'A small matter,' said Gremmidge, his eyes swivelling as if he was reading from an invisible piece of paper. 'Now, what was I to do first? Ah, yes, I was just making tea. I can offer you Dung Aromatic or Fragrant Lemon Bogey or one called Camomile that I don't care for much.'

'I'll have the last one,' said Zenda. 'I couldn't possibly drink anything with bogeys or dung in it.'

'It didn't stop you at Granny's,' grinned Toby.

'You knew?' snapped Zenda. 'Right, that's it, that's... hey, *wait* a minute old man. Did you say you were making tea?'

'Of course,' smiled the genial head.

'I see,' said Zenda, her eyes narrowing. 'And what were you doing before that? Juggling? Or maybe you were practising semaphore, or knitting a pair of bed-socks?'

'It doesn't say anything about that here,' said Gremmidge. 'Oh *dear*, and it was all going so well.'

'No it wasn't,' said Zenda. 'I know exactly what you're doing.'

'You do?' said Gremmidge. '*Oh.* Umm, well in that case, would anyone care for a crumpet? Or a buttered muffin?'

'I'd love one,' said Toby, kicking the base of the cabinet. 'Perhaps you'd like to pass a few over.'

'Me too,' said Pixy.

'On the other hand,' said Gremmidge, 'I find that a nice slice of toast can provide a welcome distraction at this time of day.'

'Alright,' giggled Toby, 'we'll have some of that too. Hand it over.'

'Umm, which would you prefer first?' said Gremmidge. 'The toast or the crumpet?'

'Whichever's nearest,' grinned Toby.

'You can stop it now,' smiled Lucy. 'You've been rumbled.'

'Rumbled?' said Gremmidge.

'Found out,' explained Lucy. 'You're just trying to slow us down.'

'Oh dear,' said Gremmidge. 'And they said it would be easy.'

'They?' said Quim.

Gremmidge darkened with fear, and Lucy decided not to push him.

'Are you going to let us past,' she said, 'or shall we open all these bags of black fly we've brought with us?'

'Black fly?' said Gremmidge, his voice trembling. 'Umm, perhaps you had better come past after all.'

'You've been a great help,' said Lucy. 'Now if you'd just like to get the lift working?'

'Oh, and by the way,' grinned Tenby. 'You *do* know you're inside one of those... *oof*, bloody *hell*, that hurt,' he said, leaping away from Lucy's elbow.

'I'm inside a what?' said Gremmidge.

'Nothing,' said Lucy. 'He was about to say what a beautiful part of the garden you're in.'

Gremmidge nodded and made a face, as though wrestling with a large lever. Moments later, a new section of floor materialised beneath them and joined the walkways, allowing them to run across to the island.

Through the clear floor of the transparent lift cubicle was a dim red glow that illuminated previously darkened parts of the cylinder. Five hundred feet below them, a thin metal gauze was stretched across the chamber. It looked like a circus safety net, but Lucy guessed that it had some other purpose – to deflect heat perhaps – and it looked remarkably like the fizzing spark-net they had seen in the kiosk maze.

'I see now how the contraption works,' said Dee, as the glow below them shifted from dim red to hot yellow. 'We are to be wafted skywards, like a leaf rising on a summer breeze.'

'Oh, *hurrah*,' said Quim. 'I *do* love a bit of poetry.'

'I've got just the thing,' said Tenby. 'I shared a hotel room once with a smudger from the Orb. He taught me all these Limericks that start *'There was a young lady from...'*

'Excellent,' enthused Quim. 'When do we begin the recital?'

'Sorry,' said Lucy, 'but this is all beginning to worry me.'

'Just close your ears when he gets to the rude bits,' said Toby.

'I'm not talking about silly rhymes,' said Lucy. 'I've heard all those from Genjamin. I meant our welcoming committee. We must be near the top of tower now, and they know we're on the way.'

'So?' said Tenby. 'There are just two angels left to deal with.'

'And we've got them outnumbered,' said Pixy. 'At least I *think* we have.'

'Perhaps the angels you fear are weak in body?' said Madimi. 'Otherwise they would not have used that poor gardener to delay us.'

'We'll know soon enough,' said Toby. 'The capsule is starting to lift.'

They moved upwards at a gentle pace – so gentle in fact that once the walkway had receded and the fire-glow had faded to a tiny pink dot it was impossible to tell if they were actually moving. There was no vibration or features passing by to mark their progress, just smooth, dark walls that might be standing still or hurtling past at hundreds of miles an hour.

After a while though, Toby spotted something. He leapt to his feet and pressed his nose against the glass.

'I think it was a bird,' he said. 'It was just gliding around, but it shot down out of view so quickly I couldn't really tell.'

'Make your mind up,' said Tenby. 'It couldn't have been just gliding and diving at the same time.'

'Haven't you ever heard of relative motion?' said Toby. '*He* was gliding around slowly, but because we're going up quickly it looked as though he was going down fast.'

'I'll take your word for it,' said Quim.

'He's right,' said Pixy. 'There goes another one.'

'And two more,' said Madimi. 'They must like the warm air.'

'Indeed,' said Dee. 'This would be an excellent place for a creature to learn the rudiments of flight.'

The sorcerer stared at Lucy long and hard, but she turned away, uncomfortable with the idea that young angels might need to fledge, just like birds. Instead, she contented herself with announcing their arrival, and on their way out of the cubicle she avoided Doctor Dee's gaze completely.

'Oh, my *God*,' said Zenda, breathing through a doubled-up handkerchief. 'What kind of horrible, stinking dump have you brought us to?'

Lucy wanted to tell Zenda that if there had been an alternative then she would have gladly chosen it, but she was too busy with her own makeshift gas mask, trying to filter the stink of bird droppings through a triple folded opera glove. The smell was like a physical presence on her tongue, as if a seagull had dropped its mess in her open mouth as she lay sleeping in a deck chair.

'I'm getting back in the lift,' said Zenda, choking and turning to go.

But she was too slow – the doors hissed shut and refused to budge, even when she battered them with a tatty high heel shoe.

Everyone else was looking at the wall perches, which, judging by the size of them, were designed to support large birds.

Lucy looked at Dee. There was a sense of foreboding in the place, as if the room knew they were here and was attempting to mask its own purpose.

'Is it used by angels?' said Madimi.

The pattern of lines on her father's face said it all.

'We must all live somewhere,' he said.

Lucy examined a pile of feathers that had been swept into a corner along with a tangle of bloodstained bandages. There was nothing unusual about the feathers, except that the shortest of them was at least four feet long.

'It's Raziel,' she said, twitching her nose. 'I can *smell* him.'

'And I suppose he moulted these and grew new ones?' said Zenda.

'It's not a joke,' said Lucy. 'He must be healed by now, and these are the last of his wrappings.'

'Do you think he left them as a message?' said Toby.

'He's laying a trail,' said Lucy, 'and we have no choice but to follow it. Wherever Raziel is, that's where we'll find Fenny.'

'Which is why I'm saving my last few shots,' said Tenby. 'Me and Zenda are going to win a Poo-litzer prize.'

'Over here,' said the reporter. 'And *I'll* lead the way if you don't mind. The press still have priority you know.'

She ran down a connecting passageway and burst into the next room and promptly tripped in the gloom. As she stood up and dusted herself off, the others came to her side, gawping in horror at the strange furniture that had brought her down. It was a long, low platform, like a mortuary slab. And laid upon it were the bodies of children, each one apparently asleep inside a sticky, semi-transparent shroud.

Shades
of Empire

Towering around them was a dark, cylindrical room, its walls lined with hundreds of cupboards. It reminded Lucy of Pobjoy's Health Emporium, where they kept all manner of chemicals in a wooden cabinet with hundreds of drawers, each fitted with a crystal knob. But to the best of her knowledge, Mrs. Pobjoy had never kept children in stock.

'Those are pupa cases,' said Pixy, pointing at the enclosed bodies. 'I had butterflies in my room once, when we lived at the observatory.' She drifted off into a long buried memory with a puzzled look, as if trying to remember more than her fuddled mind was capable of.

They stood in silent awe, staring at the life-coffins, their mouths hanging open. Then Quim surprised them all by approaching the nearest shroud.

'The poor mites,' he squealed. 'Rolled up in grisly insect skin with their heads removed. What possible reason could there be for that?'

'Maybe there isn't one,' said Toby. He stood alongside Quim, trying to determine the outlines of the children beneath the leathery skins. 'Sometimes things just are,' he sighed.

'No,' said Lucy, studying her friend's expression. 'The one thing I *have* learned in this place is that there's a purpose for everything.'

'In nature, everything is reasonable and has purpose,' said Dee. 'It is only in the minds of men that we find such aberrations such as this.'

Tenby poked one of the pupae with a curious finger. The spongy surface absorbed his fingertip, and he withdrew it with a yelp.

'The Gyptians encase their dead in pupa cases to guarantee resurrection,' said Madimi. 'Perhaps this has something to do with them?'

'Gyptians?' grinned Toby. 'The ones with the pyramids?'

'Of course,' said Madimi, somewhat vaguely.

'But there's no Gyptian part of the city,' grinned Toby.

'And nowhere beyond,' said Lucy, 'umm, apart from Farperoo – so how do you come to have stories about pyramid builders?'

Dee looked at Lucy as though she had stumbled on a great secret. 'I have often wondered that myself,' he said.

'That's all very nice,' said Zenda, examining one of the pupa cases, 'but what worries me is what happens to the heads afterwards.'

'Maybe this will explain it,' said Tenby. He whipped a dustsheet from a nearby tabletop to reveal a glass jar that bubbled with pink fluid.

'Our heggs have been piggled,' said the head in the jar.

'It's Phyllida, from the Braneskule,' whispered Toby.

'And she can talk,' said Lucy.

'Of course I can,' gurgled Phyllida. 'Two sevens are twelve, aren't they?'

'Very good,' said Toby generously. 'How clever of you to remember.'

'Maybe she can remember how she came to be pickled,' said Zenda.

'Never mind her,' grinned Tenby, removing another cloth. 'Take a look at this one – it's even better.'

'It's completely gruesome,' said Quim.

The deformed head belonged to a child that nobody recognised. Rubber tubes were attached to the jugular veins that protruded from his severed neck. Long glass rods were fitted into the corners of his mouth. And nearby, laying on a mortuary slab, was a pulsing, squishy red thing. It was attached to the jar by tubes that pulsed as the blood pumped through them.

'A Mumtaz Gubbins,' said Toby, 'like the one in the Bright Byrde.'

'If those words mean an abomination in the eyes of God,' said Dee, 'then this is indeed a *gubbins*. But there is a better word to describe such a mess of bone and hair and skin and seminal fluids. It is an homunculus.'

'It's disgusting,' said Zenda, 'and it stinks of horse dung.'

'It is an affront to all creation,' said Dee, 'so for once we agree.'

'It's like some horrific experiment,' said Tenby.

'Or a story that came out wrong,' said Zenda.

'Shhh,' said Madimi. 'I think the head knows we are talking about it.'

The eyes opened gradually, concentrating on their lip movements, and the contents of one of the pupa cases twitched. Lucy was uncertain whether it was that which made her so uncomfortable or Zenda's idea of a story that had gone wrong. But in any case her concentration was broken by Tenby rummaging through the cupboards. Most of them contained a dried out jar containing a shrivelled, blackened head that was all too clearly dead. But as he worked his way upward, the jars were in better condition and contained more fluid, and the heads inside were much less shrivelled.

'No further,' begged Madimi. 'These are too many horrors to behold.'

'Just one more,' grinned Tenby, throwing open another door.

Lucy and Pixy gasped out loud as the light crept into the cupboard, as if it was reluctant to illuminate the hairless, worm-chewed head.

'My little Neeba,' cried Dee, 'she's not dead after all.'

'But not exactly alive,' said Zenda. 'Look at all that hideous custard stuff leaking out of her nose.'

'And just look at the size of her tongue,' said Tenby, pulling his camera out. 'I have just *got* to have a shot of this one.'

Phoomph.

Zoo-weeeeee.

'What a brilliant picture,' he yelled, 'just…'

'Uh-oh,' said Toby. 'Your flashgun has started some kind of reaction. The jar is cracking.'

Spider-like lines appeared in Neeba's dome, and before anyone was able to duck it shattered, showering them with shards of glass and bubbling pink fluid. Dee tried to catch his niece's head, but he missed it, because dozens more doors sprang open and the jars inside them exploded. The heads they contained cried out as they fell, but with so much screaming going on it was impossible to hear what they were saying.

Lucy thought she heard the words 'truth' and 'death' quite often though.

'I hope you're satisfied Yates,' she screamed, as Dee tried to stop Neeba's head rolling away. 'Hanoziz was right, you *are* an executioner.'

'But it'll make a great photo,' said Tenby. 'And anyway, it's not as if any of this is real. Nothing that happens here will matter in our world.'

'How can you *say* such a thing?' cried Madimi. 'Perhaps it is your world where things have no value and nothing matters?'

'From what I have seen of his friend with the notebook I would say it's a strong possibility,' agreed Dee. He looked down at Neeba's head and began to sob.

'There'll be consequences,' whimpered Quim. 'I just know it.'

'Like those pupa cases,' squealed Pixy.

'Boring,' said Tenby. 'We've seen them already.'

'Yes, but you haven't seen *that*,' yelled Pixy, pointing.

A shroud had cracked and a body was climbing out.

'It's Bingo Sprocket,' said Lucy. 'I recognise the clothes.'

'But how can he see if he hasn't got a head?' said Pixy.

'The jar,' yelled Toby. 'Cover his head up.'

Pixy threw a cloth over Bingo, but in doing so she disturbed even more freak-show heads, whose bodies wriggled from their shrouds and stumbled to their feet.

'You can't just go wandering around with your heads chopped off,' yelled Pixy. 'It's not right.'

'That's told them,' said Toby. 'They'll leave us alone for certain now.'

'Quim was right,' cried Dee. 'Our world has meddled in things it does not understand, and we are going to pay the price.'

The zombie children headed for Zenda, who armed herself with a stout plank of wood.

'If you lot come any nearer,' she screamed, 'I'm going to give you a bloody good battering.'

'But they're just children,' yelled Quim.

'And they haven't got heads,' said Pixy. 'It wouldn't be fair.'

Just as Zenda was about to lash out, the zombies filed quietly on either side of her, apparently more interested in the rickety wardrobe propped up in the shadows. The reporter followed, pulling the creaking doors open to reveal a gaudy amusement cabinet. And as she read the newly painted name panel out loud, everyone took an extra breath.

It said '*Lucy's Folly*'.

'I suppose you know nothing about this either,' said Zenda, adding the item to her property list.

Lucy shook her head as she approached. The cabinet was deeper than others they had seen, and had a musky, almost mysterious perfume. Inside it were six crystal domes. They were decorated with gold and silver scrollwork, and the pink fluid they contained bubbled like energetic soup. The four at the back were smaller than the others, standing on mahogany bases, whilst elaborate golden peacocks supported the two at the front.

'I can't see any heads,' said Tenby. 'How come the fluid isn't transparent, like it is in the other jars?'

'Why are you so concerned? hissed Lucy. 'Nothing is real, remember?'

'Maybe we have to put a coin in the slot?' said Toby.

'What a *good* idea,' sneered Zenda. 'Well done little boy.'

'Shut your face,' snapped Toby. 'I don't hear you coming out with any brilliant suggestions.'

'It's worth a try,' said Lucy.

'Here,' said Toby, offering the contents of his pockets. 'A fluff-covered banana chew and my last three pennies.'

Lucy dropped a coin in the slot and turned the handle. The fluid in the smaller domes gurgled for a moment and then cleared to reveal four heads that looked like quadruplet sisters. Each was slightly different in some way though – a misplaced freckle for instance, or slightly paler skin colouring, or a wart with a hair growing from it.

'The countenances bear an uncanny resemblance to the Empress,' said Dee, 'but none of them is actually she.'

'Then the stories are true,' said Madimi.

'That she had four heads?' grinned Tenby.

'The old Empress had four personalities, said Madimi. 'They were known as the Shades of Empire.'

'I don't like this,' whimpered Quim. 'I want to go to the toilet.'

Lucy inserted another coin and cranked the handle. There was a farting sound, then a gurgle and then the murk cleared from the smaller of the two domes at the front. Bubbling away inside it was the head of an old, annoyed looking woman in a mop cap.

'It's Nanny Pilchard,' gasped Madimi.

'And you're the sorcerer's girl,' snapped Pilchard's head. 'What of it?'

'Umm, well, it's nice to see you,' said Madimi.

'Yes,' grinned Lucy, 'we've heard so much about you.'

'Doesn't surprise me,' said Pilchard. She took a sly glance sideways at the remaining dome, obviously trying to hide her anxiety. But finally the pressure got too much and when she yelled, a furious pool of bubbles frothed against the glass.

'What have you done with my mistress?' she gurgled.

'We don't know what you're talking about,' grinned Zenda.

'Liar,' screamed Pilchard. 'Bring her back at once.'

Lucy inserted the last coin and turned the handle again.

There was a musical fanfare that sounded like a poppadom being played on an old gramophone, and then, much to Pilchard's relief, the murk cleared and the head inside made an appearance. The Empress looked like a Punch and Judy puppet that had seen better days. Her make up was plastered on thicker than Exotica's, her hair looked like an abandoned rats' nest, and her ears were worn away to fleshy stumps. But nobody paid much attention to that. They were all too busy looking at her slime-green teeth.

'May I introduce my former patron,' said Dee, folding slightly at the waist. 'The Empress Dragonira.'

'I thought she was chucked over the side?' said Toby.

'She must be good at soft landings,' chuckled Zenda.

The head remained impassive – just a faint glimmer of activity behind the partially opened eyes.

'*We are dying*,' sang the Shades of Empire. They sounded like a cross between a barber's shop quartet and a badly rehearsed choir. '*It will be such a sweet sorrow to finally leave this field of dreams.*'

The Empress's eyelids rolled down and her head leaned forward as if she was falling into a deep sleep.

'She's slipping away,' said Lucy.

'Then let's get her out,' said Toby.

'Let's get them all out,' agreed Pixy.

'*There is little point*,' sang the shades. '*Our bodies were fed to the scarabs long ago.*'

'Lovely,' said Toby.

'Charming,' said Zenda. 'So, umm, tell me, how do you get to become Empress exactly?'

'I think it is *we* who are asking the questions,' boomed the Empress, her eyes springing fully open. 'We are the Sisters of Perpetual mercy.'

'Oh,' said Dee.

'But I thought the Sisters of Perpetual Mercy were the angels,' said Toby.

'Me too,' said Lucy.

'It was *our* name first,' snapped Pilchard. 'It was part of our master plan.'

Lucy raised an eyebrow.

'The plan to retake Assiah from our ungrateful son,' said Dragonira.

'*And then,*' sang the shades, '*exercising the most extreme form of mercy, we were going to forgive him.*'

'Or toss him over the edge,' said Pilchard, 'like he did to us.'

'Too late,' said Pixy. 'The angels have beaten you to it.'

A look of disappointment spread across Pilchard's face.

'Shhh,' whispered Lucy. 'I was going to break it to them gently.'

'Those utter, utter, utter bastards,' hissed Dragonira. 'Again they have spoiled everything. And I was *so* looking forward to killing that good for nothing scum-sucker of a son of mine.'

'The rotten, fly-blown fruit of your loins,' hissed Pilchard.

'Yes, that too,' said Dragonira.

'But how did you survive being thrown over the side?' said Toby. 'And how did you get back up?'

'*The boy child doubts us,*' sang the chorus.

'Umm, not really,' stuttered Toby, as the cabinet began to vibrate. 'But it's such a long drop, and...'

'We fell into a net, and were rescued by groundlings,' said Dragonira.

'Then they saw who they had rescued, and turned us away,' said Pilchard.

'And we spent some time in the forest,' added the Empress.

'Years,' said Pilchard.

'*With no-thing to eat but mould and berries and fungus,*' sang the shades.

'Have you got any left over?' said Pixy.

'Foolish child,' hissed the Empress.

'So, umm, how did you end up in the tower?' said Toby.

'A creature came to the forest,' said Pilchard. 'He was searching for a storyteller, and left empty handed. But soon there were more stinking angels, all desperate to find the same thing.'

'They took us prisoner,' said the Empress.

'*And extracted every bit of our knowledge,*' sang the shades.

'Except for the whereabouts of the storyteller,' said Pilchard.

'And this all happened years ago?' said Lucy, somewhat puzzled.

'Sounds like they've been looking for you for a while Luce,' said Toby.

'*You* are the one they seek?' screeched Dragonira. 'The cause of all our troubles?'

'If it wasn't for you,' gurgled an angry Pilchard, 'my mistress would still have her lovely palace and her lovely beetles and her lovely, lovely beautiful Khepri mistresses.'

'Lovely,' said Pixy.

'Do not mock us,' screamed the Empress. 'We have lost everything we ever valued. They took it all away and made it all bad.'

'*Baddy, baddy, bad, bad – bad, bad, bad*,' sang the shades.

'And poisoned people's minds,' said Pilchard.

'It sounds to me like things were going wrong already,' said Lucy. 'Why else would you need giant beetles and head cabinets?'

'For a purer world,' said Pilchard. 'A better, cleaner world, free from ugly, food stealing, shape-changing dross.'

'*Don't tell her, don't tell, don't tell her, don't tell*,' sang the shades.

'Shush,' hissed Dragonira, unaware that the shades were broadcasting her thoughts. 'She does not need to know such things.'

'Is that so?' said Lucy. 'Well it's no wonder the groundlings threw you out. I think you probably deserve to be stuck in jars – all of you.'

'Did you know about this?' said Toby, turning to the sorcerer.

'I had a certain, ah, suspicion,' said Dee with a look of shame, 'but I was busy. My work with the angelic host, you understand.'

'And look where *that* got us,' said Lucy.

'So he attracted the angels' attention to us in the first place?' said Pixy.

The shades gurgled slightly as if thinking of something clever to sing.

'Right,' said Toby. 'But if the angels are so powerful, then how come they didn't just destroy the world?'

'They wanted me alive,' whispered Lucy.

'But they bitch and squabble and have a thousand different plans,' said Dragonira. 'They spent as much time fighting each other as they did trying to find this, beautiful *child*.' She smiled at Lucy as if considering adoption – followed by a short and agonising session of child killing.

'Maybe they had lots of places to search?' said Toby. 'If they have so much power then it's the only explanation. They've been here in Assiah for certain, and we've seen them in Grimston, and in Nether Grimston. I reckon there must be dozens of other places too.'

Lucy shook her head slowly, her eyes firmly fixed on Zenda.

'I think that's enough information for now,' she said.

'Maybe you're right,' admitted Toby. He blushed as Zenda took out her notepad and wrote 'Nether Grimston' in large capital letters.

'We'll leave that little pearl for later shall we?' sneered the reporter. 'In the meantime I want to know what they were doing with the head cabinets.'

'Those are nothing to do with us,' said Pilchard. 'If they were, then do you suppose we'd have ended up inside one?'

'Good point,' said Toby. 'So where did they come from?'

'They arrived on the scene just before Lucy did,' said Quim. 'Perhaps she had something to do with them?'

It was a bizarre idea, but the more Lucy thought about it, the more reasonable it seemed. The world had been stable for the first thirteen years of its existence, but somehow her arrival had shaped its more recent history.

'She did it by magick,' said Pixy, pointing an accusing finger.

'Possibly,' admitted Lucy.

'Wow,' said Pixy. 'I got it right.'

'There's no need to look so pleased,' snapped Zenda. 'If a person spouts enough rubbish then it stands to reason they'll eventually get something right by accident.'

Toby opened his mouth to accuse Zenda of the same thing, but the floor began to shake violently.

The vibrations were coming from the head cabinet.

'Is it supposed to do that?' said Tenby.

'I would guess not,' said Toby, moving away slowly.

The handle on the front of the cabinet bucked and turned and gradually gathered speed, eventually spinning so quickly that it became a blur.

'*Our wiring is faulty and our tongues are all salty,*' sang the Shades.

'What are you doing?' screamed the Empress. The fluid in her dome bubbled furiously, making her look like a sea monster on a faulty television.

'They want us dead,' gurgled Pilchard. 'I knew it all along.'

'It's nothing we've done,' protested Lucy.

Draconira and Pilchard scowled in disbelief as the domes containing the Shades of Empire split and a torrent of head pickling fluid spewed out. The cabinet filled up rapidly, and when the fluid reached the top the glass front broke and the gunk flooded out onto the floor.

'Uh-oh', said Quim. 'Has anyone noticed that there's too much of that pink stuff? It just keeps coming and coming.'

'It's not draining,' said Pixy. She looked for plughole, hoping to become the heroine of the hour – but the floor was ankle deep and the pickling fluid was rising fast.

'We have to get out,' yelled Toby.

'Back the way we came,' shouted Pixy.

She glanced at the door, but it had disappeared.

'The phantom doors were always my favourites,' cackled the Empress.

'We're trapped,' yelled Pixy.

'No we're not,' said Toby, 'get climbing.'

Nobody moved.

'The *cupboards*,' he yelled. 'Open the doors and use the shelves as ladders.'

'Clever,' said Dee.

'I thought it was a bit obvious,' said Zenda. 'I was just waiting to see if anyone else would notice.'

There were only two ways out of the pickling room now, both located in the ceiling about forty feet above. A massive cube of steel, suspended from the other side of the ceiling, blocked the larger of two holes. The other was much smaller – just big enough for them to squeeze through.

Given the size of the footholds it wasn't a difficult ascent, but they had to use both hands, which meant they couldn't cover their noses. Some of the cupboards had been used as roosting boxes and bore a dark coating of guano that had an oily sheen to it. When they grasped it, the thin skin ruptured and spilled greenish black slime onto their upturned faces.

'Come back, you filthy bottom-feeding scum lickers,' yelled Dragonira. 'If you don't, I'll have your entrails roasted over a slow fire and eaten by crows whilst they're still attached to your insides. And then I'll have your screaming bodies set on fire, and dance on your greasy ashes.'

'Keep climbing,' yelled Lucy.

'Lucy?' wailed Pixy. 'Are we coming back this way? Only I...'

The sound of vomiting came from below. This set off a chain reaction of other noises, all sounding suspiciously like people being sick.

'Keep your mouth closed and breathe through your ears,' said Toby.

'Will that help?' said Pixy.

'No,' he replied, 'but working out how to do it will take your mind off the stench.'

'Nearly there,' said Madimi, retching as she climbed up through the hole.

'Thank God for that,' said Zenda, wiping her hands on the walls. 'I'm going to need a complete new wardrobe when we get back.'

'If we get back,' said Tenby.

Lucy looked down into the pickling room before stepping away from the vent. Then, having made sure they were all safe, she dragged an old piece of carpet over the hole to keep out the smell. It wouldn't be so easy to block the memory of those floating, swirling heads though, or the abuse that came from the Empress as she was swept away on a tidal wave of sludge.

'This chamber contains the final Lellavator,' said Dee.

'I thought you'd never been in the tower before?' said Zenda.

'Even so,' said Dee. 'I know this to be a fact.'

'How?' said Pixy.

'The first part of our journey was by a filthy waxen track,' said Dee. 'And then our travels were assisted by the power of water. Do you see? First earth and then water. After that we were lofted up by the heat, only to find this strange contraption waiting at the end of our journey. Fire and air. We have made our way to the top of the Migdal by way of the four elements.'

'Yeah?' said Zenda. 'well we haven't managed this one yet, and I for one don't like the look of it.'

'Me neither,' said Lucy, studying the mechanism. 'It looks as though this stuff will only work once.'

The tiny elevator car was nothing more than a wooden crate suspended from a wheel that was visible through the ceiling about a hundred feet up. Connected to it by a supplementary pulley, was a huge fan, to limit the speed of the steel counterweight as the crate was lifted to the next level.

'How do we get it to move?' said Pixy. 'There are no buttons.'

'I know this is going to sound a bit unlikely,' said Toby, 'but can you see that bird coop in the rafters?' He pointed to a dimly lit rack of bird boxes that obviously had an outlet to the outside world. 'If you follow the wires and catches and pulleys back far enough, that's where they end up.'

'So the weight of the perching birds is keeping the lift on this floor?' said Zenda. 'You're right, it doesn't sound very likely.'

'Tobermory is correct,' said Dee. 'There are springs beneath the cage, and the weight of the birds is keeping them compressed. If they all fly away at once then the cage will rise and touch the toggle.'

'All very clever,' whined Quim. 'But it's not explanations we need – the lift simply isn't big enough. Anyone can see that.'

Everyone had noticed, but none of them wanted confirmation, because of what it meant. The group had to split, and logically it was only those who belonged to Grimston who could continue the journey.

'It might come back down,' said Quim. 'You never know.'

Everyone looked at him in a sympathetic manner.

'Well?' he said. 'It *might*.'

'I think we all know that this is the end,' said Dee, with a sad look.

'Then it is also a beginning,' said Madimi cheerfully. 'As one thing ends another always begins – that is the way of life.'

'Oh, very good,' scoffed Zenda. 'Do you want a job at the Phibber? Why don't you apply when we open the local office?'

'It's not fair,' said Quim. 'I wanted to see all the theatres and fashions.'

'Who would *not* like to see a new world?' said Dee, scowling at Zenda. 'I also have an overwhelming desire to see Grimston, but it seems that fate has chosen Assiah as my permanent home.'

'Perhaps we can come back for you?' said Lucy. She didn't believe it, but the alternative was bursting into tears at the thought of losing them forever.

'You should go,' said Dee, his eyes moistening, 'before Quim's sobbing frightens the birds and the Lellavator leaves without you.'

'It was a pleasure to meet you,' said Dee, shaking Lucy's hand. 'And you too, Tobermory.' He patted Toby on the head and then on the shoulders and finally gave him a hug, as if he'd known him since the world began.

'What about me?' said Zenda.

'You?' said Dee flatly. 'Oh yes, well, goodbye then.'

'A most touching farewell,' said a gravelly voice in the ceiling, 'but this is no time for departures.'

They turned their astonished gaze to a shadowy area where the wooden roof beams joined to form a four-way arch. The voice belonged to an angel whose perch dangled precariously from a length of rope.

Nevertheless, he remained perfectly still, even when he moved his wings.

'Where the hell did *that* come from?' said Zenda.

'Certainly not from hell,' smiled the angel. 'I am Araxiel, of the House of Fire. I have been here for some time, listening to your theories regarding the existence of this world and the disposition of angels.'

'Eavesdropper,' hissed Pixy.

'An eavesdropper of worthless ideas,' hissed Araxiel, 'which lack clarity and insight. You appear to know nothing of our kind other than what you have gleaned through guesswork and parlour tricks.'

Dee glared, angry that his life's work had been described as if it were a party game.

'He is injured,' whispered Madimi. 'But he doesn't want us to know.'

Blood leaked from a gaping wound in his abdomen.

It dripped in bright red splashes at their feet.

'I may well be injured,' hissed the angel, 'but my hearing is exceptional. If you doubt that, then perhaps you should ask the opinion of certain others.'

Araxiel shifted his weight slightly and lifted a wing to reveal a dark shape strapped to his side. He loosened a leather strap and a lump of charred meat crashed down in front of them with a sickening crunch. The body was black with ash, but the flame-ravaged features were still recognisable.

It was Boaz.

'This one was preparing an ambush,' hissed the angel.

'He already did that,' said Zenda.

'He was planning to try again,' hissed the angel, 'but failed in his task, just as you will fail in yours.'

'Why do I think we're not going to like this?' said Toby.

'Because it involves death,' said the angel. 'Yours of course, followed closely by my own.'

'But you're hurt,' said Tenby, as the rate of blood spattering increased.

'The wound is a mortal one,' admitted Araxiel. 'Dealt to me by that flying abomination you chose to call a friend. But my power still exceeds your own, and if I cannot have you, then nobody else will. You were right about our argumentative nature. The four noble houses are seldom in agreement.'

'Selfish, aren't you?' said Zenda.

'I can afford the luxury of selfish thoughts,' replied the angel. 'Soon I will be no more.'

'You mean dead?' said Pixy.

'Worse,' said Araxiel. 'So you see I have nothing to lose by keeping from my enemies the thing they desire most.'

Dee had not been idle. Whilst the angel ranted he summoned every last fragments of his power to construct a glassy, fizzing wall of energy between themselves and their foe.

'Impressive,' said Araxiel, 'for a mere mortal. But I think you must have used up all your ingenuity in constructing those fiendish cabinets.'

White-hot flames streamed from the pouches beneath the angel's wings, crashing against the shield like a flame-thrower on a shop window. The sheer magnitude of the onslaught took Dee by surprise and he was forced to the ground, trembling and exhausted. His wall of energy popped like a bubble and vanished, leaving them defenceless.

'You shall be the last to die, sorcerer,' said Araxiel. 'The timely despatch of Lucy Blake is my priority.'

'No,' screamed Madimi, as the angel turned his fury towards Lucy. 'You cannot – the child has a destiny.'

She scooped Boaz's charred remains up in her powerful arms and held his body in front of her like a shield. Then she ran to Lucy and stood between the girl and Araxiel's fire. The force of the angel's flames was diminished now, but the pressure was still great enough to drive them against the wall, crushing Lucy into the battered metal.

'Stay as you are,' screamed Madimi over her shoulder.

Lucy had no intention of moving. To either side of her the flames were scorching rust from the walls, spinning the flakes away like fireflies to reveal the bright iron beneath. In front of them, Boaz's pathetic remains burned away in a bizarre firework display, smelling of meat and flaming cloth.

'The angel is losing his strength,' yelled Madimi. 'Stay where you are, and everything will be alright.'

Lucy nodded. But her racing heart and the blood that pounded in her ears was telling her that the battle was lost. Boaz's remains were all but consumed, and although Madimi fought valiantly to keep hold of the charred bundle it eventually crumbled in her grasp, leaving her exposed to Araxiel's fury. The sorcerer's daughter turned her back on the angel, trembling as his wrath burned her hair away and incinerated her clothes.

'Keep close,' she whispered, her lips touching Lucy's ear. 'Keep close my child, and be safe.'

Dee reached out a quivering hand towards Madimi, and then withdrew it, mentally weighing the balance. His beautiful daughter and most wonderful treasure had made her choice, and there was nothing that could turn her from it. And looking even deeper into his trembling heart, he knew she was right. The sacrifice would be worth it in the end.

'No,' screamed Lucy, 'you *can't* give your life, you *mustn't*, you...'

Madimi swallowed her own screams as the flames began to consume her, but she managed to stay upright, keeping herself between Lucy and the angel.

'I will *never, ever* forget you,' cried Lucy, the roar of angel-fire eclipsing the sound of her sobbing.

'Nor I you,' whispered Madimi.

The sorcerer's daughter slumped, her beautiful hair burned to cinders, her lithe body blackened by the raging fire.

Holding Madimi's hands, Lucy braced herself for the first lick of flames – but mercifully, having incinerated her protector, the power of Araxiel was exhausted. Lucy sighed and dropped to her knees, laying a trembling hand on Madimi's charred forehead. Then she turned her gaze upwards, directing her rage at the angel.

'You bloody murdering *scum*,' she screamed. 'You cowardly, bastard stinking piece of *shit*. I'll see you and your kind burn in hell for this. I will, I'll make it *happen*.'

But the angel was no longer listening. His grip slackened and he fell from his perch, trailing broken, smoke-stained wings as he fell.

Araxiel would never hear the voices of mortals again.

The Red Tile

It was time they couldn't afford to lose, but nevertheless they allowed an entire hour to dribble away, just sitting around in various stages of shock.

Dee's brilliant eyes were filled with thunder, his brow deeply furrowed, as he tried to work out how to rewrite history and bring Madimi back. But soon the storms cleared from his gaze, with the realisation that the course of events was in the hands of others.

'I could give you a powder to make you forget,' he suggested, looking at Lucy with something approaching love. 'You must concentrate in order to defeat your enemies, and a preparation of marillion seeds would provide a deep shadow where sadness cannot penetrate.'

'No,' said Lucy. She trembled, her blood all but drained away. 'We must keep in mind why we're fighting, and that means remembering what they have done.'

'I still can't believe it,' sobbed Quim. 'She was so lovely, and so strong.'

'We will all miss her,' agreed Dee. He glared at Zenda, who was silent for once. Then he transferred his ire to Tenby, who was busy changing his film as calmly as if he were photographing a garden fete.

'Every minute you wait,' said Dee, smiling once again at Lucy, 'is sixty seconds of additional strength for your enemy.'

'He's called Raziel,' said Toby.

Dee nodded. 'I know,' he said. 'But I fear to pronounce his name, in case it adds to his power.' He paused to listen to the faint rumblings of thunder. But there were other sounds too, from above them, and inside the tower.

'The angel is preparing to meet you,' said Quim.

'And you must confront him before his strength is restored,' said Dee.

Lucy nodded in agreement. She was light headed, and felt like she was going to faint, but at least some of her mental faculties were working.

'Umm, where has Pixy gone?' she observed weakly.

'She's cleverer than we thought,' said Toby. He pointed first at Henbeg, and then at another version of the crocodile that was standing behind Lucy. Unless of course it was other way round. 'We've lost a Pixy and gained a handbag,' he said. 'So we'll have to take both of them.'

'Or leave both behind,' said Quim. 'I could look after them if you like.'

The two Henbegs growled like drains, grunting and belching and farting in a worrying display of aggression.

'No,' said Lucy. 'I promised Exotica I'd look after him. Come on Pixy, change back *now*, otherwise you're in deep trouble.'

'It'll be a while before we know which one is in trouble,' grinned Toby.

As if waiting for a signal, the Henbegs sat up on their hind legs and pawed Lucy's coat, extending their tongues and giving her disguise glasses a thorough washing and cleaning.

'Thanks,' she said, half smiling as she wiped the spit away with the back of her hand. 'Exactly what I needed at this time of stress.'

'Take both creatures,' urged Dee, 'and go – *now*.'

As Quim sobbed into an endless supply of handkerchiefs, a solemn faced Dee supervised the loading of the tiny wooden car. He squeezed Zenda and Toby at the back, then Lucy and Tenby at the front to keep things balanced. And when they were all in position, the two Henbegs wriggled their way in, curling around legs, like reptile-based glue being poured into the workings of an intricate puzzle.

When he was certain they were safe, Dee stepped back and took a final look at them. He nodded at Quim, who clapped his hands and disturbed the birds, whose stubby, energetic wings carved the air in sudden panic. There was a clunk from the mechanism and a whirring from the fan as the steel counterweight descended into the Empress's chamber and the car carried them up through a confusion of light and feathers.

Lucy watched Dee intently as they ascended, waving gently in case she upset their balance.

The sorcerer's upturned eyes were filled with tears.

'I shall remember you always,' he called. 'Every time my daughter comes to mind, I will think of you also, Lucy Blake.'

Lucy nodded and waved again, as the tiny wooden crate bore them up through the ceiling and into the next level. And as she caught the sound of inconsolable sobbing coming up from below, Lucy wiped away a tear of her own.

They emerged onto a large, softly lit landing where the sound of music was just audible above the sound of thousands of guttering candles. The area was quite grand, but judging by the ornate wooden doors in the distance it was merely the entrance for a much grander salon. But between them and the doors was a long red carpet, and before that a tiled area, and before that a glass-fronted display case that contained items of special interest.

Lucy recognised none of the angelic stuff, but even if she *had* known of its origins and meanings she had little time to study it. For there, right in the centre of the case, was a piece of regalia she recognised only too well.

'It's my *dress*,' she said, recoiling with horror. 'The one I was wearing the first time I came here.'

'It looks like a holy relic,' grinned Zenda. 'You haven't become some sort of Goddess as well, have you?'

'Don't be stupid,' hissed Lucy. 'I've never heard anything so ridiculous.'

'Neither have I,' said Toby, 'but she might be right.'

'Not you as well,' snapped Lucy. 'Have you *seen* that thing? It stinks of pigeon droppings, even through the glass.'

'I know,' said Tenby, 'but it has to be worth a snap.'

Phoomph...

Zoo-weeeeeee...

Lucy made a feeble attempt to take the camera, but Tenby held it up out of her reach, reminding her in the cruellest way possible that whatever else happened, he was an adult and she was still just a child.

'Come on,' he urged. 'Dee said there are no more lifts, so we'll have to go the rest of the way on foot.'

'Tenby, *wait*,' said Lucy. 'This place is dangerous.'

'Why?' he grinned. 'The Sisters of Perpetual Motion have gurgled away in their own juices, and as for these so-called angels we keep bumping into, have you noticed how they keep running away? I reckon it's about time we turned the tables, beginning with a few snaps, to illustrate how we eventually came out on top.'

'Have you forgotten Madimi already?' hissed Lucy. 'Doesn't that ring any alarm bells in that thick skull of yours?'

Tenby ignored Lucy's warning and raised his camera to photograph the chequered hall from the edge of the tiles.

Phoomph…

Zoo-weeeeeee…

'Brilliant,' he grinned.

He started out in the direction of the grand doors.

But to get to them, he first had to cross the tiled floor.

There were *some* people, Lucy had heard, who experienced parts of their lives as if they were scenes in a film. And this event, where the photographer began to run, was the start of one such moving picture. For years afterwards Lucy refused to admit that the movie even existed, content to think of it as lost, or perhaps on permanent loan to someone who needed to stay awake every night.

Her first blurry impression was of Tenby. He was running across a tiled floor, making his way to the great wooden doors that were the only obvious exit from the landing. The next thing she remembered, still blurred, but clear enough to make her heart beat twice, was a single red tile, amongst all the others that were either black or white. And *that* was the first sign that something was seriously wrong. Because this time the presence of an odd tile foreshadowed something far more deadly than a pineapple falling on her stepmother's head.

The second clue was a whooshing sound just to her right. She had begun to look towards Toby, but just as the noise was at its loudest his head and shoulders were eclipsed, returning a fraction of a second later as the sound of moving air diminished. Something big – something *really* big, had passed between them, and it was heading out across the floor towards Tenby. Then, completely by chance, Lucy happened to notice another movement from the corner of her eye. It was a thread from Toby's shirt, which had somehow become detached by the wind.

'Tenby,' she screamed. 'Get *down*, it's a trap!'

The first blade moved in a direct line with their view, and was so thin that it was invisible as it raced away from them towards the red tile. The second blade however, was moving from left to right and *everyone* could see the shape of it; a curved quadrant of viciously sharpened steel, humming as it cut the air, a blue spark dancing along its razor sharp edge.

And it too passed directly through the area above the red tile, just where Tenby was standing.

The photographer paused for a moment, as if he had realised what was happening but knew there was little he could do.

And he knew that because he was already dead.

The group looked on in horror as his body collapsed into itself, no longer a whole being, but four distinct quadrants that slithered against each other as they dropped to the floor in wet, messy pieces.

There was a short delay, during which nobody actually believed what they had seen. And then the reality of it sank in. Toby dropped to his knees and was violently sick. Lucy, blinded by tears, threw up seconds later, encouraged by the smell of her friend's vomit.

'It's what Thomax promised,' wailed Zenda. 'His tongue knows what it's like to be in a mouth of a corpse.'

'We can't stay here,' said Toby, wiping his mouth. 'The whole floor might be booby trapped.'

'And we can't leave,' said Lucy, spitting out sick onto the floor. 'We've stepped onto the tiles.'

In their horror and confusion they had moved onto the tiled area, each of them occupying a single black or white square, except for the Henbegs who were both a leg short and using seven apiece.

'So what do we do now?' said Toby. 'Wait until the angels find us?'

'Shush,' said Lucy. 'I need to think.'

Zenda screamed as if Tenby was dying once again, but this time purely for her benefit.

'He's been sliced up,' she sobbed, 'like bloody carrots.'

'Shush,' said Lucy. 'Raziel is nearby – he might hear us.'

'But I don't even *like* carrots,' sobbed Zenda.

'It'll be alright,' whispered Lucy.

'No it won't,' shrieked Zenda, pointing a trembling finger. 'This is all your fault. You were supposed to be in charge, and just look what you've allowed to happen.'

'You can't talk to her like that,' said Toby, moving to defend Lucy. 'She warned you this was a matter of life and death, but you carried on treating it like a game, with your stupid threats and photographs and all this rubbish about the world being owned by your tatty newspaper. If it weren't for Lucy you wouldn't have got this far. So if you want to find someone to blame, start with yourself.'

'Alright, *alright*,' said Zenda, gathering her wits. 'I admit we could have planned the take-over better, but can we at least save the camera?'

'If you want it so badly,' said Toby, folding his arms, 'then why don't you go and get it?'

He started out by looking stern and disapproving, but made the mistake of taking his eyes off Zenda, turning instead towards the four piles of flesh that had once been Tenby Yates. And it was then, when he was reminded of what had just happened, that his mood changed completely.

His expression turned black, as if he was possessed by storm clouds.

'Toby?' said Lucy. 'Is something wrong?'

'What?' he said absentmindedly.

'Are you feeling alright?' she said. 'You look beastly.'

'I'll be fine,' said Toby grimly. 'If we ever escape from this booby trap.'

'Yes, I've been thinking about that,' said Lucy. 'And I'm pretty certain the blades won't fly again unless they're reset. But I'll ask the Henbegs to try the route first, just to be certain.'

There was a certain reluctance from one of the crocodiles, which Lucy guessed might be Pixy, but they set off side by side, walking a straight line towards the big doors. Zenda and Toby looked on in silence, expecting the worst, but Lucy smiled confidently, fairly certain that her memory of the red tile was accurate. The booby trap in the kitchen had only ever claimed one victim, and that was Lily – which meant that Assiah's red tile had also done it's worst. Not that it could *be* any worse. Unless of course she started to think about why there would be a red tile both here and in Grimston.

'Alright,' she said, when it was clear the danger had passed. 'Let's go.'

They nodded respectfully at Tenby's remains as they passed the centre of the floor. But when they finally reached the grand doorway, Lucy caught Zenda casting a wistful glance back at the lost camera.

'The *door*,' said Lucy sternly.

Zenda reluctantly turned to help, and with all three of them leaning on it, the ornately carved door eventually opened far enough for them to squeeze into the stale air beyond. The place smelt like an ancient tomb that had been waiting to exhale for thousands of years.

'This is the last leg of our journey,' said Lucy confidently. 'I can *feel* it.'

'Are you sure?' said Zenda.

'Positive,' said Lucy, surveying the scene in awe.

The entrance they had just passed through was one of four similar doors that gave access to a huge octagonal space. The doors were colour coded and highly decorated, but were overshadowed by four spectacular staircases that spiralled out of an aperture in the middle of the floor and continued upwards for hundreds of feet. Each staircase was about sixty feet in diameter and joined to its matching door by a coloured walkway.

They could go down if they wished, but Lucy knew that their destiny was to follow the single thread that was woven into the faded carpet.

And that way was upwards – on the red staircase.

Lucy paused on the way up and looked over the inner handrail to try and see where the stairs started. She could make out four tiny pools of light, but all sense of scale was lost in the sheer magnitude of the structure. The glow might have been a quartet of fireflies casting their patches of light a few feet away, or four giant lighthouses at ground level, casting beams brighter than anything the world had ever seen.

Later, when they had been climbing for ten minutes or so, she stopped on the outer edge of the spiral and looked out through the huge stained glass windows that were decorated to match the fire element.

'You can see all the way to the outer walls of the city,' she said, peering through some of the lighter coloured panels.

'So what?' grumbled Toby.

Lucy sighed as she gazed at the smoking remains of the city, but soon her attention was focused on the approaching storms, whose clouds seemed to be threatening them with a severe battering.

'We have to get to the top,' she said. 'And we need to get there before the weather.'

'Yeah? Well I've had enough,' said Toby, sitting on the steps. 'I keep thinking about Tenby and Madimi.'

'I know,' whispered Lucy, settling beside him. 'But we have to push our black thoughts away for the time being.'

'How?' said Toby, his spirit waning. 'I didn't like Tenby, but I wouldn't wish that on anyone, not even Zenda.'

'I know,' said Lucy, laying a comforting hand on his.

'I never dreamed people were made of so much red stuff,' he sobbed. 'And Madimi, the way she burned, she just…'

'Shush,' said Lucy. She drew him close and laid a kiss on his brow. 'Try to think of it as pictures – horrible ones, I grant you, but just some old pictures in a dog-eared magazine.'

'Why?' said Toby.

'Just *imagine*,' whispered Lucy. 'Now take some imaginary scissors and cut them out. Have you done that?'

Toby nodded, but Lucy could see his heart wasn't really in it.

'Now screw that piece of paper into a tight little ball,' said Lucy. 'I want you to squeeze out every last drop of anger and sorrow.'

'Alright,' said Toby.

'Good,' said Lucy. 'Now throw it into the air and let me catch it.'

Toby made a half hearted gesture and Lucy responded as if she were catching an invisible fly.

'You missed,' said Toby, smiling slightly.

'No I didn't,' smiled Lucy.

She held up her hands to show him the palms of her gloves.

They were smoking and coated with ash.

'All gone,' she said. 'Now come on – I think we're close.'

'Yes, well that was *very* clever,' sneered Zenda. 'Perhaps when we get back I should see if the newspaper needs an amateur psychologist?'

'If you don't *shut* it,' hissed Lucy, 'then I'll leave you here to rot, so help me God.'

'You wouldn't dare,' whispered Zenda.

'Just *try* me,' said Lucy.

Her stare was darker than the approaching thunderclouds.

'Just one more word from you and you'll *see* what I dare.'

As they climbed higher the spirals leaned outwards, so that instead of occupying the centre of the cylindrical room the staircases leaned away from each other and got closer to the windows. By the time they reached the ceiling the stairs would emerge at the edges of the room above.

And judging by the approaching storm clouds, Lucy, Toby, Zenda and the Henbegs would be forced to enter that final chamber in darkness.

'Toby?' she said, as they continued to climb. 'Are you alright now?'

'I haven't forgotten,' said Toby. 'If *that's* what you mean.'

'Don't *ever* forget,' replied Lucy, 'but we're going to need our wits about us when we get to the top, and I don't think the Grimston Mouth is going to be much help.'

They looked back at Zenda, who was lagging behind again.

'She hasn't helped anywhere, has she?' said Toby with a weak smile.

'Well to be fair,' said Lucy, 'she did come up with the idea of swapping the cards.'

'True,' admitted Toby.

When they reached the outer loop of the spiral he stopped for a moment and reached towards the fire-tinted glass. From a distance it looked like a single colour, but now they were closer it was clear that the tint was made from millions of shades, each slightly different – a huge diversity of colours, all contributing to the main effect.

'This is another one of your messages, isn't it?' said Toby.

'Oh,' said Lucy with a smile. 'So you believe it all now do you?'

'Ever since we visited Nether Grimston,' said Toby. 'I was just so scared of what it all might mean.'

'Me too,' said Lucy. 'Four stairways, four colours, each colour made up from so many different shades. It's scary, but fascinating too – like a room that holds the biggest secret you could ever imagine.'

'And no matter what danger lays inside, you just have to look,' said Toby.

'Ah, *there* you are,' interrupted Zenda. 'I saw we were getting close to the top so I thought I'd catch up, in case you need any help.'

'Thanks,' said Toby. 'I'm sure we couldn't manage without you.'

The Red Tile

Lucy eyed the horizon. The distant sky boiled with clouds that brewed discontent in their hearts – and they were willing to prove it by throwing thunderbolts at each other, occasionally suspending their argument long enough to join forces and hurl a spike of lightning at the ground.

'Come on,' she said, looking Toby dead in the eye. 'If we're going to get through this then we need to take control of our feelings.'

'Absolutely,' said Zenda. 'And the sooner I can sit down with a nice cup of tea, the better. I really *have* had quite a difficult time.'

As Lucy glared at the reporter, an image of Madimi's charred remains flashed into her mind, and to her eternal shame she found herself wishing that it was Zenda who had perished in the flames.

Breath of
the Cherubim

When they reached the top of the stairs, the sun was sitting low on the horizon, shining beneath the layers of storm clouds. It fired up the western skies in sheets of flame, and scattered shadows into the remotest corners of a huge temple. Like the stair-vault below, this new chamber was octagonal, but capped with a vaulted dome whose apex towered two hundred feet above a chequered floor. The dome-panels were glazed with complex patterns that joined at the centre, forming an iris whose light blue petals were decorated with tiny yellow stars. It was exactly like the opening that Lucy had seen on the Nether Grimston bandstand – an idea reinforced by the circular panel that occupied the area of floor directly below it.

The walls of the temple were filaments, woven rather than built, the one facing the sun being the only one with windows, whose five stained-glass arches reached almost to the ceiling. The leaded designs to the left and right featured angels in their elemental colours, whilst the central panel depicted a larger six-winged creature in white with an unfeasibly fierce expression.

'This place is *awesome* Luce,' said Toby.

'And we don't have a camera,' said Zenda mournfully.

'It wouldn't be any use,' said Toby. 'You couldn't hope to capture the idea of this place on a piece of film.'

'Oh?' said Zenda. 'You seem to be suddenly quite well informed. So what exactly *is* the idea of this place?'

'*Ritual*,' breathed Lucy.

She stood with her back to the window and stared at the opposite wall, where the setting sun projected a fuzzy image of the five angels.

It was like a message from God.

'Some kind of church then?' said Zenda.

'Not exactly,' said Lucy. 'This isn't about religion.'

She moved to the edge of the tiled area, which projected almost all the way to the opposite wall. Without stepping onto the tiles, Lucy turned about and faced the stained-glass angels. Everywhere she looked there was order and logic and reasons for things being placed exactly where they were.

The angels, running from right to left were green, blue, then white in the centre and finally red and yellow. And the same colour scheme was repeated all around the room. The walls in the north and west were decked by seating in red and yellow whilst those in the east and south were blue and green. The back rows of seats had nineteen positions, the row in front of that seventeen, and so on, until there was just a single seat at the front. And in front of that seat was the top rung of a spiral staircase with thread of matching colour woven into its carpet.

Lucy imagined the representatives of the four factions streaming up the stairs and taking their places in the appropriate seats. And then there would be silence as they anticipated an arrival – someone to occupy the magnificent throne at the eastern end of the temple.

Lucy didn't care if it *was* a throne or not, but that was what she was going to call it – and despite all the mental warnings that screamed at her, she knew exactly what she was going to do. It was the first time she'd felt excitement without accompanying fear since she went for a mad ride in Bentley's motor.

'I'm going to sit on it,' she said plainly.

'Good for you,' said Toby, scowling at Zenda. He half expected her to claim the room and all its contents for the Phibber, but she remained silent – probably making a mental note of the fixtures and fittings.

Lucy was almost regal on her way to the throne, decked out in important looking gloves and an elegant black coat – even if they *did* stink of bird droppings. She walked slowly, almost trance-like, and it was only when she drew level with the plate beneath the apex of the dome that she was jolted back to reality. It featured symbols she recognised from the bandstand in Nether Grimston – symbols that matched Dee's angelic alphabet. And just like the bandstand, the plate in the floor looked like it was designed to open.

But first she had to answer the call of the throne, whose seat and arms were deeply padded and decorated in gold brocade, whilst the back-rest showed a flaming sun in yellows and oranges and golds – a perfect match for the final rays of the real sun.

Lucy climbed the four short steps of the podium, and without hesitating she turned and sat down. The room darkened, but she soon realised that she wasn't to blame. The glow of the angel windows was extinguished, and dusk, for better or worse, had come to the tower.

She sat quietly and emptied her mind of pre-conceived ideas. Her presence here was inevitable, which was why she though that whatever had brought her here had a duty to reveal itself. No cards or buttons or blades or counterweights – just her and whatever message the Migdal had to offer.

She smiled slightly, amused that they couldn't even get that detail ironed out. What was this place really called? The Tower of Self Knowledge, or the Tower of Merciful Blades, or even The Migdal. But it was the phrase 'Self Knowledge' that kept returning to her thoughts, like a cat insisting on being stroked. Knowledge sounded like Nollidge, which in Assiah also meant horn. And Seff sounded like Self, but actually meant three, or was it four? She had heard it ages ago, as part of a drinking song in the Bright Byrde. So what was it then? Three horns or four?

And when she put it like that, the answer was blindingly obvious.

'Seff Nollidge,' she screamed. 'Do you *hear* me?'

There was a deep boom from below and the floor plate split into eight petals, like a camera iris. And rising up smoothly from the darkness, like a missile emerging from a silo, was the tip of what she would later refer to as the Tower of the Seasons. It was conical and pricked with portholes, behind which glimmered works designed by a madman with staring eyeballs and access to a scrap-yard full of brass tubing.

'Well I don't know where she got *that* thing from,' said Toby, staring at the emerging tower, 'but I'm glad we got to it first.'

'What is it?' asked Zenda. 'Some kind of organ? Hey, wait, those horn things on top will get bent if it doesn't stop growing.'

The upper part of the tower had sprouted four great horns. The gold one looked like an old gramophone, whereas the green horn resembled the head of some monstrous plant. The blue device was every inch a rolling wave, and the fiery red trumpet was formed by the licking and combining of various flames. All four writhed like plants searching for sunlight, rapidly climbing towards the inner surface of the dome. But despite this danger of collision the tower surged from the aperture like a mad, metallic beanstalk, threading a tube over a tube here, or a pipe through a pipe there, or adding a few extra valves whenever and wherever it felt like it.

'Hey, *thing*, erm, Toby,' said Zenda, using his name for what felt like the first time. 'Have you seen what's happening to the ceiling?'

Toby looked up and nodded. The roof iris had opened and the horns were feeling their way out into the thin, dusky air.

But then they stopped, and the upper and lower irises sealed themselves around the tower, which immediately stopped growing.

'Now what?' said Zenda.

Toby pointed at the base of the structure. Inside, pipes throbbed, levers moved and gears turned, and wherever a component was vaguely transparent or reflective it glowed the same colour as the nearest staircase.

'Lucy's message,' grinned Toby. 'The four elements combining.'

The lights strengthened and brightened, climbing the vast array of pipes inside the tower, and when they reached the ceiling and passed outside, the horns grew and grew, until it seemed the roof would be unable to support their weight.

'Hey, *wotsyername*,' yelled Zenda, 'your little friend is coming back.'

Lucy climbed down from the throne and met them at the base of the tower. Toby reached out a hand and placed his fingertips against the cool metal, feeling the power that radiated from below.

'This is *brilliant*,' he said, beaming all over his face. 'Have you *seen* in these portholes?' He pressed his nose against a thick glass window, the brilliant light of the machinery spilling out onto his hands and face.

Lucy was aware that they were losing time, but was happy to wait for Toby because he had shaken the memory of Madimi's and Tenby's deaths, if only for a while.

'We should try to blow it,' she said eventually, indicating one of the tuba-like mouthpieces that protruded from the tower.

'Any particular reason?' grinned Toby. 'And please don't just say because it's there.'

'I saw something like this at the Emperor's palace,' said Lucy. 'And I just *know* it's important. It's part of the message.'

'And it's adjustable too,' smiled Toby. 'You can slide the mouthpiece up and down or make it face the other way. And there's a thing at the bottom for emptying spit out.'

'Alright,' said Zenda, turning her nose up. 'Now I *think* I can work out what's going on here. Not the exact details you understand, but just enough to get by. And so far I've counted four mouthpieces but only three sets of lips. Are you with me?'

'Yes,' said Lucy, directing her attention towards the Henbegs. 'But there are another two sets of lips available, aren't there?'

One of them stepped up, but however hard he tried to shape his mouth it wouldn't fit.

'That won't work,' said Lucy, addressing the reluctant Henbeg. 'So my next question is, how quickly can you change back?'

'*Grrr, Rowff...*' grunted the Pixy-Henbeg. It shook its head so violently that spit flew out from the corners of his mouth.

'I suppose that means not very quickly,' said Toby.

'*Rowff,*' said the Henbeg, nodding enthusiastically.

'I don't suppose it'll work with three people, will it?' said Zenda.

'The elements work together,' said Lucy. 'On their own they are weak, but when combined they have great strength. That's the lesson.'

'What about that stuff with Doctor Dee?' said Toby. 'When he was trying to make the carpet fly you seemed to know some of his spells.'

'Or was that just a confidence trick?' said Zenda.

'If there was something I could use then I'd use it,' said Lucy. 'If Granny Moon was right then we have to be out of here by sunrise, or we'll be stuck here forever.'

'Then let's get back to the laying-on of lips,' said Zenda.

'I know,' said Toby, 'why don't you see if you can get two in your mouth at once Zenda?'

'Ah, *boys,*' said Zenda, cuffing Toby around the back of the head. 'Don't you just *love* their silly humour?'

Whilst Lucy and Zenda considered the problem, Toby went for a stroll around the tower, accompanied by the Henbegs. They were mixed up again so nobody could tell which was which, and that in itself was odd, because Henbeg was normally so aggressive they might have expected more fuss. The crocodiles were happy to trail behind though, stopping when Toby stopped and pretending to examine mouthpieces or peer through portholes when he did. They even made an effort to look surprised when he located a control panel hidden beneath a black floor tile.

'Should we take a look?' he asked.

An enthusiastic round of grunting from the handbags encouraged Toby to examine the panel. There was a lever similar to the one that Lucy had used to control the Confuser. It had two positions labelled in Enochian script, and although he was unable to read them, he hoped that one of them was *'too many mouthpieces and not enough lips'*, and the other was *'try something completely different'*. And as it turned out, that was exactly the effect that throwing the lever had.

'Toby? What have you done?' shouted Lucy.

He raced back to find her pointing around the temple using a beam of light that originated from her index finger. And as the soft illumination fell upon each item, a soothing female voice announced its name.

'Fenterum Angeli' it said, as she pointed at the huge windows.

Then she pointed at the horns.

'Seff Nollidge' it revealed.

'Murum Anniaxos', it sighed, as she indicated the wall where the images of the angels had been projected by the dying sun.

'Try the chair,' said Toby.

'The *throne*,' corrected Zenda. 'Madam Lucy's throne.'

Lucy pointed at the throne, but instead of a simple announcement they were treated to a chorus of voices, like a choir, chanting over a silent sea.

'What are they saying?' said Toby.

'It sounds like cathedral,' said Lucy.

'Actually it's *Cathedra*,' said Zenda. 'It means chair – we reporters do actually *know* a thing or two.'

'Alright clever clogs,' said Toby, 'so what are they singing now?'

The choir was chanting two words.

The first was *'Cathedra'*, and the second was all too familiar to Lucy.

'It's architect,' she said, unable to resist a smile. 'They're singing Cathedra Architectum, the Seat of the Architect.'

'It's like the talking map,' said Toby. 'But instead of teaching you about the world, it tells you about the temple.'

'I think there's more to it than that,' said Lucy. She turned to the stained glass windows, but instead of a casual wave across all of them she dwelled on the first, letting the pool of light hover on the face of the angel.

'*Terra*,' said the gentle voice. She waited, expecting to hear more, but that was it, so she proceeded to the other minor windows, and in turn managed to extract '*Aqua*', '*Ignis*' and '*Aeris*' from them as expected.

Then she turned her attention to the central window, where the dusk sky had taken on a deep purple glow.

'What are you looking for Luce?' said Toby.

'Actually I've got a question,' said Zenda. 'How come she gets to play with the pointy thing? Have we forgotten who owns what around here?'

'Fine,' said Lucy. 'Well you'd better get on with it then.'

'Get on with what?' said Zenda.

'Your idea,' said Toby. 'You keep going on about being in charge and owning the place, but you're not actually helping much. And as for ideas, I think you're only just ahead of Pixy on that score.'

'Alright,' said Zenda. 'Why don't you point at the angel in the middle?'

'I was *doing* that already,' said Lucy.

'Well keep pointing then,' said Zenda. 'And something might – *oh*, see? I *told* you something might happen.'

The lesser windows glowed as if light had been captured inside the glass and was fighting to get out. The internal radiance revealed new and exquisite detail that brought the angels to life, but as quickly as they rose they died again, contributing their brightness to the central panel. Here, a smouldering Seraphim held out an orb as if displaying it to an assembly of the faithful.

They watched in silence as the orb hinged into four floating pieces, each creating a stream of coloured light that danced and flowed like sea-blown weed.

'The light is forming into shapes,' whispered Lucy.

'Perhaps we should hide,' said Zenda.

'No,' said Toby. 'I think they might be friendly.'

'You *think* they might be?' whispered Zenda.

A corporeal shape coalesced from each stream of light, half flying, half wafting its way towards the base of the tower, its wings folded tidily behind it and long golden locks flowing down its back.

'I'm worried about all those eyes,' said Zenda, 'but they do have lovely rosy cheeks, and beautiful little noses.'

'And four faces,' said Toby. 'Their features keep changing.'

'These are Kurabi,' said Lucy. 'When Bentley came back from Lundern he mentioned guardians with changing faces.'

The Kurabi were keen to demonstrate their abilities, floating on just two pairs of wings whilst their faces changed seamlessly from human to lion, and from lion to bull and finally into an eagle before starting all over again.

'Not very talkative, are they?' said Zenda, jotting down a few notes.

'They must have been sent to help blow the horn,' said Lucy.

'Is that why you're here?' said Zenda.

None of the Kurabi answered, but each one moved to a mouthpiece and turned it inwards, placing their backs to the tower so they could address their lips to the instrument. Then they reached out their hands.

'They want us to touch them,' said Lucy.

She moved towards the rose coloured figure, trying to avoid the gaze of his dozens of eyes and taking him by the hands. They were cool to the touch, and fizzed slightly. The creature took a lungful of air, fastened his lips against the mouthpiece and blew hard into the horn.

'Finally, said Zenda. 'We get to see some action.'

The sound that emerged from the horn was pathetic – a bag of week-old fruit being run over by a milk cart. But Lucy had expected this, and indicated that the others should take their positions. Zenda took the pale green corner and Toby the blue. And the Henbegs made their way to the yellow position, standing on their hind feet, ready to join hands and claws as best they could.

'They're expecting you to say something,' said Toby.

'Yes,' agreed Zenda. 'Say something. You *know* you want to.'

Lucy *did* want to, but she didn't want to be told to do it by Freggley. It was important, and demanded respect.

'Come *on* then,' said Zenda.

'Will you please leave her alone?' hissed Toby. 'How can she think with you cackling in her ear?'

Lucy closed her eyes and tried to block out stray thoughts. She began by recalling the words of Dragonard's ceremony, but soon realised that she had to reach further back into her memory – to a time when the sky was lighter and birdsong was sweeter. A time when her mother was there, whispering rhymes and reading to her.

'In the north, height,' she whispered. 'And in the south, limitations.'

'In the east, flux,' she went on, 'and in the west, passion.'

It was all she could remember, and it was all from the Emperor's ritual.

Nothing happened.

Lucy was heartbroken.

She was filled with the dark opposite of the joy she'd experienced the day she helped Dee. On that occasion, the memory of her mother's words had lifted her heart; but now the absence of them was like a rope knotted around her stomach and cast into a dark pool with a rock fastened to the other end.

'I was expecting *something*,' said Zenda.

'It's like one of those old films where the lips don't quite match the words,' said Toby. 'You think you know what's going on, but you can never quite be sure.'

'We're doing the right thing,' said Lucy, sounding disappointed, 'but they seem to want something else.'

'What else could they possibly need?' said Zenda. 'All they have to do is *blow* the ruddy thing. And what could be simpler than that?'

Nisroc

'*Indeed,*' said a distant voice. 'What could be simpler?'

'Who's that?' said Lucy. '*Show* yourself.'

'Very well,' said the voice. 'I am your servant.'

'I don't like it,' whispered Toby. 'That sounded like *I am your serpent.*'

'I've worked with a few snakes,' said Zenda, 'so I can usually recognise them, and this one sounds *very* shifty.'

'Perhaps I should approach?' said the voice. 'To show I am no threat?'

They strained to pick out the stranger near the angel windows, but could only distinguish a silhouette and a rough shadow that stretched as far as their feet. Lucy thought it might be Raziel, but couldn't be certain until the figure spoke again.

'Did you ever *see* such a spectacle as this?' said the approaching voice.

'Umm, no,' said Zenda, cagily. 'But it's like a church, isn't it?'

'This is *not* a church,' hissed the voice. 'It is nothing quite so feeble as the monuments that man builds to honour himself.'

The figure was close enough now for the subtleties of the voice to be made out. It was female, and one that Toby and Lucy had heard before, but neither could place it, until its owner stepped from the shadows – a faltering, frail figure with a walking stick.

'Oh,' said Lucy, 'it's Miss Niblock.'

'Indeed,' said Niblock, swivelling her cane. 'And I suppose that now you have inspected the temple there will be a certain number of questions?'

'Dozens,' said Lucy.

'Starting with what she's doing here,' whispered Toby.

Lucy nodded. 'Do you know about this place?' she said.

'A little,' said Niblock. 'Do you recognise the symbolism?'

'It's all about the elements,' said Lucy. She stared at the cane, because she didn't remember the teacher having one at the Braneskule.

'Yes,' replied Niblock, 'but there is more here than a simple explanation could hope to encompass. Each of these windows for instance would require a lifetime of study in itself.'

'I see,' said Lucy. 'So who are they?'

'Who *are* they?' said Niblock. 'I was led to believe you knew such things.'

'Well I don't,' said Lucy. 'So who are they?'

'Ah, I *see*,' said Niblock. 'You think the figures have individual names.'

'Don't they?' said Toby.

'These are the *perfect embodiments*,' said Niblock. 'Each window represents an entire race of angels.'

Toby felt that something wasn't right, even though he couldn't quite put his finger on it. Lucy on the other hand seemed to have accepted Niblock's presence as if it made complete sense. The edge of her suspicion had been worn smooth by the possibility that she was going to get some answers.

'Can I just ask a very simple question?' said Toby. 'It's nothing to do with angels and it's probably going to annoy you something rotten, and I do hope you'll forgive me for asking it.'

'*Yes* Tobermory?' smiled Niblock. 'What is it?'

'Well,' said Toby, 'I was just wondering how you got in.'

'I am searching for Pixatrix Scalybeak,' said Miss Niblock.

'That's not what I asked,' said Toby. 'I want to know how you got inside the tower. And especially how you managed to get up here.'

'I *told* you,' said Miss Niblock, a little more edgily this time. 'I'm looking for the Pixy girl.'

'Yes,' said Toby, determined to get an answer, 'but how…'

'It's a good point,' said Lucy, snapping out of her dreamlike state. 'And you don't seem keen to tell him – so I'll ask a much easier question.'

'Very well,' said Niblock, seething quietly.

'What are you doing looking for her up here?' said Lucy. 'Why aren't you searching the Braneskule, or the ruins of the Observatory, or even the Bright Byrde?'

'I directed them away,' said Niblock, ignoring the question. 'When they were about to find you, I sent them in the wrong direction and allowed you to wriggle through the back of the organ.'

'Well somebody did,' said Lucy, recalling their earlier escape from the school. 'And I suppose it could have been you.'

'Don't listen to her,' said Toby. 'Even if she did help, it doesn't prove she's on our side.'

'If you're my friend,' said Lucy, 'then why did you punish me with that Lokey pole?'

'To make you afraid,' said Niblock.

'It worked,' said Lucy. 'I was terrified.'

'Which is one reason why we're not going to trust you,' said Toby. 'And the second reason is that everyone we've met seems to want to slice us up or ambush us or roast our giblets.'

Lucy swallowed hard, suddenly reminded of Madimi.

'So why don't you go and *get lost?*' she spat.

The teacher bent down and grabbed one of the Henbegs by the tail, then she swung him around her head and let go. The creature careered across the tiled floor and slammed into the wall. He picked himself up and growled at his tormentor, but didn't return for another dose of medicine.

'How did you know which one was Pixy?' said Lucy.

'There are always signs,' said Miss Niblock.

'I'm sure you'd tell us what they were if we asked you nicely,' said Toby.

'She'll know lots of things like that,' agreed Lucy. 'Like how to tell the difference between a Braneskule teacher and an angel of God.'

'*Aaaahh,*' sighed Niblock. 'Events have unfolded just as Raziel predicted.'

'Brilliant,' said Toby. 'You saw right through her.'

'You are perceptive,' said Niblock, 'but far too hasty – you should have delayed a while before letting me know that you have seen through my guise. But no matter, I shall have what I need directly. The time for treading on broken shells is at an end.'

'What did you have in mind?' said Lucy.

'Your friends will be ripped by claws and talons,' said Niblock. 'And you will surrender The Light.'

She threw her cane into the air. It paused at the apex of its flight and changed into a bird's foot with yellow, leathery skin and sharp talons. And as it fell, those razor-like claws sliced the atmosphere, giving an expectation that something might fall out of the slashes it had made. The air in the temple was restless, gently tugging at their hair and brushing their cheeks, as if trying to attract their attention. But it wasn't quite as gentle with Niblock. It rushed around her in a funnelling motion, as if she were the centre of a vortex.

'We'll be alright,' said Zenda, as the storm grew around the teacher.

'You think?' said Toby.

'The wind isn't trying to save us,' said Lucy. 'It's something she's doing to herself.'

The air thundered around Miss Niblock, tearing at her gown. She looked like a crow battling a gale, the sheets of her clothing cracking like sails on a storm-lashed ship. And just as it seemed the vortex couldn't spin any faster, it increased its velocity fourfold, tearing her garments in the mayhem. She was left naked, her flesh rippling in the intense wind, the patterns of sand dunes running across the landscape of her body.

'I don't think you should be watching this,' said Zenda.

'It's not a woman,' said an indignant Toby. 'It's not even human.'

He was right. Although Niblock was stripped naked, she bore none of usual characteristics of her sex. Like Harry's pigeon chick, she was born in the wind and had no gender to speak of.

The three stood open mouthed as the fleshy, sexless being mutated into a huge eagle-like creature. And as they turned to run it changed again, into a much more familiar shape. She was an angel with three pairs of wings and a body that was surrounded by a pale green glow.

'You *aren't* human, are you?' said Lucy, instantly regretting the somewhat obvious observation.

'No child,' hissed the creature. 'I am the angel Nisroc.'

Nisroc raised herself up, and as she gained height her feet exploded with tendrils, forcing her towards the dome more quickly than even her massive wings could manage. It was the closest Lucy had come to such an unleashing of talent and she was surprised at the expression of pain on Nisroc's face.

'Come to me,' said Nisroc.

A tendril whip-lashed around Zenda's neck, dragging her over the floor. The reporter screamed, struggling to keep her feet on the ground as she tore at the ligature around her throat.

'Put her down,' yelled Lucy. 'Put her down this instant. She...'

'As you wish,' grinned Nisroc, releasing the tendril.

Zenda dropped like a double-decker bus, the impact knocking every bit of wind from her body.

'What, whe, *h-h-h-help*,' she whimpered, raising herself on one hand and rubbing her bruised ribs with the other.

'You're just like Raziel,' yelled Lucy. 'All you care about is your precious Light – that *is* what you want isn't it?'

'You *are* well informed, aren't you Miss Blake?' hissed the angel.

Lucy watched Zenda's attempt to stand, and signalled to the reporter that she should stay down.

'And is that *all* you're interested in?' said Lucy.

'Perhaps you wish to discuss the rights and wrongs of our demands?' said Nisroc. 'Raziel tells me that you enjoy an argument, even when you possess little more than one tenth of the facts.'

'Ha,' said Zenda with a weak snort. Even though she was injured she was unable to resist the irony.

'I think we should blow the horn,' whispered Toby.

'Yes,' hissed Lucy, 'but how?'

'Is that the beginnings of an argument?' asked Nisroc. 'You know you really *must* speak more clearly.'

She lashed at Zenda with a sharp-edged tendril, whose impact brought up a huge purple weal on the reporter's left arm.

'We need help,' whispered Lucy.

'But who?' said Toby. 'Dee?'

'I can *hear* you,' said Nisroc. 'We *do* have acute senses you know.'

'Then why don't you try out your enhanced sense of compassion or your improved morality?' said Lucy, as she sidled towards the tower.

'We have compassion,' said Nisroc with a smile, 'but we don't use it too often in case it wears out. And we possess morality in abundance, although I don't expect you to understand. There is little point in discussing philosophy with a mere child, however special she believes herself to be.'

Lucy shrank back. The angel was right – they all knew far more than she did, but the way they bullied and pushed was enough to convince her that whatever else they knew, they were also wrong.

But they were strong too.

'*Luce,*' hissed Toby. 'Are we going to blow this thing or not?'

Lucy smiled. She thought about Harry, who had told her two important things. Never start a fight you can't win, and don't be afraid to ask for help. And right now, those two ideas seemed inseparable. She had no choice but to start fighting and was therefore obliged to ask for help.

Nisroc

'*Agla, agla, agla, agla,*' she cried. '*Almighty God, who art ruler of the universe and who ruleth over the four divisions of its vast form by the strength and virtue of the four letters of thy holy name. Tetragramatton. Yod He Vau He. Bless this convocation of these, thy mighty Kurabi, and bless too their divine breath. Permit them the power and the wisdom to do thy holy will, and in this action, serve our own purpose. And we shall hide under thy wings, and beneath thy feathers we shall trust.*'

Lucy panted.

Cold sweat ran down inside her dress.

But nothing happened.

'Impressive,' sneered Nisroc. 'I thought for a moment there you were asking for help.'

'So did I,' said Lucy, trembling visibly.

'*Luce,*' whispered Toby. 'Are you *sure* that's what you did?'

'The girl is out of her depth,' grinned Nisroc. 'She knows some pretty words, but on their own they are not enough. And when you ask for help it is usually wise to check if someone is in a position to respond. I simply can't imagine who *that* might be in this God-forsaken place.'

'There'll be help somewhere,' said Lucy. 'If you need it badly enough and you ask in the right way then someone will always be prepared to give it.'

'Well if they don't,' whispered Toby, 'then we're in a lot of trouble.'

And *that* was when the commotion began.

The Kurabi filled their cheeks to capacity and blew – softly this time so that no sound emerged. Instead, the tower pulsed with light, beginning at the base and working its way up, showering pools of light from every porthole and reflecting coloured beams around the temple. But the light was merely a precursor – a sign sent on ahead, to reveal the coming of the messenger.

Holding her head to one side, Lucy heard distant murmurs – a mass of indistinct voices that gradually rose to a chant and then sang one pure note that was the overture to a great work. Steady, unwavering and perfect, it spoke to her of purity, and undivided purpose.

A story without words.

The pitch slid down now, gently and steadily, and as it passed the points of harmony it set up sympathetic vibrations around her. She noticed them first in smaller items, like her spectacles and the fillings in her teeth, but as the note swung lower, larger items began to rattle and groan under its spell – the floor, the great windows, and eventually the entire fabric of the temple.

Lucy looked up, identifying the source of the sound that shook her to the core. The horns on the roof were broadcasting her message to every corner of the world, carrying her cry to every nook and cranny, every pinnacle and every chasm.

And then the call ceased, and they were left with the natural sound of the skies. It was the music of birdcall. Not just a single species, but a chorus made from every imaginable avine throat.

And so it was. Beyond the great window, the call spread, silently in some places and with great cawings and screechings in others, with every winged creature passing on the message. *Raise up your wings.*

'Is it happening?' whispered Lucy.

'You tell me,' said Toby.

'Well then,' she said. 'Why don't you go and check?'

'Go and check?' said Toby, looking completely puzzled.

'If only we had a camera,' hissed Lucy under her breath.

'A camera?' laughed Toby nervously. 'We're about to become history and you want to start taking holiday snaps?'

'Think about the people in the saleroom.' hissed Lucy. 'You know, the ones on the wardrobe?'

'Oh *yes*,' said Toby, 'well, as luck would have it I've got one here.'

He reached into his pocket and pulled out the shew stone, wrapping his hands around it so that only a small part of the glass showed. It looked just like a lens.

'Awesome,' grinned Lucy. 'But I hope you didn't steal it.'

'No,' whispered Toby. 'Dee slipped it into my pocket.'

'*No,*' screamed Nisroc, raising her wings to shield her face. 'That thing could mean eternal death.'

'A bit like the one you've got planned for us?' said Lucy.

'Can you *see* anything?' she mouthed quietly at Toby.

Toby looked into the shew stone, just as he'd done at the Braneskule. He knew what Lucy wanted, but was entranced by what he saw there. The image jittered and bounced and made him sick, but he felt compelled to watch as the stone's view approached the Emperor's palace. It was almost as if it was trying to tell him something.

In the background, just above the level of his concentration, he could hear Lucy arguing with Nisroc. But when he tried to make out what they were saying the image faltered and almost disappeared. He decided to trust her like she always trusted him, and the instant he put their conversation out of his mind he was floating above the palace again, viewing the wreckage through the eyes of a bird. On the roof, some mysterious hidden force was at work, rippling the fire-blackened slates like seawater. Lower down, the walls vibrated like mad washing machines, throwing out stones the size of tramcars. And beneath the palace the foundations were bucking and rearing, as if an earthquake had decided that today would be a good day to destroy the smouldering remains of the Emperor's toys.

But this was no earthquake.

The dragon had lain beneath the palace even before the history of Assiah had begun, and now he was shaking off all that weight, having heard the call that freed his soul. All he had to do now was thank the girl who had uttered the cry, and perhaps enquire where she had learned such words.

Satisfied that his wingtips were released, he flexed the muscles along his back, sending a shudder through the palace. And with an ear splitting scream and a spinal spasm that threatened to tear him apart, the dragon was free, the charred timbers and roof slates dripping from his back like water falling into an abyss.

Toby felt a dig in his ribs and realised that Lucy was shouting at him.

'Take a picture *now*,' she screamed.

'Yes, go on,' said Nisroc, 'take a picture, why don't you?'

'Alright then,' said Toby, pressing an imaginary button.

The glow around Nisroc brightened as she realised that her instinct had been correct.

'Just as I thought,' she said triumphantly. 'Nothing but a ruse. Did you *really* think that you could deceive me with that thing?'

The Transform-o-Matic

Toby gazed into the shew stone, desperate for a sight of the palace – but it was gone, replaced by a pile of smoking rubble.

'Oh,' he said, searching the barren landscape.

'Have your plans all come to nothing?' sneered Nisroc. 'There is no need to deny it boy; I can see it in your face. Your kind is so transparent, wearing every little emotion on the outside. There is nothing in the glass object that can possibly help you.'

'Do you *think*?' said Lucy. She took the stone from Toby and held it up, pretending to see what he had. And to her surprise she did see something, albeit rather hazily.

'But you can't use it properly,' whispered Toby.

'Be quiet,' snapped Lucy.

'Yes, be quiet,' grinned Nisroc. 'Let the silly girl have her moment.'

Lucy held the shew-stone to her eye. The image was fuzzy, like an out of focus holiday snap in some long forgotten seaside town.

'So,' said Nisroc, 'what can you see in your camm-er-ah?'

'Friendship,' said Lucy. 'And loyalty.'

'Then child, perhaps you *are* worth saving?' said Nisroc. 'If you can detect abstract emotions in an old piece of stone then you must be capable of even greater things. Can you also see love in there? Or *hatred*?'

With a vicious tendril lash from Nisroc, Toby was dragged away gurgling and choking, his face turning a pale blue. One of the Henbegs snapped at the plant-wire, but another tendril wrapped his forelegs and cracked him away like a whip. He tumbled end over end, crashing into the banisters and falling into the blue stairwell. He reappeared with one of his legs broken and tried another attack, but Nisroc simply brushed him aside, wrapping Zenda in a stranglehold and hoisting her up like a puppet.

'I think *pain* might be a good place to begin,' cackled Nisroc.

The tendrils holding the two prisoners exuded a sticky sap that brought their skin out in hideous boils, but it was the plant-growths themselves that caused the most suffering. They coiled round Toby like a tightening spring, covering his body with energetic tubes that were determined to squeeze the life out of him. Zenda was similarly entwined but held upside down, with blood rushing to her head and hair hanging down like a beard.

But then Lucy noticed Nisroc's expression, which echoed the reporter's agony.

'Are *you* in pain too?' she said, slightly incredulous.

'What do *you* think?' screamed Nisroc as she increased the pressure on Toby. 'Do you imagine that power can be exercised without a corresponding effort? Would *you* be able to support a weight above your head for a whole day without tearing the strength from your muscles?'

'Umm, no,' admitted Lucy.

'Whatever talent we may have is brought about by effort,' said Nisroc.

'You're strangling yourself?' said Lucy in disbelief.

'Not only myself,' said Nisroc.

'So you think those two will die before you do?' said Lucy.

'I *know* they will,' said Nisroc. She increased the pressure on Zenda, who passed out like a limp rag doll. Toby's eyes bulged and his tongue protruded as he struggled in the tendrils' iron grip.

'Alright,' said Lucy, seeing that Nisroc meant to kill them both. 'Stop what you're doing and I'll co-operate.'

'Now *that* is exactly what I wanted to hear,' said Nisroc. 'If you'll just pass The Light over to me, I will make the necessary preparations.'

'What kind of preparations?' said Lucy.

'When The Light is secure we will return from whence we came,' said Nisroc. 'And you will see your mother.'

'My *mother*?' Lucy's knees weakened and she dropped slightly before regaining her stance. 'But how can that be?'

'Did Raziel not tell you?' said Nisroc. 'It has always been our intention to return you to your mother's side.'

'Luce, don't listen to her she's...'

The rest of Toby's words were choked away, as tendrils curled around his waist and bent him over backwards so he was unable to see his friend.

'Don't listen to him,' said Nisroc, feigning warmth. 'He can't *possibly* know what it's like to be without a mother.'

Lucy blinked away the tears. She knew Toby was in pain, but the mention of her mother had drawn a veil over his suffering, as if Maggie might appear now that her name had been called. And once she *was* here, she'd be certain to put things right. All Lucy had to do was hand over The Light and they'd be reunited – it seemed so obvious. And she had never *really* been entitled to The Light, having stolen it, and if anyone knew where her mother had gone then it would surely be the angels.

'Can you really take me to her?' whispered Lucy.

'By all that is holy,' grinned Nisroc. 'May the Grand Architect of the Universe strike me down in flames if I tell an untruth. Hand over The Light and I will take you to your mother.'

Lucy knelt, searching her pockets for the manuscript – but when she finally laid her hands on it, the book wouldn't come out.

'Get off, Lucy Glake. Get off it. Not for giving away to nasties.'

'Genjamin, give me the book,' insisted Lucy. 'I'm warning you.'

'No, no, no, *no*,' said Genjamin. '*Nasty*. Listen to Togy.'

'Give me the book this instant,' demanded Lucy.

She gave an extra hard tug and the manuscript tumbled out, landing a short distance in front of her.

'*Aaah*,' sighed Nisroc, her vulture-like eyes falling on the book as if it were a carcass. 'At last, we have The Light. Good. *Gooooood*.'

'No give The Light,' screamed Genjamin, 'no give...'

Genjamin's last words were muffled as Lucy closed the pocket.

She took The Light and stood up, holding it towards Nisroc.

'*No* Luce,' said Toby, choking the words out. 'You mustn't.'

'You said it yourself,' replied Lucy. 'All they have to do is threaten my friends and I have to give in. But this way she'll stop hurting you and I'll get to see my mother.'

'But help is coming,' said Toby, suddenly able to speak clearly. Nisroc knew that it wouldn't further her cause to continue throttling him. After all, she had *won*, hadn't she?

'We don't *know* any such thing,' said Lucy.

'I promise you,' said Toby. 'I saw our friend, sitting on a low hill near the palace – and he's waiting for something.'

'Well your imaginary friend had better arrive soon,' smiled Nisroc. 'Your time is running out. You *do* know that?'

'We must leave before sunrise,' said Lucy, 'or the world will be sealed.'

'And if that happens you will never see your mother,' said Nisroc.

'Don't listen Luce,' said Toby. 'I *told* you, help is on the way – look in the shew stone if you don't believe me.'

Lucy had forgotten about the stone, but now felt the weight of it in her pocket, pressing gently against her thigh. She put The Light on the floor and rested a foot on it. Nisroc accepted the fact, knowing that the girl was bound to give her The Light eventually.

'I can see the sky outside,' said Lucy, taking out the stone.

'Is that so?' said Nisroc. 'And your mother?'

'No,' said Lucy, feeling slightly queasy. 'I really *can* see the sky – it's like I'm flying.'

'Like an angel,' said Nisroc. 'And does it feel good, this flying?'

'No,' said Lucy. 'I feel like vomiting.'

A sickness rose in her throat as she peered into the stone. It was like looking through world's most powerful telescope – but she saw what Toby meant. An inky cloud was rising over the Forest of Skeels, and as Lucy flew down into the black mist she recognised the creatures that Gusset mentioned when they escaped from the Braneskule – the same ones that had gathered at her window and settled on Miss Pubrane's bed.

She looked even more closely as the image wobbled and swam in her head, until she could taste the vomit at the back of her throat.

And then she broke into a broad, beaming smile.

The living dragons' scales had responded to the call of the horns, a message that spoke to the spirit inside every creature capable of flight. They were flocking in the direction of the Emperor's palace, and when they got there they would dive onto the waiting dragon and attach themselves to his wings and tail and fuse with the mountainous ridge of skin that ran along his back.

'So,' said Nisroc, jarring Lucy from her vision, 'now that you have failed to find anything of interest in your stone, perhaps we can do business. I'll take The Light if you please.'

'Umm no, I don't think so,' said Lucy. 'Our call has been answered. And in any case I don't believe that you can take me to my mother.'

'My oath was sincere,' said Nisroc. 'We *can* take you there, because she…'

'I have heard *quite* enough of this,' screamed a familiar voice. 'And *you* my lady Nisroc were about to reveal far too much.'

'*You*,' hissed Lucy. 'Well I thought you might at least have dressed for the occasion.'

'In feathers?' said Raziel. 'Oh yes, well I *do* enjoy that when the occasion demands it, but at other times I prefer the clothing favoured by mortals. It may even turn out to be their one saving grace, the ability to cut cloth and prepare such divine wrappings.'

Lucy frowned, part in surprise and part relief. She had expected Raziel to arrive on powerful wings, but he was dressed as he was on that very first day, in a black frock coat and top hat.

'I think we mortals might be good at more than that,' she said. 'And now of course, we have help.'

She gestured towards the Kurabi, who had been cowering in a corner since Raziel arrived – and now that Lucy had pointed them out they were cringing all the more. With a flap of wings all four of them took to the air, wheeling off in different directions, as if a hawk had appeared amidst a flock of smaller birds.

'Did you see something fly off just then?' said Raziel. 'I think it might have been vermin.' He gave a thin, cruel slit of a smile that Lucy hadn't seen before, even when he had killed poor Morana.

'Fly away my beauties,' he yelled. 'But don't go too far, or I might not be able to reach you.'

Raziel spread his hands and showed his palms, the bony fingers curved toward the tiled floor. A stream of liquid light burst from the tip of each finger, spitting and crackling and filling the air with incandescent trails.

By their glow, Lucy saw the Kurabi cowering in the apex of the dome.

'There is no escape,' yelled Raziel. 'If you wanted to live then you should have ignored the girl's summons.'

'We have served her well,' shouted the one with the bull face.

'And are proud to have done so,' said the one who looked like an eagle.

'Then you shall die filled with pride,' said Raziel.

The liquid fire-streams snaked towards the ceiling space, slowly circling the tower as if Raziel was enjoying dragging out the hunt. Then with a quick flick of his wrists they homed in on the Kurabi who flapped like pigeons against the yellow stars. As the burning plasma found its mark the victims let out a joint scream – four gut-wrenching notes of pure misery. Lucy couldn't bear to look as the angelic bodies were ripped asunder, showering the floor of the temple with dripping blood and lumps of flesh.

She stared at her feet as a blanket of feathers floated to earth – a red stained shower of forlorn hope.

'*You* killed them, didn't you?' yelled Lucy, her eyes filled with tears.

'You saw plainly enough,' said Raziel. 'So why ask?'

'Not the Kurabi,' she screamed. 'I'm talking about Harry's pigeons – and what did that old man ever do to you?'

'Nothing,' said Raziel.

'Then why?' yelled Lucy.

'Because birds are not angels,' said Raziel, 'and it gave me pleasure to injure the old man in a lasting way. If I had killed *him* then that would have been that. But now he suffers every time he looks into the empty loft.'

'And you did all that because he gave me The Light?' said Lucy.

Raziel laughed like a bad actor playing the part of a mad woman.

'You *still* don't understand, do you?' said Raziel.

'Apparently not,' said Lucy.

'And perhaps it is best that you remain in ignorance,' said Raziel. 'At least until you have been taken into protective custody.'

'I can imagine your kind of protection,' said Lucy. 'Which is why I don't intend to go anywhere with you.'

'Oh, I think you *will*,' said Raziel. 'Once you see what I have in store for your little friend.'

There was a movement in the shadows behind Raziel, but it was too dark to make anything out. Now that the sun had set, the only illumination came from the inner workings of the tower.

Raziel beckoned, and the shapes emerged from the shadows.

The Transform-o-Matic

'These are our newest assistants,' he said.

The dark forms hovered, awaiting his command, their faces covered with swirling mist. One of them carried a small casket. The other had something heavy concealed under its stinking robe.

'Vooghuls,' said Lucy, turning her nose up at the smell.

'But not just any Vooghul,' said Raziel. 'These are special – and look who they have brought with them.'

The figure with the pregnant cloak released its folds and Fenny dropped to the ground in front of Lucy. She was alive and apparently unharmed.

Lucy stood for a moment trying to take it all in. After all the time they had spent searching for Fenny she couldn't think of anything to say.

'I'm sorry,' she said eventually. 'I should have come back for you that day on the pier. And then none of this would have happened.'

'It would,' said Fenny, getting unsteadily to her feet.

'You're just trying to make me feel better,' said Lucy.

'Enough,' spat Raziel. 'We will close the business that my lady Nisroc seemed to find so difficult to complete.'

There was a hiss from Nisroc. Her feathers brightened, illuminating the carnage that lay all around – the matted, bloodstained feathers, the pieces of light, honeycomb-filled bone and the severed head with the face of a lion that lay at Lucy's feet.

'What happened?' said Fenny, her complexion turning white.

'Nothing that concerns you,' said Raziel. 'Your part in all of this is to look pretty – and vulnerable.'

Lucy felt hatred rising in her heart. Raziel was enjoying himself *far* too much – but it wasn't just that. She hated him because his tactics were so effective. She only had to look at the remains of the Kurabi to realise what the angel was capable of. And then she recalled what Granny Moon had said about how she might want to change hatred into love.

No, she thought to herself. She hated Raziel, and that was that.

'I'm sorry it's come to this,' said Lucy, trying to hide her rage.

'You did your best,' said Fenny.

'But it wasn't good enough,' said Raziel. 'And I will show you why.'

The Vooghul carrying the casket stepped forward, giving Lucy the full benefit of its stink. It opened the lid and tilted the box so she could see the contents. The item was about six inches long and two in diameter, made of a dull metal that looked like frozen mercury. At each end was a small horn, like those on the tower, but just a few inches in diameter at the wide end.

'What is it?' said Lucy, almost hypnotised by the twinkling lights that danced over the mystery item.

'A converter,' grinned Raziel. 'It fell into my possession after the inventor had a little accident.'

'I see,' said Lucy, thinking of Byron. 'And what does this converter *do?*'

'It combines the souls of the dead with the bodies they inhabited in life,' said Raziel. 'But it can also put that same soul into a different body.'

'Well if it's true,' said Lucy, 'then it's a disgusting idea.'

'Oh, it's certainly *true,*' said Raziel. 'I only wish I had thought of it myself. Just think of all those souls who can live forever in the body of their choice.'

'As long as the body lasts,' said Lucy. 'Have you *smelt* these two?'

'An unfortunate by-product,' said Raziel, 'but the bodies *will* live forever. And so will the souls.'

'But they don't *choose* that, do they?' said Lucy.

'They can be persuaded,' said Raziel. 'That's why we needed a machine to talk to them. Even angels can't communicate with the dead you know.'

'And what if they don't *want* to join you?' said Lucy.

'Then nothing we can do will make them convert,' said Raziel.

'There's something else,' said Fenny. 'He's keeping something from us.'

'I know,' said Lucy. 'And I don't expect it's very pleasant.'

'We need Vooghuls to help in our quest,' said Raziel. 'And if we have the body soon after death then we can force the matter. The machine can make a Vooghul whether the soul likes it or not.'

'And what happens when the conversion is complete?' said Lucy.

'Then the new being is bound to do the will of whoever performed the conversion,' said Raziel.

He signalled the Vooghul who held the device.

The mist inside its hood cleared to reveal a recognisable face.

'Blueface,' screamed Lucy. 'What have they done to you?'

'Didn't I just *tell* you that?' sneered Raziel.

He bore little resemblance to the boy who performed for the Emperor. His eyes were like bottomless pools, full of despair and sadness.

The Transform-o-Matic

'*Blueface*, can you hear me?' said Lucy. The vomit rose in her throat again as she noticed that his body was made up of thousands of wafer thin sheets, each one glowing like a slide in a projector.

'Of course he can hear,' said Raziel. 'But he can answer only with my permission. Now, are you ready to give me the manuscript, or do you need another example of how hopeless your situation is?'

Lucy said nothing. Raziel took her hesitation as a refusal and signalled the other Vooghul to reveal itself. Was it the Emperor? Or the Dung Juggler? Or perhaps the Magician with some of his doves?

The face that presented itself was divided neatly down the middle of the nose and forehead, and leaning slightly to one side she could see that it was perfectly halved front and back as well, at least half an inch between the four sections of his head.

'Oh God, *no*,' said Lucy, feeling very, very sick.

She didn't attempt to speak to Tenby; instead she let out an involuntary whimper that made her feel even more insecure. The telltale signal didn't escape Raziel – he saw her resolve weakening and decided to step in with his final threat.

'You have less than thirty seconds to decide,' he said. 'And when those thirty seconds have passed I will kill your little friend. Not only that, when she is laying there, pretty, but quite, quite lifeless, then I will use the machine to create a new Vooghul. And when *that* is done you will still come with me, because you have no choice. Unless you would rather remain trapped in one strange world, with no chance of seeing your mother again?'

At this, Fenny began to cry, the tears pouring down her face like a stream in flood. Even though her eyes were red and puffed up Lucy couldn't help but notice how beautiful she was.

'You heard what I told Nisroc,' said Lucy. 'I don't believe all that rubbish about my mother. She died years ago.'

'Suit yourself,' said Raziel. 'But Nisroc told the truth. And now you have only twenty seconds remaining.'

Nisroc bristled and glowed again, but it was clear that she didn't dare to challenge Raziel for possession of Lucy.

'You know what I'd like to do Fenny?' said Lucy.

'No,' sobbed Fenny. 'What?'

'I'd like to explain to you what all this is about.'

'Ten seconds,' said Raziel.

'I'd like to tell you all about The Light, and how we came to be here and what we've done. I'd like to tell you all about the people we've met and the things we've seen.'

'Five seconds,' said Raziel.

'I'd like to show you the diamond sphere we saw in Dee's laboratory. I'd take you in my arms and wrap us both inside it to protect us from *him*.'

'Of *course* you would,' said Raziel. 'And when you have both suffocated inside this impossible contraption? What then?'

'Then we'd both be away from you, master Angel.'

'And I would take your bodies for conversion,' said Raziel. 'You would be mine forever. Now, do you want to watch your pretty little friend die in agony and be made into a Vooghul, or will you be sensible and hand over the manuscript?'

The angel flexed his fingers and extended them, palm upwards towards Lucy. As they stretched to the limit, a look of pain crept across Raziel's face.

Lucy felt the sweat run down her back as the angel's fingernails extended into short, razor-sharp knives. And when he put those evil looking blades next to Fenny's throat all the fight went out of her.

'I believe you're mad enough to do it,' said Lucy.

'Of *course* I am,' hissed Raziel. 'Madness and passion are all one.'

'But before I hand this thing over,' said Lucy, 'just tell me one thing.'

'Another one of your tricks?' said Raziel.

'No,' said Lucy. 'I *promise*. I just wanted to know why you allowed us to blow the horns.'

'Is that *all*?' said Raziel. 'Of all the questions you might ask an angel of God, you wish to know that?'

'Yes,' said Lucy.

'To satisfy your curiosity,' said Raziel. 'The fewer questions that remain in your head, the fewer barriers there are to your returning with us.'

'He's lying,' screamed Fenny. 'I can see right inside him, and he's lying, as plain as anything. He *had* to let you use the horns, because that's what you were always supposed to do. Ever since the tower was built, the horns have been waiting for you.'

'What do you mean?' said Lucy.

'This whole world was made for you,' yelled Fenny. 'The angels don't belong here, but you do Lucy. I can see it inside him.'

'Rubbish,' screamed Raziel.

'Don't listen to her,' barked Raziel. 'She's just a mere girl.'

'That'll be the same as me then,' said Lucy. She turned to Fenny with an almost invisible smile of pleasure dancing on her lips. 'Is that right Fenny?' she said. 'Is this place *really* here just for me?'

'Yes,' screamed Fenny, 'and that's what scares him the most.'

'The girl will say anything to save your skins,' screamed Raziel.

'We're dead anyway,' said Lucy. 'Why would she need to lie?'

'I'm not lying,' insisted Fenny. 'He had to let you get this far before he could do anything. He's scared of *you* Lucy.'

'This is complete nonsense,' said Raziel, puffing himself up.

'He watched you sit on the throne,' said Fenny, 'and that's when I saw his stomach all churned up in black and violet. He was terrified.'

'But why?' said Lucy.

'There *is* no why,' screamed Raziel. 'And there *was* no fear.'

'*Liar,*' screamed Fenny. '*Liar, liar, liar.*'

'Be *quiet*,' hissed Raziel, pressing the blades against her throat. 'Nothing you say can make the slightest difference. Either Miss Blake gives me The Light or you die. Whether I fear her or not is irrelevant.'

A look of disappointment spread across Fenny's face. She'd believed that revealing Raziel's thoughts would end it all. But she saw now that he was right – the angel held all the winning cards.

'Lucy, *please* don't give him what he wants,' said Fenny. 'I don't know what it is, but he wants it *so* badly. And he shouldn't be allowed to have it.'

'It's alright,' smiled Lucy, 'I'm not going to.'

'What?' said Raziel and Nisroc together.

'I've changed my mind again,' said Lucy. 'Us girls are like that.'

'Bring me the machine,' growled Raziel.

Fenny formed a silent scream as the angel's claws sliced her dress and drew four rivers of blood from her shoulders. She didn't cry out though, and more importantly for Lucy she didn't faint either – but the pain was written on her like the lines on a gargoyle's face.

The Transform-o-Matic

Blueface held out the Transform-o-Matic, but as Raziel was about to take hold of it he saw Nisroc cocking her head, as if listening for a noise. She rose into a hover, dragging Toby and Zenda into the air, their heads hanging like pendulums.

'What is it now?' hissed Raziel.

'A disturbance,' said Nisroc. 'I sense something approaching.'

'Our friend,' said Lucy, indicating the shadow that was gradually eclipsing the windows. 'Why not look for yourself? He's right behind you.'

'*Behind* me?' bellowed Raziel. 'Do you *really* think that a creature who fought in the first wars of heaven will fall for such a ruse? And suppose I *did* turn around – what do you intend to do then? Disappear into thin air, like your mother?'

Vovina

In the years that followed Lucy Blake's time in Assiah, the most popular myth by far was the story of Vovina, a dragon who spent countless centuries sleeping beneath the Imperial palace. Then, for a reason that nobody was able to explain, the creature awoke and rose out of the ground like heavenly fire in the west. Some say he dived into the setting sun, dragging the heart from the star to trail behind him in celebration. Some believed that the flames were a message from God, whilst others reckoned that the fire in the sky was the dragon's own. But all of them agreed on one thing. Having been freed from the weight of the palace and newly reunited with his scales, there was only one thing on his mind.

He intended to give thanks to the ones who set him free.

Vovina's sharp snout crashed through the vast central window, spraying shards of glass into the air then turning them to globules of flame by the fiery blast of his breath.

'*Duck,*' screamed Lucy. '*Fenny*, get *down.*'

Fenny did as she was told, but Raziel also removed himself from the firing line as the edges of the dragon's wings broke through in a shower of sparks and molten lead.

'He's got the angel,' squealed Fenny.

Vovina sailed over their heads and crashed down onto the temple floor.

'He's got the angel, he…'

Her words were lost amidst the sound of twisting, bending metal and the rushing air that tried to suck them out of the window.

But nobody was going anywhere.

Lucy grabbed hold of a stair rail. Vovina's white-hot feet were fused into the floor and Nisroc was anchored securely in his one free claw. Toby and Zenda in turn were tethered to Nisroc, so as long as she held them they were relatively safe.

Raziel hung onto a balustrade and Fenny clung on beside him, her hair streaming like flames in the wind. The torrent of air tested Lucy's grip, and she wrapped her legs around the bars to take the strain. Fenny copied her, but so did Raziel, who had shed his dark coat and began to grow his wings.

Lucy glanced at the dragon.

She could see why the angel was preparing to flee.

Vovina had collided with the central tower, shattering the structure into a million twinkling fragments. He was stunned and shaking his head to gather his wits, but he was still an awesome sight. His transparent skin revealed the fires that burned inside him – already glowing white-hot, but with an urgency that suggested they intended to grow even fiercer. Even so, he had a fight on his hands. Nisroc flapped and struggled, refusing to release her captives and even attempting to lift the weight of the dragon from the ground.

There was a creak from above as the roof dome started to collapse at the point where the shattered tower had torn free. Lacking support, the four horns tore through the ceiling and crashed down into the temple.

The golden horn of the air element smashed the throne of the Architect into tiny fragments, whilst the blue one disappeared into a stairwell in a pall of dust and debris. The green horn in turn destroyed most of the mosaic floor, sending up an explosion of black and white tiles that poured like rain in a bad dream. And the remaining fire horn fell on Vovina's back, ripping his scales and sending them flying in all directions. There was a yelp from the shadows, which Lucy recognised as one of the Henbegs. They had taken shelter from the falling debris, but now, having been pelted with dragon scales, they were running wild and looking for enemies to bite.

Lucy glanced at Raziel, whose wings were grown now and fully extended. He hovered above Fenny with some difficulty, but the rush of air through the window had lessened now and it was clear that he'd soon be able to take flight.

And when he did, Lucy knew that he would take Fenny with him.

She turned to Vovina, who was bleeding from his back, but had shaken off the impact of the horn. In fact he looked taller now, his maw belching white-hot flames and filling the temple with the stench of sulphur. Inside him, clearly visible through his skin, every artery, vein and capillary pulsed with white-hot liquid fire.

'He's going to take Fenny,' yelled Lucy.

'Actually I'm rather busy,' screamed the dragon. '*This* one is not going down without a fight.'

'This one is not going down at *all*,' bellowed Nisroc. She relinquished her hold on Toby and Zenda, dropping them unconscious onto the tiles.

Lucy shuddered as they hit, and the shock increased when she moved in closer. Fat oozed from their pores and flames burned in tiny, fizzling pools on the surface of their skin.

And there was nothing she could do to help. Vovina burned with such ferocity that it was impossible to approach them without being incinerated.

The Henbegs saw an opportunity though and rushed in. Protected from the heat by their thick skins, they licked every bit of exposed skin they could find, extinguishing the flames and simultaneously salving Toby and Zenda's wounds with their own special blend of spit.

'Oh, well done both of you,' yelled a tearful Lucy.

But Nisroc's tendrils were free now and sought Vovina's limbs, wrapping his forelegs and neck and encircling his scaly head. But the angel was no match for a dragon in full flame. Wherever her green shoots made contact they scorched and fizzled away, leaving nothing but curling bursts of flame and puffs of sulphurous gas.

And very soon there were no tendrils left.

'I'm *still* not going down,' screamed Nisroc.

But it was a forlorn cry.

Vovina held the angel in a single scaly claw, from which there was no escape. He lifted her level with his snout but didn't breathe on her straight away. Instead he turned to look at Lucy, as if seeking permission.

Lucy felt sick to her guts, because she knew what the dragon was asking and knew that it was wrong. But if she dithered then Raziel would escape. It was Nisroc's life or Fenny's, but even so, Lucy was determined to give the angel one last chance.

'Promise you won't hinder me if I try to stop Raziel,' she said, looking Nisroc straight in the eye.

'*Never*,' said Nisroc. 'We are both duty bound.'

'Then you leave me no choice,' said Lucy, nodding to the dragon.

'You have been a worthy adversary,' said Nisroc. 'Your mother...'

Nisroc never completed the sentence. The mouth they emerged from evaporated in a white-hot blast from Vovina's snout. There was no time for a scream and no time for Lucy to feel guilty, even as the burning flesh and scorched feathers tumbled around her. She *had* to stop Raziel taking Fenny.

But whilst she had been dealing with Nisroc, her sworn enemy had flown out of the window where the lead ran like a silver river and images of angels sagged into molten pools.

Lucy stood motionless, unable to believe how close they had come to rescuing Fenny. Raziel was powerful in flight, and already hundreds of feet from the tower.

He glanced back just long enough to sneer at Lucy.

'I could melt him from the skies if you wish,' said Vovina.

'You'd hurt Fenny,' said Lucy.

'Then climb onto my back and we will follow,' said Vovina.

'Have you *any* idea how hot your scales are?' said Lucy. 'I'm practically melting as it is – and my friends are hurt.'

She glanced at Toby and Zenda. They were groggy and stumbled as they tried to stand, eventually deciding to stay on the floor until they recovered.

'I'm sorry I took such a long time to answer your call,' said Vovina. 'I had to wait for my scales to return. Perhaps if I had come sooner things might have been different?'

'It doesn't matter,' said Lucy. 'We can't change what has happened.'

'Then we should take some time to talk,' said Vovina. 'I have a thousand tales from the old wars.'

'Some other time,' said Lucy. 'I really *would* like to make friends with a dragon, but we have to leave soon, or we'll be trapped in this world.'

'Is the place not to your liking?' said Vovina.

'It is,' said Lucy, 'but none of us belongs here.'

Vovina bowed and shuffled his way through the glass shards, settling on the narrow ledge outside the window. But he was only there for a matter of seconds before popping his great head back through the window.

'You have visitors,' he said.

'Well I hope they're friendly,' said Lucy. She was exhausted, and didn't relish the prospect of another fight.

'Oh yes,' smiled Vovina. 'I think these *must* be friendly.'

Lucy made a path through the debris. And when she finally made it to the outside ledge she couldn't believe what she saw. The visitors were baby ornithopters, all crowded together and shivering with the cold.

'I am the flight-child known as Blink Bonny,' said the closest bird. 'First daughter of our mother, the Once Visible.'

'Who?' said Toby.

Lucy glanced at Toby and Zenda. They were on their feet and looked like they had spent far too long under a sun lamp, but apart from that they seemed alright.

'Our mother,' repeated the ornithopter. 'She who was Once Visible.'

'And now presumably isn't?' sneered Zenda.

There was a round of squawking from the other birds, but Blink Bonny lifted a wing to silence them.

'We have a mission,' she said. 'To carry Lucy Blake to freedom.'

'Brilliant,' said Toby. 'And me?'

'Of course,' said Blink Bonny.

'And, umm, what about me?' said Zenda.

Blink Bonny turned to Lucy.

'Is the insolent one to be carried also?' she asked.

'Unfortunately,' said Lucy. 'But if you accidentally drop her I don't think anybody will mind.'

'I see,' said Blink Bonny. 'Umm, is that a joke?'

'Only just,' said Lucy.

'I thought so,' said Blink Bonny. 'Flatty, our nest-mother, did mention that you had a sense of humour.'

'Do you mean he, umm, I mean *she* is still alive?' said Lucy eagerly; not wanting to admit that she had believed Flatty to be a boy.

'Only in our memories,' said another, nuzzling his way to the front. 'I am Minoru, brother of Blink Bonny, and most honoured to meet the great Lucy Blake.'

'Pleased to meet you,' said Toby, grinning as he gestured at the rest of the flock. 'And who are all this lot?'

'Our brothers and sisters,' said Minoru, lifting a wing to introduce them. 'These are Firdaussi and Tracery and Ladas who fly on my right wing.'

'And here are Bayardo and Coronach and Hal o' the Wynd,' said Blink Bonny. 'They fly on my left wing.'

'Well we're very pleased to meet you all,' said Lucy, trying to keep track of all the flapping wings and bobbing heads.

'And we're all honoured to meet *you*,' they squawked at once.

'I can't believe it,' shouted an enthusiastic bird at the back. 'We're actually in the presence of the creator.'

'Finally we get to meet her,' screeched another.

'Hey, you at the front, get your head down,' squawked another. 'I can't see a thing. Is the famous Lucy Blake still there?'

'Yes I am,' smiled Lucy, turning to speak to Minoru. 'So, could you really help us to escape?'

'We are not fully grown,' said Minoru, 'and our cockpits are not properly developed, but you could fly on our backs if you can stand the cold.'

'And if you can make use of the scant air,' said Blink Bonny. 'You must not expect to breathe normally until we lose some height.'

'Then what are we waiting for?' said Toby, stepping over the remains of Nisroc. 'There's nothing left for us here.'

'It would seem not,' said Blink Bonny, poking her head through the window to survey the damage. 'So *now* all that remains is to decide which of us will carry the larger one.'

Zenda's expression turned from 'dead calm' to 'monsoon', but just as quickly it turned back again to 'slightly ruffled' when she realised she was going to have to be pleasant.

'Maybe if she sits astride *two* of you?' suggested Toby, stepping out onto the ledge. The Henbegs followed him, each eyeing the other suspiciously and growling with a note so low it was almost inaudible.

'Whoever carries her we must move quickly,' said Minoru. 'Only then will we have a chance of catching up with the angel.'

'You mean you can out-fly him?' said Toby.

'There is only one way to find out,' said Blink Bonny.

Precious seconds were leaking away, but Lucy was reluctant to leave. She stepped back into the temple for a final look. Even with all the destruction they had wrought, it was still a beautiful place. And she was still convinced

Kovina

that the charred and melted wreckage had messages for her – if only she had the time and the ability to read them.

'Luce, we have to go,' urged Toby.

'I know,' she said, stepping back onto the ledge.

'Umm, yeah, *about* that,' said Toby as he waited for his friend. 'There's just one thing I want to know before we set off.'

'Yes?' said Minoru impatiently.

'Where exactly are we going?' said Toby.

'We had intended to follow the angel,' said Blink Bonny. 'Is that not your wish?'

'It is,' said Lucy, emerging from the temple. 'But I think we'd all be a lot happier if we knew where he was going.'

'I think we might *all* be happier with that knowledge,' sighed Minoru, 'but surely only the angel himself can know that?'

1083

Bright Squadrons

The ornithopters were overjoyed at the thought of rescuing the creator and fulfilling their mother's prophecy, so most of them didn't protest as their passengers mounted, even when great handfuls of back-feathers were pulled out in the attempt.

The exception was Toby's designated carrier, who was Blink Bonny.

'If you pull any more out, I might not be able to fly,' she complained.

'I don't *think* so,' said Zenda, slipping around on Firdaussi's back. 'You fly with wing feathers, not the ones on your body.'

'She was just being polite,' said Toby. 'Look underneath the feathers at the base of the wings you'll find a handle.'

'A handle?' snorted Zenda. 'On a *bird*?'

'Actually it's a bone,' laughed Lucy, climbing onto Minoru. 'But it's just as well they've got it – we'd have no chance of staying on otherwise.'

'Are we all prepared?' squawked Blink Bonny.

'I think there might be another problem,' said Toby.

'It's the dragon,' said Zenda. 'He's frying us all with his heat. But once we get away from him we'll be fine.'

'That's not what I meant,' said Toby. 'Look at the net – it's closing in.'

'*Net*?' said Zenda.

When Vovina flew in from the palace he blasted through the cordon of scarabs protecting the tower, but they had regrouped now, into a deadly spherical blockade.

'Vovina?' said Lucy. 'Can you make a gap?'

'Certainly,' he grinned. 'Would you like huge, or absolutely massive?'

'Let's go for absolutely massive,' yelled Toby.

Vovina trotted a few steps, and then, with a scratch of claws on stone he disappeared over the edge in a most inelegant flying manoeuvre. It was more of a controlled stumble, and nothing like the take-off they expected from an ancient warrior. But after dropping twenty feet or so, Vovina spread his great wings, and as they filled with air they gave a thunderous crack, which startled the ornithopters. It was like a hundred leather rugs being beaten at once – an invitation to witness him rising into the dusk sky, his body glowing like a furnace, his wings turned to fiery sheets of lava.

'I'm glad he's on our side,' said Ladas.

'And I'm glad he got off our perch,' squawked Bayardo. 'My feathers were beginning to singe.'

'Look,' said Coronach, 'he's flying straight at the scarabs.'

As the dragon approached, the scarabs gathered into a tight bunch where they thought he might break through. It was a good idea, or at least Vovina thought so, because the closer they got the more he could take out in one breath – and the longer it would take them to regroup.

'Are you all ready?' shouted Lucy.

Everyone nodded and one after another the ornithopters made a short run and took to the air, all managing much more elegantly than the dragon.

'Umm, *wow*, you've got *legs*,' observed Lucy, as they left the ledge.

'Of course,' said Minoru. 'Haven't you ever heard of evolution?'

'No,' said Lucy, with a nervous smile. 'But I've heard of miracles.'

She looked across at Zenda who was scowling fit to burst. Firdaussi had dipped severely just after take-off, and she took it as a personal insult.

Lucy glanced down, gripping the bony handles tight. There was nothing but ten thousand feet of sky below them, and *that* was followed by a lot of very hard looking ground.

'If the dragon doesn't make it,' yelled Zenda, 'I'm turning back.'

'You are *not*,' shouted Lucy. 'If he doesn't get through then we'll fight the scarabs ourselves.'

'*Whoo-hoo-hoo*,' yelled Minoru, picking up speed as he went into a shallow dive. 'We're going into battle with the creator. What a story we'll have to tell our chicks.'

'*If* we survive,' said Lucy, so that only Minoru could hear.

'I know,' he whispered, 'but we must encourage the others, mustn't we?'

Lucy smiled, shivering deeply in air that blasted her face and flowed like an arctic blizzard over her back. The cold was turning her skin to gooseflesh.

Up ahead, the scarabs tightened their net further, giving the impression that they might be able to stop the dragon. With less than a hundred feet to go, Vovina took a huge breath. His insides dimmed, like a densely populated city suffering a Lectric cut.

'What's happening?' screamed Zenda. 'He can't do that, he....'

A rush of air blasted from the dragon's snout, turning into words that none of them could understand as it emerged.

'*Eeshiah, Heebeyow, Fanori, Cheekoru, Kabah,*' he screamed.

And with less than fifty feet to go, the words and the air surrounding them turned to flame – a ball of searing cosmic fire summoned from the heart of a star by a spell that only dragons know.

The scarabs at the centre of the blast simply ceased to exist, vaporised by bolts of pure, dancing plasma. Those on the outer edges of the fury fared no better, disintegrating slightly before they too were turned to gas. Further out still they were swamped in hot, blue flames that consumed their outer shells and sent their charred innards plummeting towards the plains.

'I think that will do for now,' said Vovina. He turned to make sure that the ornithopters were following.

'I'm right behind you,' squawked Minoru.

'We all are,' shouted Blink Bonny.

'Then we're on our way home,' yelled Lucy, her boundless joy floating on the cold air.

'It's getting dark,' said Minoru eventually. 'But if you look below you'll see the outer wall.'

Lucy leaned to one side and saw the curtain wall approaching. It was a lot closer than she expected.

'We've lost height,' explained Minoru. 'I came lower to keep you warm.'

'Th-thank you,' said Lucy, her teeth chattering.

'This is the northern edge,' said Minoru. 'Just below us are the Winding Crayns – possibly the last you will see of this world.'

Lucy stared in awe at the huge, spindly crane-forms that stood like tall seabirds watching for crabs. Then she buried her head in Minoru's feathers and tried to forget all the things they were leaving behind. After all that had happened, there was a small part of her that didn't want to leave.

'Minoru,' she said, leaning forward to whisper in his ear. 'I think I want to see Assiah for one last time.'

There was no sign that the ornithopter had heard, but the colour of the sky lightened and Lucy saw that they were turning gently, peeling away from the rest of the group. Ahead, and slightly below them, were Ladas and Hal 'o the Wynd, who were carrying the Henbegs. They hesitated slightly when they noticed Minoru's change of course, but kept following the dragon as he in turn pursued the angel.

'You *will* be able to catch up, won't you?' said Lucy.

'Possibly,' said Minoru. He gave a shudder that might have been a belly laugh. 'But we must be quick – the scarabs will be organising a pursuit of their own.'

Lucy had heard that if you flew high enough you could see the curvature of the earth in space, and although she never thought to witness that sight in her own world, she was able to confirm that the same principle worked in Assiah – only it wasn't a curve she saw.

They were out beyond the encircling wall now, and for the first time she was able to divine the true shape of the city. It was built on the uppermost surface of a conical plug of rock that was riddled with a maze of huge pipes. It looked as if someone long ago had banished the city to the skies, scooping it up from wherever it had grown, complete with sewers and subways and secret underground tunnels.

She sighed, knowing that she would never explore its mysteries. Then her heart sank as her gaze moved back to the upper surface of the world. The Migdal was a distant sliver of darkness against a backdrop of storm cloud, but even here Lucy felt its threat. But it had once had a good side, and it was *that* which she was searching for, as if she needed to see the face of virtue before she departed the world forever.

'We must go,' said Minoru, turning to resume their original course. 'And you must say goodbye to this world forever – but you will see many others.'

'How do you know?' said Lucy.

'Our Mother, the Once Visible told us,' said Minoru. 'She said the creator will travel to many worlds, and that we would be the ones to help her escape from this.'

'I hope she was r-right,' shivered Lucy.

'She was,' said Minoru proudly. 'And now it's time to rejoin the others.'

'You can see them already?' said Lucy.

'No,' he said, 'but I can hear them.'

Swoosh.

'What was that?' hissed Lucy.

She ducked as a dark shape brushed against her.

'Hundreds of insects,' screeched Minoru. 'We have come back too far – and now we must fight.'

'No,' yelled Lucy, as another scarab skimmed past. 'We'll out-fly them. You can *do* that, can't you?'

'But what about the stories?' said the ornithopter. He wheeled quickly on one wing, reversing their course. 'The nest-tales will say that Minoru was the only one to run away.'

'The hero will be the one who carries the creator back to Farperoo,' said Lucy. 'And that's you.'

'But the scarabs,' said Minoru.

'There are too many,' yelled Lucy. 'Don't you know there's a time for fighting and a time for running?'

'Thank you for reminding me,' said Minoru.

'Then *f-fly*,' shivered Lucy. 'F-f-fly like the wind.'

Minoru shuddered as his powerful wings bent into the task of pursuit and they left the scarabs in their wake. For a while their only companions were a huge flock of starlings lofted up on the darkening weather – but eventually even they were unable to keep pace.

'We have left them behind,' said Minoru. '*All* of them.'

'I kn-know,' said Lucy. She shivered with the intense cold, but her voice was trembling for another reason.

Quim and Dee and Madimi were slipping quietly into her past.

She buried her face in Minoru's back, hoping that he wouldn't hear her cry. But the sobbing vibrated his bones, and as he dutifully carried her into a gathering darkness that even he didn't understand, the ornithopter shed a few small tears of his own.

The Nexus

They had all noticed Minoru's deviation from the route, but the rest of the ornithopters had stayed on the angel's trail, stretching into a dull, straggly line behind the brilliant point of light that was Vovina. Safe from harm now, they began calling to each other with long, mournful honks – and it was the sound of this secret language known only to the birds, that led Minoru back.

'They're just ahead,' he said. 'And the dragon is still with them.'

Lucy peered into the darkness. There was a dim red glow in the distance, and she could just hear the call of the ornithopters.

'Minoru?' she said. 'What does all that honking mean?'

'It is the birth of a legend,' he replied. 'The first ever telling of a story called *The Bright Squadrons and the Escape to Farperoo*.'

'Then shouldn't you should be telling it as well?' smiled Lucy.

Minoru nodded and bellowed like a goose with a sore throat. It was even louder than the Grimston foghorn, and when *that* thing spoke, everyone for miles around listened. The only people who didn't cover their ears were the ones trying to stop their false teeth dropping out.

'*Honka, honka, hoo-onko-onko-onk,*' he called. '*Honk, hoo-onko-onko-onk.*'

They quickly bore down on the rest of the group as the others spotted them and slowed down. The dragon dropped to the rear of the squadron, and as they passed him Lucy felt a welcome blast of heat. She waved at Vovina and received a snort of flame in reply. Then she waved at the empty ornithopters who were bringing up the rear, and those carrying the Henbegs and Zenda. And finally she waved at Toby as they flew past Blink Bonny and took position at the head of the squadron.

'And now what?' she whispered, staring into the dark skies ahead.

'Now we continue,' whispered Minoru, his powerful wings carrying them straight into the void.

The Nexus

For eight whole hours their flight had been purposeful and direct, but now, with a subtle change in their surroundings there was a decision to be made. The sky was dark above them and even darker below, and in between those two infinite limits was a band of purplish-violet haze that Lucy found it difficult to look at. Within the glow was a complex maze of pipes that constantly joined and separated, making and breaking what she felt sure were connections to other places.

'Where are we?' she whispered.

'This is a crossroads,' said Minoru, 'but not quite so simple as two dusty tracks meeting on a level. There *are* dusty tracks here, I'm sure, but there are glistening crystal highways too, and paths laid with spikes. There are paths written on smoke, and roads and byways that exist only for as long as the storyteller speaks. And each of these ways crosses with every other, in order to confuse the unwary traveller.'

'But what about you?' said Lucy. 'Are you confused?'

'We fly by instinct,' shouted Blink Bonny, flapping alongside. 'We were born with a purpose, and in taking you home we will achieve it. As for those other routes – we could no more navigate those than an ant could navigate the stars. We follow a golden thread, laid by a weaver of tales.'

'Umm, yes,' said Lucy, 'but what…'

'*Scarabs,*' yelled Vovina, brightening at the prospect of conflict. 'Below us, above us and behind us.'

Lucy twisted round.

The dragon was surrounded by a swarm of insects flying in such a tight formation that they interfered with his wings.

'They're crowding him out of the sky,' shouted Toby.

'Then the time for glory has arrived,' screamed Minoru.

The ornithopters broke formation and wheeled back to ram the insects and forcing them to drop away from Vovina. The dragon gave a grateful nod of the head, then shot them down in a sea of flame.

'Keep at it,' shouted Minoru, 'and you'll all be in the legend.'

'That would be lovely,' yelled Lucy, holding on tight as they turned and dived. 'But can we try to make sure this legend has a happy ending?'

'They haven't a chance against all of us *and* a dragon,' said Minoru.

Seconds later, Lucy's teeth rattled in her head like she'd been hit with a plank. In his enthusiasm, Minoru had smashed into a scarab too hard, and as he struggled to recover the enemy had managed to embed his claws into the ornithopter's neck.

'*Minoru*,' screamed Lucy, her knuckles whitening.

With the insect firmly attached he began to fall, dragging Lucy down with him. But this was no time for panic – the scarab's head was just inches from Lucy's and it was trying to pull forward to get at her. She dodged from side to side as the sticky tongue darted towards her, leaning back out of reach of the snapping jaws. But there was a limit to how far she could move – she needed to keep a grip on the handle bones or be dragged off Minoru's back by the rushing air.

And then the insect worked it out. Instead of reaching for Lucy's head, he snapped at each of her hands in turn. All she could do was let go with the hand he was attacking then reach back and grab hold again as he turned his attention to the other.

'Luce, get your head down,' cried Toby.

'I can't,' screamed Lucy. 'I have to see which hand he's after.'

'You have to *trust* me,' shouted Toby. 'Get down, *now*.'

Lucy closed her eyes and buried her face in Minoru's feathers, expecting to feel the scarab's jaws on her neck. Instead, there was a flash of heat, and she glanced up to see Vovina's battle-scarred belly sailing over the top of them. He was soon gone though, and so was the scarab.

Lucy watched impassively as the insect fell into the void, dragging a trail of flame and smoke behind it.

'*Whoo-hoo*,' yelled Toby. 'A brilliant precision burning.'

'Thank you,' shouted Vovina, turning sharply.

'And thanks from us too,' said Minoru. 'For a moment there I thought the legend was going to end badly.'

'Me too,' said Lucy, searching the skies for their saviour. '*Vovina*? Where did he go?'

'He's gone after the other scarabs,' shouted Toby.

'Then we have to help,' said Lucy.

The smell of her own singed hair was fresh in her nostrils.

'If we delay,' said Minoru, 'then we will lose the angel's trail.'

'And you will remain here forever,' said Blink Bonny.

The ornithopters circled so their passengers could see what was going on around them. The sky had turned a dusky pink, but in the direction that Vovina had flown a shimmering blue curtain hung in the sky.

It extended upwards and downwards as far as the eye could see.

'We have crossed the veil,' said Firdaussi.

'We'll wait until he returns,' said Toby, 'then *he* can cross it too.'

'I'm afraid that cannot be,' said Minoru.

'Why?' said Lucy.

'Yeah, why?' asked Toby. 'We could definitely use a dragon at home.'

'Look into your hearts,' said Minoru. 'You already know the answer.'

Lucy thought for a moment, and then it all became clear.

'The sun has risen,' she said. 'Assiah is sealed.'

'Just so,' said Blink Bonny. 'A new day has dawned.'

Lucy kept glancing backward as their journey continued, hoping to catch sight of the friend they had left behind. But of Vovina there was no sign, not even the faintest of pink stains in the darkness that might have marked his distant return. There was just a touch of heat on Lucy's skin, as if some fragment of his warmth had been left to console her. And it was whilst she bathed in the comfort of that thought that she heard the faint sound of wind chimes and detected the merest taste of a sea breeze on her lips.

'The stars have disappeared,' said Toby, 'and the ornithopters are flying closer together.'

'And the sky is suddenly much darker,' yelled Zenda.

'Minoru?' said Lucy. 'What's happening? Where are we?'

'I know,' grinned Toby. 'Just look straight down and concentrate on the dark and tell me what you see.'

'Dark,' said Zenda.

'And, umm, I *think* I can see floorboards,' said Lucy. 'They're a long way down, but it certainly *looks* like a wooden floor.'

'And now look up,' said Toby, unable to stop smiling.

Lucy glanced up, and for a moment it looked as though the stars were back. But if they were, then someone had arranged them in a neat row.

'Lights,' she said, 'I can see old broken light shades, and Lectric bulbs.'

She glanced sideways and spotted doors and picture frames flashing by. And as the birds slowed down, the paintings and the ceiling and the floor got closer. Soon their surroundings were so cramped that the ornithopters had to retract their wings and they dropped rather gracelessly onto the polished wooden floor, skidding along like fairground ducks.

'I think we're there,' said Toby.

Blink Bonny skittered to a halt.

'Then our task is done,' said Minoru, piling in like a goose landing on ice.

'I suppose that means *you* can't stay either,' said Lucy.

'Either?' said Minoru, as Lucy dismounted. 'Are you *still* thinking about the dragon?'

'I knew there was no hope of him coming with us,' sighed Lucy. 'But we didn't even get a chance to listen to his stories.'

'Ah, yes, the story,' said Minoru, with a serious face. 'Does the escape to Farperoo end here? I was hoping we could…'

'This is not our world,' said Blink Bonny. 'But the legend of the Bright Squadrons will be told in nests for generation upon generation, and the names of the chicks who returned the creator to her own world will become part of history.'

'Goodbye Lucy Blake,' said Minoru.

'Yes, *goodbye*,' came the cries from further back down the corridor.

'And goodbye Toby,' said Blink Bonny.

'Yes, *goodbye Toby*,' came the echo from the rest.

Zenda sat astride Firdaussi, her head cramped against the ceiling. She waited for a farewell but the ornithopter found some urgent scratching to do and she had to climb down and wait for ages before he succumbed to her icy stare.

'Umm, bye then,' he said reluctantly.

'*Bye then*,' echoed the others.

Zenda snorted. Then a smile spread across her face as she realised there was still a problem to be solved.

'I know we're all very clever around here,' she said, 'apart from myself that is – but how exactly were you intending to leave?'

'Back the way we came,' said Minoru. 'We cannot return to Assiah, but we should be able to reach the veil of the Nexus.'

'Go on then,' grinned Zenda, 'let's *see* you.'

There was a lot of shuffling and flapping, but they soon discovered that none of them could move.

'I see what she means,' said Blink Bonny. 'The corridor is only slightly wider than an ornithopter chick, and we cannot turn around.'

'It *is* a bit crowded,' said Lucy. 'Can you make it to the door at the end?'

Minoru waddled along as best he could, with Toby and Lucy going on ahead. When they got to the door they found it open and were able to squeeze inside. Lucy called the others to follow and when they were all safely inside and the corridor was empty she turned each ornithopter around. Then she gave each one a hug as they left, saving the biggest of all for Blink Bonny and Minoru.

'Thank you ornithopters,' she said. 'You saved our lives.'

'And thank *you*,' said Minoru. 'The name of Lucy Blake will be kept alive forever in the legend – and yours too Master Tobermory.'

'What about me?' said Zenda. 'Will I be in the legend as well?'

'Firdaussi might insist on the truth being told,' said Minoru.

Zenda beamed at him, and turned to smirk at Lucy.

'But then again,' said Minoru, 'he might say that he came along simply to protect our wings, and that he flew without a passenger.'

And with that, the bird waddled out into the corridor and with a single soulful honk, he was gone.

FX-3

'Close the bloody door will you?' snapped Zenda. 'We don't want those stupid ornithopters coming back *do* we?'

'No chance of that,' said Toby. 'Anyway, you're only upset because they didn't want you in their legend.'

'Yes, well we're back now,' smirked Zenda, 'and just in case you need reminding, I'm an adult and you two are a couple of scrawny kids. And as for *you* two,' she added, looking at the Henbegs.

The crocodiles gave a threatening growl, then wandered off to sniff at the skirting boards, eager to discover a way out before anyone else did.

'So where exactly are we?' said Lucy.

'Some kind of store room,' grinned Toby. 'You know how to travel don't you Luce? Janitors slop rooms, airing cupboards, and now *this* place.'

'Well it's not a store room,' said Zenda cocking her head. 'Umm, wait a minute, is that voices I can hear?'

'Not you and your voices again,' sighed Toby.

'She was right last time,' said Lucy.

'The press is *always* right,' said Zenda, holding her hair back to listen better. 'And the voices are coming from the other side of this wall.'

'Yes, I've been looking at that,' said Toby. 'It's more like a bit of wobbly plywood than a wall. In fact it looks so thin it might just be cardboard.'

'And I know this sounds unlikely,' said Lucy, 'but I could *swear* I heard someone mention Doctor Dee just then.'

'Impossible,' said Zenda. 'We're in Inguland, I just *know* we are.'

'And how do you work that out?' said Toby.

'Two things,' said Zenda. 'The name stencilled on the plywood says *Fred Green and Sons, Streatham.* Now correct me if I'm wrong, but all the time we were in that other place we didn't come across a single Fred Green or Herbert Jones. They all had stupid names like Bendysquirps Popsqueak or Gruntfondle Fartsprocket.'

A growl emerged from the Henbegs, but it was difficult to say which. They were exploring the far reaches, sticking their snouts into dark corners in the search for interesting doors, or failing that, edible insects.

'That's true,' said Toby. 'Not that I like to agree with you. And what was the second thing that makes you think we're back home?'

'The air,' said Zenda. 'It *smells* different.'

Everyone took a careful breath, as if they were tasting a fine wine.

'I hate to admit it,' said Lucy, 'but I think she's right again.'

'Of course I am,' smirked Zenda. 'Now, are we going to stand here for the rest of our lives or shall we break down the wall?'

Toby fished in his pockets and surprised himself yet again by producing Quim's favourite scissors. It seemed that every time he put them away he managed to forget all about them, and every time he found them again it felt like he was discovering the lost continent.

'These will do nicely,' he said, hacking a hole in the cardboard.

They punched their way into the space beyond and were surprised to find a large, matronly woman standing with her back to them. She was on the other side of a huge sheet of glass, and unlike the group of people she was talking to, was blissfully unaware of the strangers who had appeared behind her.

'One of John Dee's first achievements was the production of a play by Aristophanes,' she said. 'It was called *Peace*, and required the use of some very special stage props. In fact Dee was almost tried as a sorcerer, because people were unable to see how it was done. The only explanation they could come up with was that he had used some kind of dark magic.'

'I *told* you I heard Dee's name,' whispered Lucy. 'And look at the stuff in this display. It's exactly like we saw in his library.'

'Don't you think we should be getting out?' said Zenda, tapping on the glass to attract the woman's attention.

It worked a lot quicker than she had expected.

'What on *earth* are you doing in there?' screamed the guide. 'Get out at once, you idiots. Those are priceless exhibits.'

'Open the door then,' mouthed Lucy through the glass.

The guide did so and stepped inside, intending to issue a stern lecture about how to behave in a museum – but then she spotted something in the corner of her eye, which looked worryingly like a crocodile.

When she looked again it was gone, but the tour group were still there; faces eagerly pressed against the glass and waiting to see what she did next.

'I don't know how you got in here,' said the guide, her eyes narrowing, 'or why you look like survivors from a warehouse fire, but I have a sneaking suspicion that if I ask the question I'll get a load of nonsense in return.'

'So?' said Zenda.

'So I'm not going to give you the satisfaction,' snapped the guide. '*Now*, would you mind getting out of my museum?'

'I thought museums belonged to everyone?' said Lucy.

'Do you see this badge?' screamed the guide. 'It says *official* guide – which means that the museum is a lot more mine than it is yours. It also gives me the right to ask what you're doing here – only I'm not going to.'

'We were looking at the exhibits,' said Lucy, 'and we came from, umm, well actually now I come to think of it I forget – it runs in my family.'

'What does?' said the guide.

'I can't remember,' said Lucy.

'Amnesia,' said Toby helpfully.

He watched a small boy on the other side of the glass pick his nose.

'I've heard enough,' said the guide. 'I'm going to call security.'

'We're going,' said Lucy, 'and we weren't trying to steal your exhibits. In fact I've seen enough of them to last a lifetime. We're sick of fighting angels and we just want to get home.'

'*Angels?*' said the guide, tapping Lucy on the shoulder. 'Did you say angels? *Hello?* Are you listening to me?'

'Umm, no, I mean yes,' said Lucy, looking distracted. She shot a glance at Toby. 'I thought I heard something in the corridor.'

'*Corridor?*' said the guide. 'What corridor?'

'Behind the display case,' said Lucy. 'That's how we got in.'

'Impossible,' said the guide. 'It's a solid wall.'

'Well in that case,' said Lucy, 'I must have been hearing things.'

'The only thing *you're* going to hear is the sound of a cell door slamming,' said the guide.

'Oh please, not another one,' said Toby. 'We've had enough of that too. We thought people might be pleased to see us when we got home.'

'Of course,' said the guide. 'Security will be extremely pleased.'

'In that case,' said Lucy, pushing past her, 'we'd better be going.'

It was suddenly busier. Another group, all craning their necks to see what was going on, had joined the tour.

'I saw something just then,' said the nose-picking boy. 'It was a handbag that looked like a crocodile.'

'What have I told you about telling lies?' said the boy's mother.

'No, honestly,' he said, looking for somewhere to wipe his bogey. 'It was looking straight at me.'

As Lucy pushed past the boy she gave him a friendly smile.

'Keep up the work with the lies,' she said. 'You never know, one day they might just come true.'

'Hey, come back,' shouted the guide. She ran after Lucy and grabbed her by the shoulders, having realised that there was something deeper going on. 'I heard the boy,' she said. 'Something about a crocodile?'

'*Two* actually,' said Lucy. 'They're called Henbegs. Although now I come to think of it, one of them isn't *really* a Henbeg. She's just pretending.'

The guide frowned, unsure where the story began and reality ended.

'Oh, and by the way,' smiled Lucy. 'Do you remember what you said about Doctor Dee and the scarab? Well he did it with wires and magnets and smoke and mirrors. Oh, and something else, called a Pax rope. In fact I just happen to have one of those in my pock...'

'You've met John Dee?' scoffed the guide. '*Doctor* John Dee – a man who lived in Elizabethan times and died some three hundred and fifty years before you were born?'

'Of course,' smiled Lucy. 'I first met him at the big house near the Morty Lakes.'

'Yeah, me too,' grinned Toby. 'The Emperor was after us, so we jumped from the overhang window and crashed through the dome and ended up in his library, and...'

'Yes, yes, I'm *sure* you did,' said the woman. 'And I suppose he let you in on all his great secrets as well?'

'Some of them,' said Lucy. 'We know how to use the shew stone.'

'Oh you *do*, do you?' said the guide.

'Yes,' said Lucy, 'and by the way…'

'Ye-es?' said the guide.

'You see those Sigillum Dei you've got under the table of practice?'

'*Ye-es?*' she said, her eyes narrowing to slits.

'Well you've got them under the wrong corners,' smiled Lucy. 'Do you want me to show you the correct way?'

'No, actually, I don't think I *do*,' said the guide.

'Oh well,' said Lucy. 'It's up to you.'

'Yes, actually it *is* up to me. I'm the senior person here, and I think I can safely say I know more about John Dee than you do.'

'Ah,' smiled Lucy, 'but you haven't *met* him though, have you?'

'And neither have you,' said the guide.

'We have,' protested Toby.

'Then you'll have seen some interesting books,' sneered the guide. 'When you were visiting the dead sorcerer's library all those hundreds of years ago.'

'He had *thousands*,' said Lucy, 'but there were just twenty four of them in the main circle – twelve of them standing on lecterns and the others hanging from the ceiling on long chains.'

'Twenty four?' gasped the guide. 'But we only know of twelve volumes.'

'Well you learn something new every day, don't you?' laughed Lucy.

'Apparently,' said the guide, suddenly eager. 'Umm, is there anything else you can tell me about these chained volumes?'

'Loads,' said Lucy, cupping her ear, 'but we don't have time – I think we might be being chased by giant scarabs.'

'Oh, God, *yes*,' said Toby. 'I can hear them. They must have followed us down the corridor.'

'Yes, and *I'm* Helen of Troy,' said the curator with a knowing smirk.

'Suit yourself,' said Lucy, 'but if I were you Helen I'd duck.'

Lucy and Toby dived to the floor as one after another four giant insects crashed through the cardboard partition, then through the glass and out into the museum.

'I can't understand it,' shouted Toby. 'I thought Vovina got them all.'

'Perhaps these are the clever ones?' shouted Lucy.

She ducked as one swooped overhead. People screamed and ran in all directions, their hands raised in horror.

'They must have been on this side of the veil when the world was sealed,' said Zenda.

'For *once* we agree,' said Lucy.

'Tell me about the chained books,' screamed the guide. She was hiding behind a glass display case, peering through the mechanism of a giant orrery.

'Actually I think we're going to be a bit busy,' shouted Lucy, 'perhaps next time?'

In a matter of seconds the scarabs had changed a sedate museum into a cattle stampede, apparently intending to destroy the exhibits in their attempt to escape. One of them toppled a huge Gyptian Mummy, whilst two of its companions munched on the remains of a rare three million year old fish. But the fourth creature was hovering, eyeing the place carefully; as if it knew exactly what it was looking for.

'That'll be the clever one,' said Toby, squatting down behind a Gyptian sarcophagus. 'The one with the beady eyes.'

'But he hasn't seen us yet,' said Lucy.

'Great,' grinned Toby, indicating an emergency exit. 'Shall we run for it?'

'Go,' said Lucy, 'and pray that scarabs can't read exit signs.'

'Actually,' said Toby, 'I've just noticed another very slight problem.'

'Don't tell me,' sighed Lucy. 'If I turn round now, I'm not going to find Zenda, am I?'

'Right,' said Toby, 'so that's *half* of the bad news out of the way.'

'Don't you just *love* her?' said Lucy, turning to speak to the one remaining handbag. 'And I suppose you're the *real* Henbeg are you?'

'*Growwf,*' said the creature.

'So Zenda has taken Pixy,' said Toby. 'I can't imagine what she's thinking of, but I'm willing to bet it involves instant fame and a pile of money.'

They burst through the emergency exit and ran down a narrow alley to the front of the museum where they raced down the broad stone steps and out through the black iron gates. A cluster of hawkers was gathered in the street outside. They were selling souvenirs and maps, but one in particular caught Lucy's attention. He was roasting chestnuts that smelled good enough to eat. And they *looked* good enough to eat too, which for Lucy was the final proof that they had actually left Assiah.

'Hey, get your money out or move on,' said the nut roaster, 'that smelly coat of yours is interfering with the waft of my produce.'

'*Waft?*' grinned Toby. 'Is that some kind of advertising talk?'

'Might be,' said the vendor. 'So are you buying, or what? There's a queue forming behind you.'

'Mum told us to come and get our dinners from you,' said Lucy, realising that they had spent their last penny.

'Oh, *did* she now?' said the nut seller. 'And did this mother of yours give you any cash?'

'No,' said Lucy, speaking up so everyone could hear. 'But you've been told over and over again that you're not allowed to charge your own children for their dinners.'

'You *what?*' said the nut man, looking bewildered.

'This is our dad,' said Lucy, turning to the woman behind her. 'He takes all of our mum's money and then tries to make us pay for our tea.'

'Yeah,' said Toby, latching on. 'Mum sends us out hunting with this huge handbag so we can collect scraps of food from dustbins. And just look at the state we get into.'

'It's disgusting,' said a man in a bowler hat. 'The poor things look as if they've been to hell and back.'

'Well I'm certainly not buying nuts from *him*,' said the woman with the cloche hat. She eyed the Henbegs with vague distaste.

'Me neither,' said the man behind her.

Soon, everyone in the queue was talking about how mean the vendor was, and seconds later Toby and Lucy were presented with a steaming pile of salted chestnuts.

'I hope they chokes you,' whispered the seller between gritted teeth.

'Thanks dad,' said Lucy with a huge beaming smile. 'It's a pleasure to be back in the real world again, and an even bigger pleasure to be telling honest-to-goodness lies just for the sake of it.'

'Eh?' said the vendor. 'Are you bonkers or something?'

'I'm really very sorry,' whispered Lucy as she popped a hot nut into her mouth. 'But we're starving. I'll send you the money by post.'

FX-3

She gave him a little smile and they ran until they reached the bookshop on the corner. It was closed, which according to the sign on the door meant it was either Sunday, when they were closed all day, or Wednesday, when it was half-day closing.

'Delicious,' said Lucy, as they pressed into the doorway. 'The first food for ages that doesn't taste like eleven kinds of dung.'

'Brilliant,' agreed Toby, stuffing his face, 'but I could do with a cup of tea as well. And then some sausages, and umm, bacon and maybe a few beans, and then some toast.'

'And a double egg sandwich with Snogg's sauce,' said Lucy. 'And a bacon sandwich with marmalade, and then I want, umm, *hey*, wait a minute,' she said, 'it's just occurred to me. We don't know how long we've been away.'

'And we don't know where we are,' said Toby. 'Do you know your way around Lundern?'

'I know some of the place names,' said Lucy, after a bit of thought, 'but I don't know where they are. What we need is a map – or a policeman.'

'Let's stick to the map,' said Toby. 'I think we'll be talking to the police soon enough.'

'I've got a better idea,' said Lucy. 'Why don't we just get someone to take us to the station?'

They were about to look for help when a smashing noise came from the museum, and four scarabs flying in perfect synchronisation crashed through the windows, the glass raining like brilliant hailstones into the courtyard.

Just then, a taxicab pulled up alongside them.

'Hey, what was all that noise?' said the cabbie.

'That?' said Lucy innocently. 'Oh, it was nothing to worry about.'

She leaned through the luggage bay window, distracting the driver whilst Toby carefully opened the door and crept onto the back seat.

'Are you sure?' said the driver. 'It didn't sound like nuffink to me.'

'You're right,' said Lucy. 'The nut seller's stall has just fallen over.'

'Doesn't surprise me,' said the cabbie. 'There's been a big fuss up at the moo-seum. Kids smashing up cabinets and stuff.'

'How did you know that?' said Lucy. 'It's only just happened.'

'Ah,' said the cabbie, tapping his nose. 'That's the cab driver's bush telegraph that is. Sometimes we know stuff that's goin' to 'appen even before it 'appens.'

'That must be handy,' said Lucy.

'Well we need to keep one step ahead, see?' said the cabbie. 'Specially round the moo-seum of anti-kwitties. There's *always* stuff goin' on in that place – people seeing angels and stuff. It's not natcherel if you ask me, not that anyone ever *does* ask me.'

'They probably can't get a word in,' whispered Lucy.

'Wotsat?' said the cabbie.

'Nothing,' smiled Lucy.

'No, well if they asked us cabbies, then the world'd be run a lot better'n it is today, know what I mean?'

'Umm, yes,' said Lucy, 'but what about these angel stories?'

'Crackpots, the lot of 'em,' said the cabbie. 'That's what I reckon.'

'Probably,' said Lucy, 'but what have they been saying?'

'Weird stuff, that's what,' he said. 'Just the other day, right, someone saw this bloke wrapped up in bandages, like one of them Hegyptian mummies.'

'Raziel,' said Lucy.

'Ra-*who*?' said the cabbie. 'Nah, I don't think they got a name for him, not that he even existed. Someone said they saw him walking up the Spottenham Port Road, but they counted all the mummies in the moo-seum and they was all there. Anyway, where did you want to go?'

'We don't know,' said Lucy. 'We have to find someone first.'

'Sounds complicated,' said the cabbie, 'but then I do *like* the odd bit of complication. It's ferrying lazy lard-bottoms from the Arse of Commons to the nearest Pox Factory that I can't stand. Don't get me wrong, I mean it's a living, innit? But we all need something a bit special now and again.'

'In *that* case you're the very man we're looking for,' grinned Lucy.

'*We*?'

'Me and my friend Toby,' said Lucy. 'He's right behind you.'

'Hey, this isn't one of those stick-ups I've been hearing about is it?'

'It's *much* more interesting than that,' said Lucy. 'Have you ever dreamed of someone leaping into your cab and shouting *follow that cab*?'

'Have I *ever*,' enthused the cabbie. 'Come on then, get in.'

'*Henbeg?*' said Lucy. '*Find Zenda.* Understand?'

'Growwf,' said Henbeg.

'And Henbeg?'

'Growwf?'

'Don't get too far ahead – and don't bite anyone until I say so.'

Lucy placed the handbag on the road in front of the cab where the driver could see it. Then she climbed in and stood up in the luggage compartment at the front.

'Are you ready?' she said.

'Umm, ye-es,' replied the cabbie, still not sounding totally convinced. 'My name's Ernie by the way.'

'Alright then Ernie,' said Lucy. 'Now I want you to listen *very* carefully – are you listening?'

'Ye-es,' said Ernie, straining to see Henbeg over his steering wheel.

'Good,' said Lucy, 'because I want you to *follow that handbag.*'

The Gargoyles of Saint Pancreas

As the taxi moved off, Lucy leaned out of the window screaming *Eeekah, Eeekah, Eeekah.* But Henbeg didn't need any encouragement, and shot off up the road, stopping every hundred yards or so to sniff the tarmac. He wasn't accustomed to traffic and caused a few upsets, especially when he insisted on overtaking vehicles by running underneath them at the back and then out again at the front.

'He can't do that,' shouted Ernie, 'he's got to indicate, and then he's got to pull out, all proper like.'

'Never mind giving out scores for road sense,' shouted Lucy, 'just don't lose him.'

Every time Ernie looked in his rear view mirror there was some new scene of destruction caused by the runaway crocodile. But eventually the traffic calmed down and so did Henbeg's overtaking.

Ernie settled visibly in his seat, despite Toby's enthusiastic yelling.

'So,' he sighed, as they turned into Eweston Road, 'you're going up north are you?'

'Umm, why?' said Lucy cagily. 'Do we look like the sort of people who might be going up north?'

'Not necessarily,' said Ernie. 'But if you're heading south then I wouldn't recommended King's Cross as a point of departure see? I only mention it because that's where we seem to be heading.'

'Ah,' said Lucy. 'It really is that simple, isn't it? You'll have to forgive us Ernie, but where we've just been we had to be suspicious of everyone and everything. It was a nightmare.'

'Yeah?' said the cabbie. 'Sounds like my ex-mother-in-law's house.'

A gap appeared in the traffic, and Henbeg accelerated into the space so he could stop for a really good sniff. When he eventually took off again he surprised a nun, who fell off her bike. And it was during this delay, whilst the cab was at a standstill that Lucy's heart missed a beat. They had stopped near a newspaper kiosk that displayed a message apparently directed at her. It was written in huge black letters on a headline board.

'*Surrender The Light*,' it said in foot-high script.

And underneath, in letters that were merely six inches high, it said :-

'*Giant Bird Kills Three More. Northern town under siege.*'

'Here we go again,' said Ernie as they moved off. '*Hey*,' he screamed to a cabbie on a parallel route. '*Parsley*, wind yer window down.'

The man called Parsley duly obliged and Ernie filled him in on all the exciting happenings, trying to keep one eye on the road, one eye on Henbeg and the other on his friend.

'You wouldn't believe it would you?' shouted Ernie. 'I'm *only* following a bleedin' crocodile for God's sake.'

'Nah,' said Parsley. 'Pull the other one.'

'Straight up,' grinned Ernie. 'Anyway, must run.' He pulled his head back in just as a bus screamed past, its horn blaring. The double-decker had just swerved to avoid something that looked like a leather suitcase with six and a half legs.

'Here we are,' said Ernie, skidding to a halt behind Henbeg. 'King's Cross and Saint Pancreas, just like I said. That'll be fifteen bob, not that you've got that much money.'

'Yes, *thanks*,' said Lucy, absent-mindedly. She was still stunned by the message on the newsstand. 'Umm, this stuff in the papers, I don't suppose you happen to know where it's happening?'

'Could be anywhere,' said Ernie. 'It's just *north* innit?'

'I suppose,' said Lucy, 'and I'm sorry about the money, but we haven't got any.'

'No problem,' said Ernie. 'I knew that before we set off.'

'Umm, look,' said Lucy. 'We need to go and collect someone and then we need to be off doing something really interesting. Are you with me so far?'

'I reckon,' said Ernie. He made a rude gesture at the person behind, who was sounding his horn.

'Well we're going to need transport,' said Lucy. 'And we'll probably need an understanding driver too. So do you want a bit of adventure?'

'You've got a deal,' grinned Ernie, not even stopping to think. 'But only if I can have my photograph taken with your handbag.'

Lucy expected Henbeg to charge into the railway station where she'd find Zenda arguing with a porter or trying to cram Pixy into a left luggage locker. But Henbeg had other ideas, and led them to the station next door, which was ten times more impressive than King's Cross.

Saint Pancreas the maroon and yellow sign declared.

'Wow, *this* is brilliant,' said Toby. 'Now if *I* was going to kidnap someone from another world and use her as a prize in a newspaper competition, this is definitely where I'd hide. It's like a huge castle, with battlements and towers and everything.'

'It's fabulous,' said Lucy, leaning back to take it all in.

'But just one thing though,' said Toby. 'Why are we looking for Zenda instead of Raziel?'

'Because the angel is already back in Grimston,' said Lucy gravely. 'And Freggley is still here. In fact I think Henbeg might just have found her.'

There was a huge commotion in the lobby of the Midland Grand Hotel, and for once it wasn't Lucy to blame. An enormous woman in a tweed suit had fainted into a chair and was being fanned by a grinning bellboy. Behind him was a waiter with an ice bucket and flannel, who was waiting to mop her brow.

'I'm telling you, I saw it *move*,' she insisted. 'I was simply admiring the craftsmanship of the item when I realised that it was obviously lost, and then, when I merely went to pick it up, purely to hand it in to lost property you understand, it moved. And I swear it even *looked* at me.'

'And when was this madam?' said the waiter, winking to his friend. 'Was it before the bar opened, or just now?'

'Don't be insolent young man. I don't need to take a drink to see moving handbags. I'm telling you the thing was moving.'

'Ah, there it is,' said Lucy, calmly walking over to claim the lost item.

'Is this yours young lady?' said the woman, sitting up slightly.

'Of course,' said Lucy, turning to leave.

'Wait a minute,' said the woman. 'Can you prove this handbag is yours?'

'Why?' said Toby. 'Would *you* like to try and claim it?'

'*Yes*, umm, on second thoughts *no*,' said the woman, hearing a low growl from Henbeg's direction.

'Very wise,' said Lucy. She made her way to the front desk, aware that the woman was still eyeing up Henbeg. But there were more important matters to deal with, and finding Zenda La rotten Freggley was right at the top of her list.

'Yes?' said the receptionist, staring at Lucy's clothes. 'And how may I help you, umm, *children*?'

She was a pleasant looking woman of forty who believed she was twenty-five and had all the makeup to prove it. She flashed a pearly white smile at Lucy, and even managed to *keep* smiling when she smelled the pungent whiff of scarabs mixed with angels.

'Me and my friend here,' said Lucy, 'we're planning a surprise for a friend of ours. She's staying in your hotel.'

'I see,' sniffed the woman. 'And what kind of surprise would that be?'

'If we *told* you then it wouldn't be a surprise, would it?' said Lucy. 'We discussed it yesterday with your manager.'

'*Oh*?' said the receptionist. 'Well it so happens that our manager has been in Feastbourne all week, at a cutlery and napkin folding conference.'

'Has he?' said Lucy. 'Whoops.'

'Yes, *whoops*,' said the woman, turning to answer the telephone. When she turned back, Toby and Lucy were gone and the hotel register was open at the page where Zenda's had scrawled her signature. 'Security?' she screamed, breaking a fingernail in the telephone dial. '*Security*? There are children in the hotel. Dirty, filthy, stinking, rotten, lying children – and I want them found.'

'Did you hear what she called us?' said Toby, stopping part way up the staircase to listen to the racket.

'We need to find Zenda,' panted Lucy. 'We have to stop her getting to a telephone, or we're all dead.'

Running up the staircase they paused to look at the ceiling, attracted by the sight of a sky blue dome sprinkled with yellow stars.

'Luce? Have you *seen* this?'

'Uh *huh*,' said Lucy. 'It's like the temple in the tower, but smaller.'

'If I was the suspicious type,' said Toby, 'then I'd say the person who designed this place had a hand in that temple.'

'Yes,' smiled Lucy, 'but we're *not* suspicious, *are* we?'

'Of course not,' said Toby, turning back to the hunt.

Toby talked them into Zenda's rooms with a few choice lies about the mad relation who had wandered out of the house without her special blue pills. He told the chambermaid that if she didn't get her medicine, their aunt Zenda would turn into a loud-mouthed, self centred bigot with a razor sharp tongue and flappy ears. The poor girl had practically fallen over herself to let them into Zenda's suite, claiming that the process had already begun.

And for his splendid effort, Lucy had awarded Toby a record breaking five out of ten.

The suite consisted of a huge living room and an even bigger bedroom that had last been decorated a hundred years ago. The curtains were closed, giving the room a spooky feel,

And there was a lump in the bed that was breathing.

'We have to sneak up on her,' whispered Lucy.

'Then what?' whispered Toby. 'Hit her with a shovel?'

'I'm not sure,' whispered Lucy.

'That's alright then,' smiled Toby. 'As long as you've got a plan.'

Lucy tiptoed over to the bed. She decided to jump on Zenda and sit on her chest until she agreed to return Pixy-Henbeg. But when she leapt onto the shape it was Pixatrix Scalybeak who yelled out in terror.

'*Pixy!*' said Lucy. 'You're safe – but where's Zenda?'

'She went out for a stiff drink,' said Pixy, sitting up and rubbing the sleep from her eyes. 'What does that mean?'

'It means we've got time to get you out of here,' said Lucy. 'Come on, we've got a friend waiting for us downstairs.'

'I can't,' said Pixy.

'Why not?' asked Toby.

'Because, little boy, she is chained to the bed,' said Zenda.

The reporter was silhouetted in the doorway.

'Freggley,' said Lucy. 'How nice of you to drop in.'

'Yes,' said Zenda, 'and I'm pleased to see you as well.'

'I'll bet,' said Toby. 'Where did you get handcuffs?'

'They're standard newspaper issue,' smirked Zenda. 'You never know when they'll come in handy.'

'Well you're right about that,' said Lucy. 'Because we're going to chain *you* up with them. Now hand over the key.'

'Not bloody likely,' said Zenda. 'I'm going to call the manager and have you thrown out. In the *real* world, Zenda Freggley is queen.'

'We'll see about that,' said Lucy. 'Henbeg – start with her ankles.'

'Alright, alright,' screamed Zenda. She jumped up onto the bed to get out of Henbeg's way. '*Have* the rotten key.'

'Thanks,' said Toby. 'We will.'

'Umm, just as a matter of interest,' said Lucy, 'how did you manage to get the Pixy Henbeg to go along with your plan? Didn't she try to bite you?'

'Oh, haven't you even noticed *that* yet?' mocked Zenda. 'If you close the clasp on the handbag it can't turn back into a crocodile.'

'Oh,' said Lucy, as she unchained Pixy, 'well that's interesting.'

'See?' smirked Zenda. 'You still don't know everything.'

Lucy gave a little grimace, wondering if the reporter had any more tricks up her sleeve. But then she noticed Toby peering through the curtains.

'Hey, Luce,' he said. 'When we looked at this place earlier, were there any gargoyles or scarab statues perched on the battlements?'

'Umm, I don't think so,' said Lucy.

'*Oh,*' said Toby, letting the lace curtains float back into place. 'Shall we get a move on then?'

'I won't argue with that,' said Lucy, listening at the door. 'I think our friend the receptionist has just worked out where we are.'

'But what about me?' said Zenda. 'I need to get back to Grimston too.'

'Don't worry,' said Lucy. 'You're coming too, just as soon as we can get these handcuffs on.'

They dragged Zenda downstairs, pausing to look at the blue-sky ceiling again before rushing her through the lobby. They performed a body-swerve around the receptionist but then failed to squeeze past the fat lady who had decided on a last-ditch effort to take possession of the handbag. But she jumped back when Henbeg snapped at her ankles and swallowed one of her shoes.

'It's stealing my clothes now,' she screamed. 'Why doesn't somebody *do* something? Do you know how much those cost? I say, you there, chase after him, he's going out into the street.'

'Now, now madam,' grinned the bellboy. 'I'm *sure* those nasty visions will go away, just as soon as your pre-dinner drink wears off.'

'It's not fair,' screamed the woman, flopping into a heap. 'I would simply have *loved* a handbag like that.'

'You wouldn't,' yelled Lucy, as she ran through the revolving doors. 'He's not your type.'

'Over there,' yelled Toby, as they spilled onto the street. 'It's our cabbie – the one who likes the north, even though he doesn't know where it is.'

'Thanks for waiting,' said Lucy, as they climbed into the cab.

'Don't mention it,' grinned Ernie. 'I don't want to miss a thing.'

'*Right*,' said Lucy. 'I want to get moving as soon as possible, but first of all, Ernie needs to know who he's dealing with. And more importantly, he needs to know who he's *not* dealing with.'

'Brilliant,' said Ernie. 'So who's who?'

'The small strange-looking one is Pixy,' said Lucy. 'And the big one with the ears is Zenda. Rule number one, don't listen to anything that Zenda tells you. For now, she is the enemy.'

'Enemy,' said Ernie. 'Right, and what about the Pixy thing?'

'Neutral for the moment,' said Lucy, 'she's on unfamiliar territory and easily confused.'

'And very hungry,' said Pixy.

'Maybe we can stop and get some egg sandwiches?' suggested Toby.

'Will I like them?' said Pixy. 'These egg sandwich things?'

'I don't see why not,' said Toby. 'You seem to like everything else.'

'I've got a sausage roll she can have,' said Ernie. 'And there's a flask of tea as well.'

'That's very kind,' smiled Lucy. 'Perhaps later. *Now* Ernie, to continue, Toby and me are friends, and we're the only ones giving orders. Right?'

'Right,' said Ernie.

'But the handcuffs are biting into my wrists,' moaned Zenda. 'Can't you just take them off and trust me?'

'Handcuffs?' said Ernie, raising an eyebrow.

'I told you,' said Lucy, 'she's the enemy and can't be trusted. You'd be safer trusting Pixy with a bag of cakes in an empty room.'

'So that's a *no* then, is it?' said Zenda.

'You heard the boss,' said Ernie. 'The handcuffs stay on.'

'You're learning fast,' said Lucy.

'Blimey,' said Ernie, pointing at Henbeg. 'And what about this handbag thing? Is he a friend too?'

'Ah, *no* Ernie,' said Lucy, 'please don't do that or he'll...'

It was too late. Henbeg snapped at Ernie who jerked back in surprise and knocked his head on the drivers' side window.

'*Aaagh*,' shouted Toby, pointing in Ernie's direction. A scarab head was pressed up against the glass and the matching wings were wrapped around the windscreen and down the side of the car.

'Oh, my *Gawd*,' screamed Ernie, staring into the dripping, insect jaws. 'Is this your idea of a joke?'

'It's the start of that adventure I was telling you about,' said Lucy. 'Now tell me Ernie, do you *really* not know which direction north is?'

The Great
North Road

The ancient cab rattled along far more quickly than Bentley's motor had ever managed, but mainly because it was getting lighter by the minute, as various bits fell off and were left by the wayside. The wobbly red dial on the dashboard indicated eighty miles-per-hour, but Lucy recalled it saying that earlier, when they were standing still back at Saint Pancreas. One thing was certain though – they weren't going *nearly* fast enough.

'Are you sure we're going the right way?' said Zenda.

'*Course* we are,' said Ernie. 'Didn't you see the sign back there?'

'I was busy worrying about my hands falling off from gangrene,' moaned Zenda.

'Don't worry,' said Pixy. 'If they *do* then I'll be here to help scratch your nose.'

'Just watch it, you bloody pipsqueak,' said Zenda. 'And just wait until we get back – *all* of you. Then you'll see the power of the press.'

'Yeah, right,' said Toby. 'We can hardly wait.'

As if recoiling from the events of the last few days, they all fell eerily silent, and as the telegraph poles whipped by at regular intervals they lapsed into a kind of stupor, unaware of how much time was passing, or even if it was passing at all. But they were soon woken from their daydreams by the sound of enthusiastic screeching.

'*Look*, it's another one of those sign thingies,' said Pixy, bouncing on the worn-out leather seat. 'What does it say? What does it say? What does it say?'

'Nothing that actually helps,' said Toby, as the sign flashed past. 'It just said *to the north*. But it didn't say how far.'

'That depends which bit of the north you want to get to,' said Lucy.

'Yes, and how *fast* you go,' said Zenda.

'Hey, this is my pride and joy,' said Ernie. 'It's precision engineering at its best. When I first bought the little beauty I was the only one in our street with a jam jar.'

'A *what?*' said Toby.

'Car,' said Lucy. 'Jam jar rhymes with car. And we're driving on the frog and toad – road. See?'

'So this is the Great North Frog,' said Toby. 'Does that mean you're a Cocker-knee then Ernie?'

'It *serpently* does,' said Ernie with obvious pride. 'I was born and bred within the sound of Bow Bells, and my old mum, well she's a Pearly Queen you know. In fact there was this particular time when…'

'Umm, I think the story might have to wait,' said Toby. 'I don't want to worry anyone, but the scarabs are back.'

'The thing that tried to suck my head through the window?' said Ernie.

'About a quarter of a mile behind us,' said Toby.

'There are two of them,' said Pixy, peering out of the back window, 'and then one, and then another one.'

'Very funny,' said Zenda. 'But if you knew how to say two the first time then why didn't you say two and then another two?'

'I wanted to keep the suspense up,' grinned Pixy.

'That's *almost* a joke,' said Toby. 'And I'd be killing myself laughing if they weren't capable of eating through this cloth roof.'

'I know I'm going to regret asking,' said Lucy, 'but can we go any faster?'

'We *could*,' said Ernie, 'with a bigger engine, or less weight on board. You *do* know I'm only supposed to carry four passengers?'

'Henbeg counts as luggage,' said Lucy, 'so we're not breaking the law.'

At this, Henbeg curled up beneath her feet and assumed his fashion accessory form, even though she hadn't asked.

'Doesn't matter if he's luggage or not,' said Ernie. 'We're doing nearly sixty as it is, and that's the tops.'

'What a pathetic *heap*,' moaned Zenda.

'Of course,' said Ernie, 'we could probably manage sixty five if we threw Miss Handcuffs Houdini overboard.'

'Now that's a *really* good idea,' grinned Pixy.

'Right, *you*, driver, and *you*, Pixy thing,' hissed Zenda. 'I'm putting your names and addresses in my little black book, and it's *not* the one I use for sending out greetings cards.'

'Yeah?' said Ernie. 'You know where I live then, do you?'

'I can find out,' said Zenda.

'And *I* can afford a new cab,' said Ernie.

The view from the back window wasn't encouraging. Toby sat with his nose glued to the glass, eager to report every detail as if it might help them escape the threat. But the scarabs were catching up, flying straight and true, their wings almost touching the tarmac.

'Luce? Do you remember the scarab you spiced at Saint Pancreas? Well it's back again, and it doesn't look very happy.'

When Ernie first caught sight of the scarab stuck to his window, Lucy had blown some of Weazenock's spice into its face. The scarab shot across the station forecourt and demolished a W. P. Sniff's newsstand, sending a flurry of newspapers into the air like huge snowflakes. And when the crowds spotted the insect and his ugly friends, all the winds of hell were let loose, and possibly some of those from purgatory as well.

'Hey, wait,' said Toby, 'there's another car coming.'

'Seen him already,' said Ernie, 'driving all over the road in that bleedin' great big motor as if he *owns* the bleedin' place.'

'It's getting closer,' said Toby, 'and there's something funny...'

'I *thought* there might be,' said Zenda.

'Let me have a look,' said Pixy, pushing Toby out of the way.

'Oh,' she said, 'umm, what's that thing on the front?'

'A radiator mascot,' said Toby, pushing back. 'Wow, just look at the *size* of that stuffed parrot – and it's flapping its wings!'

'Parrot?' said Lucy.

'They're trying to overtake us on the inside,' said Ernie, '*Oi*, mate, don't they have driving licenses where you come from?'

The car drew level. The driver ignored them all, but then, without even looking in their direction, he winked.

'It's Bentley,' yelled Lucy. 'He's wearing a silly cap and a stupid uniform, but I'd recognise him anywhere.'

'Look Ethel, it's the magic girl, over there in the other car.'

Lucy didn't actually hear the words, she just saw the lips moving and then recognised the face they were attached to.

'Toby,' she screamed. 'It's the woman from the bus stop.'

'What bus stop?' said Toby. 'What woman? Where?'

'The other car,' said Lucy, uncertainly. 'The Bentley, the Priory, I mean the magic trick at the bus stop, they were chasing us they, erm...'

'Who was chasing you?' said Toby. 'You're not making any sense.'

'*She* was,' shouted Lucy, pointing an accusing finger at Zenda.

'Oh, *that's* right,' said Zenda, in a sing-songy playground voice. 'Blame it all on the press. Everyone else does.'

'I *will*,' blustered Lucy, 'and when I explain all of this later it's going to make a *lot* more sense than it does now.'

'I hope so,' said Toby, shaking his head.

Lucy wound the luggage bay window down and leaned out to shout at Bentley, but a scarab landed on the cab, and began to eat his way through the roof.

'If it gets in, we're dead,' said Toby. 'Even if we escape from the cab, there's nowhere to go.'

Everyone peered out. They were passing through flat, desolate farmland and there was nowhere for them to hide.

'Why didn't you pick a cab with a proper metal roof?' moaned Zenda. 'I *hate* these old cloth covered jobs. They're always so draughty.'

'Don't worry,' said Lucy. 'You'll have a scarab breathing down your neck soon – that ought to warm you up nicely.' She picked up an umbrella lost by a previous passenger and jabbed the soft roof with it.

The scarab didn't budge.

'Bentley,' she bellowed. 'We could do with some help.'

The ladies in the back of Bentley's motor smiled and waved, apparently unflustered by the giant insect that was eating its way through the cab roof.

'Bentley?' screamed Lucy.

The scarab had chewed a hole big enough to get its snout through. Lucy and Ernie were safe for the moment, but everyone in the rear compartment had to get down on the floor to avoid becoming the creature's dinner.

'That wouldn't happen in *this* car,' shouted Ethel helpfully as she rolled her own window down. 'It's a limousine, you see, so it's *built* properly.'

'Oh, well thanks very much ma'am,' shouted Ernie. 'I paid good money for this cab.'

'No, *really*,' shouted Ethel. 'What I mean is that you should all come over here. We have lots of space, don't we Gladys?'

'Oodles,' said Gladys.

The two ladies were ready with their umbrellas and when the scarab flew over to them it retreated after a sharp poke in the eye. Then it turned back to the cab and the tender delicacies that lay inside.

'I think we should listen to Ethel,' shouted Lucy. The scarab's jaws were reaching further inside now. 'Can you get alongside them Ernie?'

'I think so,' said Ernie.

He manoeuvred so that the running boards on both cars touched. Then he juggled their relative positions so that the doors lined up.

And then they flung open the doors.

'*Jump*,' screamed Lucy. 'All of you, get across into the other car, *now*.'

'Limousine,' corrected Gladys as she leaned back into her seat to make way for the newcomers.

Zenda went first followed by Pixy, then Toby pitched Henbeg across and finally jumped himself.

That was the *easy* part.

'Now us,' said Lucy, turning to Ernie.

'You *are* joking?' said Ernie.

'I'm deadly serious,' said Lucy. 'Unless of course you *want* to stay here.'

The scarab had eaten through the roof. Ernie looked over his shoulder and saw an ugly insect snout pressed against the partition glass.

It was spreading snot all over the inside of his precious cab.

'You first,' he said.

Whilst the two ladies battled the scarab away, Lucy opened her door and stepped onto the running board. Ernie dropped the cab back to line her up with the limousine.

'Ernie, go to the other side,' she shouted, as she leapt across.

The cabbie dropped behind the limousine, then accelerated up the inside and jumped across as soon as the doors were lined up.

Now the only occupant of the cab was the scarab.

'Have you met my new employers?' said Bentley. 'I gave up the private dick business when these ladies offered me a job as their chauffeur.'

'But how did you know to follow the cab?' shouted Lucy.

'It was the only one for miles being chased by giant insects,' said Bentley. 'I thought that was probably a clue.'

'I don't want to stop your reunion,' said Toby, 'only…'

'Yes, I think we'd best get out of here,' said Bentley, as the cab wobbled and the cars veered apart.

'Yes Benters, give it some *gas*,' shouted Gladys, whooping and screaming with delight.

They pulled ahead of the cab as the scarab climbed out onto the roof.

'*Keroosh, splam, bash*,' shouted Ethel. 'Look at that thing *go*…'

'Yeah,' said Ernie mournfully, 'just *look* at it.'

The cab veered off the road, ran across a patch of scrubland and hit a huge oak tree. The petrol tank exploded and engulfed the tree in flames.

'My precious cab,' said Ernie, 'and my ride back to Lundern.'

'We'll see about that,' said Ethel. 'But first we have a few things to get out of the way.' She swivelled in her seat to look at the flame-tree, searching for signs of the other scarabs.

But the sky was deserted, and so was the road.

Everyone sighed and sank into their seats. For a moment nobody spoke. They just stared at each other across the vast central space of the limousine's rear cabin.

'Is it just me dear,' said Ethel eventually, 'or have those beetle things got a lot bigger since we were girls?'

'I don't recall them being that size,' said Gladys, 'but I was never any good at biology, or whatever *ology* it is that bugs belong to. And I don't ever recall seeing a handbag that looked like that either.'

'Ladies,' said Lucy, not wanting to dwell on the handbag. 'Thank you both very much for rescuing us. And you too Bentley. It was lucky you came along when you did.'

'It wasn't luck,' said Gladys, still eyeing Henbeg. 'He *knew* you'd be back eventually, so we just went down to Lundern and waited.'

'Waited?' said Lucy.

'For the trouble to start,' said Gladys. 'Bentley said if the mayhem begins in Lundern then Miss Lucy Blake won't be far behind.'

'Oh *did* he now?' said Lucy.

'I was *right*, wasn't I?' said Bentley. 'And we had a lovely time whilst we were waiting.'

'Yes,' said Ethel. 'Gladys and I have been doing a lot of visiting.'

'And I've been doing some snooping,' added Bentley.

'You naughty boy Benters,' said Ethel. 'You *do* say the wickedest things.'

'He does,' grinned Gladys, 'and that's why we like him.'

'Me too,' said Lucy. 'But it seems ages since we last met. How long is it now. Would it be *days*?'

Bentley flicked an eyebrow upwards, trying to give Lucy a clue.

'But no,' she said, 'it must be *weeks*, mustn't it?'

Bentley gave another twitch.

'It can't be months, can it?' said Lucy. 'We've only just – umm, yes, yes, I suppose it *must* be months.'

'Three and a half months, to be precise,' said Bentley.

'*Ah*,' said Lucy. 'Well that's going to take some explaining, isn't it?'

'Just a little,' said Bentley. 'But you needn't worry about that until we get back to Grimston.'

'Is something wrong dear?' said Gladys. 'Only you appear to be grinning like a sack of split peas.'

'It's nothing,' smiled Lucy. 'I was thinking how nice it sounded, that's all. *Going home to Grimston.*'

'Well it would be,' said Ethel. 'If it wasn't for all this giant bird nonsense.'

'You know about that?' said Lucy.

'The papers have been full of it for days,' said Ethel. 'But I don't think we're being told the whole story, do *you* Gladys?'

'They're keeping us in the dark,' said Gladys. 'You know what the papers are like.'

'That's right,' grinned Toby. 'We *all* know what they're like.'

'Can we cut the cackle?' said Zenda. 'And can this heap go any faster?'

'Faster?' said Ethel, spotting the handcuffs. 'Why would we want to go any faster? And what *is* this modern obsession with speed? When I was a girl we were told that if we did more than twelve miles an hour our brains would get sucked out through our ears and we'd suffocate.'

'Can we *please* hurry?' said Zenda. '*Pretty* please? I've got the hottest story ever here, and I need to get it back to my editor.'

Lucy bit her lip. Events were closing in, like thousands of threads coming together and threatening to bind her. And when Zenda finally escaped their control she would tell the whole world what had happened.

'Hmm,' said Ethel. 'I can imagine how desperate you must be to have your story printed, and I'm sure it's a very nice story too. But there's just one problem, as far as I can see.'

'Problem?' said Zenda. 'Can I help?'

Toby and Lucy swallowed hard at the thought of Zenda providing help. Pixy wrinkled her nose and was about to poke her tongue out when her eyes grew to the size of saucers.

'I don't think so,' said Ethel. 'Not unless you can clear those insect things off the outside of the car. *Without* removing your handcuffs I hasten to add.'

The job of driving had suddenly become more difficult, due to the huge scarab that had fastened its face to the windscreen. Fortunately it had never heard of windscreen wipers, and when Bentley turned them on they tickled the insect's feet so much that it fell off and demolished a traffic light.

'What do they want?' shouted Bentley, pretending he hadn't noticed the red light.

'I don't know about yours,' shouted Toby, 'but I think this one wants to suck my brains out with a straw.'

Toby wound his window up as the beast attached itself to the door, trapping the scarab's jaws between the glass and the doorframe. Its foul smelling tongue lashed around the cabin like a whip, so Toby whipped out Quim's scissors, trying desperately to get his fingers and thumbs into the holes. It was like trying to juggle jelly on a bike – and all the while the insect was nudging his head further inside the car.

'Squish it,' shouted Gladys.

'No, grab hold of its tongue,' shouted Toby.

'Oh *yuck*, no,' said Pixy. 'That's *disgusting*.'

'Don't look at me,' said Zenda, lifting her hands to show the cuffs.

Lucy leaned forward and held her gloved hands in front of the scarab's mouth. And the next time the tongue appeared she grabbed it, bracing her foot on the door to stop it reeling her in like a fly. Toby leapt into action, slashing at the slimy tongue with his scissors and finally managing to cut it off near the base.

'Oh, *God*,' screamed Zenda. 'I've never seen anything *quite* so disgusting.'

The scarab was surprised, but held on long enough to belch.

'On second thoughts,' said Zenda. '*That* is the most disgusting thing I have ever seen.'

A half-digested head appeared in the scarab's gaping mouth, the victim looking not horrified at being eaten, but strangely surprised.

'It's Mongy Twelvetrees,' said Pixy.

'Good grief,' said Ethel, 'what *have* you all been up to?'

'I want to be sick,' said Zenda.

Toby pushed the remains of the tongue out of the window, then levered the scarab away from the car with an umbrella. The insect resisted, but was weakened by blood loss and soon fell off, cart-wheeling down the road and finally getting run over by a huge Scammel lorry.

'Look out,' squealed Pixy. 'There's another one.'

They got a close-up view of Pixy's scarab as the head smashed through the window next to Ethel.

'I've got just the thing,' she said, fishing in her capacious handbag, much to Henbeg's amusement. 'Here it is, one canister of *Puffy-Poof-o-Poo* hairspray, extra large size.'

'Give it a bloody good squirt,' squealed Gladys. 'Quickly.'

'Now, now,' said Ethel, 'lets mind our language, shall we?'

'Just get *on* with it,' screamed Gladys.

'But it seems such a pity,' said Ethel. 'Look at the beautiful wing casings and all those wonderful colours on the body.'

'And look at all those matching teeth,' said Toby.

'For God's sake,' screamed Gladys. '*Spray* the bloody thing will you? It's slobbering on my best dress.'

Fsssst…

Yeeaaagh…

Fsssst, Fsssst…

Yeeaaagh, Yeeaaagh…

Fsssst, Fsssst, Fsssst…

'I think that might have done the trick,' said Ethel.

Fsssst…

'I'll say,' said Gladys, breathing hard. 'He's not very happy, is he?'

The scarab clung on for a moment, but the carefully applied layers of *Puffy-Poof-o-Poo* finally proved too much. The beast fell off the speeding car and skidded away into a field, finally coming to rest with its legs in the air.

'We're not going back to turn *that* one the right way up,' said Lucy. 'I don't care *how* many times we get struck by lightning.'

'Can anyone see the other one?' asked Pixy.

There was a whistling noise, followed by an ear-splitting thump and the sound of tearing metal.

A scarab crashed in through the roof. Everyone leapt back in their seats and pulled their feet up as it dropped into the space between them.

'Get the *Puffy-Poof-o-Poo* out again,' yelled Gladys. 'I think we might have another customer.'

'Save your hairspray,' said Toby. He pointed to the ceramic insulator that was embedded in the insect's head. 'It must have got fried when it crashed into a Lectric pole.'

'I *still* don't trust it,' said Pixy. 'Can we kill it again, just to be sure?'

'Perhaps you might like to *Puffy-Poof-o-Poo* it?' suggested Zenda.

'You'd better be quick then,' said Bentley. He pulled up about a hundred yards short of a vaguely visible barrier. 'I think this is as far as we're going to get, and we appear to have a welcoming committee.'

'But we're not even in town yet,' said Gladys, peering out. 'This is just the boundary sign.'

They all crowded towards the windows, and read the sign that greeted every visitor as they came into the town on the main road to the south.

"Welcome to Grimston-on-Sea - Home of You Won't Bleevit"

Beyond the sign was a checkpoint with a striped barrier. The army were turning back everyone who tried to get past.

'Well if *that's* the kind of welcome we get,' said Ethel, 'I wouldn't like to see it when they were trying to keep us out.'

'Absolutely,' said Gladys. 'Those chaps with the big boots and rifles don't look friendly at all.'

'Which is why we need to do something about Pixy,' said Ethel. 'Now don't get me wrong, I think she's a perfectly wonderful little thing, but if anyone in authority sees her, umm, *unfamiliar* face, well there are going to be certain questions asked.'

'Embarrassing questions,' agreed Gladys.

'You're right,' said Lucy. 'Would anyone like to see a magic trick?'

'Wonderful,' said Gladys. 'Who's going to disappear this time?'

'Nobody,' crowed Zenda. 'The Phibber has taken custody of your special piece of paper, or had you forgotten?'

'Then you won't mind being blindfolded,' said Lucy.

There was a brief struggle as they forced Ernie's coat over Zenda's head, and another frantic moment as they tied the ends of the sleeves to stop her peeping through the armholes.

'Right, close your eyes please ladies,' said Lucy. 'You too Ernie.'

'It's nice to be back amongst people we can trust,' said Toby.

There were a few muffled words of complaint from Zenda, but nothing that anyone wanted to listen to.

'Ready?' said Lucy. She delved into her pockets and produced the last remaining fragment of her toy theatre – the gateway to Nether Grimston.

'What are you doing?' said Pixy.

Lucy put a finger up to Pixy's lips and whispered. 'We're going on a little trip,' she said.

'No,' said Pixy, 'I don't think I want to.'

'There are things to eat,' whispered Lucy. 'Do you like nuts?'

'Oh, well that's different,' said Pixy out loud. 'Let's *go*.'

'*Go?*' said Zenda, trying to rip the blindfold away.

'No you don't,' said Toby, holding the coat in place. 'You know the rules, no looking, and no peeping.'

Zenda struggled, but the ladies hit her with handbags, so she sat quietly and tried to figure out what was going on. But Lucy's words were audible to no one but her and the magical fragment of plywood.

'What's happening?' said Zenda eventually.

'Yes,' said Ethel, 'may we open our eyes yet?'

There was an almighty bang, followed by the smell of Lectric.

'You can look now,' said Toby, glancing out of the window. A guard had seen Bentley turn the headlights off and was marching towards them.

'Been anywhere nice Luce?' grinned Toby.

'Just to the bandstand,' said Lucy.

'*What* bandstand?' said Zenda, ripping her blindfold off. 'Oh,' she said, gathering her wits. 'The Pixy creature has disappeared. Now how on *earth* did you manage that?'

'Don't you ever listen?' said Gladys. She smiled at the guard as he tapped on the window. 'It was magic.'

Gladys wound the window down whilst Ethel dragged a travel blanket over the scarab to hide it from the prying eyes of the army guard. He was a thin, weaselly man with two stripes on his arm and a bright brass badge on his beret.

'Evening ladies,' he said, poking his head inside. 'Oh, and gentlemen, and children too. My, you *have* packed them in, haven't you?'

'We have plenty of room, thank you corporal,' said Ethel, 'not that it's any of your business. Now, what can we do for you?'

'This is as far as you can go I'm afraid. The town has been evacuated.'

'Has it?' said Ethel. 'But it has never been evacuated before.'

'Most unusual,' cooed Gladys. 'Umm, why are you looking at our car like that corporal?'

'Well,' he replied, 'we've had reports of unusual incidents on the Great North Road.'

'Yee-ess?' said Ethel innocently.

'And a car just like this one was involved,' said the guard.

'*Was* it?' said Gladys. 'Oh, well they *are* quite common you know.'

'No they aren't,' he said. He poked his head through the window, eager to find something amiss. Henbeg didn't like it, and gave a low growl.

'Hey, what was that?' he said.

'What was what?' said Lucy.

'Don't play smart with me,' he snapped. 'You heard it as plain as I did.'

'It was my stomach,' said Lucy. 'Listen.'

They all held their breath, waiting for Lucy's stomach to make a noise.

Eventually it did, but it wasn't quite the same sound as before.

'That wasn't what I heard just now,' said the guard.

'It doesn't make the same noise every time,' explained Toby. 'That would be boring, wouldn't it?'

'Hmm, alright then,' said the guard, 'but if I find out there's been funny business there'll be trouble.'

'I can assure you there has been no funny business in this vehicle,' said Ethel. 'We've had a *very* quiet trip.'

Everyone nodded and then yawned, as if working to a script.

'Yes,' said Lucy. 'A very boring trip.'

'Mind numbing,' said Toby.

'I slept the whole way,' said Zenda. 'Umm, but if you could arrange for me to have a private word with your commanding officer…'

Lucy glared at Zenda.

She stroked Henbeg to extract a warning growl.

'On second thoughts it can wait,' said Zenda.

'Yes,' said the guard, examining the hole in the roof. 'It probably can.'

'I see you've noticed our little mishap,' said Ethel. 'I keep meaning to get it repaired, but have you seen garage prices these days? It's scandalous.'

'Appalling,' said Gladys. 'We'd rather spend the money on treating our nieces and nephews. They just *love* going on day trips.'

'And where exactly did you go?' said the guard.

'*Blockpool*,' said Ethel.

'*Skragness*,' said Gladys, at exactly the same time.

'Actually we went to both,' said Lucy quickly.

'In one day?' said the guard. 'This car must be quite a mover.'

'It goes by magic,' said Lucy innocently. 'When the meteorite crashed through the roof it transferred some kind of strange power into the car, and now it can travel at the speed of light.'

'I see,' said the corporal, 'and who's the story teller?'

'This is my talented young niece,' said Ethel, tidying Lucy's coat and straightening her glasses. 'She likes dressing up.'

'And the grim looking handbag?' said the corporal.

'It's mine,' said Gladys. 'But our niece looks after it when we travel.'

'I *see*,' he said. 'Well if I could just have a look inside it?'

He reached out for the bag, but Henbeg's growl was louder this time and the guard cracked his skull on the window frame as he pulled away. Zenda gave a little snort of pleasure, but the guard regained his senses and stepped back, cocking his weapon.

'Upset stomach,' said Lucy hopefully.

'Handbag, no*w*!' he shouted, waving the rifle in Ethel's face.

'*Really* corporal,' said Ethel. 'If you insist on continuing with this boorish behaviour then I shall have words with your commanding officer. Don't you know that the contents of a lady's handbag are a private affair between her and the almighty?'

'That's right,' grinned Toby. 'Handbags are sacred ground – like inside a church.'

Henbeg gave another growl, even louder and more obvious. Lucy rubbed her stomach and gave a weak grin, but the guard wasn't convinced.

'Out of the car,' he screamed, '*all* of you – and bring *that* thing too.' He pointed at Henbeg, who had disobeyed Lucy and opened his eyes. But only because he'd sensed danger.

'It seems we have no option,' said Ethel, smiling broadly at the guard.

'You're *not* giving up are you?' said Lucy.

'Not bloody likely,' screamed Gladys. 'Step on it Benters.'

The car accelerated, throwing Lucy and Toby into the ladies' laps.

Bentley crashed the car through the barricade as a hail of bullets whistled past. But they escaped unscathed, and were soon hurtling down Saint Jacob's hill towards the town centre.

'You ladies are as bad as the girl,' said Zenda. 'I thought you might be old enough to know better.'

'*Old* enough?' said Gladys, looking deeply hurt. 'We like adventures, don't we Ethel? And we love the odd lie too, just like Lucy. I told them all the time when I was her age, although I don't recall ever getting *this* deep in trouble.'

'I blame the parents,' grinned Ethel. '*Now*, what are we going to do when we get there?'

'I suggest we start by avoiding *that*,' said Gladys, pointing at the sky.

'What? Where?' said Ethel, peering through the window. 'I hope you're not having us on again?'

'It was up there behind that line of trees,' said Gladys, 'but it went behind a cloud – I think it was an angel.'

'Have you been taking those pills like I told you?' said Ethel.

'*Yeees*,' said Gladys.

'The blue ones *and* the green ones?'

'*Yeees, and* the pink ones,' insisted Gladys. 'But I *still* saw an angel.'

'I believe you,' said Lucy. She concentrated on the patch of sky where Gladys had pointed, but there was nothing to see.

'You *do*?' said Ethel.

'Of course,' said Lucy. 'We've *all* seen them, haven't we?'

Everyone except Bentley and Ernie nodded, and it was only then that Gladys began to suspect what was going on.

'You're all just humouring me, aren't you?'

'No, really,' said Lucy. 'We've seen lots.'

'Honestly?' said Gladys.

'I believe her,' said Bentley, as he slowed the car. 'And if you don't, then perhaps you should have a look at what's happening up ahead.'

Nobody noticed the car as Bentley coasted up to the second checkpoint, because the guards were shooting into the air. Encouraging them was a more important looking soldier with crowns on his lapels, who was peering at the sky through huge binoculars.

'Keep going,' yelled Zenda. '*Ram the barrier.*'

'Yes, floor that pedal,' shouted Gladys.

'No Bentley, *stop*.' shouted Lucy. 'They're shooting at the cherubim.'

Bentley piled the brakes on, and as they screeched to a halt Lucy leaped out of the car and ran towards the marksmen.

'Leave them alone,' she screamed. 'You have absolutely no idea who they are. I'm *ordering* you to stop.'

'Sergeant, tell the men to cease-fire will you?' shouted the Major.

As he marched towards Lucy the four cherubim inclined their heads in her direction, climbing until they were nothing but a dim smudge of light in the night sky. Lucy watched with a heavy heart, as if they were deserting her in an hour of need. But then, she realised, they might not even know about her.

'You're right,' said the Major calmly. 'I *don't* know what those things are, but I have no idea who *you* are either. And I haven't a clue how you and all your friends managed to get through.'

'The corporal was very helpful,' said Ethel, leaning out of the window.

'That's right,' said Gladys, pushing Ethel out of the way. 'We told him we were on a very important mission and he just let us through.'

'I see,' said the officer. He stroked his chin slowly and stared at Lucy as a man with a large backpack radio approached them.

'Skews me, *sah*! Radio for you, *sah*!' He handed a telephone handset to the Major, who listened for a moment, nodding and frowning.

'I see,' he said. 'Damage to the barrier? I see. Large car with a hole in the roof? I see. Suspicious handbag? Yes, I see. Something else under a blanket? I see. I see, yes, I see, I see – yes, *well* corporal, I think we might have all that under control now, thank you corporal. *Oh*, and corporal?'

There was a delay whilst the man at the other end answered.

'Thank you *so* much for letting these people through. As you know we have very little to do down here at the command post, so we *do* appreciate being given something to keep us occupied. *Now*, can you still hear me? You can? Oh, *good. WELL DON'T LET ANYONE ELSE THROUGH, YOU BLITHERING HALF-WITTED IDIOT. DO YOU UNDERSTAND?*'

'Oh *dear*,' grinned Ethel. 'Have we got him into trouble?'

'Only in a very deep and serious way,' said the Major. 'Which is exactly the kind of trouble all of *you* are going to be in if I don't get a convincing explanation.'

'In that case, *I'd* like to say something,' said Zenda, her voice suddenly muffled by Toby's hand.

'What was that?' said the Major.

'Nothing,' said Ethel, kicking at Zenda. 'Young Lucy here will do all the explaining. We'll just sit here very quietly and listen, *won't* we Zenda?'

'Of course,' said Zenda, feeling Henbeg's teeth cutting into her ankle.

'I'm Major Pilkington,' explained the officer as he escorted Lucy to the command post tent. 'I'm the O.I.C.O.G.T.F.T.O.O.G.'

'And what's one of those?' said Lucy.

'Officer In Charge Of Getting The Flying Thing Out Of Grimston,' said Pilkington. 'I command a highly trained elite force of handpicked men. *Now*, do you see that man over there? The one with the huge round mouth and the red face? Well he got that way by yelling orders at the men who serve under him. And would you like to guess who gives *him* orders?'

'I don't suppose it would be you?' said Lucy.

'Right first time,' said the Major. 'That's the way it works in the army. It's called the chain of command.'

'But why are you telling me all of this?' said Lucy.

'Procedure,' said Pilkington. 'All this *ordering* nonsense you were shouting at me just now.'

'*Ah*,' said Lucy.

'Quite,' said the Major. 'The only person who can give *me* orders is Brigadier Bobbingberry. So if you want to order me to do something then you'll have to speak to him. That way he'll give *me* the orders and I'll give the orders to Sergeant Babington and *he* can give the orders to the men. But only in that order. *Now* do you understand?'

'Can I make a request then?' said Lucy. 'Instead of giving you an order?'

'You can always try,' said Pilkington.

'Please don't hurt the cherubim,' said Lucy. 'Despite what you may have read in the newspapers they're not giant birds and they don't intend you any harm. They're angels.'

'I know,' said Pilkington. 'Anyone with half a brain can see that. What *we* want to know is whose side they're on.'

'They're not on *anyone's* side,' said Lucy. 'At least not the way you mean. If anything, they're arguing amongst themselves.'

'You seem to know a lot about them,' said the Major.

'Not really,' said Lucy, 'but I probably know more than you.'

'So whose side are they on?' said the Major.

'I just *told* you,' said Lucy, frowning.

'Indeed you did,' said the Major. 'But you didn't give the answer I wanted to hear. The modern army is always interested in hearing answers, but only if they belong to questions we have asked ourselves. You see we don't actually have a philosophy regiment as far as I'm aware, so we limit ourselves to simple questions of allegiance. And that boils down to yes or no, black or white. Are you on *our* side? Or are you on *their* side?'

'I'm on *your* side,' said Lucy quietly.

'Pleased to hear it,' said the Major.

He held open the flap of the tent and motioned Lucy inside.

'But the cherubim are on your side too,' she said, stepping into the musty gloom. 'Which is why you ought not to be firing at them.'

'Well it doesn't seem to make much difference in any case,' admitted the Major. 'No matter how much we shoot at them they just continue to hover, as if they're waiting for something.'

'Or some *one*,' said Inspector Trembley.

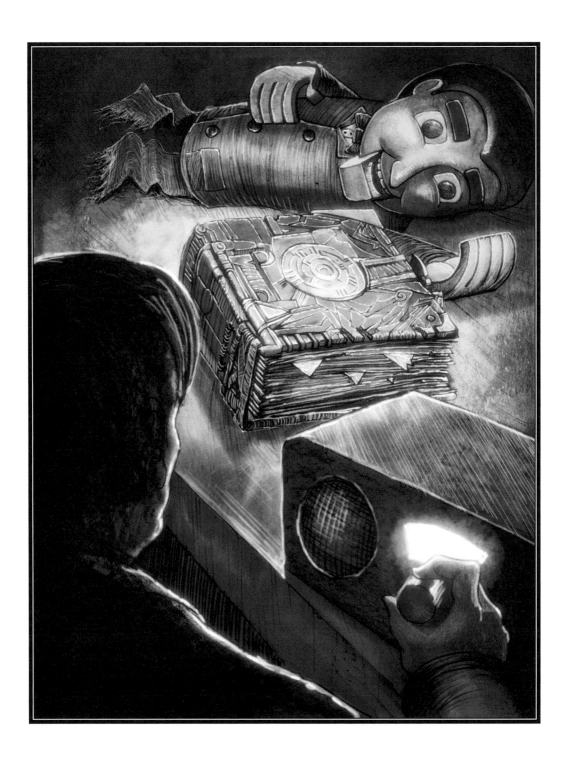

Blue Underpants
on the Promenade

A hurricane lantern spilled light onto the large, folding table where they forced Lucy to sit. At the back of the tent, a man twiddled a radio receiver, extracting all manner of bizarre noises from it, but very little else. And it was here, on the table next to him, that Lucy could just make out Genjamin and the rest of her confiscated possessions.

'Let's have a look through the list of confiscated items, shall we?' said Trembley.

'If you must,' said Lucy, 'but can we do it later? There are a few urgent things that…'

'A business card belonging to Bentley Priory,' said Trembley, ignoring her plea. 'A Mimsy Muggeridge postcard. A picture of Harry the pigeon man with a bird. A pack of tarot cards, and another strange postcard that looks to be at least a hundred years old. We *have* been busy, haven't we?'

'You have no idea,' sighed Lucy.

'I'm not finished,' said Trembley. 'We also found a length of rope that's practically invisible. Almost hanged the sergeant with that one.'

'It was a present,' said Lucy, 'from a very dear friend.'

'Name?' said Pilkington.

'Yes, he had one of those,' smiled Lucy.

'*Name?*' insisted Pilkington.

'Quim,' replied Lucy. 'Do you want his address?'

'Not just now,' said Trembley. 'We're more interested in the other items. The ventriloquist's dummy for instance, and the book.'

'It's just an old diary,' lied Lucy. 'It belonged to Exotica Pubrane.'

'Rank?' said Pilkington.

'Fortune teller,' said Lucy with a straight face.

'And why do you think a fortune teller would need access to encrypted information?' said Pilkington.

'Excuse me?' said Lucy.

'The *book*,' he barked. 'The whole damned thing is written in code. And naturally we want to know what it's about.'

'When I find out myself, I'll let you know,' grinned Lucy.

'And the sword,' said Trembley. 'Will you be telling us about that?'

'Of course,' smiled Lucy. 'In the fullness of time.'

'And, umm, that coat of yours,' said Pilkington. 'The pockets, umm, ahh, how did you manage to fit all those things inside?'

'It has a special lining,' lied Lucy, 'sewn by my two dear old friends.'

'Ah, yes, the *ladies*,' said Trembley. 'They seem a bit confused.'

'Their minds have gone,' said Lucy with a smile. She knew that Trembley would interview them later and wanted to distance herself, in case they gave something away.

'I *see*,' said Trembley. 'So why exactly *were* you sharing a car with a couple of mentally defective octogenarians?'

'They ran us off the road,' said Lucy. 'The Great North Road.'

'Ah-ha,' said Trembley. 'A shred of truth.'

'It's the best way,' said Lucy. 'Without an element of truth our lies are so much easier to spot.'

'I see,' said Trembley, recalling their previous interview in horrendous detail. 'And where did you read that, Reeble's Digress?'

'Look,' said Lucy, 'I know you've got a lot of questions, but couldn't you just write them down and post them on to me or something?'

'*Post* them?' said Trembley, his eyes widening with amazement. 'Did you hear that Major? She wants us to conduct a murder investigation by mail.'

'*Murder*?' said Lucy. '*What* murder?'

'I'm asking the questions,' said Trembley. 'And I'm going to get some sensible answers. You're not going to smart-Alec your way out of *this* one.'

'No,' sighed Lucy, 'it doesn't look as though I am.' She rubbed her knees, which were sore and bleeding, and then her palms, which were covered in gravel rash. It was the first time she had ever been rugby tackled onto a concrete path, and was hoping it would be the last.

'So,' said Trembley, wriggling in his chair. 'Let's start again, shall we?'

'What if I decide to co-operate?' said Lucy. 'Will you let me go?'

'Why?' said Trembley. 'Have you got an emergency appointment?'

'People's lives are at risk,' said Lucy.

'We know,' said Trembley. 'We've had a few deaths in Grimston recently, on account of this huge bird that picks holidaymakers up and flies them out to sea for a pleasure trip – whether they want it or not.'

'*Not*, I'd say,' grinned Pilkington.

'Quite,' said Trembley. 'The point is we're up to our ears in it, and you, Miss Lucy Blake, are not helping. Unless of course you'd like to tell us what '*Surrender the Light*' means. We keep finding it written in the strangest places. Carved into the roof of the Winter Gardens for instance, or ploughed into the beach in hundred foot high letters. One woman even found it engraved on the head of a pin that was pecked into the top of her head by a pigeon.'

'Amazing,' smiled Lucy.

'Quite,' said the Major. 'But do you know what it means?'

Lucy shook her head. If she revealed *that* particular secret they'd take the book for certain and probably destroy the town in the process. Dee had told her that the power of heaven was unknowable, and the very *last* place that knowledge needed to be was on the inside of Trembley's head.

'You've never heard of this expression?' said Trembley. 'The Light?'

'No,' lied Lucy.

'Hmm,' said the Inspector, 'now why do I think you're lying?'

'I'm not capable,' lied Lucy.

'Really?' said Trembley. 'The report we got from St. Mallydick's describes you as a psychopathic liar who wouldn't recognise the truth if it marched along the promenade dressed in blue underpants and playing a trombone.'

'And that's a proper medical report is it?' said Lucy.

'Just a snippet I got from Doctor Veraciter,' said Trembley, 'who, I might add, is quite eager to have you back.'

'I'll *bet* he is,' said Lucy. 'But he'll need to get in the queue, I've got quite a few other people to see before I get around to him.'

Trembley got up and paced around the tent, as if trying to imagine how he was going to phrase the next question. Then he sat down, elbows on the table, and made a steeple with his fingers.

'Miss Blake, how well do you know Morana Fay?'

'Why?' said Lucy. She knew she was blushing, but even worse, she knew that Trembley had seen it. Her face was lit up like a warning beacon.

'It's just that I mentioned a small matter of murder,' said Trembley. 'And you didn't even think to ask who the victim was.'

'And is it her?' said Lucy quietly.

'Morana Fay was found floating face down in the model boat pool about three months ago,' said Trembley, 'just after you vanished for the second time, when we hadn't even had an explanation for the first.'

'So you think I drowned her?' said Lucy.

'Ah, well now we're getting somewhere,' said Trembley. He opened a fresh notebook and wet a pencil on his tongue.

'I think we both know she didn't drown,' said Lucy.

'Oh, *do* we?' said Trembley.

'Yes, but I haven't got time to sit around discussing it,' said Lucy flatly, 'I keep telling you, there are things I have to do.'

'Take a note Major,' said Trembley. 'The accused knew that the victim wasn't drowned. And she has better things to do than talk to us about it.'

'Yes,' said Lucy. 'And can you also make a note that she has to go and attend to the angel?'

'*Angel?*' said Trembley, choking on his words. 'Who mentioned anything about an angel?'

'That's what your giant bird is,' said Lucy. 'He's an angel and he's pretty damned mad.'

'Yes, *we* know that,' said Trembley. 'But how do *you* know? You need a code purple clearance for that. Even the Major here didn't know until this morning.'

'I don't care about your code purples,' said Lucy. 'Or even your code blues or your code reds. I just want to get into Grimston.'

The Major took a notebook from his breast pocket and leafed through it as if he had lost something.

'Sorry,' said Trembley, 'but access to Grimston is out of the question.'

'That's right,' said the Major, frowning as he reached the end of the book and flipped back to the start. 'Grimston is completely O.O.T.Q. for L.B.'

'Then what are you going to do with me?' said Lucy.

'We're going to have a very long conversation,' said Trembley. 'Followed by a short cup of tea and another very long conversation.'

'About anything in particular?' said Lucy, glancing at the tent flap. It was guarded by two soldiers who had their rifles pointed in her direction.

'I think we can come up with something,' said Trembley. 'Zenda Freggley for instance. *She* has some interesting tales, not that I claim to understand any part them. And then there's the kidnapped Lindstrom boy, who also told us some strange things – but only after we tortured him of course. Then we have the famous Bentley Priory, and Ernie Crowley, whose cab you appear to have wrecked. Will any of *those* stories do?'

'Has the angel mentioned anyone by name?' said Lucy.

'No,' said Trembley. 'I don't think it has, has it Major?'

'I don't think so,' said Pilkington.

'Yes it has,' said the radio man, taking his headphones off. 'There were all those screams we got over the radio. Those bloody awful voices yelling 'surrender The Light, Lucy Blake'. That was the name they said right enough. Umm, *oh*, or was that supposed to be one of those code purple secrets?'

Inspector Trembley's eyes rolled back in his head, like a cast-iron moneybox Lucy had seen once in a shop window. Only this time there was no need to put a penny on the policeman's tongue to get him to work. The Major buried his face in his hands, and when he finally emerged Lucy just *knew* he would be the colour of pickled cabbage.

Lucy *hated* pickled cabbage.

'*Un-be-bloodywell-lievable*,' he screamed. 'You've told the blasted enemy *everything*. Unless of course there's anything you'd like to add?'

The radio man gave an embarrassed shrug and returned to his corner, replacing the headphones in the hope they might make him invisible.

'But I'm not the enemy,' said Lucy. 'The angel is. The big one, not the little ones you were shooting at.'

'There's a difference, is there?' said the Major.

'They're on opposing sides in some kind of heavenly disagreement,' said Lucy. 'But don't ask me what.'

'Hmm,' said Trembley. 'Well that would seem to agree with our friends in the two congregations.'

'Are we telling her about that as well?' said the Major. 'We might as well hand over command of the whole operation if you ask me.'

'It can't hurt if she knows,' said Trembley. 'And she might even be able to help.'

'Possibly,' said Lucy, sensing an opportunity. 'So who are these friends of yours?'

'*Ah*,' said Trembley. 'When I said friends, I wasn't being entirely serious. I think a more accurate description might be loonies. Although they do seem to have some interesting ideas.'

'Such as?' said Lucy.

'That would be telling,' said the Major, 'and as the inspector has already pointed out, this is *our* interview, not yours.'

'Hey,' said Trembley. 'What was that?'

'What was what?' smiled Lucy.

'I *heard* something, just then.'

'I'm sure you did,' said Lucy innocently.

'No, he's right,' said the Major. 'I heard it too.'

'And I'm the one that needs to go St. Mallydick's?' said Lucy.

'It came from the radio,' said Trembley. 'And it sounded like one of those voices.'

'The screaming ones?' said the Major.

'The boring ones,' replied Trembley. 'Remember when we had all those incredibly tedious people interfering with our transmissions?'

'How could I possibly forget?' said the Major. 'We were attempting to organise troop movements and *they* were all complaining about not being able to buy non-smell insoles for their shoes or wondering why the number fifty-three bus doesn't stop at the cemetery any more.'

'Yes,' said Trembley, 'and they're back – listen.'

Sssss – Zzzzz – Snackle – Freeeeeeeee……poppp…

Vzzzzzzz…

Snuzz…

HISSSsssss…

Nnnnoonngg…

Vzzz…

Gronk…

Phartsss…

Sput.

They listened carefully to the voices, trying to identify what they were saying, but there was an explosion outside, and something soft landed on the roof of the tent. It was hot, and burned a hole in the canvas, then dropped onto the table in front of them.

It smoked and sizzled and smelled strongly of burning feathers.

'Oh, *look*, it's a flame-wrapped, stuffed parrot,' smiled Lucy. 'Now where could that have come from?'

Trembley and the Major leapt to their feet and ran out of the tent, their faces illuminated by the flames that leapt from the blazing limousine. Lucy leaned back in her chair and spotted Toby standing near the car. He was holding a pair of Jump-o-Start leads, and his grinning face was covered in grime.

'That's *amazing*,' said Lucy, wandering over to the radio table. 'Have you seen what's happening outside?'

'I'd better keep an eye on you,' said the radio man. 'You've already got me in trouble once.'

'Yes, but I'm not going anywhere, am I?' said Lucy. 'There's only one way out of the tent.'

'I suppose,' said the radio man. He removed his headphones and moved towards the tent flap, eager to see Toby's explosive distraction. Lucy sneaked back to the table and grabbed her coat, loading it up only with items that wouldn't slow her down.

'Don't look at me like that,' she whispered to Genjamin. 'You're heavy, and I need to run. And I need you to take care of things at this end.'

Genjamin said nothing. He just stared at Lucy, not even blinking as she drew the obsidian sword and cut a long slit in the back of the tent. She gave Genjamin a quick smile and stepped into the night air, with just one thing on her mind. Even though the town was empty, there was someone whose advice she desperately needed to seek.

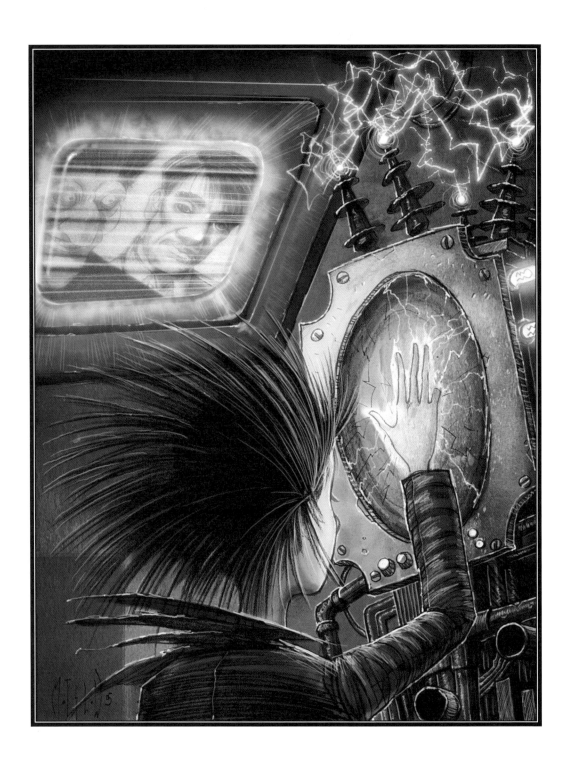

Lectrical Language

The Lectric had been turned off during the evacuation, so the Winter Gardens auditorium was bathed in darkness. Even so, sufficient moonlight filtered through the dome to show the vague outline of the Confuser. It was bigger than Lucy remembered, and on closer examination she saw that the original design had been supplemented with extra control panels and flashing lights to make it more attractive to the punters.

She located the main switch and brought the machine and its immediate surroundings to life. The rest of the Winter Gardens remained in darkness, and for the moment at least she was glad not to be attracting any attention. The only creatures that might notice her would be sleepless birds that were over-flying the dome, or late night balloonists with extremely good eyesight. Or angels. And if there were any of those about she hoped they would stay away, at least until she was ready.

She had once joked that the Yakky Morto might be a machine for putting jam inside circular biscuits, and now she almost wished that it was. It didn't seem right, having something that let you talk to dead people, because when they were gone, they were gone. Even so, she was determined to use it just this once. There were things that she needed to hear, and only the dead were capable of saying them.

The original swivelling seat had been replaced with a comfortable leather chair, but the control panel was exactly as she remembered it. The engraved nameplate had been replaced by a brightly painted sign that proclaimed the Yakky Morto as the eighth wonder of the world, but just behind it was the same tiny piece of sticking plaster that Toby had taken a dislike to. Whoever moved the Confuser must have thought it necessary to keep things working. Lucy screwed the seat down until her eyes were level with the curved glass screen. Then she dithered, and dithered some more, drumming her fingers on the three position switch that was still marked 'CWPWHPO (OKAD)', 'Dangerous' and 'Experimental'. For the moment she left it in the 'converse with people who have passed over (otherwise known as dead)' position and placed the palm of her right hand on the screen.

There was a vibration in the floor. Somewhere over to her left, a pointer moved to indicate 'red hot lover', but she ignored the display, entranced by the sudden smell of Lectric and showering of sparks. Her heart filled with joy as she realised the machine was actually *working*. The room filled with the sound of tiny glowing angels, each singing at the top of its voice. She was *so* glad to hear the song of the thermionics again, even if it meant having a hairstyle that was only a slight improvement on a wire brush.

When the transformer began to whine and the main relay clicked, Lucy knew the device was ready. She smiled as the familiar yellow-orange sheets of flame appeared. They danced between metal rods, just as they had in Byron's laboratory, but here in the great hall, the upper rods were suspended from a balcony, so the aurora curtains were taller and their thunderous call that much deeper. They still folded and flexed and touched at their edges though, and when they *did* touch, tiny blue sparks leapt between them as before – only now they reminded her of Blueface and his exotic dance.

With a touch of sadness Lucy sat still for a moment and listened to the sound of the sparks, wondering if it was some kind of Lectrical language they were speaking.

The curtain of lights thinned and dimmed, and the noise from the valves died to a gentle hiss as sounds emerged from a loudspeaker buried deep in the gubbins.

Phlebbo,
Phlebbo,
Phlebbo,
Phlonk…

There was a flash of light on the screen and a vague image appeared – a dim patchwork of lines and dots with hardly any shape. The pattern hesitated for a moment, then gathered strength again, gradually forming the outline of a face.

But it wasn't Byron.

Lucy was confronted by a thin, ruddy-cheeked man whose hooked nose was trying to make contact with his huge up-curved chin. She was glad the picture lacked clarity, because it meant she didn't have to look too closely.

'My name is Professor Mennabungus,' said the face.

'I was expecting someone else,' said Lucy.

'In that case I'm sorry to be a disappointment to you, Lucy Blake.'

'*Oh*,' said Lucy. 'You *know* me. But I don't know you, do I?'

'Not yet you don't.'

'Not *yet*?' said Lucy.

'That's exactly what I said – but you *will* do.'

'I don't understand,' said Lucy.

'Neither do I,' said the Professor, 'at least not properly – I *think* I knew you once, but then I came here. My memory is a little bit hazy.'

'Not as hazy as mine,' said Lucy. 'How did we meet?'

'I remember a small tent,' said the Professor. 'There was an argument and someone got thrown out of a window – and after that I don't remember a thing. In fact I don't even remember if I *liked* you. We might be enemies for all I know.'

'I hope not,' said Lucy. 'So where did all this happen?'

'Ah, well now,' said Mennabungus, 'that I *do* remember.'

'*Yes*?' said Lucy expectantly.

'Wait a minute,' said the Professor. 'No, I don't remember now I come to think of it.'

'Are you related to someone called Granny Moon?' smiled Lucy.

'Never heard of her,' said the Professor. His face broke up into a series of horizontal bands. 'But there were red and white stripes on the tent, if that's any help…'

Flebb.

Snokkit.

'Professor?' said Lucy. 'Hello?'

As the face faded, Lucy realised that she didn't *really* know how to use the machine and had just dialled the equivalent of a heavenly wrong number.

Fzzzt.

Vizzzzzzz.

Spozz.

'Hello dearie,' said a feeble voice. 'Have you brought those cough sweets I asked for?'

'No,' said Lucy, trying to make out a face. There was nothing but static though, and the voice faded quickly, replaced by more ridiculous noises from the Yakky Morto.

Hosssss….

Peeyong.

Vzzzt.

'I *told* them I was ill, didn't I? And did they listen? No, they did *not* – and look what happened.' The new voice sounded upset, and was accompanied by the vague outline of a man. He had pale green skin, and poked his tongue out as if looking in a bathroom mirror for signs of some horrible disease. 'Is that a healthy colour for a tongue?' he said.

'I don't know,' said Lucy. '*Look*, can you actually hear me?'

'Of course I…'

Gronnnk.

Phlobb.

Nubbocks.

Sput.

'This is *not* going very well.' said Lucy under her breath.

'*Hello?*' said a vague voice with an indistinct face. 'Is that the complaints department? I've been trying to get through for three months now…'

'No, it bloody-well *isn't* the complaints department,' snapped Lucy. 'Now would you please go away? I'm trying to reach someone else.'

She pressed harder on the glass, and as sparks continued to leap between the strands of her hair, Lucy concentrated on the screen so hard that she almost hypnotised herself.

And then he appeared – as thin and as worried as he'd looked the last time, still apparently haunted by some terrible tragedy.

He looked about furtively, as though someone might be eavesdropping.

'Uncle Byron?' smiled Lucy. 'It's me, Lucy. Can you hear me?'

'Yes,' said Byron, his voice accompanied by the sound of crackling.

'I need advice,' said Lucy, wiping away tears of joy.

'What sort of advice?' said Byron, still hissing and popping.

Fazzz.

Burp.

Phlopp.

'Uncle Byron, can you still hear me? *Uncle Byron?*'

The image on the screen broke up, and although his mouth was moving Lucy couldn't hear what Byron was saying. If *only* she'd brought Genjamin with her, the dummy would have been able to translate. She felt certain it was something that a person with wooden teeth would be good at.

Fronnnng…

Plap.

Weeble.

'Uncle Byron?'

Lucy studied closely, picking up the odd word-shape on his lips. 'Mother' was one, and 'angels' was another, but everything else was scrambled by the interference, including the faint outline of his face.

'Hello again,' said a cheery Professor Mennabungus.

'*You,*' hissed Lucy. 'I thought you'd gone.'

'Ah,' he said. 'Well what we have here is a crossed connection. It happens all the time.'

'Would you mind awfully just going away?' said Lucy. 'This is a private conversation.'

'Actually I don't think it is,' said the Professor. 'There are at least half a dozen of us listening to this one.'

'And why would you want to do that?' said Lucy.

'Because it's a lot more interesting than *not* listening,' he said. 'And if you had to lounge around in the afterlife doing absolutely nothing all day then I'm sure *you'd* be eavesdropping on private conversations too.'

'Perhaps I would,' said Lucy politely.

And then she realised that she was having a perfectly understandable conversation with the Professor, without any interference.

'Would you mind passing on my uncle's messages?' said Lucy. 'He seems to be having some difficulty doing it himself.'

'I *might* do,' said Mennabungus. 'Ah, but no, I can't you see, because you said it was private.'

'I'll make an exception in this case,' said Lucy. 'And if I'm ever in a position to do you a favour then I will.'

'Anything at all?' said the Professor.

'Anything,' repeated Lucy. 'If it's within my power.'

'Then swear,' said Mennabungus, 'on your mother's life.'

'I swear,' said Lucy, without hesitating. Only *then* did she realise what she had committed to, and where the promise might lead.

'Oh dear, I'm afraid he's gone,' said Mennabungus. 'Your uncle seems to have just sort of fizzled away.'

'Fizzled away?' said Lucy. 'To *where*?'

'Things are never very clear here,' said the Professor. 'But I remembered some of what he said.'

'You *do*?' said Lucy eagerly.

'You did swear to help us, didn't you?' said the Professor.

'Of course,' said Lucy.

'Anything at all?' he said, 'as long as it was within your power?'

'Yes,' said Lucy. 'Now come *on*, tell me what Byron said.'

'Alright,' said Mennabungus. 'Now it's not all that clear you understand, what with interference and all, but there was something about your mother.'

'What *about* my mother?' said Lucy.

'You are in a great deal of danger,' said Mennabungus. 'Apparently the four worlds, umm, or no, perhaps it was five? Well anyway, however many there are, these worlds have been infiltrated by something or someone called the Dominion.'

'But what about my mother?' said Lucy.

'Oh it's all to do with her alright,' said the Professor. 'Whatever is going on, your mother is very definitely involved.'

'I *knew* it,' said Lucy. 'She's alive, and she's coming back.'

'Umm, no-oo,' said Mennabungus. 'There was no mention of that.'

'Was there anything else?' said Lucy.

Mennabungus faded and for a moment Byron's face reappeared.

He was only just recognisable, and his lips moved feebly, like a dying fish.

'Uncle Byron? Can you hear me? What's going on?'

'*Preparation*,' said Byron.

'For what?' said Lucy.

'Part of you knows the answer,' said Byron, his voice almost obliterated by static noise. 'And the part of you that doesn't know must wait and see.'

'Uncle Byron, *please*, don't go,' pleaded Lucy. 'What about my mother?'

'Trust no-one,' said Byron, his image fading rapidly.

The instant his face disappeared, Lucy detected a shadowy movement overhead. Of course it *might* have been a cloud passing over the dome, but it had cast a shadow over her heart too. And now that she looked more closely there were shapes up there. Pieces of dark but identifiable meat, and huge, sticky-red flight feathers were stuck to the glass.

Raziel had been at work again.

Lucy gave a deep sigh that seemed to pull air from a dark place buried deep inside her. There had been joy in her heart as she freewheeled towards the sea front on a stolen army bicycle, but the flames of that passion were melted now, and she was reduced to a cold, icy hatred of what the angel and his kind stood for.

Sprimpo,

Webbit, Whee, Whee, Whee…

Crump…

The Yakky Morto was plunged into blackness. Either it had broken down again, or the Lectric had been cut off.

Lucy sat in the dark with her hair still standing on end and a horrible feeling of isolation in the pit of her stomach. If the visit to Assiah had taught her anything, it was that she made her best decisions under pressure, perhaps even when she was afraid – like now. There was no need for the Confuser any more, or even advice from Byron. Lucy Blake, the one the ornithopters called the creator, had decided *exactly* what she must do.

On the way out of the auditorium Lucy tripped in the dark, and when she recovered she found herself sitting in a dusty aisle between two blocks of seats. Scattered around her were handbills, advertising the wonders of the Yakky Morto. She paused, listening to the wind as it funnelled through the main entrance and chased round the empty seats like a demented ghost.

Then she heard a voice.

Or perhaps it was just the air, taunting her.

'*Hello?*' she said. 'Is anyone there?'

It was a stupid question, which she regretted it at once. But as long as it wasn't Raziel that answered, any sort of company would be welcome. Even Trembley, or God forbid, Zenda.

'Hello?' she said again, in a quieter, almost feeble voice.

There was no answer – just a vague sensation of loss as the breeze swept long forgotten cobwebs out of corners. Lucy picked herself up and walked up the sloping aisle into the main lobby, pausing for a moment at the cash desk before stepping out into the deserted street. Once outside, she made her way to the post office by way of the back alleys, in case anyone was left behind and watching. She went round to the back door and reached through the cat flap, and there, dangling on a piece of string, was the key, just like Malcolm had said.

It was wrong to be sneaking into the shop, but certain things sometimes *had* to be. She had to attract Raziel to a certain place at a certain time, and as Bentley once demonstrated, this particular method was the most effective way of sending a message ever devised.

She took a pencil and two postcards from the counter. The first one she addressed to the post-mistress, promising to pay for the cards. The other one she wrote for Raziel, in block capitals that could be seen from a distance.

When it was done, Lucy taped the card to the window, facing the street. Then she set the post-mistress's alarm to go off at six o'clock and crawled under the counter, settling down to sleep amongst the sacks of letters.

Do you seek *enlightenment?*
Come to 47C Kronk Street at 10 a.m. tomorrow,
where you may hear something to your advantage.
(Oh, and P.S. Why don't you bring a *friend?*)

The Patrons of Darkness and Light

Lucy rose from her nest of mailbags before first light and made her way to the northern end of the promenade where a great mound of earth known as Monkey Island was to be found. There were no monkeys of course, and never had been, but it was the best place in Grimston to watch the sun rise, and Lucy's favourite place for thinking. She sat amongst wild grasses at the high point of the island, watching the tide flow gradually around her and considering her plan. She still wasn't certain it would work, but there was one thing that she *was* certain of.

When the day had run its course and the sun was ready to set in the east, only she or Raziel would be left alive.

The sky was clear all the way to the horizon, so when the sun appeared on the lip of the world and the first fragments of light appeared they rushed across the waters unimpeded, painting Grimston in a gentle, pink mist.

But the glow didn't last.

Soon after sunrise, a cloudbank closed in and wrapped the town in a dull, silver blanket, as if it were about to catch a chill. The sea was calm, its surface a flat and strangely unreflective pool of mercury. A skylark twittered overhead, its call punctuated by the cries of a gull that wheeled around her, as if it knew who she was and why she was here. Lucy smiled at the sight of him as her thoughts turned to Blink Bonny and the other ornithopters. She wondered where they could possibly have gone, now that Assiah was denied them.

As she walked back to town, past the concrete pyramids and the rows of brightly painted chalets, Lucy began to worry that the sea was unusually empty. At this time of day the fishermen would usually be on their way to lay crab pots, but the waters were ominously quiet, all except for one small craft about a mile out to sea. It looked like a navy boat, and was surrounded by thousands of birds in a funnel-like formation. But it wasn't just gulls in that bird-storm. There were hundreds of species massing in the darkening sky, and as they got closer, it was clear that they were not following the boat.

They had gathered with a much darker purpose, and today, of all days, that could only mean one thing.

They were here because of Raziel.

Lucy carried on walking as she watched the developments at sea, and was so entranced by the bird funnel that she arrived at the pier without realising it. But she was soon brought to her senses when she walked into a lamppost and fell to the ground, clutching her head.

And then it all went black.

Upon waking, Lucy let out an involuntary scream. She was surrounded by men who fortunately for her, seemed concerned with her welfare. She shook her head, but they were still there, and quite probably real.

'Umm, my head hurts,' she said, somewhat dozily.

'Of course it does,' said a man in a brown overall and bow tie.

Lucy noticed that he was wearing a black armband.

'We believe in the dark,' he said, helping her to her feet.

Lucy frowned, but only for a moment.

'You're Mister Brown,' she said. 'The bicycle repair man.'

'Correct,' said Brown. 'But we can repair bicycles and *still* believe in the darkness, can't we?'

'I'm sure you *can*,' said Lucy, regaining her composure. 'But tell me, how did you all get here?'

'The army couldn't possibly hope to seal the town off completely,' said Brown. 'Especially since old Albert here used to work for the Corporation Sewers.'

'Hello,' smiled Albert. He grinned like a piano with missing keys.

'Yes, *hello*,' said Lucy, watching him with great interest. He squinted like a mole, as if he'd spent the whole of his life underground.

'He wasn't the only one though,' said Brown. 'We had other help, *didn't* we lads?'

Some of the men nodded, but others were less well informed and shook their heads.

'Did we?' said one of the head shakers.

'Of course,' said a nodder.

'Alright then,' said Lucy. 'Who was it that helped?'

'The angel,' said Brown. 'He emptied the town so nobody else could hear what he had to say. Then he let us come in and talk to him. We're the chosen ones.'

'Oh, yeah, that's right,' said one of the shakers. 'I *remember* now.'

'I can't see the angel helping anyone but himself,' said Lucy. 'And as for you lot being the chosen ones, well…'

She was about to say something she might later regret, and was grateful when she was interrupted by voices nearby. Only when the owners of those voices finally swept around the corner, she wasn't so sure. There were twenty of them, many of whom she recognised from around the town. They wore white ribbons on their chests, and like the wearers of the black armbands their faces glowed and their eyes burned bright with a new found faith.

'What are you lot doing here?' said Brown.

'I could ask you the same thing,' said their bowler-hatted leader.

'Well I asked first,' said Brown.

The man in the bowler hat ignored the bicycle repairman and turned to Lucy, smiling like a snake that's about to try and swallow a pig.

'We saw you in the Winter Gardens,' he said. 'I'm councillor Grumpton by the way. You'll have heard of me, of course.'

Lucy studied his face and decided that she didn't like him. His dark eyes were too close together, and his fat, greasy nose was far too red.

'Ah,' she said. 'So it was *you* up on the balconies?'

'Of course,' said Grumpton, breathing through his teeth. 'That's why we came looking for you. We saw you talking to God, on the machine.'

'Talking to God?' snapped Lucy, uncertain why she was so annoyed by their accusations. 'I've never heard anything so bloody ridiculous.'

'Well if that *wasn't* God,' wheezed Grumpton, 'then how come he knew so much about the angels?'

'Yeah,' said the second-in-command. 'And how did he know about the Yakky Morto? Nobody else that appears inside that thing knows anything about it. They think they're having a normal conversation. It's not natural, that thing isn't. Not natural at all.'

'Of *course* it isn't natural,' said Lucy. 'My uncle Byron *built* it, so how can it be natural?'

'She's keeping summat back,' said Grumpton. 'I can tell when people are lying. You need to, in my business. We should take her back to the church for questioning. All in favour?'

Lucy laughed out loud as Grumpton counted the votes. But he seemed to take this as a personal insult and directed his henchmen to take Lucy by the elbows.

'Did I say something funny?' he said.

'I was just thinking of something a friend once said,' said Lucy.

'Oh?' said Grumpton, breathing the smell of digested cabbage over her. 'And what exactly *was* it that he said?'

'He wanted to know why nobody was ever pleased to see us,' said Lucy.

'But we *are* pleased,' said Grumpton. 'We're *ever* so glad to have you on our side.'

'Hey, less of that,' said Brown, squaring up to Grumpton. '*We* saw her first, and she's on our side – she as good as promised.'

'I did no such thing,' insisted Lucy. 'And anyway, I'm on my own side.'

'You won't be for long,' said Grumpton. 'Just wait until we get you back to our church and show you what we've discovered.'

'Yeah? Well she's not going with you, *is* she?' said the repairman. 'She's coming with us, to teach us how to worship the angel.'

'And what has the angel done to deserve that?' said Lucy. 'I thought he'd been carrying people out to sea.'

'He's been picking out the unworthy and destroying them,' said Brown.

'That's right,' said one of Brown's men. 'I heard about a family who left Poonsnake's Bed and Breakfast without paying, and sure enough the angel descended and whisked them out to meet the fish.'

'That's power for you,' said Grumpton, trembling with admiration.

'Being powerful doesn't make him right,' said Lucy, 'or even worthy of your respect. Especially not this one.'

'And how would *you* know?' said Brown. 'Have you met him?'

Lucy shook her head, but he saw through her lie.

'You *have* met him,' said Brown, turning to his followers. 'I vote we take her to the bicycle repair shop, umm, I mean chapel, so we can interrog…, umm, I mean find out what she knows. We can make *her* worship the angel too. That's bound to please him.'

'I'm certain it would,' said Lucy, 'but you don't worship angels. They're only messengers.'

'Who says?' said Grumpton.

'Bentley Priory,' replied Lucy

'That crackpot?' said Brown. 'And how would *he* know?'

'He just does,' said Lucy. 'He knows all sorts of things.'

'Well if the angel is a messenger,' said Grumpton, 'then why is he taking people out to sea and dumping them?'

'Or is that part of the message?' said a faint voice at the back.

'Don't be ridiculous,' snorted Grumpton.

'It *might* be,' said Brown. 'We need to work it out, and write it down.'

'We'll be doing that as well,' said Grumpton. 'We're going to write down everything that happens so that future generations will know the truth. But there'll be a proper vote taken as to the what actually constitutes the truth, and we certainly won't be writing it on those greasy bits of paper that bicycle accessories come wrapped in.'

'Neither will we.' said Brown. 'It's *our* descendants who will know the real truth – yours will just be grubbing around in the dark.'

'Well *I* think you should all just shut up and go home,' said Lucy.

'And you should keep your opinions to yourself,' said Brown. 'What do *you* know about matters of worship and angels? You're just a silly kid.'

'Maybe,' said Lucy, 'but a few minutes ago you thought this silly kid had been talking to God.'

'Perhaps we *were* a little hasty with that,' admitted Grumpton, 'but you've been talking to *him* though, haven't you? The angel?'

'That's right,' said Brown, 'you have, and if he really *is* a messenger then you can tell us what he's trying to say.'

'Haven't you listened to anything?' said Lucy. '*Surrender The Light.* That's what he keeps saying. *That's* the message.'

'And what *is* The Light?' said Grumpton. 'None of our committees have heard about it.'

'It's just a book,' said Lucy, regretting the utterance immediately.

'And I suppose you just happen to have it with you?' said Grumpton.

'Of course not,' lied Lucy.

'We'd better look,' he said, 'just in case.'

The councillor pushed Lucy to the ground and tore at her coat, but just as he was about to delve into her pockets there was a loud 'ping' and a hole was chipped out of the pavement right next to his undersized feet.

'It's the army,' shouted a nobody at the back. 'They're shooting at us.'

'Well isn't that the absolute *limit*?' said Grumpton. 'Don't these people know who I am? I'm chairman of…'

The sound of rifle shots echoed around them as another hail of bullets splattered into the road.

'*Run*,' shouted Brown.

'I agree with Brown,' shouted Grumpton, 'but *only* on this point. We disagree with him on every other issue of faith. *Run…*'

The white ribbons and black armbands scattered in opposite directions as Lucy got up onto one knee, shielding her eyes from the sky and trying to see where the shots had come from. Then she spotted a glint of light near a tall chimney pot. A reflection from binoculars perhaps? And there was a shadow that might belong to a soldier. Yes, *there* he was, a sniper with a large rifle.

'Do not shoot the girl,' squawked a familiar voice in a loudhailer. 'I repeat, do *not* shoot the girl.'

'*Pssst*,' said another voice, also in the loud hailer.

'What is it *now*?' said the first.

There was a whispering in the background.

'And put your raincoats on,' said the first voice. 'There appears to be a storm coming.'

Distant

Voice

Lucy glanced out to sea, where lightning flickered between the clouds, as if the deep, black bags and their Lectric guts had followed her all the way from Assiah. The birds were more numerous now, but increasingly difficult to make out, as day turned to night.

But in the midst of all that darkness was a single point of brilliance that grew brighter by the second. Lucy recognised the flight signature of an angel, even at a distance.

And she had absolutely no doubt who that angel was.

It was Raziel.

'Umm, is that what I *think* it is?' said Trembley, laying an unsteady hand on Lucy's shoulder.

'I wish it wasn't,' she replied, continuing to stare at the horizon.

'You don't seem surprised to see us,' said the Major, stepping up to join them. He adjusted his walkie-talkie, trying to silence it, but it kept bursting out with noisy static.

'Not really,' said Lucy. 'I heard your radio ages ago.'

'And you didn't run?' said Trembley.

'There's no point,' said Lucy, with a growing look of despair. 'How do you run away from *that*?'

The bright swirl of sky gradually formed a distinct figure whose body feathers glowed like mirrors, glinting in the little sunlight that remained.

And against every urge to the contrary, Lucy found herself admiring him – an angel of God, his powerful wings picked out in radiant gold against the backdrop of a dark grey sky.

'I think we should hide,' said the Major, his binoculars trained on the funnel of birds that circled above Raziel.

'That's the first sensible thing you've said since we met,' said Lucy.

As they dived for the post office doorway Pilkington's eyes narrowed, and Lucy knew that if she was ever back under his control she'd regret her words. But it was worth it, just to see Inspector Trembley attempting to hide a grin.

'Oh,' said the Major, 'so *you* think it's funny too, do you?'

'No,' said Trembley, still smiling. 'I think the girl has appalling cheek.'

'She does,' said the Major, 'but she'll be laughing on the other side of her pretty face soon.'

He barked a command into the walkie-talkie and a volley of shots rang out from the rooftops. They were aimed at the angel who was now hovering overhead.

'Absolutely useless,' said Trembley. 'They just go straight through him.'

'You won't hurt him like that,' agreed Lucy.

'Well unless you have any better ideas,' said the Major. He leaned out of the doorway as Raziel swooped down towards the rooftops. 'Oh my *God*,' he shouted. 'That abomination has taken one of my men.'

They looked on in horror as Raziel carried his victim out over the sea and released him. The soldier screamed as he plummeted end over end and then crashed through the rusting pavilion roof at the end of the pier.

'We must *do* something,' sighed Trembley.

'Absolutely,' said the Major. 'We need a plan.'

'I've already got one,' whispered Lucy, 'but you won't let me use it.'

'What was that?' said the Major.

'Nothing,' said Lucy, smiling at Trembley. 'I was just wondering who I could trust.'

Raziel flew to the stumpy lighthouse in the harbour and disappeared from sight for a while. And then, just as they began to think he might have met with some kind of accident, the foghorn sounded. Not with its usual monotonous moan though. It was the deepest, loudest sound they had ever heard, and modulated by the speech of the angel.

'Surrender The Light,' it boomed.

'SURRENDER THE LIGHT.'

'Isn't it time we did just that?' said the Major, looking pointedly at Lucy.

'What do you think Miss Blake?' said Trembley.

'We have to choose the moment,' said Lucy.

'Absolutely not,' said the Major. 'That thing is liable to attack us at any moment, so if you have what he wants then I suggest you hand it over.'

'Don't be silly,' said Lucy. 'He mustn't actually *get* The Light. That's just the bait in the trap. We have to defeat him.'

'You mean kill?' said Trembley.

'Yes, *kill*,' said Lucy, steeling herself against the word. 'He'll never allow himself to be captured. He's duty bound. They *all* were.'

'Pity,' said the Major, 'we could do with interrogating a chap like that.'

He followed Raziel with his binoculars as the angel circled the South Bay, obviously waiting for a response. And that gave Trembley a chance to talk to Lucy on her own.

'You're going to *kill* him?' he whispered. 'And do you have that flame inside you? The ability to take the life of another?'

Lucy thought of Morana, floating face down in the boating pool. But *that* wasn't the image that burned her mind. It was the sight of the poor woman writhing in agony that haunted her, and it was Raziel's hand poised on the fateful dial. In fact it was *his* hand that was poised everywhere, she'd come to realise. And it was a hand that needed to be stilled.

'Yes,' said Lucy eventually. 'I *have* got the flame.'

'Then you might also have killed Morana,' suggested Trembley.

Lucy gave a deep frown, the way Lily sometimes looked at Percy when she wanted to reduce him to a quivering jelly.

'No,' said Trembley meekly. 'Perhaps not.'

Major Pilkington's radio burst into life with a voice that Lucy recognised instantly, even beneath all the squealing and crackly interference.

'Gingo leader calling nunger three.'

'Gingo leader calling nunger three.'

'Grigadier Gogginggery here – is that *you* Pilkington?'

'Yes sir,' replied the Major. 'But…'

'Gut *nothing*,' said the voice. 'Something is wrong with this damn-fool radio. Every time I say the letter *G* it comes out as the letter *G*.'

'You're right,' said Pilkington, somewhat perplexed. 'It *does*, but I can still understand you quite clearly.'

'Oh, *good*,' said the voice. 'Now listen very carefully.'

Distant Voice

'*Fzzz. Fzzz.*'

'Are you listening?'

'*Fzzz.*'

'Yes,' said the Major.

'*Fzzz.*'

'Good, well I want you to get out of there – at the duggle.'

'*All* of us?' said Pilkington. 'At the double?'

'That's what I *said*, wasn't it? Oh, and gring that policeman with you. What's his name? Trengley?'

'*Wait* a minute,' said the Major, regarding Lucy with suspicion. 'How do I know this is the *real* Brigadier Bobbingberry?'

'This is a Code Purple priority order,' said the voice. 'You *do* understand orders, don't you?'

'Of course,' said the Major. 'But I have to be sure they're coming from the right place. So tell me, what's the name of my Sergeant?'

'Gagington,' said the voice.

'And the password?'

'Rugger Duck. Now get out of there, and leave Lucy Glake to get on with the jog.'

'Jog? Oh, yes, *job*,' said the Major.

At Pilkington's command the soldiers disappeared from the rooftops, but Inspector Trembley stayed put, eyeing Lucy with mistrust.

'I don't know how you did that,' he said to Lucy, 'but you're not going to fool me that easily.'

'I haven't a clue what you're talking about,' said Lucy, smiling at the Major as he marched away.

'You have something in mind, don't you?' said Trembley. 'Remember what I told you about all those years of interviewing criminals? I can tell when there's something going on inside a head.'

'Well if there was I wouldn't tell *you*, would I?' said Lucy.

In avoiding Trembley's gaze, she made the mistake of glancing at the window behind him. The detective turned, and immediately identified what she was looking at. It was a small white feather. and it was stuck to the window with a drop of blood. Beneath it was Lucy's handwritten postcard, clearly showing the time and place of her meeting.

'A-*ha*,' said Trembley. 'And suddenly everything becomes crystal clear.'

'What?' said Lucy innocently.

'This meeting,' he said. 'You were planning to go alone I assume?'

'I *have* to,' said Lucy, not bothering to deny it.

'I disagree,' said Trembley. 'Whatever you have planned, it will be better if we went together.'

'*No*,' snapped Lucy. 'It won't.'

'Then you're not going at all,' he said. 'I can't let you risk it.'

'And Raziel will have won,' said Lucy.

'*Raziel?*' said Trembley. 'Is that the angel's name?'

Lucy didn't reply. Further argument was pointless. And she had just spotted the ideal way to remove Trembley from the equation. About fifteen yards away, in the middle of the road, was a manhole cover left open by Mister Brown and his sewer crawlers from the Congregation of Darkness.

'What are you looking at?' said Trembley.

'Nothing,' lied Lucy.

'*Ah* – the manhole,' said Trembley. '*See?* I can always tell.'

'Alright,' admitted Lucy. 'So what am I thinking now?'

'You want to get rid of me,' said Trembley, 'so you can execute some kind of bizarre plan. One that probably involves mayhem and destruction.'

'Correct,' admitted Lucy. She took off her opera gloves and pocketed them, then held her hands in front of her, the palms facing each other.

'You *do* know I could take you into custody at any time,' said Trembley. 'You *are* just a little girl after all. Or were you planning to wrestle me to the ground?'

'Something like that,' said Lucy.

She wasn't really certain *what* she was doing, but there was a vague feeling that everything would work, just so long as she trusted to memory. She was aware of a gift that Blueface had passed on to her – something that had been fermenting away inside her ever since that fateful day in Dragonard's theatre.

'Interesting,' said Trembley, watching Lucy's palms. 'But I'm not likely to be overpowered by a parlour trick. What is it? Some kind of glow in the dark powder?'

Lucy stared at her hands, fascinated by the tiny blue sparks that danced on her fingers. But even more interesting was the hum that increased in pitch and volume as she brought her palms closer together.

'*Ah*,' said Trembley, somewhat nervously. 'Now, I *think* you'd better stop doing that, whatever it is.'

'Don't worry,' grinned Lucy, 'I'm just a little girl, so you can't come to any real harm, *can* you?'

Trembley's face fell as the sparks danced over Lucy's clasped hands like a thousand demented fireflies – and it fell even further when she opened them again. A loop of blue flame leapt from her palms and encircled his head. The searing cloud set fire to his hat and scorched his hair, surrounding him in a vibrating cage of sparks that made his nose bleed and eventually knocked him to the floor. Lucy stumbled, surprised that the shock affected her almost as much as Trembley. But unlike him she had remained conscious, and when she finally regained her senses she was able to drag his body to the manhole and feed him into it, feet first.

'It's alright,' said Lucy, when he came round. 'You'll be safe down here.'

The detective rubbed his head, examining the slimy brick walls and the iron ladder that led back up to the street.

He was chained up with his own handcuffs.

'Handy, aren't they?' smiled Lucy. 'I believe they're standard issue for newspaper reporters.'

'Really?' sighed Trembley. He felt for his hat and was a little shocked to discover that he had no hair left. 'And what exactly is it I'm going to be safe *from?*'

'I'm planning a little surprise for the angel,' said Lucy. 'And I don't want anyone else to get hurt.'

'Is that why you cleared the soldiers out of the way?' said Trembley.

Lucy nodded.

'So it *was* you,' said Trembley. 'Really, this is all a bit too much.'

'Actually,' said Lucy, 'I'm hoping it will be just the right amount.'

'Well it's certainly enough to get you into some very deep trouble,' said Trembley. 'Kidnapping a police officer is a serious crime, and the hat you set fire to was a birthday present. I think you really *have* gone too far this time.'

'That's an interesting little phrase,' laughed Lucy. 'Have you ever met my step-mother?'

'Just the once,' admitted Trembley.

He rattled the handcuffs against the ladder.

'So now you know why I turned out like I did,' smiled Lucy. 'Anyway, I've already stolen a priceless work of art, kidnapped Toby Lindstrom and murdered Morana Fay, so a few more crimes won't make much difference.'

'Probably not,' said Trembley, as Lucy stepped onto the first rung of the ladder. 'Umm, just before you go, I don't suppose you're going to tell me how you managed to overpower me and get me down here?'

'No,' smiled Lucy, 'I don't suppose I am.'

'That's a pity,' said Trembley, 'because my superintendent will probably ask me the same question, and I was rather hoping to have an answer.'

Magdala

Lucy settled into the battered chair and watched the clock as it ticked away the seconds. She was certain that Raziel had seen the post card and that he would arrive dead on time – because *he* would be spending every waking moment thinking about her, just as *she* spent every spare moment thinking about him. As the minute hand edged towards twelve there came a tap on the window. A brilliant white bird was perched on the sill outside, dozens of tiny raindrops laying on his feathers like magnifying glasses.

It was Lucifer.

Lucy smiled and he returned her a slow blink. She half expected to see a message tied to his leg, then realised that Lucifer himself was the message.

Harry had sent his last surviving bird to remind her of his words.

'There's some dark in the brightest white, and some bright in the deepest black. They need each other see? Dark needs light and bad needs good.'

On the stroke of ten, the door flew open and a smell like burning oil and smouldering hair floated in. It was Raziel in human form. He was swathed in black, and his stare filled with loathing, like a thousand angels hating her all at once.

'You escaped from Assiah,' said Raziel.

'Obviously,' smiled Lucy.

'I had confidence,' he said, glancing at the window. 'Although by now I thought you might have got rid of your fascination for these sky-rats.' He flicked his cane and hissed at Lucifer, who took off in a flurry of feathers.

His departure left Lucy empty and cold.

'There's beauty inside every creature,' she said, watching the window and wishing for Lucifer to return.

'And darkness too,' said Raziel, 'even in such as you.'

Lucy nodded, but resisted the temptation. It would give her enormous pleasure to win a war of words with Raziel, but there were more important things to be done.

'Did you bring a friend?' she asked.

'If you have brought The Light then I have brought a friend,' he said.

'In that case, yes,' said Lucy.

'Good,' said Raziel, with a sickly smile. 'Oh, and by the way, I liked your clever little note. A nice touch, and spelt correctly too.'

'It wasn't my idea,' said Lucy, suddenly wondering what was happening to Bentley and the others.

'No? Well I wouldn't worry,' said Raziel. 'Our very best schemes and ideas are seldom our own.'

'So I've heard,' said Lucy. With Lily, it was often a good idea to try and provoke a reaction. But there were also times when provocation bordered on foolishness.

'And what do you mean by that?' snapped Raziel.

'Well it wasn't *your* idea to come looking for me, was it?' said Lucy. 'You were just sent here on an errand. The Lady Nisroc told me.'

Raziel hissed. The veins on his forehead throbbed in sixty shades of blue. And as if to answer her accusation he threw open his cape to reveal Fenny cowering inside. The kidnapped girl stumbled as he pushed her forward. She fell in front of the desk, then crawled underneath it to emerge next to Lucy.

'Here is the source of your fatal weakness,' said Raziel.

'Are you alright?' whispered Lucy.

'Of *course* she is,' snapped Raziel, 'otherwise she would be no use to me. You know the bargain well enough. You and the manuscript in exchange for the girl's life.'

'There are a few matters to sort out first,' said Lucy. 'That's why we had to meet here.'

'Ah yes, *that*,' said Raziel. 'Now why *this* place particularly?'

'No special reason,' lied Lucy, 'apart from the fact that I like the decor.'

The angel glanced briefly at the tatty curtains, bare light bulb and scarred wooden floorboards. Apart from the wall clock, a desk and a battered chair where Lucy sat, there was little else worth describing.

'It has a certain minimal charm,' admitted Raziel. 'But there is a smell of despair about the place too. And as for your connection with it…'

Lucy fiddled with a triangular wooden sign on the desk, turning it around so that the angel could read it.

Mr. McGuffin.
General Manager.

Magdala

Acme Confuser Corporation.

'Mr. McGuffin doesn't exist,' said Lucy. 'Just like the person responsible for my uncle Byron's death doesn't exist.'

'Are you *still* annoyed with that?' smiled Raziel.

'Disappointed,' sighed Lucy, 'because you don't value life, and you don't care when you take it. It was you who killed him, wasn't it?'

'An opportunity arose,' said Raziel. 'I needed help with the machine at Saint Mallydick's, and he was good with Lectric. And by some bizarre chance he also happened to be your uncle.'

'That was lucky,' said Lucy.

'*Lucky*?' said Raziel with a grin. 'Coincidences like that don't just happen child, they are made in heaven.'

He smiled and pulled back his coat tails to reveal the radiant lining.

'Don't look,' screamed Fenny. 'That's how he caught me.'

Every fibre in Lucy's body told her not to look, but her gaze was drawn towards the brilliance that radiated from the raiment and the creature that danced in its golden folds. It looked like a kingfisher when she glimpsed it in the saleroom, but now, despite its jewelled plumage and bird-like appearance, she could clearly see that it was an angel. It hovered in a bare, cubical room that existed not as part of a house, but purely in itself – a stage erected in the middle of nowhere, for the enactment of a short but very special play.

'That's enough of *that* I think,' said Raziel, closing his coat.

'What?' said Lucy. 'Umm, no, no you can't. I was watching the…'

'Oh very well,' grinned Raziel, 'but only because it's *you*…'

Fenny screamed another warning, but Lucy turned her face back to the glow, even though she knew it to be a trap. She was desperate to see what was going on in there, and believed herself strong enough to look away if she wanted.

Well *wasn't* she?

The angel in the vision alighted gently, gradually absorbing those great glowing wings into its back. Then, just like Pixy, it melted and remoulded itself into someone that Lucy thought she would never see again.

'Do you *see* her?' said Raziel, his lip curling in a terrible grin.

'Yes,' said Lucy, wiping away a tear.

Ω૪ଧ୪୪ଧଧ૪૮

Magdala

The vision was like a film of Maggie disappearing, but it was being played backwards, so her mother went from angelic manifestation to human form, and then appeared in a locked room. And if *that* was true, then Lucy finally had the answer she'd sought for so long. Her mother had turned into an angel, and *that* was why she had disappeared.

'You do see her, don't you?' grinned Raziel. 'Her reflection is painted on your face, like a blessed radiance. What a joy has been sent to greet us.'

'Lucy, *please* look away,' screamed Fenny.

But Lucy's eyes were glazed over. She had embarked upon a journey to a land where Fenny's cries were all but inaudible.

'It's her,' said Lucy in a faint whisper. 'I'm not imagining it, am I?'

'And she wouldn't come without good reason, *would* she?' said Raziel.

'Mum,' said Lucy weakly. 'Can you hear me?'

'Perhaps she is trying to tell you something?' said Raziel.

Lucy stared open-mouthed. Maggie held out her hands, gesturing as if telling her daughter to give something away.

'Wake up,' screamed Fenny, shaking her friend by the shoulders. 'Please Lucy, wake up.'

'*No*,' yelled Lucy, her blank look clearing slightly. 'I'm being tricked. My mother would never tell me to give up The Light.'

'That's right,' said Fenny, yelling encouragement. 'Her mum would never tell her to give anything to you.'

'But she already *has*,' whispered Raziel. 'What she sees in the raiment is not a mere fantasy – it has already happened.'

Lucy stared into the coat, going past her mother to the landscape beyond. It was a dark, featureless plain – a flyblown prairie, where lights twinkled on the distant horizon.

And there was a smell on the air, like rotting flesh.

Lucy felt a chill in her bones. The skin on the back of her neck crawled at the thought of what had happened in this place. Then her mother faded and another took her place – a fabulous creature, who despite her femininity, was as black as oil on the inside. There was another whisper on the prairie-wind, and Lucy strained to hear the angel's name pronounced – but Raziel closed the coat, releasing Lucy from its influence and depriving her of the vision.

Lucy gasped, realising that she had been tricked.

Magdala

The room was filled with murderous tendrils that blocked the exits and choked every square inch of the walls, bathing them in an eerie green glow.

It was the most perfect form of snare Lucy could imagine, and she, in her eagerness to see her mother, had fallen into it.

And as the trap slowly tightened, she heard the name of the black angel whispered again. It hissed through the green mass that entwined them, like a mournful wind blowing through sand-choked grasses.

'*Mag-da-laaaaaah…*', it sighed.

The Tongue of Demiurge

The growths took Lucy by surprise. She was accustomed to seeing them emerge from angels' feet, but Raziel was in human form now, and they burst like rabid weeds from his palms and his fingertips and his groin.

'We're trapped,' squealed Fenny.

'What did you expect?' said Raziel with a thin smile. 'That I would let you go, after all the trouble I have gone to?'

Lucy's heart stalled.

The tendrils wove a deadly web that threatened to fill the room, and for a moment she forgot her plan and panicked. Unable to think of a way out, she was suddenly fearful that he might have other surprises in store – things she didn't know about him, that might yet defeat her plans.

'Such beautiful colours and patterns,' she whispered, half mesmerised.

'They are an essential part of who we are,' said Raziel with a nod. 'Each angel of the house of earth produces a different growth, with unique leaves and flowers and scent.'

'A strange match for your violence and hatred,' said Lucy.

'Ah,' said Raziel, pretending to look offended. 'But I made this display purely for your pleasure.'

'No you didn't,' yelled Fenny. 'You only ever think of yourself. I've seen what he does when you're not there Lucy – he hates you.'

'I think he hates all of us,' said Lucy.

'Hate is such an *awful* word,' grinned Raziel, 'and it implies a level of equality that simply doesn't exist. It would be like *you* Miss Lucy Blake, declaring everlasting hatred for an earthworm.'

The angel threw down his cane and took off his cape to reveal a tatty and exceptionally filthy tunic, which he also removed. He was naked from the waist up, his chest and arms covered with barely healed scars.

'He looks awful,' whispered Fenny.

Lucy drew the girl to her side and they both took a pace backwards.

'Yes, I do look awful,' hissed Raziel, his ears twitching. 'Would you not agree Miss Blake? Or do you not recognise your own handiwork?'

He turned so that Lucy could see his back. It was covered in whiplash scars, which in turn were covered by a transparent, liquid-filled membrane that reminded her of a blister.

'You brought it on yourself,' said Lucy. She was trying not to look at the sticky bag of flesh that clung to the angel's back.

'Of *course*,' said Raziel. 'How silly of me. I electrocuted myself, didn't I? It was nothing at all to do with you or your accursed little friend.'

'You were hurt by your own actions,' said Lucy. 'If you hadn't followed us to the laboratory then you wouldn't have been injured. And anyway, it would have been much worse if I hadn't switched the thing off.'

'Yes,' hissed Raziel, still facing away. 'You saved me, and *that* was your first mistake.'

Lucy hadn't noticed until now, but Raziel was quite scrawny beneath that cape of his. Below the sticky layer of skin that adhered to his back, every rib was visible – but it was the prominent shoulder blades that demanded most of her attention. They were broader than usual, and covered in layers of hard muscle that rippled and shimmered.

And in the valleys between those muscles, bones were emerging, their sharpened ends breaking through the flesh as if his body was a construction kit filled with the relics of dead birds.

'If you will excuse me for a moment,' said Raziel.

'What's he doing?' said Fenny. 'He, it, oh *no*, it's disgusting…'

The blister on the angel's back burst, flooding the room with the foul stink of rotting flesh.

Lucy gasped as Raziel's transformation accelerated.

First to emerge were the wingtips, then the delicate metacarpals and the main spars with their articulated joints and knife-like extensions. Then came the coverings of flight feathers and coverts – not white as she expected, but of every shade of brown and black, each with the sheen of a peacock feather, but none of its beauty.

Raziel lifted his arms and flexed his stubby wings, flicking the stinking blister-fluid about as he did so. A few drops of the liquor landed on Lucy's forehead, and as she tried to wipe them away, even more fell on her lips.

She took a deep breath.

Her tongue was dry and needed to find air, and to her horror it did so without any thought or command from her. And *that* was how she first came to sample the angel's fluid. It was like salty bath water, and had the strangest effect on her. But before she could work out what the consequence was, Fenny screamed, like a tiny creature caught in a vicious trap.

'The *plants* Lucy – they're *changing*.'

Lucy wrapped her arms around Fenny's shoulders as the tendrils began their own transformation, their fresh leaves and strong, dark stems turning to brown, twisted growths. Every branch was suddenly shrivelled, rotting into a putrid mush that stank of decay and extreme age. They were trapped in a forest of rotting flesh and slime.

Raziel laughed like a demented soul in a deep-well prison.

His breath smelled like an explosion in a septic tank.

'No,' screamed Lucy, 'please, not *those* things.'

The angel's wings clothed themselves in lightning, but the display of fire dimmed slightly as the stomata emerged from the tendrils.

Fenny panicked, her face a picture of unspeakable horrors. They were surrounded by grinning mouths whose rotten teeth parted only to belch out flies.

The insects had cellophane wings and teeth like needles.

Lucy trembled, trying to reassure Fenny, but shadows of influence were emerging from the tendrils – patterns of darkness that consumed whatever they found and regurgitated it in nightmare form. The Stomata were feeding on her thoughts, twisting them into unmentionable forms and then throwing them back in her face.

Lucy choked as her own feelings rose up to attack her.

And then she heard Lundrumguffa.

He was talking to her as if she was already dead.

'Have you seen her?' he asked.

'Go away,' screamed Lucy. 'You're not real.'

'Have you *seen* her?' repeated Lundrumguffa.

A figure appeared before her.

It was hunched over a theatrical dressing table – a head covered by a hood and surrounded by dozens of bare light bulbs. The hood dropped – frayed as if it had suddenly aged ten thousand years, and the face it revealed was her mother's. She gazed at Lucy, not directly, but as a reflection in the mirror, as if she daren't face her daughter in the real world. But Maggie's face was already fading, melting away to nothing as her skin peeled away in hot waxen sheets.

'This isn't real,' screamed Lucy. 'You're meddling with my head.'

She closed her eyes and opened them again, blinking the tears away and praying that the vision would be gone. Her mother was still there, but her outline was vague, like breath on a windowpane.

And she was mouthing something.

'What is it?' pleaded Lucy. 'Have you a message?'

Before Maggie could reply, the image vanished like burning tissue, and Lucy could hear Raziel laughing.

'Now you have seen what you must fight against,' he said. 'Wouldn't it be simpler to hand over The Light? Then we can all share in its wisdom.'

'I'd rather read it on my own,' yelled Lucy.

The angel lowered his head and turned awkwardly, the tips of his wings inscribing arcs on the slimy ceiling. His talons scraped similar grooves in the floor, leaving deep, unvarnished wounds in the boards.

'Do you like what you see?' said Raziel, his wings aglow. 'You really *should* you know – it's within you as well.'

'I doubt it,' said Lucy. 'We're not all as ugly as you on the inside.'

'But we are,' smiled Raziel. 'Even gentle, kind Fenny, who wouldn't hurt a soul. I'll bet you have a darkness in you too, don't you child?'

'Don't worry,' whispered Lucy. 'He's just trying to scare us.'

'He *is* scaring me,' whimpered Fenny.

As Raziel lifted his head up, his face became a skull, the hair replaced by stubby feathers coated in dark oil and swept back to grow through the top and sides of his hat. Lucy glanced briefly at his staring eyes and the mouth, which had warped into a beak-like shape. The lips were formed by a semi-transparent parchment, their sharpened edges protecting a thin, black tongue that darted impatiently as if it had a mind of its own. Even more horrifying were the bony breastplates made from rows of close-knit ribs fused down the middle. These formed a solid mass over his abdomen, but higher up where they were set further apart she could see his heart beating through the cellophane-thin skin. The organ was black, like his tongue, and pulsed with great stealth, like a clock measuring out his life in precise amounts.

'You're shocked,' snarled Raziel. 'And please don't bother to deny it. I smell your fear. It floats on the air, like the scent of prey.'

'You're a *daemon*,' hissed Lucy. Her eyes were riveted on his waxen hands, whose skin was so transparent she could see the complex network of bones laid out beneath. 'I just *knew* you couldn't be an angel. I *knew* it.'

'You really should keep such displays of ignorance to yourself,' snorted Raziel. 'Whether we go by the name of angel or daemon, we are all the same, differing only in our intentions. We are one race, as ancient as the skies, and as widespread as the stars.'

'But you still haven't learned any manners,' said Lucy. 'Or how to tell the difference between right and wrong.'

'Would that be *your* idea of right and wrong?' said Raziel. 'And *your* idea of black and white? All very limited I'm afraid.'

Ever since Raziel had removed his tunic, Lucy had wondered about the row of leathery purse-like bags, knitted into the skin around his waist. And even though she was in imminent danger, she still wondered – now more than ever, because they had begun to breathe.

'Why did you wait all this time to show yourself?' said Lucy, her eyes fixed on the pulsating sacs.

Raziel thought for a moment then smiled, as if something amusing had happened, but only in his thoughts. To Lucy, his smile was still an evil leer, the taut skin around his mouth buckling and wrinkling like a withered prune.

'An angel will show you as much of himself as is necessary,' said Raziel. 'I began by showing you nothing at all, but little by little you have surprised me. Step by step you have raised the stakes of our game, to the point where we are both gambling with our lives. *That* is why I do you the honour of showing you my real self.'

Lucy was shocked. Even though she'd had the same thought herself, it was a body blow to hear Raziel say it.

One of them was going to end up dead.

The Tongue of Demiurge

Fenny screamed as one of Raziel's waist-sacs opened, like a flesh wound inflicted by an invisible weapon. The ragged mouth resembled a Venus flytrap, but instead of catching flies it released them – just a few at first, then hundreds, and then, as the other pouches burst open, thousands.

They filled the air with a buzz that drowned their conversation.

Lucy swept a dozen or so blowflies from her forehead and spat a couple out onto the floor.

The time for talking was at an end.

'My mother once told me a story,' she yelled, through half-pursed lips. 'It concerned a daemon who fought the forces of good and ended up spending his last few minutes of existence talking to a silly girl in a fly-filled room.'

'And what happened to this poor creature?' grinned Raziel. 'I suppose the ever resourceful girl defeated him in the end?'

'Of course,' shouted Lucy. 'She kept him talking just long enough for his wings to catch fire.'

'Really?' said Raziel. 'How unfortunate for him.'

Lucy kept a close eye on Raziel's stubby wings, but nothing happened.

'Did you hear me?' yelled Lucy. 'The daemon's wings caught fire.'

'I heard you,' laughed Raziel. 'But I don't see anyone perishing in flames.'

Lucy shook her head, swatting the flies that forced their way into her mouth and settled on her eyes. Raziel was right, nothing *was* happening, and it couldn't have *not* happened at a worse time. She had only just started to believe in her storytelling ability, and now, when she needed it most, it had failed her.

'Do you have any more ideas?' sneered Raziel. 'Or shall we get down to business?'

'Actually I have got *one* idea,' said Lucy. She took her opera gloves off and put them in her pocket. Then she brought her bare palms close together, smiling as the blue sparks danced across her skin. Raziel seemed surprised, and expressed shock when Lucy separated her hands. With a blinding flash of light she brought every single insect down from the air.

'Impressive,' hissed Raziel. One by one, the waist pouches snapped shut as he surveyed a floor carpeted with dead flies. 'But you cannot defeat me; not with this, and not with your talent for lies.'

'They're inventions,' insisted Lucy. 'Doesn't anybody *ever* listen?'

'Whatever you decide to call your so-called gift,' said Raziel, 'you cannot use it on me.'

'Why not?' said Fenny, her hair thick with fallen insects.

'Because, you stupid girl, I believe her,' grinned Raziel. 'Whatever lie she chooses to tell me, I believe it with my whole heart, because I know what she is capable of.'

'And why does that make a difference?' said Lucy.

'Because for any lasting effect, your inventions must be told to those who do *not* believe,' grinned Raziel.

He looked as though he wanted to laugh hysterically.

'Can you *imagine* anything more ironic and more perfect?' he said. 'Those who *want* to believe you will never benefit from your efforts. And those who disbelieve will reap the rewards, such as they are.'

'Well *I* don't believe it,' said Fenny, hoping to help out.

'It's no good pretending,' hissed Raziel, the spit foaming on his lips. 'You really must *not* believe, in your heart, and in your soul. Because *that* is where it all happens.'

'He's right,' said Lucy. 'I can sense he's telling the truth – but it doesn't matter. We might not be able to set *this* daemon on fire, but there were other stories. Like the one about the diamond sphere – do you remember that?'

'You told me about it when we were in the temple,' said Fenny.

'So?' hissed Raziel. 'You believed her, didn't you?'

'Yes,' said Fenny, with a triumphant smile, 'but *you* didn't – you laughed and called it an impossible contraption.'

Lucy had never been certain of tempting the angel into her trap, but now that he was here and Fenny had spoken the words, the die was cast.

And so the rest of the device needed to come into being.

Lucy hadn't given it much thought on previous occasions, but now she realised just how it all came to be. Inventions never came without effort, and like angels' talents they never came without pain either – but at least now she knew *why* they came. It was when they were needed – and the story she told in the temple was needed now, which was why her eyelids felt like they had tiny lead weights sewn into them.

She reached deep inside herself, into a place that even she wasn't familiar with. It was like opening the door of a darkened library and stumbling in the shadows to look for a book. Only she couldn't be certain what the volume was until she had removed it.

And by then it would be too late.

'*Shemara, partica, hem-sham foresh,*' she intoned.

'*Lementa, peekora, omnium accheos.*'

There was a moment of silence, like the part of the day that follows the stroke of midnight – the one, single second when the dead can all breathe again.

And then came the thunder. Not the simple clash of clouds or discharge of Lectric, but a rage connected to the bowels of the universe – an echo of some great power that had lain dormant for aeons.

A power that was waiting for the turn of a key.

The force radiated from her in waves that acknowledged boundaries only so it could smash through them. It burst through the tendrils and the walls and surged out over the town in every direction – a radiant, rippling glow that washed every shop and house, every bicycle and every lamp post in its gaze.

It sent out a message that was wrapped in the tongue of magick.

I, I, I am the power.

I, I, I am the irresistible call.

I, I, I am the will of the creator.

Bring me your elements that I, the epicentre of this power, demand.

Bring them here now.

Bring them here, to me.

There was a moment when it seemed like the command had failed.

But then it began.

The sky shook.

Pavements cracked.

Railway embankment fences collapsed like concertinas.

Bricks jostled each other, suddenly eager to be individuals, and not just a part of some ancient wall.

The whole of Grimston bent to her will.

'Wow,' whispered Lucy.

Fenny tugged at her sleeve.

'Lucy, are you alright?' she said.

'I don't know,' said Lucy, keeping her eyes closed.

'But the noises,' said Fenny. 'Something isn't right.'

'Shh,' said Lucy. 'I think it's happening.'

'What is?' said Fenny.

'It,' whispered Lucy. 'The *invention*.'

It started with a noise near the door, like a key vibrating in the lock. It was a tiny sound, but enough to make Raziel frown, because it simply didn't belong.

It was just as Fenny had said.

Something was *going on*.

'What was *that*?' said Raziel, spitting the words.

'What was what?' said Lucy innocently.

'Don't play games with me,' hissed the daemon. '*You* heard it.'

There was another sound, thin and metallic this time, like a key falling onto a bare, wooden floor. Before the key had chance to bounce the daemon span to face the door, fearing an attack. But there was nothing there, and when he turned back Lucy was staring at him with the most innocent look she could muster.

'It's *you*, isn't it?' he said.

'It might be,' she smiled.

Vibrations emanated from every surface, as if some giant creature was shaking the building to death – but it wasn't just inside the room. All over Grimston, the mournful, elephant-song was loosening anything that wasn't nailed down.

Pictures fell from living room walls.

False teeth dropped out of bathroom cabinets.

Pennies tumbled like never before in abandoned amusement arcades.

Half-sucked gobstoppers rolled about in the fluff in school desks.

But something else was happening – something that united every form of blackness in a common cause.

All over town, coal lifted from cellars and crashed up through the roofs of outdoor bunkers. It slipped away from the staithes in railway sidings and levitated from parked delivery lorries. And the soot from twenty thousand chimneys loosened, rising to form a jet-black cloud that blotted out the rays of the sun. Even at sea, vast fields of black diamonds were lifted from the ocean bed and spirited into the air.

'Can you feel it?' said Lucy, her eyes ablaze.

'What?' said Raziel, his sunken eyes darting about.

'Soot and coal and dust,' whispered Lucy. 'It's coming here because of my invention – because I *wanted* it to.'

'Then I shall stop it,' hissed Raziel. 'I will pack this room with filaments, tighter and tighter until there are no gaps left.'

'Have you ever *seen* a molecule?' she said.

'Of course not,' said Raziel. 'Even angels…'

'Nobody has,' interrupted Lucy. 'They're absolutely microscopic, so no matter how close you pack your filaments they'll find a way through.'

'Then let them come,' said Raziel.

He grimaced with the effort, but it was too late. Black powder flooded the room, like a billion dark stars in a universe of air. Lucy's heart filled with wonder at the sight of her invention come to life. And her grin broadened, with the realisation that Raziel's grip was slipping.

As the room turned to blackness, Raziel's feathers bristled, like a large bird shaking rain from its back. He reinforced them, so that even the softest was changed to leathery armour.

But still the dust came, leeching through every nook and every cranny to gather at the centre of the room. At first, the cloud just hovered, but soon the leaves on Raziel's tendrils began to move, as if disturbed by a slight breeze. It was an insignificant occurrence, but all three of them backed away from the phenomenon, Raziel towards the door, and Lucy and Fenny to the opposite wall, their eyes fixed firmly upon the dust cloud.

'I can feel the air moving,' whispered Fenny. 'And the angel's colour has changed – you've got him worried.'

Lucy smiled and lifted a fingertip to her cheek. It felt cooler than she expected and there was a breeze on the back of her hand.

'Stand your ground,' she whispered.

The grime cloud rotated clockwise, dragging the air behind it like a blanket as it increased speed. Lucy set her feet apart and leaned to the right to counteract the airflow. It felt like a storm whipping in from the sea. She and Fenny managed to remain upright as the speed steadily accelerated, but so did Raziel. His wings juddered and flapped in the draught, but there was every sign that he was preparing to stand and fight.

Lucy was relieved, because she wasn't finished with him.

Not just yet.

A bare light bulb dangled undisturbed at the centre of the maelstrom, but at the edges of the room it was a different matter. The air tore the curtains away and despatched Raziel's filaments in the same way, ripping them from the walls as the intensity of the storm grew.

And amidst it all the three figures remained untouched, like a group of lighthouses in a raging sea, a constant point of reference in a swirling vortex of froth and foam.

'I'm scared,' said Fenny. 'It's going to get *us* next.'

'Don't worry,' said Lucy. 'This is *my* invention, remember? It's nothing to do with him.'

The room was bare, stripped of all detail by the wind, but none of them was concerned with that. Instead, their attention was fixed on the whirling mass of carbon that first surrounded and then absorbed the desk. The cloud glowed a deep, almost invisible red, then progressed to yellow and then to white and finally a brilliant, searing blue that was impossible to look at – a globe of light, spinning in the darkness.

And like the distant stars it resembled, it gave off no heat.

'This is the rest of my invention,' smiled Lucy.

'But what *is* it?' said Fenny.

'I'm *hoping* it's a sphere,' said Lucy.

The rotating shape slowed, the cloak of dirty air it had dragged around dropping away to reveal the gem located at its centre.

They were just as Lucy had once described – two hemispheres of pure diamond, one half resting on the creaking floor, the other just touching the dangling light bulb. The two halves were similar to Dee's, but six feet in diameter and with walls at least a foot thick.

'They're beautiful,' said Fenny.

'A nice trick,' sneered Raziel, 'but completely without relevance.'

'Then you won't mind if we have a look inside, *will* you?' said Lucy.

'I have all the time in the world,' grinned Raziel.

'Maybe you do,' said Lucy, stepping into the lower half of the sphere. 'And maybe you don't.'

She beckoned Fenny to follow. It was cool inside and quite slippery, so they had trouble standing. But they eventually steadied each other and faced the daemon with the best stare they could manage.

'This is pointless,' sneered Raziel. 'You *do* realise that when you die inside that thing The Light will be mine by default?'

'If we die then you can have it,' said Lucy.

'Oh *good*,' hissed Raziel. 'That is *just* what I wanted to hear.'

Lucy smiled as the upper half of the sphere descended and joined the bottom section with a hiss. She felt strangely isolated. The join between the two halves was no longer visible, and all sound from the room outside was blocked. But in the midst of that hush, Lucy could still hear something. At first she thought it was Fenny, but then noticed that the sound matched the movements of Raziel's breast. It was his *breath* she could hear, wheezing like a bellows in a draughty passage.

But the sound wasn't coming through the diamond wall.

It was present *inside* her.

'Don't speak to me,' she thought, 'I don't want to hea...'

'*Finally*,' hissed Raziel. 'The Light will return with me.'

Lucy recoiled in shock.

Every fibre in her body was cold, like she had plunged into a freezing, dark lake. Raziel's voice was inside her – and his emotions were there too. They wrapped his words in layers of hatred and conceit, like icy hands massaging her internal organs.

'Can you hear him too Fenny?'

'He's in my lungs and he's breathing my air,' she whimpered. 'He's so cold Lucy. And I can't breathe – he's taking my air away.'

Fenny was right. The sphere had been joined for just a couple of minutes and already the air tasted stale.

'We shan't be here for long,' said Lucy confidently. 'And we shan't need to listen to *him* for long either.'

She knelt on the hard crystal and removed The Light from her pocket, placing it gently in front of her. Outside the sphere, Raziel stared though the impenetrable shell, his face illuminated by a self-satisfied grin – there was nothing the stupid child could do now to deprive him of the prize.

Lucy smiled at Raziel with thinly disguised hatred, keeping clear in her mind the reasons for her actions.

She reached into the very bottom of her pocket – and there, amongst old pieces of greaseproof paper, half chewed pencils and balls of grey fluff, she found a tiny box with two buttons and a blinking red light. She held out the device so Raziel could see it. And then she smiled, thinking of Morana and Tenby and Madimi and all the others who had died because of him.

'Goodbye,' she said, pressing the larger of the two buttons.

But nothing happened.

Lucy clicked the button again and again, but the angel was still there.

Her heart sank into a well of despair as Raziel's expression turned from smile to evil grin. Lucy Blake had *finally* lost the game. All he had to do now was wait for the stupid girl's air to run out.

'What's he doing?' whispered Fenny.

'Gloating,' whispered Lucy.

'He thinks he's won, doesn't he?' said Fenny.

'He has,' said a dejected Lucy. 'We can't stay in here forever, and if we go outside then I finally have to give him what he wants.'

'No,' insisted Fenny.

'I do,' whispered Lucy. 'I've run out of ideas.'

'I know how much the manuscript means to him,' said Fenny. 'After he took me prisoner he spent days staring into space, and it was the book he was thinking about. I saw it in his colour. And if it means that much to him then he mustn't have it.'

'I know,' said Lucy. 'But the choices are that we both die or just one of us does. If only the button had been connected. I just *knew* I shouldn't have trusted that old duffer. He was as mad as a hatter.'

'I can *hear* you,' said Raziel.

'Actually, we don't really *care*,' yelled Lucy.

She bashed the control box against the sphere until it was a pile of bits, all the while staring at Raziel's beak, which horrified and fascinated her at the same time. He was grotesque. She wished his black tongue and foul smelling wings were connected to control wires, like some puppet that Dee might invent. And then at least she'd be able to pick him up and put him back in his box and it would all be over. But he was no toy, and there was no box big enough for an angel of the Lord.

With a sigh she wiped away a tear and turned to Fenny. She intended to apologise to her friend for letting her down, but before she could open her mouth the daemon broke into her silence with his ice-wrapped words.

'What was *that*?' he hissed. His grin had disappeared, his beak deformed in an expression of panic. 'Did you hear a tick just then?'

'No,' said Lucy truthfully.

'Perhaps not,' said Raziel, 'but the noble race has excellent hearing, and I heard it quite clearly. It was the sound of lives leaking away.'

'You mean time passing?' said Lucy. 'How can you hear that?'

'I keep telling you child, we are not *like* you. Our perceptions are not the same. We see and hear and smell things differently. Unlike your miserable species we comprehend the flow of time as numerous streams of possibility.'

'I see,' lied Lucy, wishing that she *did* understand.

Raziel moved closer, squelching across the carpet of dead flies.

He placed his hands on the outside of the sphere, pressing his waxy flesh against the cold diamond. Then he sniffed the air. But it wasn't a smell he detected. There was something else – something that he could sense and she could not.

'Yes, I see it all,' he said, 'but I had not really believed it until now.'

'Believed what?' said Lucy.

'You really *are* one of the architects,' said Raziel.

'Is that good?' said Lucy hopefully.

'For you, perhaps,' said Raziel. 'For the others, I think not. The tide has begun to turn.'

'Tide?' said Lucy. 'What are you talking about?'

'It isn't for me to tell,' said Raziel. 'But look at the evidence we have in this room. Only God can create matter, but there are some in his realm who have the ability to re-form that which he produces.'

'Like Demiurge?' said Lucy.

'You speak his *name*?' hissed Raziel. 'And just how much do *you* know of the Grand Architect of the Universe?'

'Only his name,' said Lucy meekly.

The Tongue of Demiurge

Once again, she'd been given all the clues and left to divine the obvious answer. She recalled her conversation with Bentley, about creating something from nothing, and things gradually began to fall into place. There had once been a man called Kolly Kibber who didn't exist. Then she told a story and he was suddenly real, as large as life. And then he was gone again. And then, many stories later, came the tale of a diamond sphere. It must have come from the same place as Kibber, and was presumably going back there. But what might happen to it in the meantime? And what about all her other stories? Where had *they* gone?

'What do you know about *Creatio Ex Nihilo*?' said Lucy suddenly.

'The creation of something from nothing?' smiled Raziel. 'You may be surprised to hear that I know everything – apart from how to do it myself.'

'Then tell me,' said Lucy, 'before...'

'Before what?' said Raziel.

'Umm, before...'

Lucy bit her bottom lip so hard that it bled. But she welcomed the taste of her own blood, because it washed away the scent of Raziel's bath water.

'What *exactly* is it that you have done?' he said.

'Nothing,' said Lucy. She had a vague impression that she had somehow won, but now she was wishing she hadn't, at least not yet. Raziel was a party to everything she needed to know, and it sounded like he was willing to tell.

'Nothing?' said Raziel, sniffing the air again.

And suddenly he began to laugh. It was a gruesome sight on a daemon's face, which clearly wasn't designed for such expressions.

'What is he so amused about?' said Fenny.

Raziel stared at the girl, with the intention of making her wet herself.

'The curious ability of small things to upset the course of much grander plans,' he said. '*That* is what I find so amusing.'

Eophian
de Madriax

In the room below them, the slow passage of time continued just as it always had. The moth-eaten curtains flapped gently in the breeze. The old leather chair creaked imperceptibly, slowly releasing the shape of the person who had sat there last. A pool of marmalade soaked into the filthy carpet and seeped through a crack in the floorboards.

In the room below that, a solitary fly explored the parts of its world that seemed most interesting, unaware of events that were unfolding nearby. But in coming to rest on the dust-laden windowsill it had a sudden sense that all was not right. It squeezed through a crack in the glass and without looking back it flew towards the safety of the sea.

Below the fly-room was a cellar, and here too, time was ticking away, leaking to wherever time went when it was finished with. But it was also disappearing in a much more visible way. There was a large blue box, with a tiny hole in one side where brightly painted numbers were visible – figures formed by pieces of wire that glowed white hot, like the inside of a light bulb. And the filaments formed shapes, which in this world, represented a system of counting.

Numerals.

They were moving backwards.

Eight…

Seven…

Six…

In the room above Lucy it was a similar story. Here were dozens of wooden filing cabinets, filled with everything anyone needed to know about fish, providing its name began with a letter between 'K' and 'P' inclusive. Where the rest of the alphabet had gone was anyone's guess, but it certainly wasn't in as much danger as the 'Khaki-Keeble-Kipper' or the 'Mongolian Banjo Fish' or even the 'Moon-faced Noonyboggers'.

On the floor above the fishy filing cabinets was an empty storeroom, where dust-balls chased each other in the breeze – and above that was an attic, which contained another blue box.

But this box was different.

The white-hot numerals it displayed were lower…

Five…

Four...

Time passed inside the sphere, but all sound had ceased. Even the rasp of Raziel's breath was gone.

Lucy and Fenny had become characters in a silent film.

And in the cellar and in the attic, the count was *still* reducing…

Three…

Two…

One…

For a moment it felt like time had stopped.

Lucy turned to her friend, who was part way through blinking her eyes. Fenny's lips were slightly parted, as if she was about to say something. Lucy passed a hand in front of her face, but she didn't react.

Outside, Raziel slumped against the sphere, his face flattened grotesquely on the diamond surface. In other circumstances Lucy might have smiled, but this was a daemon who had killed repeatedly, and would do so again, if it suited his purpose.

And *that* was what Lucy tried to remind herself of as the look of sadness crept across Raziel's face – because she almost felt sorry for him.

'Do you wish to see what you have won?' said the daemon.

His voice was weak.

'I don't understand,' replied Lucy.

As Raziel lifted his fly covered coat, Lucy noticed the angel's hands. They were pale and waxen, with blue-stained knuckles and purple blood showing beneath long, sharp nails – the hands of someone clinging to a precipice. His wings were bent lower too, his limbs forced into a squat, as if being pressed from above.

And then Lucy realised what he had meant about time. The daemon was experiencing the effects of his immediate future.

'You think I want to look into the coat?' said Lucy. 'After all this?'

'I know you do,' said Raziel. 'I *always* know.'

'Well I don't,' lied Lucy. 'You're trying to trick me again.'

'This is not a trick,' whispered Raziel, wiping away the dark blood that leaked from his sunken eyes. 'It is a gift from the vanquished to the victor. You have defeated seven of God's angels, so the vision I offer is yours by right of conquest.'

Before Lucy could protest he exposed the lining and she was inside – but this time it was not a simple vision. She was actually there, experiencing with each of her senses what Raziel wanted her to see.

It was night, and she was flying over a smoking cornfield. Sparks and scattered flames were still visible amongst the stubble. But flying lower, the story changed. It was not the glowing remains of a crop, but the aftermath of a bloody battle, where the cries of the wounded flew up from the shadows to meet her. But there was no time to stop and help. There was no time to stop and examine the fragmentary battle-machines either, the broken remains of which were strewn everywhere. There was no time for anything but flight, because a dark malevolence was in pursuit; sensed only by the silent beat of wings in her head and the pulsing sadness in her breast.

Up ahead, a walled city offered refuge, but as she flew closer it became apparent that the citadel too was under siege. Mile-high walls protected it, but the armoured gates had been forced open by hordes of warriors who bore shields and wands. Some of them reminded her of Dragonard's men, but were more heavily set, as if carved from solid iron. Some were thin, like wraiths, their bodies almost transparent. And others were made of fire, like Vovina, but with the bodies of men and the faces of creatures she didn't recognise. Lucy was mesmerised. She wanted to stop and remember every last detail, but the flight continued through crowded and devastated streets where the sick and the wounded called up to her.

And then she reached her final destination.

She flew up the steps of a cathedral-like structure, floating soundlessly through a maze of corridors until she came to the temple. It was like the one in the Migdal, but larger. Angels poured up from below on the four spiral staircases. Some were already seated, their great wings folded away, whilst others still swooped and dived in the vast space above the tiled floor. And some simply stood in awe, staring at the fabulous empty throne.

Lucy's insides turned to jelly, as if she was witnessing something intensely private. And that was when she heard her name being called.

'*Lucy Blake*,' said Raziel. 'Have you seen enough?'

'N-no,' she replied, her heart beating in her stomach. 'I saw too much.'

'Indeed you did,' whispered Raziel.

'Was it *real*?' said Lucy.

She was back in the real world, sealed within diamond walls.

'Oh yes,' said the daemon. 'I was there when it happened, fighting in the Wars of Heaven.'

'When?' said Lucy quietly.

'Thousands of years ago,' said Raziel. 'But the memories are still fresh.'

'But why did you show it to *me*?' said Lucy.

'You have proved a worthy adversary,' said Raziel. 'You deserve to see the Dominion of which you will eventually become a part.'

'*Will*?' said Lucy. 'But all that death and suffering was in the past.'

'History has a habit of repeating itself,' said Raziel. 'Like mankind, the race of angels never seems to learn from its mistakes, so we are doomed to repeat them.'

Lucy gazed back into Raziel's coat, but the temple was gone, replaced by flames with the vague outline of angels. They spread to the lining, causing the raiment to flare up and catch fire. Raziel dropped the smoking remains of the garment at his feet and faced Lucy.

'And now we have seen the future,' said the angel. 'Yours is yet to come however, whereas mine has already arrived. Overdue in fact – even *I* cannot hold back the stream of time for long.'

'You stopped time?' said Lucy, her mouth sagging. 'But *how*?'

'Does it matter?' said Raziel. 'Even *with* that talent I have been unable to defeat you. You have resisted me with innocence, and that, it would seem is a powerful tool in the hands of the just.'

'So you have lost?' said Lucy. 'But how?'

'You already *know* how,' said Raziel, 'you just don't know it *yet*.'

'So you punished me with that vision?' said Lucy.

'It was mercy,' snapped Raziel. 'I could have left you in the dark, but instead I chose to give you a warning of what will come.'

'But *why?*' said Lucy.

'Because it is written,' said Raziel. '*Even evil itself shall pity.*'

'So you *are* evil,' said Lucy.

'There are always degrees,' said Raziel.

'I'm not sure that I understand,' said Lucy.

'You will,' said Raziel, his voice fading. 'You will…'

Lucy was free of his influence. The warmth had returned to her guts and the voice in her head was gone. But for a moment she found herself listening to the echoes of his words and regretting her actions.

Raziel had seemed almost reasonable.

Parts of an Angel

Six tons of dynamite was not a force to be argued with, and to prove it, the shock waves emanating from the attic and the cellar set about reducing the room to rubble, like vengeful hands crushing a ball of paper.

The force of the blast was invisible and inaudible, but Lucy still felt its immense power. It vibrated her guts like a roller coaster and made her feet and hands tingle where they touched the sphere. The floorboards below her splintered and cracked, the nails flying from the bending wood like seeds spraying from a melon. Above them, the ceiling turned to dust as the light bulb was ripped away and annihilated itself against the hard diamond surface.

Outside the sphere the twin pressure fronts moved Raziel's bone-baked skull and tendril-torn feet closer together. He seemed to resist for a moment, but the wave fronts were relentless, compressing his body until wings were crushed and bones were shattered and the angel's silent cries rang out for nobody to hear.

And suddenly there was nothing left for Lucy to hate.

Raziel disappeared like a television picture in a power cut.

For a moment he was a single line of dots, full of rage and nothing else.

And then he was just a point of light.

And then he was gone, replaced by a sucking cloud of dust and the vague impression that they were falling, falling, falling...

As long as the explosion lasted, the sphere was supported by the equal and opposite force of two blasts, but now that the pressure waves had cancelled each other out there was nothing to hold it up. The floors and the ceilings were all blown out, and there was nowhere to go but down.

They plummeted towards the place where the cellar used to be, and as they fell, the sphere disintegrated.

Parts of an Angel

By the time of impact it was gone – a sea of shining fragments glistening in the half-light.

Lucy choked on brick dust and struggled to stand, believing that she had survived the fall unscathed. But her body had other ideas. As she slumped and her mind slipped towards darkness she caught a glimpse of the birds.

Only they were *not* birds.

They were what remained of the enemy.

Most of the feathers fell straight to the ground, weighed down by the evil that had spread throughout Raziel's body. Some though had flown high into the air, and others span like sycamore seeds, torn between heaven and earth. Lucy knew she was about to pass out, but struggled to keep her eyes open, just to confirm that the daemon was gone.

As she slumped next to an unconscious Fenny, she wondered about what the angel had said, about there being evil in everyone. Because according to Harry, that also meant there had also been good in Raziel.

And she had destroyed him.

Lucy inhaled, drawing in the smell of burning feathers and damp soil to remind herself what Raziel had been made of.

He was earth.

He was air.

He was fire.

He was water.

But he was no longer of this world.

Or any other.

The Kronk Street Crater

When Lucy regained consciousness the offices of Dewey, Cheetham and Howe had gone – in fact nothing remained of *any* of the buildings that formerly stood in Kronk Street. The nearest structure to withstand the blast was a cinema that Lucy had once disappeared from, which was more than a hundred yards away on the northern edge of the crater.

And it was at the bottom of this newly created hole where Lucy Blake and Fenny Savage found themselves – a deep, saucer shaped depression, from which they could see only sky and the silhouettes of the hundreds of townsfolk who had gathered at the edge.

Lucy blinked slowly to make sure she wasn't seeing things.

But when she opened her eyes again, they were all still there.

'There she is,' shouted an unidentified voice. 'And she's got the missing girl with her.'

'Yeah,' yelled another. 'That's Fenny alright – the Blake kid must have taken her hostage or something.'

Lucy sighed, unable for the moment to bring herself to speak. It seemed as though half the population of Grimston had turned up to see the 'loony schoolgirl murderer' or whatever it was the Phibber was going to be calling her when the story got out.

'I always knew that family were no good,' said another voice.

'Yeah, well you have to wonder, don't you? She disappears, he dies, then the kid disappears, and then those weird stepparents find the Yakky Morto thing and get filthy rich. Then the kid disappears again. If you ask me there's something not quite right with that family.'

'Can we discuss this later?' shouted Lucy. She felt as though her trial had started already. 'Only I'd like to get out of this stinking pit first.'

'Me too,' shouted Fenny.

'Stay exactly where you are,' screamed a loudhailer. '*All* of you.'

A round of rifle shots caused everyone to duck.

'Hey, they're firing at us,' yelled a voice in the crowd.

'They won't shoot us just for looking,' said someone else.

More shots rang out, and this time the bullets whizzed by a little closer.

'Yeah, I see what you mean,' said the first voice.

'They're firing because they want you to stop you thinking about the big, huge, giant, enormous marble,' said a familiar voice. It was Tarquin, speaking from the relative safety of his mother's skirts.

'What's the kid talking about?' said a man with a notepad.

He had some of Zenda's look – roving eyes and twitching ears.

'He's talking rubbish,' said someone at the back.

'I'm not,' protested Tarquin. 'I saw a big glass marble thing through my frenockliars. And Lucy, my step-sister, was inside and couldn't breathe.'

With that he grabbed his own neck, to demonstrate that he'd learned absolutely nothing from almost being hanged. Unless you counted the fact that if you ate purple sarsaparilla and poked your tongue out it looked as though you were choking to death.

'Step-sister you say?' said the man with the notepad.

'Never you mind what he said,' snapped Lily. 'And as for you,' she said, turning to Tarquin, 'you can stop telling stories about giant marbles, unless you want to end up like her. And put that disgusting tongue away.'

'But mum,' said Tarquin, 'I saw it, honestly.'

'Shut up,' hissed Lily. 'Don't you realise what this means? If Lucy is back then we can fix the Yakky Morto – and you can have that new bicycle.'

She shouted towards the girls in the crater.

'Lucy, my *darling*, is it really you? We all thought you were dead my love.'

'Miss Blake?' shouted the man with the notebook. 'Zack Tawdry of the Sunday Lyre. What's all this about you and a big bird?'

'It wasn't a bird, it was an angel,' shouted Mister Brown, the leader of the Congregation of Darkness.

'Yeah?' said Zack. 'Well that was never in the papers.'

'Have it your way,' said Brown. 'But when the time comes to be counted by the dark angel you're going to be standing in the wrong queue chum.'

'Whatever,' said Zack, winding a finger at the side of his head. 'So, Miss Blake, this giant bird – is it a secret army project, like people are saying?'

'Work it out for yourself,' yelled Lucy. 'Now will someone *please* help us out of here?'

'*Stand perfectly still*,' screamed a loudhailer. It was Pilkington.

'*Yes, everyone stay where they are*,' blared another. This time the amplified voice belonged to Inspector Trembley, and he didn't sound happy.

But nobody seemed worried by their warnings, even when shots began to ring out again.

'Halloo? Miss Blake?' said a silky feminine voice. 'I'm Perdita Hotchkiss of Curl-Up and Dye magazine. Can I ask who does your hair?'

'Yeah Perdita,' shouted another reporter, 'that would be wonderful. But how about a proper quote, regarding the giant insects that were seen on the Great North Road?'

'Yeah,' said Zack. 'Tell us about that.'

'Miss Blake I absolutely *forbid* it,' screamed the Pilkington loudhailer. 'These people have no security clearance, and this area is under strict control of the army.'

'Oh yeah?' shouted Zack. 'Well you're not quite strict enough, are you? Otherwise how did all these people get back into the town?'

'*Well* Major?' yelled Miss Hotchkiss. 'I'm sure our readers would like to hear your views on security.'

She turned to her photographer and whispered, 'Grab some shots of him Eddie, and make sure the girl's in the background.'

'Hey, put that camera away,' shouted the Pilkington loudhailer.

'Get lost,' shouted Eddie. 'I can photograph what I like. Haven't you ever heard of the freedom of the press?'

'I have,' yelled Pilkington as he approached, 'and if you don't put that camera down right now I'm going to take it off you and stick it where the sun doesn't shine.' He was still yelling through the loudhailer, even though Eddie was only standing a few feet away.

'You and whose army?' yelled the photographer.

The laughter was so loud that even with the loudhailer the Major couldn't make himself heard, and he wandered off shaking his head.

A boy who had pushed his way through from the back took his position at the crater's edge.

'Miss Blake,' he shouted. 'Tobermory Picklegruber of Outdoor Catering and Picnic Gazette. I have an important question that our readers would like answered.'

'*Ye-es?*' said Lucy with a smile.

'If you absolutely *had* to choose,' he said, 'what would be your all-time favourite sandwich?'

'What's he talking about?' said Miss Hotchkiss.

'Haven't a clue,' said Mr. Brown. 'He's probably mad, like those two.' He pointed to a pair of old dears who were jostling their way through the crowd.

'Yoo-hoo! Loo-cy,' shouted Ethel. 'It's *us* dear. Come on, let me through will you? I'm a fully qualified old person.'

'We both are,' said Gladys. 'And Lucy *needs* us.'

'And who exactly is *us?*' said Zack. He licked his pencil and prepared to make an entry on his pad.

'Never you mind,' shouted Zenda, 'they're my clients and that's all you need to know. The Grimston Phibber has an exclusive on this story.'

'In your dreams,' said Zack. 'Whatever she's offering you, the Sunday Lyre will double it. So, umm, old lady, what's the story?'

'We had a lovely day out in Lundern,' said Ethel, smiling vaguely.

'*And?*' said Zack.

'That's it,' said Gladys. 'But it *was* a lovely day.'

'You're hiding something,' said Zack. 'There must be a story, or the local hacks wouldn't be sniffing.'

'Hey,' said Zenda. 'Less of the hack.'

'Can *I* just say something?' yelled Lucy.

'What was that?' said Zack.

'The girl in the crater wants to say something,' smiled Toby.

'She can wait her turn,' yelled Zack. 'This isn't about her, it's about the freedom of the press.'

'Nothing doing,' snapped Zenda. 'I didn't get chased through palaces and fight off insects and have my photographer sliced into pieces just so I can hand the story over to *you.*'

'Uh-oh,' said Toby, 'slightly too much information.'

'A-*ha*,' grinned Zack. 'So you were *involved*. Well you can't possibly write a story *and* be in it. Haven't you ever heard of impartiality?'

'I *have*, and I frigging-well *can*,' screamed Zenda. 'And *you're* not going to stop me.'

She knocked Zack's hat off and stamped on it, then pulled his hair. And in a final flash of inspiration she pushed a sharpened fingernail up his nose.

It was the final straw for the Lyre reporter. He took a swing at Zenda, and in the tussle that followed they slid into the crater, rolling and tumbling through the rubble. They ended up a few feet from Lucy and Fenny, who were standing in powdered diamonds. The reporters in contrast were up to their ankles in a combination of brick dust and sewage.

'Serves you right,' shouted a man at the crater's edge. It was Grumpton, head of the Congregation of Light. 'And now you can get on your knees and beg for Miss Blake's forgiveness.'

'You *what*?' said Zack, trying hard to look dignified.

'You heard,' shouted Grumpton. 'This girl has spoken with God.'

A murmur spread as the crowd discussed what the announcement might mean. Some of them didn't seem to mind, but a more vocal group started up with cries of 'shame' and 'blasphemy'.

'I think we ought to be leaving now,' whispered Lucy.

'Did you *really* speak to God?' whispered Fenny.

'I'm surprised you need to ask,' smiled Lucy.

'Only I'd believe you, if you said yes,' said Fenny.

'Well I *didn't*,' said Lucy. 'Now, have you got any idea how we're going to get out of here?'

'We should let them get on with their arguing,' said Fenny.

'You mean encourage them?' smiled Lucy.

'And slip away whilst they're busy,' said Fenny.

Lucy waved her arms above her head.

'Hello? Mister Brown? I've decided that I like the sound of your sewer patrols,' she yelled, 'so I want to join your congregation. But there's a small matter to be cleared up first.'

'And what's that?' shouted Brown.

'The other congregation,' said Lucy. 'They have to disband and join us.'

'You're *right*,' said Brown, filled with enthusiasm. 'We'll see to it.'

'Yeah?' shouted Grumpton. 'I'd like to see you come *here* and say that.'

The rim of the crater erupted as fights broke out between the factions of Darkness and the Light. There was trouble brewing in the blasphemy group too, who were murmuring about God and the idea that some cheeky slip of a girl had managed to get hold of his telephone number.

'I think that might be our cue to get out of here,' said Lucy.

She and Fenny scrambled up the side of the crater with some difficulty, closely followed by Zack and Zenda who made much harder work of it.

'You needn't bother following,' shouted Lucy. 'There's no story here, and even if there *was* nobody would believe you.'

Zack stopped and steadied himself against Zenda. He stared up at Lucy, who was leaning on a wrecked telephone box at the top of the slope.

'Ah,' he said, 'but if there's no story then there'd be nothing for people to not believe – so there must *be* a story, right?'

'If you say so,' said Lucy. 'I tell you what, if we ever meet again I might just consider telling you one.'

'But be careful,' smiled Fenny. 'They have a habit of coming true.'

'That's right,' said Toby, emerging behind them. 'She told a story about bacon and marmalade sandwiches once and *that* came true. Look.'

He held out a greasy paper bag, first to Fenny and then to Lucy.

'I don't *believe* it,' said Lucy, squealing with delight. 'At long *last*, we get to eat some real food.' She grabbed a sandwich and stuffed it into her mouth all in one go.

'Come on,' she said, chewing with some difficulty. 'Let's get out of here before anybody thinks of a *really* embarrassing question.'

The friends turned to run, but had only covered a couple of paces when the wrecked telephone rang.

'Leave it,' said Toby.

'But it might be for one of us,' said Lucy.

'I thought it was broken,' added Fenny.

Lucy picked up the receiver.

'*Hello*,' said a pinch-nosed voice. '*Is that Lucy Blake?*'

'It might be,' said Lucy.

'Good,' said the voice. 'I have something for you.'

'What is it?' said Lucy. 'And who are you?'

'Wait there,' said the voice.

And then the line went dead.

'Luce, I'm getting an awful feeling about this,' said Toby.

'Something's not quite right,' said Fenny.

There was the sound of an engine starting in the distance.

Seconds later a van screeched to a halt beside them, and a man in white overalls jumped out.

'Miss Blake?' he said. 'I have a delivery for you.'

'What if she isn't Miss Blake?' said Toby.

'The package goes back to the depot,' said the driver. 'It has to be signed for, see?'

'It'll be your writing prize,' said Fenny.

'I doubt it,' giggled Lucy. 'I made up all that stuff about winning the competition.'

'Another invention?' smiled Toby.

'No,' giggled Lucy. 'That one was just an ordinary lie.'

'Look, do you want this thing or not?' said the driver.

'Open it Luce,' said Toby.

As Lucy took the package, she noticed Zenda and Zack eying her from a distance. She tore open the brown paper to reveal a rosewood box. The lid was decorated with concentric rings and Enochian symbols were engraved on some of the smaller parts that were obviously designed to slide.

'It looks like a lock,' said Toby.

Lucy fingered the glassy symbol at the centre of the motif. She applied the tiniest amount of pressure on the design, and the scarab beetle inside the bezel changed from green to blue. Then the insect changed shape, mutating into a crocodile with wings.

'It's open,' said Fenny, as the catch gave a click.

Lucy lifted the lid. It was foggy inside the box, like a sea mist creeping ashore.

'Be careful,' said Fenny, 'I see bad colours.'

Lucy nodded, then screamed in agony as spring-steel coils lashed out of the mist and snaked around her wrists.

'*No,*' screamed Fenny, 'not after all she's been through.'

'It is *because* of what she has been through,' said the driver.

'*No,*' screamed Lucy, 'you can't…'

The driver smiled and pulled a referee's whistle from his pocket. He blew hard, and the back doors of the van burst open. Lucy's blood froze as two hooded figures jumped out and pinned Toby and Fenny to the ground. Another of them, this one wearing a carnival mask, dragged her inside and strapped her into an ambulance bed.

'Toby,' she yelled, 'find Trembley and tell him they've got me.'

'Shut it,' said her captor, his breath hissing through the mask.

He tightened the straps, climbed out and slammed the doors, enclosing Lucy in a world of metallic shadows that smelt faintly of mothballs.

'Who's there?' she whispered.

She could hear breathing in the dark.

A leather chair creaked, as if a great weight was shifting position.

The breathing got nearer, and Lucy felt a cold sensation on her arm, as though she was being dabbed with a piece of wet cotton wool.

She screamed as she felt the unmistakeable scratch of a needle.

And darkness came to visit her…